I0633315

Summer of Speculation

2021 Edition: Catastrophe

A Cloaked Press Anthology

Published by:
Cloaked Press, LLC
PO Box 341
Suring, WI 54174
https://www.cloakedpress.com

Cover Design by:
Steger Productions Design
https://fantasyandcoffee.com/SPDesign/

ISBN: 978-1-952796-03-6

Cloaked Press is proud to present:

Lindsay Pugh
Sandy Stuckless
David Castlewitz
Katie Kent
Nickolas Urpí
Alex Minns
Daragh Kennedy
Max Turner
Barend Nieuwstraten III
Kara Race-Moore
S. C. Burns
David Richie
Elana Gomel

Contents

The Paper Boat

by Lindsay Pugh

1. *The Paper Boat*

The River Styx was flooding, and Hades was on the phone. "C'mon, Hera, I know he's there," he said, and Persephone paced, worried about her pomegranates. He paced, and the water rushed towards their gleaming bone fortress, heavy and forceful with human tears, discarded dreams, gurgling wails, fiery flare-ups, forgotten names, all things left behind, all things trapped. Charon's boat bulleted forward, his oar lost in the waves, and the ones waiting on the shores tried to make chase, screaming, shrieking *WAIT* even though they had waited a thousand years already. And the librarian, Sophia, cannibalized the spines and pages of books to make an escape boat no one thought they'd need.

Sophia asked the shades guarding the palace if the bones would hold. Would Persephone be crushed under them?

"Femurs, ma'am," one chittered in Ancient Greek, which Sophia was conversational in. "They will hold."

She took the novel she'd been reading along, a few of the fist sized rubies Hades grew in the garden, just in case.

She asked one more time, to be sure.

Persephone wouldn't come.

2. *Mojitos*

The librarian ate the pomegranates she'd packed, sucked the flesh off the seeds and spat them out into the water. The Styx had deposited her into the Mississippi, and a friendly bull shark had said hello as she bobbed by, unafraid of the lingering stench of death on the pages. Her soaked loafers and knee socks dried in the sun as the river lollygagged, sending her into the Gulf of Mexico. She'd kill for a margarita in Cancun. Was Hades still on the phone?

El Nino swept her past Cancun into Florida. She found Amelia Earhart in the Bermuda Triangle. Amelia had befriended some extraterrestrials and built a plane that hopped dimensions. "Now, hon," she said, "why would I go back to 1937 when I can go to the sun if I like? When I've slipped through time?"

The aliens were excited to meet her. They asked endless questions of her humanity and her half-death when she descended with Persephone into the Underworld, the last semester of undergrad, enticed by a pomegranate smoothie and promises of every book ever written.

"And how did you meet the goddess?"

"She was my botany TA." They chattered, recorded her voice, took notes, asked her what she'd studied in botany. She'd mostly forgotten. It had been so long ago. She had wanted to be a regular librarian then, get a Master's of Information Sciences and help students write their dissertations.

"What is she like, Lady Kore?"

Deceptive was the word that jumped to mind. Not maliciously, even. One had the urge to protect her from even the wind, worried she would disintegrate and blow away with the breeze. She appeared translucent, especially in the gloomy, craggy darkness of Hades. But she was brutal. Sophia had to admit even that. Her beautifully translucent eyes always glowed with a faint sense of rage.

"Lovely," she said, ever considerate.

She had drinks with pirates, Navy men, Atlanteans who sipped a briny brew from golden mugs. "What do you do here?" she asked them. "Sunbathe, mostly," said a young man from New York who was zapped here in 1955.

"And the sirens make killer cocktails," a honeymooner said. He had a sunglasses tan and defined pecs beneath a parrot-patterned Hawaiian shirt. His husband was playing shuffleboard with a Plutoan, a blue, skinny humanoid shape with a jangly skirt. "You *need* to try Zafara's mojitos."

She agreed to a mojito before she went. The limes were wonderfully fresh.

3. Hell is Empty

Eventually the librarian floated so long that she ended up on the dusty banks of Hell. The river she had been on evaporated beneath her, and the pages disintegrated. The gate said- UNLOCKED. ENTER AT YOUR OWN RISK. IF YOU KNOW YOUR PARTY'S EXTENSION, SHOUT IT REALLY LOUD AND HOPE SOMEONE ANSWERS.

"Excuse me," the librarian said in her quiet voice, unused to talking above a whisper. "Ahem. Ahem. Excuse me!" No one. Perhaps Hell *was* empty. "*Diabolus,*" she shouted, and someone said, "Oh, hello. No one's called for me that way in ages."

The Devil was in a vest and fedora. He had a tattoo of a goat on his neck. He looked about thirty-five. One curly ram's horn poked out from the brim of his fedora. One eye was blue, the other brown—or it was for a second. When she looked back, the right eye was green, and the other blue.

"Do you know the way to the Underworld?" she asked. "That's where I intend to go."

"Oh, darling," The Devil said kindly, "I am nowhere as cruel as Hades. Everyone who comes here is given a special punishment for eternity. I don't make them stand in fields and fade. They are someones here. Much more than they were someones when they lived."

"And what will you do to me, then?"

"Hmm," The Devil said. He scurried forward and tapped her forehead. "Oh, my. Librarian of the Palace of Death. And you never even got your master's."

"Lady Persephone hired me."

"Yes, yes, I know, she's very persuasive, it's the sad, lonely eyes, just tugs the heart strings, but don't cast her too white, she did damn you to eternity in that dingy place, yeah?"

Sophia had left behind some friends, a set of introverted parents, a roommate who must've been angry at her. It felt like a loss someone else had suffered. The days luxuriated in her hall of books, those she'd read and those that had been lost for centuries. Lady Persephone was there, often. Sophia did miss her when she ascended, but she never asked to return to the surface with her.

She even liked Hades, and Persephone loved him, much to her surprise.

"I'm afraid my mother is quite the control freak," Persephone explained. "When I saw an out, I took it, and my husband is kinder than anyone could know. He gets a hard reputation because of his job."

"So why go back in the Spring?"

Persephone shrugged. "Oh, it's so gloomy here sometimes. I sometimes feel I might fade into shadow if I don't see the sun for just a while."

When Persephone was gone, Hades would come read between meetings and councils and long-distance calls to Olympus that left him with migraines. His voice was melodic and sad, when he spoke, which was rare. He was pale and thin in a way that suited him. It must be terribly lonely to be here all the time, the librarian thought, and yet, she herself was not lonely.

"Well, I—well, yes," Sophia admitted. "The pomegranate smoothie was very good, and she had been such a nice TA."

"Oh, she can be nice, but so can I," the Devil chuckled. "We're fond of her of course, you see her in the hell circles. I've been here longer than most, the parties were frightfully dull before the Greeks. And that puppy of yours, he's just a riot!"

"Surely God is entertaining?" She'd read the Bible in Greek, Hebrew, and Latin. She thought she preferred the Greeks.

"God and I had a falling out, of course. You know how friends get when they're cooped up too long. But we're working on it. We do lunch on Tuesdays."

"And He keeps his dates?"

"Mostly. He likes to make me sweat by running fifteen minutes late. Are you sure you'd like to go to Hades? You can stay, grab some fresh clothes from our lost and found. I have a pink velour tracksuit that should fit."

"Yes, I'm sure. I evacuated for a flood, but I'm sure it's been sorted by now," she said. "Where is your library? I'd like to visit it, before I go on my way."

"Of course. All we have is *Ulysses,* missing the last page, *Atlas Shrugged,* Reader's Digests from the nineties, and the various autobiographies of dead Senators. Also, none of it is alphabetized."

"On second thought," she said. "Where's the nearest waterway?"

"Eek," he said. "That's our sewage system."

The librarian sighed. "Well, there was enough of that in the Styx. Lead on."

The wastewater trickled into a river where she nearly plowed over some children bathing and their mother washing clothes, and they directed her towards the best place to buy a lunch. She circumnavigated the world and read the pages that hadn't been smeared blank, looking for the Styx's mouth. She had never descended without Persephone, and she had always had a poor sense of direction.

It was Poseidon, in the end.

She had dismounted onto a small island, to bathe and switch her clothes. Her loafers were in terrible condition. She'd have to ask for more.

She hadn't meant to come across a major god nude and distracted by a nereid, and she squeaked in embarrassment. Poseidon covered himself with his trident, badly, while the nereid grinned lazily, her blue-tinged breasts fully exposed.

"Now, Amphitrite and I have an agreement," he said awkwardly. "Thousands of years together, you know, you have to spice things up a bit."

The librarian stammered, "Please don't feel like you need to explain to me, my Lord." She hadn't seen a nude male form outside of manuscripts in years. It wasn't a pleasant surprise.

"Awfully odd to see a mortal here," Poseidon said. "And yet, you're not quite. You're not dead, but pardon me, *are* you alive?"

"I'm not quite sure, my Lord," she answered honestly.

"My niece!" He shouted. "Ah, that's it. She's shown me your Facebook. You are the librarian?"

"I am, my Lord."

"And why are you here, then? Didn't you-?" He mimed drinking a smoothie.

"I did, but there was a flood."

Poseidon glanced at the nereid. "Tell you what. I appreciated the book newsletter you emailed out for Christmas. The beach read section was a nice touch. I'll send you back." He raised his trident, spoke quietly, and the tide swelled to her ankles, bringing with it her battered paper boat.

"I'll give you a nudge the right way," he said. "I liked that beach romance book I read. Good luck, not-quite-mortal."

She stepped into the boat. Bubbles floated to the surface just ahead of the boat, then popped. The boat glided forward. It wasn't until she reached the mouth that a green sea serpent poked itself out of the water. His eyes were wide and sympathetic. He chirped and inclined his head to the dark cave, and she understood that this was as far as he could go.

"Thank you," she said, and he sank into the water and disappeared.

There was new dam circumventing the water into an eighth circle. She rowed home with planks she lucked from the murky water; her own set had been lost, though she didn't recall how anymore. She saw a stray palace femur bone, and worried after the shades who had been confident, and after Hades and Persephone, foolishly immortal and reckless. Signs of the damage were everywhere. She wondered if the dead had been displaced, and if they even cared much. Perhaps they were relieved.

"Oh, Sophia," Persephone said when she knocked on the gate, soaked, cold, exhausted. "I have been so worried. Hades wanted a new librarian after we started to rebuild the library, but I wouldn't hear of it, wouldn't even look at any resumes. Would you like a smoothie? We managed to save the pomegranate trees."

Lindsay Pugh is a full-time grad student pursuing her masters of Social Work, and she lives in Richmond, VA, with two sweet tabby cats and her partner. She writes mostly urban fantasy infused with magic realism, and she reads anything she can when she can.

Hot Wings

by Sandy Stuckless

Milo Elwood sat in the back of Mess Hall #4, leaning on his hand as he stirred the greyish protein gruel in the bowl. It had all the nutrients to get through the day, but it tasted like a dirty sock. He stirred in another couple shakes of hot sauce, but he doubted the slop would be any more appetizing.

Milo shoved the bowl aside and dropped his head to the table. Unfortunately, he couldn't afford the premium gruel. The last few excursions hadn't been all that lucrative. He'd tagged only a few battle bots, earning barely enough to rearm and go back out to do the same crap again. So much for the 'Earn a Living, See the Galaxy' BS they sold on the recruiting poster.

Milo would've been better off in the standard military earning a steady paycheck instead of this specialized 'pay per kill' unit. Being a mercenary wasn't all it was cracked up to be. No chance of getting out though. Even if he sold his mech for parts, it wouldn't earn him enough to pay off his debts and hop a shuttle back to Earth. He was stuck for the time being. If he could bag a comms bot or a couple harvester bots that might be worth something.

A command and control bot, affectionately called the brain bot, was the crown jewel. Bag one of those and the geeks back home would pay him a ton. They kept on about how one of those would help them figure out how these things ticked.

Ever since they got word that the colonists were interested in peace talks, government folks back home were keen on gaining the upper hand. Milo didn't know about any of that. He was only a mech pilot that went where he was told to go and shot what he was told to shoot.

Judging from the data dumps the outpost received every week, very few back home trusted the colonists were really interested in peace. The Sector Seven Ambush was a cautionary tale to any new mech driver. Take nothing at face value.

Neither side banked on a homicidal, mech-driving, space pirate throwing a monkey wrench into things. Apparently, peace wasn't good for the pirate business. Sovereign Noble and his army of battle bots were a major thorn for everyone.

Milo picked up his head at the sound of the mess hall airlock hissing open. Any remaining appetite disappeared with a gurgle in his stomach. Jordan Prince was the last person he wanted to see. Not that he had many places to hide on the outpost.

Jordan was one of the most successful mech operators in the sector and made sure everyone knew it. The other thing he liked to do was loan money to the less fortunate and then extort them for repayment. Milo really wished he hadn't needed to borrow the cash to recertify his mech. They wouldn't let you fly with expired tags and you couldn't renew the tags on an unsafe mech. Milo almost threw up when he saw the final bill.

Jordan bypassed the serving counter, making a bee-line straight for Milo's table. His three amigos followed him in. Gyro, Tin Can, and Sabre, the only girl in his crew. Milo didn't know too much about the others. Jordan was the only one who gave him a hard time.

Milo pulled the bowl back in front of him and choked down another spoonful of cold gruel. "How nice to see you again, Jordan."

"Stow it, Elwood. Where's my money? You had three sorties this week. Plenty of opportunity to earn out."

"Funny thing about that. Hunting wasn't as successful today. Seems the bots didn't want to play."

Jordan leapt across the table at Milo, who managed to slide back out of his reach.

Milo wagged a finger. "Careful. Hurt me too much and I won't be able to pilot my mech. How will you get your money then?"

"The loss will be worth seeing your useless hide in a body cast." Jordan drew his shoulders up and crossed his arms. "Besides, I'm surprised you can get that hunk of steel out of the space dock."

The airlock hissed open again, admitting the outpost commander and saving Milo from Jordan's threat. "Attention on deck!" the duty officer shouted.

Everyone bolted to their feet and saluted.

"At ease," the commander ordered. She moved to the front of the mess hall, her boots thudding on the carbon fiber floor, and surveyed the crowd. "I need three squads for a critical sortie. Pays double the normal rate. Any takers?"

Several mech drivers jumped at the opportunity, but the

commander stayed put. "What about it, Prince, Elwood? I have a special assignment that's right up your alley."

"There you go!" Jordan said, glaring at Milo. "Perfect opportunity to get my money."

Milo leaned back, locked his fingers behind his head, and plopped his feet up on the table. "Yeah, that's not going to work. Got reservations for the new steak joint on the Outer Ring. Kinda looking forward to it."

Jordan towered across the table over him and lowered his voice so as not to be overheard. "Take this mission and get me my money or I'll take that heap of scrap you call a mech instead. What I don't get for the mech, I'll take in broken bones."

"You drive a hard bargain, Jordan. You're ugly and your breath stinks, but you drive a hard bargain." Milo got up from the table and worked his way to the front of the mess hall. "What's the mission, Commander?"

"You know that's not how it works, Elwood," she replied. "First you sign on, then you get the details. Take my word for it, though. You don't want to miss this one."

Milo hesitated for another second. Double pay meant it was three times as dangerous. On the other hand, if it went according to plan, he'd earn enough to pay back Jordan, fix up his mech and maybe book a trip back home. He'd had enough cold dark space to last a lifetime. His first stop would be Buffalo, New York for a plate of hot wings. Then maybe he'd pick up a commission escorting luxury shuttles to Mars and back. "Alright, Commander. Count me in."

"I'm in too, Commander," Jordan said. He glared at Milo. "You didn't think I'd let you go out there alone, did you? Either you come back with enough kills to pay me off, or you don't come back. Consider this insurance on my investment."

Tin Can, Sabre, and Gyro rounded out the team and the Commander nodded. "Briefing Room Three in ten minutes. Don't forget to log your mech IDs on the active roster so you get paid."

Jordan turned back to Milo after the airlock door had slid closed behind the Commander. "You better get that metal disaster tuned up. Wouldn't want any mishaps on the mission."

Despite Jordan's crass tone, he wasn't wrong. In its current state, Milo would be lucky if he didn't explode before leaving the docking ring. Without a steady income, keeping up a mech was hard. He'd go see Wrench. Wrench would help him. Maybe.

Sabre hung around for a minute after Jordan and the others left.

She palled around with the boy wonder and his crew, but seldom engaged in the harassment. She brushed a string of red hair from her face, revealing her brilliant blue eyes. "Are you sure you want to do this? Never mind endangering us with an unreliable mech, I'd rather not see you bite it out there."

"Gee, Sabre. You almost sound like you care. Anyway, I don't have much choice, do I? You better go catch up with your friends. Wouldn't want to start any nasty rumors. I'll be along in a few minutes after I see a girl about some new cooling coils."

On any outpost without Jordan, Milo maybe would've taken a shot. Not here, though. It wasn't worth the aggravation.

#

Wrench McNaughton was tucked in the smallest repair alcove on the far side of the docking ring. She also happened to be the only one remotely willing to work on Milo's mech without question.

Milo weaved amongst mech parts on the floor. There was even a new grappling hook spool over in the corner.

Wrench side-stepped Milo to get to an already over-full shelf, kicking a bucket of bolts out of her way. "I can't do it, Milo. You still haven't paid for the last round of repairs and I need the money too. I'm only working on mechs for people who can pay. Got my eye on a bigger alcove closer to the active docking bays. Do you know how much of a pain in the ass it is carting all my tools halfway across the ring? It's hard enough getting these bot jocks to take me seriously as it is."

"Come on, Wrench. I just need the bare minimum. A couple new cooling coils and a power booster to get me through the mission. If this trip is a success, I'll be able to pay you back with interest. I'll even paint your logo on the side of my mech. You can be my sponsor. The dynamic duo."

"And if it isn't a success? The parts and labor still come out of my budget."

Milo shrugged. "Then I'll be dead and you'll never have to see me again." Milo flashed her some pouty puppy dog eyes. "Please, Wrench. I really need this one or Jordan is going to fillet me like a fish."

Wrench huffed and raked her greasy hand through greasier hair. "Fine. I'll take a look. You better come back alive or I'll kill you. No promises on the coils or the booster. Those things aren't free, you know."

"Excellent. One more thing. I need it done in an hour."

Milo's conversation with the armory went much the same as it did with Wrench. The list of people to whom he owed money seemed to grow by the minute. He did manage to score a FEMP charger and a magazine of low yield nuc burst torpedoes. A mech pilot was nothing without a Focused EMP cannon. He tried for a couple of the larger nuc launchers but was laughed out of the armory.

Milo arrived last to the briefing, earning more than one annoyed glance from Jordan and the other pilots. Somehow, he managed to piss off thirty other people by barely lifting a finger. Milo sat in one of the chairs in the back row. Of course, Jordan and his merry band were at the front of the room like good little teacher's pets. "Sorry. Had to make sure the mech wouldn't get a flat on the way out."

"Shall we get started?" the commander said and hit the button on the vid screen. "Ninety days ago, Earth launched a resupply shuttle for the sector that has become disabled and veered off course past the front. It is imperative we recover that shuttle."

"Must be some high-valued supplies to double the pay rate and risk an excursion into colonist territory," Jordan said.

Images of a disabled shuttle drifting past outpost defense nets continued to scroll across the screen. "Very high-valued. There are some sorely needed outpost upgrades along with some new weapons and intel that might come in handy. Wouldn't surprise anyone if the colonists made a play for it. They could use the supplies as much as we can."

Milo sat up a little straighter. Maybe he'd finally get that new targeting computer. Hard job to kill Bots when you didn't know which way your guns were pointing.

"Does this have anything to do with the rumored peace talks, ma'am?" Jordan asked.

"I'm limited in how much I can say. Intelligence briefings are still highly classified. But, yes. There is some relation. The colonists want us to defend them against the pirates."

Milo had no sympathy for the colonists. He knew the history of their ancestors' attempts to start a civil war. They wanted their own way of life and they got it. They were all guilty of treason, in his opinion. Even Sovereign Noble and his band of space pirates were a direct result of the colonists abandoning Earth. Not everyone wanted governments telling them how to live all the time. "Maybe they should've thought of that before sending their killer bots after us. Not as easy to overthrow a pirate as it is to overthrow a government, apparently."

"I'm sure there are regrets on both sides," Sabre said. "Nobody's perfect."

Milo dropped the argument. This was a military briefing, not a political sciences class. "Just tell me which way to aim the barrel, commander."

"We'll need their intel on the Bots if we're going to take down the pirates," Jordan added. "Be nice to know how Sovereign Noble is hacking them."

"Well, if the rumors are true," Gyro said, "he's a former colonist engineer so he'd have inside knowledge. Maybe we should try to hire him."

"We don't need the pirate," the commander said. "There's a case onboard that's supposed to make the difference in this fight. There's a chance this means the difference in us going home or staying out here."

Milo dismissed the notion almost before the commander had finished saying it. They claimed that every time hopes for peace were high. It always fell apart at the end and the shooting started again. Milo had a better shot affording that steak dinner he mentioned earlier.

Milo was luckier than some on this outpost. He didn't have a bunch of family to go home to. Guys like Jordan had wives and kids on Earth. They had no choice but to be out here. This was where the real money was.

Tin Can raised his hand. "You think Sovereign Noble will make an appearance?"

"I was just getting to that. It's an attractive shipment so we're expecting strong resistance."

"You'd think a shipment this important would have some kind of escort," Milo said.

"It did," the commander replied. "The bots hit it in numbers and wiped it out. The shuttle didn't take a scratch."

Jordan nodded as he tapped his finger on the metal table. "Sovereign Noble loves to send in the bots to soften us up. No doubt he'll be waiting for us."

"I'm told there's a special delivery for the mess hall. I guess they figured we could use a crate full of chicken wings and craft beer. Someone back home is thinking about us."

Milo bolted straight up in his chair, almost falling over backwards. This mission had just become personal.

The tech and intel were one thing, but a few days without having to stomach that horrid protein gruel was worth a hundred battles against Sovereign Noble. Milo couldn't remember the last time he had a decent plate of wings and a cold beer.

"I've uploaded the star maps and projected intercept points that give you the best chance of recovering the shuttle. The bots aren't going to make your welcome a warm one."

"All part of the job, Commander," Jordan said, acting all cocky. Milo would love to shove a boot right up his arrogant ass. "What other support are we looking at?"

"Three other outposts are sending reinforcements, but we were the first stop for the shuttle so this one's mostly our problem. I have three other squads running interference and Dreadnaughts inbounds from another mission. They'll join you when they're able. You five are to focus on the supply shuttle. Our early uplink attempts have failed. Somehow, the bots have hacked it and steered it into their space."

"How are we supposed to regain control?" Tin Can asked. "We don't have the tools to override that."

"Your best bet is to find the bot controlling the hack and destroy it. Given what we know of their range, it can't be too far from the front line. Any other questions?" When no one else spoke up, the commander nodded. "All right then. Get your mechs on station and let's do this. Happy hunting."

#

Milo walked around his mech, inspecting the welds on each of the legs and arms suggesting something stitched together from disparate parts. In a way, it was. Milo came here with nothing and couldn't afford one of the fancy pre-fabbed mechs. He cobbled together what he could find from parts no one else wanted. "Frankenstein," he said. "That's what I'm going to call you. You're practically stitched together anyway."

Everything else looked to be intact, including his lightning harpoon clutched in the mech's right fist. One of these days, he'd get to use that. He didn't get the new cooling coils he'd asked for, but the second-hand ones Wrench installed were in decent enough shape. The real test would be when he pushed his mech to the limits.

"How you've managed to stay alive in that thing is beyond me."

Milo peeked out around the left leg of his mech to see Jordan strolling up. *Give me a break,* he thought. This guy just didn't know when to quit. "What can I say? She's a good girl and I know how to treat her."

Jordan scoffed. "That's a load of crap. You've been lucky so far. Sooner or later that luck is going to run out."

"Yeah, well, you better hope it's not today."

The commander's arrival saved Milo from further conversation. "You boys ready?"

13

Milo zipped up his flight suit and pulled on his helmet. "Gonna be a picnic, ma'am. Just finished loading up the chips and beer."

"You watch yourselves out there, you hear. This could be nothing more than a colonist trap to launch an attack on the outpost."

"So you don't believe the rumors of peace talks either," Jordan said.

"Let's just say I've been burned too many times to take anything at face value. I'm counting on you to end this quickly and get your asses back here."

Milo slapped the side of Frankenstein. The commander left as Sabre and the others walked up. "You good?" Sabre asked.

"As good as I'll ever be, I guess. Let's party. I can already taste those wings."

Sabre giggled and it was almost cute. "You always think with your stomach, Elwood?"

"Makes up for what I lack in other areas."

"Hopefully, we're not the ones getting fried," Gyro added.

Jordan led the flight of five mechs out of the outpost for the simple fact that he was the first one out of the outpost docking ring. Milo wasn't complaining. He trailed behind just trying to keep his mech from overheating and killing him. Wrench really had done the bare minimum to keep it space worthy.

Three other squads followed them out, turning left away from them to cut off the bulk of the resistance. They had the harder and probably the better paying job. Maybe Milo joined the wrong team.

Milo took a minute to appreciate the view. Beyond the battle group in front of him stretched the black expanse of deep space. Some called it a void. To Milo, it dripped with possibility, worlds untapped, stories untold. No matter how many times he came out here, it always blew him away.

That appreciation wouldn't last though. They were only a hundred miles from the Front so it didn't take long for the heat to get turned up. Once they crossed that imaginary plain, it was game on.

"Elwood," Jordan called over the battle frequency. "You're with Sabre and Gyro on battle bot duty. Keep those oversized can openers off our ass long enough to establish the uplink and turn the shuttle around. Don't miss and don't die. At least, not until you've paid me back."

Milo's head slumped forward and his shoulders dropped. Battle bots were practically worthless. He'd be out here for hours and still not earn enough to pay off his debts. "Whatever you say, Jordan. You go get all the glory. That's what you live for, after all."

Milo smirked at the dead silence that came back through the radio. Jordan was an arrogant, attention-seeking man-child who hated when people smacked him in the face with it.

"You shouldn't agitate him," Sabre called over Milo's private comms link. "You know it only pisses him off more."

"I know, but it's so much fun. Let's go kill some bots. If I get more than you, you let me buy you dinner."

"Ha," she barked. "You can't even afford to buy your own dinner."

Milo activated his targeting radar, the screen flickering until he punched it several times. He'd have to have a word with Wrench. This wasn't the quality he expected for work he hadn't paid for. "Reading five clusters on screen. These bots have colonist transponder signals."

"That doesn't mean anything," Sabre replied. "Latest intel on Sovereign Noble suggests he can mask his transponder signature. We're probably flying into a trap."

"They're staying tight together. How nice of them to help us out like that."

"I have the supply shuttle on my scope," Jordan called. "Twelve miles out at thirty-seven degrees. Looks like we'll have to go through that swarm to get to it."

As they got closer to the cluster, Milo got a better look at what they were up against. Battle bots chopped up and stitched back together, kind of like his mech. Definitely not colonist level manufacturing. Sabre had been right on the money. These were Sovereign Noble's bots. "Keep your eyes open. Our pirate friend is around here somewhere."

Milo activated his FEMP cannons and magazines of nuclear burst torpedoes. Not the top of the line weapons, but he'd manage. They'd have to thin the herd before engaging in close-in combat.

The radio crackled with Jordan's irritating voice once again. "All right you three, go sweep the floor. Tin Can, you're with me. We're going for the shuttle."

Milo, Sabre, and Gyro broke off from the pack and hit the swarm head on. Three burst torpedoes exploded in rapid succession, thinning out the bots and scattering the rest. Chunks of bot bounced off his mech as he flew through the debris field. He checked his meter. Fifteen thousand credits. A good start, but not the forty-five he owed Jordan or the thirty he owed Wrench.

Milo jetted towards a small cluster of bots forming up on the edge of the battle zone, fixing to take a run at Jordan and Tin Can on the shuttle. Sabre and Gyro took similar tracks to separate clusters. Clutter started to build in this sector as more bots were destroyed. It made picking out viable targets all the more difficult.

Milo checked his gauges. FEMP cannons fully charged so he opened fire. Another three bots bought it before they knew they were under attack. Another ten grand in the bank.

"Sabre," he called over the radio. "I'm going to draw this cluster into your crossfire. Be a peach and light them up, will you?"

"Copy. Ready when you are."

Milo swooped in low and to the right, dragging four bots in with him. He dodged high-powered laser cannon fire and space junk like he was on some kind of obstacle course. Out his left window, a blue and grey mech exploded.

"Ah crap," Milo called. "We've lost Gyro. No sign of an escape pod. I say again. We've lost Gyro."

Milo cut back towards Gyro's flaming wreckage. Four more bots fell to his FEMP cannons. Another twelve percent gone from his power reserves in that little skirmish. He was okay for now, but a second wave would mean real trouble. His backup batteries were a last resort.

He'd hoped to go a little longer before engaging the bots close in, but they were spread out too much for proximity weapons to be effective. "What's the deal with the transport, Jordan? This frying pan is getting a little hot."

"I'm locked out. I can't access the uplink. It's going to take a few minutes to break through these firewalls. Keep the bots off me for a bit longer."

Easy for you to say, he thought. *They aren't shooting at you.*

Another check of his gauges. Voltage and amps on the batteries still showed full. Engine temp was creeping up, but still okay. Milo didn't think he could push it much harder, though.

He scanned his visibility field. Amongst all the battle debris and fighting, Milo spotted a strange bot he'd never seen before. The bot swerved away from him, but it didn't move quickly. "What the hell is that?" He clicked his mic. "You see that, Sabre?"

"Yeah. What do you suppose it is?"

Milo engaged his thrusters, full power. His mech shuddered as it picked up speed. "Must be some new kind of command and control unit. Seems the bots got a few upgrades of their own." It had to be worth ten times the battle bot. "I'm taking a run at it. Watch my six."

"Roger that."

Maybe the colonists weren't as interested in a peace treaty as everyone believed. Else, why the military upgrades? The government spooks back home would love to get their hands on this thing.

"Take it out fast, Elwood," Jordan called. "It's jamming my uplink signal."

Six battle bots popped up from behind the strange jamming bot. Figured they wouldn't leave it unguarded. Milo's FEMP cannons jolted his mech every time he pulled the trigger.

Milo dodged the explosions and debris on his way to the control bot. Milo hit it with his FEMP cannons, but it continued to evade him. Interesting, he thought. It has shields. "Seems like we're not the only ones adapting to the fight."

Milo selected his nuc burst torpedoes, but nothing happened when he pulled the trigger. "No, no, no. Not now." Milo pulled the trigger again and again. before punching the dashboard. There was never a good time for his targeting computer to crap out. He thought Wrench fixed it. In a flurry, he turned off his targeting computer and turned it back on. If this didn't work, he was screwed.

Another alarm on his console sounded. Damn it. His thrusters were overheating. Much harder and he'd melt his whole chassis, and that Wrench couldn't fix.

To hell with it. No guts, no glory. Milo pushed forward on the stick demanding full power. By the time he got within range of the command bot, his targeting computer had rebooted. He unleashed a wave of nuc burst torpedoes. They struck the rear of the bot near the starboard nacelle, but the machine barely even shuddered.

"We've got a problem here," Milo called over his radio. "Our weapons are ineffective against this new bot. Anyone got a Plan B?"

"Figure it out, Elwood," Jordan replied. "I can't get into the supply vessel until that thing is disabled."

Great, Milo thought as he reconfigured his mech for Battle Bot mode. Just like Jordan to expect him to go all kamikaze just so he could get the glory of rescuing the supply vessel. Milo pushed forward on his boosters to gain on the comms bot. Good thing his mech was tough as nails.

Sabre kept the bots at bay while Milo figured out his next move. She was a good person. Genuine. Milo couldn't understand what she was doing chumming around with Jordan.

Milo hit the bot with several Rolling Frequency Jammer tags. It was a long shot, but maybe it would take down its shields or disrupt the signal long enough for Jordan to establish a link. A few of the battle bots shut down, but the resupply shuttle maintained its course into enemy territory.

Looks like I'm going to have to do this the old fashioned way. With brute force.

As he closed in on the bot, Milo looked for weak spots in the hull. It was smooth and shiny, like the side of an airplane. There! Near the front. Some type of antenna. It looked vulnerable. He kept an eye on his instruments as he swooped in underneath the bot. Engine temps were getting close to red. He fired his grappling hook from the mech's left arm into the bot's underbelly. "I'm hooked on," he called. "Retracting."

The high-tensile steel cable spooled back onto its drum, pulling Milo in. The laser cutter made quick work of the antenna. He slashed the laser across the engine cowling, shearing off chunks of sheet metal. "Just like carving a turkey," he cackled. The bot lost its drive, sending it adrift. Milo tagged it with his mech number and detached to move on to the next bot. "Target disabled, Jordan. Begin your upload." Milo did a quick check of his count. Fifty thousand. "You'll be happy to know. I have your money." *And once this mission is over, hopefully I'll never have to speak to you again.*

"Yeah, stow it until we get back. Job's not done yet. Whatever you did didn't work. Those firewalls are proving to be a pain in the ass."

Milo let his head fall back. Son of a... Probably a good thing anyway. He hadn't earned enough yet to pay off Wrench and the armory. "Elwood to Battle Group. There's a command and control over that here that's almost completely intact. I'm claiming the kill."

He left the command and control bot to help Sabre, but his mech had other plans. Alarms went off all over the place. Engines overheating, targeting computer going nuts. Even his FEMP cannons were being stubborn. He clicked his mic to call for help, but even that was dead. His thrust dropped out, leaving him floating like a piece of space junk in the middle of the biggest dog fight he'd ever been a part of.

On the plus side, all of the scrap floating around made him look like another dead mech. The bots tracked active power signals and Milo didn't have one of those just now.

Milo powered down everything except life support, which he had tied to his backup batteries. Hopefully, that wouldn't crap out too. He wouldn't last ten minutes. The diagnostics computer spat out a list three pages long of things wrong. Some systems he could do without, but he was useless without his engines and weapons.

Milo flipped up the cover on his master reset switch. He had no choice. He held it for three seconds and it felt like the whole mech took a deep breath before everything powered down.

The next three minutes felt like a lifetime. He pictured Jordan and

Sabre screaming at him through the radio. He'd help if he could.

Movement outside his port side window caught his attention. "Oh damn…" A second wave of battle bots was inbound. Milo jabbed his finger on the master reset switch and flipped every other switch he could. The mech shuddered and whined as power supplies and systems came back online. He tried to will it to go faster, but it was painfully slow. Finally, all of his systems came back online and the first thing he heard was Jordan's frantic voice through the radio.

"Goddamn it, Elwood. What the hell are you doing? We're getting clobbered over here. There's a second wave inbound."

"We're sorry," he replied in his best comms center voice. "We are currently experiencing some technical difficulties. Please hang up and try your call again later."

"Save it," Jordan snapped. "There are pirate mechs inbound with them. Intercept it. Now. Tin Can and Sabre will support you."

Milo noticed that. It was a bit unusual. The pirates didn't usually join the battle until after the bots were through. Sovereign Noble must really want this shuttle. "What about you? What's the deal with that uplink? We can't keep this up forever."

There was a hesitation from Jordan. "Still working on it."

"Have you tried unplugging it and plugging it back in?"

Jordan growled before switching off his mic. That boy could use some happy pills. Hopefully the folks back home sent some. If all else failed, there was always the beer.

There had to be a mech around here somewhere calling the shots. Milo futilely scanned his star field. "This is Elwood to outpost. The pirates must really want this shuttle. Their mechs have joined the party. You might want to consider sending another squad or two out here."

"Roger that, Elwood. Three squads of Dreadnaughts are inbound. Help's on the way."

Excellent, he thought. Would it get here in time? Dreadnaughts were badass mechs, but not exactly the fleet's fastest.

The second wave hit them like a tsunami. Milo and Sabre avoided the onslaught, but Tin Can wasn't as lucky. His mech broke apart and the last thing Milo heard was his screaming through the radio. "This is getting out of hand, Jordan. We can't afford to lose any more mechs. We need to pull back and let the pirates have the shuttle."

"Negative. Hold out as long as you can. I'm going to try to board the shuttle and take control manually."

"How are you going to unlock the door? I don't think we get Triple A out here."

"I'll figure it out. Just go kill some damn bots."

They were all going to die and nobody was going to get paid. Shame. He'd accumulated enough to pay off his debts and put some aside. "One of these mechs must be running interference."

They blasted through the battle bots and Milo saw an opening. Maybe he could buy Jordan more time and find out where that mech was hiding. Never mind that it'd get them out of all this debris so they could see what they were shooting at. "Sabre, follow me. We're going to lead these hunks of scrap metal on a wild goose chase."

"Where are you going, Elwood? That's deeper into enemy space."

"Exactly."

Milo raced ahead of the drifting shuttle. It wasn't long before a thick cluster appeared on his scope. Probably too much for him to handle on his own. He should really wait for backup. He pushed forward on his accelerator.

"Jesus Christ, Elwood," Sabre called. "You're barely holding that tin heap together and you're going to take on a whole cluster? You're going to get yourself killed."

"Probably," he replied.

Out his port side window, six mechs in colonist livery joined the fur ball. "This is Elwood to Command. Colonist mechs have decided to lend us a hand."

"What?" came the frantic reply. "How can you tell?"

"Does shooting at the pirates count? I hope they don't expect me to share my chicken wings. They can get their own."

"Watch your ass, Milo," Sabre called. "Just because they're shooting at the pirates now, doesn't mean they won't be shooting at us later. That shuttle could be worth a lot of dough."

She wasn't wrong. Colonists were opportunists. Cowards until conditions turned in their favor. Then they jumped in to claim the spoils. "If one of them even twitches in my direction, waste them."

As he sped toward the cluster, something else popped up on his scope. Not a cluster of battle bots, but a single, larger vessel. "Outpost, this is Elwood. I think I've located the command mech. It's Sovereign Noble. Starting my attack run now." How much would they pay him for taking down the deep space version of Blackbeard, he wondered.

"Negative, Elwood. Hold your position until the Dreadnaughts arrive."

"This is not a good idea, Milo," Sabre added. "He'll tear you apart."

He wasn't that big, though he made Frankenstein look puny. Almost every inch was armor plated and Milo lost count of the weapons ports it had. Nice paint job though. Be a shame to dent it. He patted his dashboard. *Hold together a little longer, baby.* "You ready to crash the party, Sabre?"

"Hell now, but I'm not letting you take him on alone."

Milo set his nuc torpedoes to 'proximity' and fired off three shots. Sabre let three go as well. The resulting explosions were like the fireworks on the Fourth of July. The cluster scattered, but reformed almost instantly, noticeably smaller though.

Giant 'angel wings' folded out from the mech's bulbous shoulders and down in front of Sovereign Noble's cockpit as the blasts pushed him back. When the explosions cleared, he was still in one piece.

The cluster broke apart, making their proximity weapons useless. All they had were their FEMP cannons now. This wasn't going to be pretty, but they didn't have much choice. He wasn't about to engage Sovereign Noble in close combat. No need to make Sabre's prediction a reality. "Lead them back to the main battle group," he called over to Sabre. "Try to even the odds a little bit. I'm going to see if our pirate friend would like to dance."

"Sounds like a plan to me," Sabre responded. "See if you can draw him into the main group."

Milo charged toward Sovereign Noble, activating his Battle Mech systems along the way. He had to be crazy to take on the most notorious space pirate this side of Saturn. They stopped posting his kills on the outpost board because it was scaring off the other mech drivers. Some of the Outpost Battle Groups flat out refused to engage him. Even the Dreadnaughts were reluctant to mix it up with him. Milo had never had the pleasure of encountering the infamous rogue. Until now.

His targeting computer locked on with the grappling hook. "Here we go," he muttered and pulled the trigger. The hook sped towards Sovereign Noble and Milo didn't breathe the whole time. The hook never came close to the mech. Sovereign Noble dodged to one side and grabbed onto the cable.

"Well, that backfired," Milo said and reversed his engines. Maybe Sovereign Noble was into waltzes.

Milo's engines at full thrust did nothing to stop his collision with Sovereign Noble. He fired his FEMP cannons and nuc torpedoes, but nothing worked. No wonder this guy was an ace. Nothing hurt him.

"Where the hell are those Dreadnaughts?" he screamed into his radio. "We're getting decimated out here."

"Dreadnaught ETA, three minutes," an unknown voice replied.

"Excellent! We'll be dead in two."

Milo swooped low, hoping to wrap his tow cable around the legs, but Sovereign Noble was smarter than that. He slashed down across the steel cable with a long blade from his mech's left arm.

That was a problem. How was he supposed to go bot fishing without a proper line and hook? Wrench wasn't going to be happy. Milo knew then he couldn't go up against Sovereign Noble alone. To take down this pirate would require a concerted effort.

Milo raced toward the main battle group with Sabre and Sovereign Noble trailing behind. Milo's mech rocked from the pirate's cannon fire. Alarms sounded everywhere. Engines were running hot again. If Sovereign Noble didn't kill him, his own mech would. "Hey, Sabre. You think you can give this guy something else to think about while I take a minute to not die?"

"I'm trying, Milo, but that thing's got armor everywhere. It must weigh a ton."

There had to be a weakness on it somewhere. A seam between armor plates to jam his laser cutter or something. They just had to get in close to find it.

Milo pulled up on his stick, pitching his mech up over Sovereign Noble. He juked and jived, but the pirate was having none of it. Sabre cutting between them gave Milo the chance to disengage. "You're a lifesaver, Sabre. Literally."

"Outpost Battle Group, this is Elwood. We're bringing the party to you. Hope you set out some hors d'oeuvres."

"Copy that, Elwood. The table's set."

Milo cut back towards Sovereign Noble, who was mixed up with Sabre, and unleashed his cannons. The shots were like mosquito bites to the pirate, but it got his attention as Milo sped away towards the main battle group. He hoped the pirate took the hint and chased him.

"I think you pissed him off, Elwood," Sabre called. "He's on your six and closing fast."

"All part of the plan, my friend. All part of the plan."

Milo's mech rocked as laser fire bounced off his rear deflector plates. He silenced the wailing alarms and pushed his mech harder. Outside his starboard window, Jordan hovered over the resupply shuttle while a defensive line of mechs kept the heat off him. Still no sign of the Dreadnaughts.

"You guys up for some target practice?" Milo called. "Coming in hot."

Sovereign Noble didn't feel like playing that game though and veered away from the battle front. "Looks like we're playing tag," Milo called over his radio. "Any volunteers to join in?"

Three mechs joined Milo and Sabre in chasing the pirate down. Sabre hit Sovereign Noble from the left flank, trying to drive him into the main attack force. Sovereign Noble hit the brakes and Sabre didn't have time to react and flew in front of the pirate. The missile hit Sabre on the rear starboard flank, shearing off a leg and sending her tumbling through space.

"We've lost Sabre," Milo radioed. "Looks like her pod is still intact, but she's adrift."

"Roger that. SAR unit has a fix on her transponder. We're inbound."

Sabre's sacrifice changed the course of the fight. Forcing Sovereign Noble to slow down allowed the main battle force to close on him. Torpedoes and FEMP cannon fire slammed into Sovereign Noble, spinning him out of control.

Milo still had the lightning harpoon. He just needed to find a soft spot on the hull for it to penetrate. He circled in Sovereign Noble and spotted an opening between the engine nacelles. It was a tight shot, especially for a weapon with no guidance system.

Milo wouldn't get a better opening. He closed the distance to Sovereign Noble and launched his lightning harpoon. It embedded itself in the soft metal between the mech's legs and upper torso. Milo flipped the switch to electrify the harpoon and the sight was beautiful. "It works," he screamed.

Milo's radio crackled with an unusual voice. "You fight well, Little Mech. Until we meet again."

"Yeah, can't say I'm looking forward to it," Milo responded.

"That did the trick, Elwood," Jordan called. "Get your ass up here to that shuttle."

Sovereign Noble's disabled mech drifted away from the shuttle. Milo didn't dare go any closer. A wounded animal was a dangerous one. After a few minutes though, the mech broke apart, leaving a small escape pod.

"Battle Group, Sovereign Noble is disabled and adrift in Sector Two. I think the polite thing would be to offer him a lift back to the outpost, wouldn't you agree?"

"Roger that, El- Stand by. Colonist forces have engaged the battle group and are going after the shuttle. All remaining units provide close fire support."

The commander's hunch was right. The supply shuttle was too good an opportunity for the colonists to pass up. Letting the pirate go to fight another day was a mistake, but the shuttle was the priority. Milo watched Sovereign Noble's escape pod jet away into deep space.

By this time, he'd earned enough to pay back Jordan, Wrench, and bank some for a trip home. Or he could buy a new mech. Decisions, decisions.

"I'm dead stick, Elwood," Jordan radioed. "They've hacked my systems and shut me down. You need to board that shuttle and regain control."

"On my way." He altered course toward the shuttle. "Elwood to Battle Group. Sovereign Noble is bugging out. Took him down with my lightning harpoon. I'm heading for the supply shuttle now."

"Roger that, Elwood. Well done. We'll see you soon."

With Sovereign Noble defeated, the codes for the resupply shuttle worked again. Milo established a solid uplink and slowed the ship down. He swooped up behind it and opened the cargo bay doors.

Milo cut the engines and his mech dropped to the cargo bay floor with a loud 'thang'. The cockpit hissed as he released the pressure and popped it open. He hated the cold eerie silence greeting him. Probably why he went into mech piloting instead of shuttles. Ninety days in deep space all alone? No thanks.

He hopped out of the cockpit and worked his way along the cargo bay. Sealed crates lined both walls. The beer and wings were in one of those. Soon, he thought. First, he had to regain control of this flying apartment building.

The main section of the shuttle was meant to be manned, complete with crew quarters and a galley. Not exactly a luxury cruise shuttle, but better than a kick in the ass. Most of the time crews only went halfway before switching it to auto-pilot and disembarking, leaving it unmanned for the second leg of the journey.

Milo figured the outpost crew sent out to retrieve it got taken out with the armed escort. Hopefully, they put up one hell of a fight before they bought it.

Milo made his way forward toward the bridge. The first thing he had to do was get the shuttle turned around and headed for the outpost. He grinned mischievously. Maybe he'd stop and pick Jordan up along the way.

Milo sat in the left hand pilot's seat and oriented himself with the controls. Not a lot different than his mech. Just a few more buttons to push. He found the switch to open the blast shields over the windows.

He expected to see quiet space filled with bot parts that'd look good once they were converted to cash. What he saw, however, was entirely different. Battle bots surrounded the supply shuttle, weapons systems hotter than a plate of suicide wings. The six colonist mechs hovered behind the line.

"This is Elwood aboard the resupply shuttle. I am decidedly outgunned here."

"This is Dreadnaught One inbound. We have your mechs on screen. Taking out the trash for you now."

Long range plasma torpedoes slammed into the colonist mechs, scattering them across the star field. They did nothing for the bots latching onto the hull of the resupply shuttle though.

The commander's voice came over the radio then. "The case, Elwood. You have to deploy it. Transmitting you the activation codes now."

"That's great, Commander. Where do I find this case? There isn't exactly a blinking arrow pointing the way."

"There's a safe in the supply closet on the bridge. The access codes are with the packet I just sent."

Milo scrambled around the bridge while several bots latched onto the hull. That wouldn't have bothered him so much except for the giant metal saw blades slicing through.

"Hull breach imminent," the computer announced. "Proceed to the nearest escape pod."

"Thanks for the update, ya giant hunk of tin. How 'bout you deploy some countermeasures?"

"Command not recognized."

Of course not, Milo thought. That would be too easy.

Milo found the closet and the safe inside. Thankfully, the codes the commander gave him worked like a charm. The case inside looked like one of those metal briefcases the old US presidents used to carry with the nuclear launch codes in it. The 'Football' Milo remembered it being called. Ah, the good old days. Before you could pick up nucs at your local hardware store.

"Hull breach imminent," the shuttle reminded him again. "Proceed to the nearest escape pod."

Milo ignored the computer and opened up the 'Football'. A small screen and several switches laid out before him. "You still there, Commander? I have the case. What now?"

"There are five codes that have to be entered in order. It should take about thirty seconds after the last code for the signal to go out."

Five codes? Couldn't these people ever keep things simple? "Any chance I can get some help cleaning off the barnacles? I don't know if this tub has thirty seconds left."

"We'll see what we can do," the commander replied.

The shuttle rocked and pitched as mechs scraped the bots off the outside. The bots kept coming though. Milo pushed it from his mind and focused on the case. Each code was twelve characters. Milo swore these computer programmers did this on purpose just to piss users off.

"Hull breach in aft cargo hold," the computer announced.

"Seal it off," Milo ordered. Hopefully, they didn't lose any of the cargo. Milo was really looking forward to those wings.

He'd gotten to the fourth code when the shuttle screeched and shuddered. Milo lost his balance and the case slid to the far side of the bridge.

"You better make it quick, Elwood," Jordan called. "That shuttle is about to become scrap metal. I'll be really pissed if you lose all that delicious cargo now."

I'm working on it. I'm working on it. "I'm on the last code," he called over his radio. "Decided to take a coffee break."

Milo crawled across the floor to the case and punched in the last code, having to backtrack a couple times after hitting the wrong button. He hit the 'Execute' key and flopped back. He should try to make it back to his mech, but the cargo bay was sealed and he'd never make it before the bots tore the ship apart anyway.

He leaned against the wall and closed his eyes, waiting for the end to come one way or the other. "This is Elwood. I have control. You might want to send out a cleanup crew. There's a lot of tagged junk."

"You did it, Elwood," Jordan squawked in his ear. "The bots are breaking off. They're nothing but space junk now. Gotta hand it to you. You did good. Beers are on me tonight."

"But dinner is on you, Milo," Sabre cut in.

Milo laughed and laughed and laughed. "No arguments there. Let's get the hell out of here."

#

Three days after the excursion Jordan was paid off, Wrench was paid off, the armory was paid off, and Milo had a rebuilt mech. He also had a date with Sabre at the Outer Ring Steakhouse.

But first thing's first. Milo pulled the plate of steaming poultry in close, savoring the aroma of the spicy coating. A pint of amber lager sat on the table next to it. This right here was what it was all about. He closed his eyes and bit into the first hot wing of the day.

Sandy Stuckless writes in fantasy, sci-fi, and a little paranormal. He enjoys outdoorsy stuff like camping, hiking, and throwing snowballs at his kids. He lives with his family in Toronto.

To learn more about Sandy and his work, connect with him at: Twitter: @SandyRStuckless

Blood Rain

by David Castlewitz

Head down, Brandon Wiles shuffled to the dome's exit, his hands clenched into fists that bounced against his expansive waist, his eyes on the filthy pants legs in front of him, which was all he could see in the corridor's dim light. Nearby, two test subjects were yanked from the line before they stepped out of the dome. The subjects rolled up their sleeves, baring wrists and forearms, and grimaced when hit with a spray of hot water. Both tester and subject then watched for wriggling red worms beneath the epidermis. Many victims of blood rain suffered only mild itching and discomfort in their extremities before the worms went to the brain and turned them mad.

At the sound of "Yo!" Brandon stopped at the gate. He looked at the sunlight outside the dome. Anxious to be outside again, he fished his wooden work chip from his pants pocket and held it yellow side up to prove his non-tyro status. The guard let him pass.

The activity around the narrow gauge railway tracks and the very long line of freight cars filling up with trade goods told Brandon he had a good chance of getting assigned to the train, not just to the loading crew that stayed behind. The train would be long, the cars heavy to push.

"Big guy," the train master called out as he pointed at Brandon. A braided red rope looped under the epaulets on his right shoulder spoke of the train master's many years of service.

Brandon dropped his hands to his sides and looked straight ahead, mindful of not staring into the train master's hooded eyes. He watched several men as brawny as himself manhandle an overloaded freight car onto the tracks from a siding. More men pushed at the merchandise stacked in the car's bed to keep it from toppling until a crew of youngsters tied it down with coarse leather straps.

"Handle a car before?" the train master asked.

Brandon nodded, though he'd only been a loader. At age 20 he was too old to have missed out on so many chances to work a swap meet. Just bad luck, his parents told him. And the preparations outside the

29

dome weren't for some ordinary meet; this was for the winter solstice rendezvous.

He looked around to gauge his chances at a plum assignment. Watchers in sleek caps with long rounded visors kept their eyes on the sky. Group supervisors scurried around grabbing workers they knew or liked. Skinny kids lined up beside the freight and passenger cars, grease cans at hand. They'd keep keeping the train moving. More men and women trundled alongside the tracks pushing wheelbarrows and empty carts.

"Car 27," the train master said. "Now roll up your sleeve."

Brandon unbuttoned the cuff and pushed the rough denim up to past his elbow. The cool morning breeze peppered the faint blonde hairs on his forearms, making them dance. A woman in a white sack-dress hurried over and sprayed the underside of his wrist with hot water. Brandon knew he'd pass the test. He hadn't been out of the dome in months. No chance of being caught in a blood rain.

"I'll take that one." A tall redhead approached, hands in the pockets of his knee-length coat, which fanned out around him. A shiny belt buckle and glossy trousers spoke volumes about his status.

"Not this time, Jamerson," the train master growled.

"You want to push some cart back there," Jamerson said to Brandon, pointing to the rear of the train, "or get in with my peeps and maybe make some extra money?"

"He's got no say in this," the train master countered. "Anyway, I already gave you your good luck charm."

Jamerson grinned, his light blue eyes twinkling. "I got a skinny dopey looking guy pushing. Not my first pick, that's for sure."

"Clean," the woman in the sack-dress announced with a tap on Brandon's wrist before she hurried away to test someone else.

Brandon relaxed and let the train master and Jamerson work out their argument. It had nothing to do with him. He'd take whatever work he got, though he'd really like to be a watcher or a checker or, perhaps, a rail-fitter. There were always broken railway ties that caused the steel rails to buckle.

"You know there's a cut for everyone involved," Jamerson said, and hooked his thumbs beneath his wide cloth belt. "Give me the kid and you'll get a piece."

Brandon liked what he heard. There could be treasure hunting.

The train master nodded. "Send your dopey kid over to car 27."

Brandon followed Jamerson. Near the front of the train, they stopped at the rear of a passenger car with three rows of cushioned seats, each occupied. These were Jamerson's peeps, Brandon surmised. Gruff and dirty and tough, the men and the women. One carried a long handled pistol, the kind of weapon that required a special license.

"Back bar," Jamerson ordered. "Take the middle spot."

Brandon grinned and hurried to do what he was told. This was a crew of hunters. They looked for treasure most of the time; they sought rare and costly prey. The cloud-like monsters in the sky that rained down murderous blood nodules sometimes crashed. That's when men like Jamerson and his "peeps" – as he called them – sprung into action.

Excited, Brandon took his place at the back of the open-air carriage. Three pushers, Brandon in the middle and one to his right, the other to his left, combined with three pullers up front – center, left and right – would keep the carriage moving. Considering the weight of the passengers, the job required big guys, not skinnies.

Someone brought Brandon cloth gloves and a bar of resin. He donned the gloves and shoved the resin in a shirt pocket. He didn't care if he looked like an excited kid, eager to please. He didn't care if his fellow pushers shook their heads and laughed at him.

A grease girl – one of three greasers assigned to the carriage – traded a glance with Brandon. With her unevenly cropped red hair and small stature, she looked like a ten-year-old boy, but her soft face and puckered lips painted a compelling picture.

The other loaders shied away when she came close. They snapped curses in her direction, and spat at her feet. The girl didn't react, didn't speak or flinch. She squirted grease on the steel wheels and when Brandon looked directly at her, she stared back. He wondered how her ugly cropped hair looked when she was a kid. Long and flowing. Beautiful, he decided. And how long ago was that? He couldn't say.

"Don't get too close to that freak," a blue-rope wearing group supervisor said, chuckling as he passed.

A heavy-set matron pushed past the girl. She adjusted her round crown-less hat so it didn't fall, threw a gray furry wrap across both shoulders, and walked to the very first car in the train, a large passenger carriage that required ten push-pullers instead of the usual six.

Brandon overheard a few remarks, enough to identify this matron as the judge, one of the dome's administrators. In the story books he read as a child, administrators were always pictured as wise, professorial men and women.

At the upcoming swap meet, the judge would make the final decisions about what to buy, what swap was fair, what should be considered junk, and what trades were ill-advised. Most judges, Brandon often heard, shied away from engines and motors, electrified tools and batteries. Although the habitats relied on solar energy for electricity, most relied on able-bodied men and women, not machines. Like Brandon, they were always available to push a cart or a railway carriage, bike-pedal dome leaders to places they needed to go, and provide whatever muscle power some electrical contraption would otherwise replace.

A whistle's shriek sounded, followed by more whistles up and down the line of train cars.

Brandon looked to the sky, fearing a blood-rain attack, but the clouds were white with patches of blue, like lake water interspersed with land on a map.

At the blaring of horns, the open sides of some of the railway carriages suddenly filled with rigid shutters made of wooden slats and heavy canvas. Roofing was propped up above the heads of Jamieson's squad sitting in the carriage. Pushers ducked down. More wood curtains rattled. Greasers dived for cover, rushing to their assigned spots.

The girl with the ugly hair wedged herself between Brandon and the curtain to his left. A few tugs on an overhead rod at the back of the carriage caused a rigid shell to pop out of a receptacle. In seconds, the pushers and the grease-girl were nestled together in a shell of wood and canvas. Narrow slits in the side screens offered a view of supervisors prancing alongside the train. They pointed and shouted orders, or made notes in small books with stubby pencils. Demerits? Brandon wondered.

The grease-girl shivered.

"I think it's just an exercise," Brandon whispered to soothe her fears.

"I know that," she snapped. Still, she shuddered.

"I'm Brandon."

"I don't care. I'm not looking for another friend. I've got Jamerson."

Brandon straightened his back to relieve a cramp. The overhead slats rippled across his shoulders and a supervisor shouted an admonishment. "Be still over there. In an attack you gots to be quiet and still so the blood don't go through the curtains."

"Why'd you jump in here with me?" Brandon asked. "If you don't want – "

"It's my assigned station. You've never been went out before, have you?"

"No."

"Then why do you act like you know what you're doing?"

Brandon glared at her. Used to being big and muscular, he'd learned long ago that people discounted him at the start, never expecting more than heavy-duty lifting and pulling, with no particular smarts to go along with his physical strength.

"Why're you shivering?" he asked to change the subject. "You been out before, so why're you scared."

"I'm not." She turned away. Her small body didn't disturb their cocoon.

A few quiet moments passed. Brandon peeped through a rip in the canvas and watched the supervisors huddle with the train master. He guessed they were scoring the results of the drill.

"Markie," the grease-girl whispered. "My name."

Brandon grinned.

"Don't ask any more questions," Markie said.

#

The thin slice of mealy white bread surprised Brandon because he'd thought he'd have to buy breakfast using one of his few precious chits. A half-cup of hot cider complemented the meal and he sat content, his back against the train car. Here and there, watchers scanned the sky, inadvertently producing some excitement when one of them pointed to a blood-red cloud in the distance. But no warning horn sounded. No protective shields and screens went up. Brandon didn't hunker down at his assigned car.

Oddly, Markie didn't react at all. She sat munching her slice of bread, sipped from her tin cup, and didn't even look up at the source of the commotion.

Two teenaged boys passed by, pointing at her and laughing. One made a remark that Brandon didn't understand.

"Get too close to her and she'll put a worm down your throat."

Again, the derisive laughter, followed by another taunt:

"Don't kiss her. You won't like it."

Brandon started to stand, thinking he should protect the grease-girl, but she touched the top of his hand and shook her head.

"I hear that stuff all the time," she said.

"Why?"

She shrugged, but Brandon suspected she knew the answer to his question. Later, Jamerson strolled over and asked Markie if she wanted more to eat. They had leftovers. She refused the offer.

"He likes you," Brandon said after the redheaded hunter moved out of earshot. "Why're you his good luck charm?"

"Why do you ask so many questions?"

Brandon mentally searched for a good answer.

"We're not going to be friends," Markie continued.

"We could be."

Markie laughed.

"Guards!" someone shouted.

Brandon stood. His legs creaked from being in a bent position too long, and he used the side of the railway carriage to pull himself to his feet. Not far off, several ragged people appeared outside a nearby building.

The supervisor conferred with Jamerson. An older woman escorted the judge away from her ornate carriage and surrounded her and her assistants with guards armed with stout clubs. The people from the building advanced. None were armed. Their clothing was little more than rags tied together and patched — makeshift shirts and skirts. Behind them, two cages rattled against one another in the bed of a wagon pulled by several men as ragged as the others. Naked captives, both males, sat in individual cages, hands on the wooden bars, feces and urine pooling around their bodies.

"Don't let them get too close," the train master said. Immediately, four of the convoy's guards advanced.

Jamerson spoke up. "They probably got a couple of misfits to sell." He turned to Markie and gave her an order with just a nod. She scrambled to her feet, her face flush.

"Take the big guy with you," Jamerson said.

Markie bristled. "I don't need a bodyguard."

"Spit some worms at them," someone shouted. A round of snickering laughter erupted, and Jamerson glared at those standing close by.

"What's he expect you to do?" Brandon asked as he hurried to Markie's side.

Markie lowered her head and trudged ahead, her arms stiff at her sides. The ragged visitors parted to let her pass. She went immediately to the wagon and its cages, her nose wrinkling. Brandon stayed close to her.

He eyed the strangers. More of them emerged from the nearby building. They were hardly equipped for a battle, Brandon surmised with contempt. Towering over Markie he smiled to himself, happy to be playing the role of protector.

"I need space," Markie said. "Don't hover."

Brandon backed off a step while Markie examined the caged men. Both prisoners had splotches of purple and red interlaced with oozing welts across their backs. Brand watched for either or both of the men to reach out through the wooden bars.

"Are they infected?" Jamerson asked. He'd advanced towards the wagons, but didn't come too close. He cast a wary look at the people standing around him.

"We're taking them to the swap meet," said one of the men from the building. A dirty sheet wrapped around his body was his only item of clothing, but he had the bearing of a leader.

The train master approached a leather club in one hand. The decorative gold chains around his thick neck jingled, clinking against one another.

"The judge doesn't want to buy them," he said to Jamerson.

The leader interjected with, "We're not selling."

"What do you want then?" Jamerson asked.

"Transport. We can't pull this wagon all the way to the meet up. Not overland. Put us at the back of your train, on the tracks. Assign a greaser. We'll push-pull."

The train master bent to check the wagon's wheels. He shook his head when he rose up. "Two wide. Wrong wheels. No flange."

"Put the cages at the back of your train," the ragged leader said. "On one of your less full freight cars."

Jamerson shook his head. "Looks like more trouble than it's worth."

The leader dropped to a squat. "Let's talk."

Brandon stood by, curious but unable to hear everything said while Jamerson and the train master negotiated with the stranger. Meanwhile, one of the captives hissed at Markie and spat at her. That drew Brandon's attention and he slapped the wooden slats of the cage with his hand.

"If they're not infected, why are they caged?" Brandon asked Markie.

"We got rained on," one of the captives said in a raspy voice. "But we ain't crazy. Ain't going crazy, either."

The other captive added, "Ain't got no worms in the brain."

"But you got soaked in an attack?" Markie asked.

Both captives nodded.

"It happens," she added in a soft voice. "Not everybody succumbs, I guess."

Brandon had never heard of anyone who didn't go crazy from worms in the brain if they got soaked.

"Is that what happened to you?" he asked Markie. "Did you get soaked?"

"No," she replied.

"Then where'd you get your powers?" one of the captives asked, a trembling smile on his narrow face.

Markie walked away from the cages.

"Do you have some sort of power?" Brandon asked her.

"I sense things."

"Because you survived an attack?" Brandon pressed.

"I wasn't attacked," Markie snapped at him.

Brandon stared down at her, intent on knowing more. He hated being in the dark about things.

"My mother got soaked," Markie finally said. "Okay? Now you know. I was born while she screamed, probably with the worms eating her brain and driving her insane."

#

"All I said…" Markie's voice trailed off, her round face full of irritation.

Brandon exchanged glances with the pullers up front. They looked amused, as did the pusher to his right. Amused at his expense. He didn't like that, and he put extra muscle into his work.

Moved to the last car in the train, he thought his slender car-mates would appreciate his contribution. "Jamerson sent me back here," he told Markie. "Wasn't my idea."

"Not mine, either," she said.

The prisoners in the two cages strapped to the floor of the freight car banged their fists against the thick wooden bars that enclosed them.

Markie slapped the front wheels with grease from the can she carried, and the prisoners settled down in their cages, arms crossed. Three of the captors sat huddled together at the back of the carriage with blankets over their heads. When Brandon looked at them, they lowered their eyes, refusing to make contact.

In the distance, thick clouds drifted high in the sky. The clouds were not the fiery red he'd seen in picture books at school. Nor did they drip with blood, as some storytellers would say. More pink than crimson, they assembled into a V formation, the largest of the three at the point position.

"See that?" Brandon said to Markie.

"Too far away."

The train came to a stop, each of the railway cars slowing and then halting before bumping into the push-crew ahead of them.

"Do we take cover?" Brandon asked. He didn't see a protective curtain or anything to duck into. This car wasn't as well-equipped as the carriage he'd been assigned to before.

"Has to be a break in the track up ahead," Markie said. "That's why we stopped."

The train tracks were ancient artifacts uprooted from mines in the mountains, then replanted across the plains. Track was often pried from the timbers set in the ground and carried away by scavengers. Bands of people like those sitting close by, roamed the wild lands outside the domes.

The clouds continued to drift, meandering like baffled hunters not quite certain of which direction to travel.

All along the train, watch crews fanned out, their eyes on the sky. Many of the carriage handlers crawled under their cars. The three wild men scrambled to cover their captives' cages with a patched tarp before throwing blankets over themselves. Markie crawled under the railway car and Brandon followed her lead, though he was too big for the space between the wheels and had to stretch out face down across the wood ties.

"Thought you said they were too far away," he said to Markie.

She grunted in response.

A horn sounded. Then another. Shouting erupted. The commands and warnings ganged up on one another like insects in a fight. All of it was just noise to Brandon. Above his head, the prisoners banged at the bars of their cages.

"Not even close," Markie said after a few minutes. "I was right."

"How do you know?" Brandon hadn't seen much more than feet running. He couldn't see the sky.

"I just know."

"Is it safe then?"

"The watchers are probably waiting for something. Don't know what."

In his imagination, Brandon saw the clouds turn towards the train, their bodies now crimson instead of dull pink. They'd soon unleash a furious rain of thick blood-like particles, each of which contained parasitic worms intent on finding a home in a warm human body. According to everything he'd ever heard about these cloud monsters, they came from a far away mountain covered in ice and snow..

"All clear," someone shouted.

Brandon squirmed backwards and out from under the freight car.

In the sky, two of the three clouds drifted away.

"One went down," Jamerson said in an excited voice as he sprinted from the front of the train.

The train master joined him and they conferred with one another for a few minutes.

"I'll catch up," Jamerson said in an assuring voice. He turned to Markie. "You're coming with me. You got shoes for a hike?"

Several men and women from his crew joined Jamerson. He picked two men and two women to accompany him.

"What's going on?" Brandon whispered.

Markie gave him a grim look. "Jamerson's going on a treasure hunt."

Brandon narrowed his eyes. "What about the swap meet?"

"Markie!" Jamerson ordered. "Get yourself together. Find some better shoes. I'm not going without you."

"Take Big Guy," Markie said, pointing her thumb at Brandon.

"Good idea."

Brandon didn't balk when Jamerson put a hand on his shoulder. "You'll come in handy."

"And what do I do about this?" the train master asked, pointing at the railway car with the caged prisoners and their captors.

Jamerson pushed his thick blonde hair back with one hand and leaned close to the burly master. "Scrounge around."

Several large wheelbarrows appeared and the four people in Jamerson's hastily assembled team each took one. Brandon was given a two-wheeled pushcart to handle. Markie ran off and returned with a straw hat on her head and heavy boots on her feet. She smiled and hugged Jamerson like a child going off on an adventure with a loving uncle.

\#

Brandon pushed the unwieldy pushcart across the jagged rocks, lifting the cart over slabs of dark stone embedded in the ground, straining to keep up with Jamerson and the others.

Still, he couldn't help stopping now and then to gaze at the scene before him. So much tantalizing clues about what may have existed at this site long ago. Old walls towered over him and spoke of lofty buildings. Here and there, he spied printed letters chiseled out of the rock. Most of the words were weather worn and illegible. Perhaps they denoted owners of the buildings. Perhaps the words spelled out directions.

"Don't stop to gawk," Jamerson chided. "We cleaned out this place years ago."

Brandon caught up to him with a burst of new energy, though his upper arms had begun to ache with the effort.

"Some city. Some town." Jamerson said. "That's what you want to know, right?"

Brandon nodded.

His hands shading his eyes, Jamerson scanned the sky.. Brandon pushed past him while, up ahead, one of the wheelbarrows keeled over, spilling several broad-blade knives and a hand axe. Some in the party laughed at the unfortunate teammate when he stumbled across the broken concrete trying to retrieve the weapons. Brandon hurried to help out. As he retrieved the implements scattered across the rocks, a stone slab caught his attention. Wind-worn lettering puzzled him. He made sense of individual letters, but couldn't discern any real words.

"Do you know what that says?" he asked Markie.

She shrugged. "Does it matter?"

"Just curious."

"Somebody's name, I guess. Maybe it's the name of the building."

They moved on, with Brandon in the rear of the line of wheelbarrows. Markie tagged along beside him, skipping, clapping her hands. The terrain slanted uphill, and the air filled with curses and grunts until they topped the rise, drew clear of the rocks and debris, and looked directly ahead at a blacktop full of evenly spaced metal bars, all of them upright like trees. Another mystery from the past.

Markie pointed to a spot in the distance. "That way. I can feel it." She dashed ahead, her slim legs stretching to increase her pace. Jamerson reached out for her, but neither his order to slow down nor his entreating hands had any effect.

"Go after her," Jamerson said with a flick of his hand at Bandon, who immediately dropped his pushcart and ran after Markie. He easily caught up to her.

"I know what I'm doing," she complained.

Brandon grabbed her by the arm. She wrenched herself loose, but when she turned away she didn't run. She walked. Brandon followed, certain that that's what Jamerson wanted him to do. Somehow, he reasoned, he'd gone from porter to protector, and he liked the idea.

Markie pointed at a gently sloping hill ahead of them. The rest of the team caught up to them.

"I don't see anyting," Jamerson said.

Markie walked on. Brandon followed, but stopped at the top of the hill and stared at where she pointed. A bubbling red mass hugged the ground. Thick tendrils oozed between the crevices and dripped from upright rusty metal bars.

"Alive or dead?" Jamerson asked.

"I can't tell," Markie admitted. "I gotta get closer."

Brandon hurried to Martkie's side. She could be under attack at any moment. The mass had to be a cloud, he thought. Fallen from the sky, but still deadly. Silvery worms wiggled across the cracked cement, winding around the rebar, and slithering along the surfaces of old granite and marble slabs.

"I need to get closer," Markie said. When Jamerson nodded, she moved towards the shuddering red mass. She ventured close enough that tiny fingers of red gel lapped at the toes of her leather boots.

A finger of red slime rose in the air; several more quickly joined it. A crimson wave reeled back, like a blood-red sling, and heaved itself at Markie, drenching her. Brandon tried to get to her, but Jamerson held him back, shaking his head, mouthing a soundless, "Don't."

Markie peeled off her shirt, pulling it up over her head. She slipped out of her loose fitting trousers and kicked them and her shoes to one side. Silvery worms crawled across her round face. She plucked them off, threw them to the ground, and stamped on the ones that didn't get away.

Someone said, "She's immune. It's true."

Markie stepped backwards, closer to where Brandon and Jamerson stood watching. Quickly, Brandon undid the ties keeping his shirt closed and tossed it over Markie's shoulder. A large garment, it fell well past her hips, effectively covering her naked body.

"The worms," someone said, pointing.

Brandon looked down at his shoes. Several of the silvery objects huddled at the toes of his boots. He stomped on them. Elsewhere, the wiggling creatures trembled in their death throes. Markie picked one up.

"Dead?" Brandon asked.

"Kinda," Markie said. "But not really. The cloud, neither." She took in a deep breath. "Something in between."

Brandon mulled that over. He didn't fully comprehend what she meant. Meanwhile, Jamerson urged the crew towards the fallen cloud, and they attacked it with long handled blades and the hand axe. They dug into it and pulled out pieces of its innards.

Jamerson sent Brandon to retrieve the pushcart he'd abandoned at the base of the hill. When he returned, he bent to the task of scooping up the cloud's strange interior parts. Blood clung to his clothing, but easily peeled off. The worms didn't threaten. They didn't move.

Something that looked like a pump, a device made of plastic, lay at Brandon's feet. He picked it up, examined it for a moment, and then tossed it into the pushcart. Writing on the pump spelled out words he didn't know. Glancing sideways, he watched Markie squat on the ground, her round face pale, her eyes downcast. Elsewhere, the team stripped the cloud-creature of its interior parts. Flexible piping and bellows and bottle-like containers filled the wheelbarrows and the pushcart, while sticky globs of thick red gel were tossed away, along with the stringy material that bound the plastic parts together.

Brandon soon backed away, his pushcart full. The team redistributed the booty amongst the four wheelbarrows to balance out the load.

"Somebody built these, didn't they?" Brandon said to Markie.

She looked up. "Maybe. Don't ask me. Why would I know?"

"But you've got this… this – "

"Affinity? Yeah, that's what I got." She toyed with one of the dead worms. "I don't understand it. Nobody does."

"There must be somebody who knows."

"They're all long dead." Markie gestured at the cloud on the ground. It was no longer blood-red. Now it was pink in the center and white at its extremities. "Hybrids," she said after a short silence. "Mechanical parts mixed with organics, I've been told. Like cyber-men in those old books they read in school."

Brandon pretended he understood. He'd never been told such stories.

Jamerson sauntered over. He waved at the pushcart. "Get going. We gotta catch up to the train."

Markie stood. She pulled off Brandon's shirt and handed it to him. He looked away while she dressed in her still-slimy clothes.

"Any of those things get in you?" Jamerson asked.

Markie shook her head.

"What're we going to do with this – stuff?" He pointed at his pushcart.

"There's usually a couple of science types at these swaps," Markie said. "They'll probably buy some of the stuff we pulled out."

"They study the clouds?" Brandon asked.

"They'll probably buy those two prisoners, too," she added.

#

Scores of camps, with many fenced off from their neighbors and some a sprawl of wagons and bedding and pitched tents, covered the site of the mid-winter rendezvous. A canvas pavilion, capped by a domed roof spiked with fluttering flags of various colors representing traveling clans, underground villages, and the domes, overflowed with merchants and hawkers. They spilled from the edges. A mix of acrobats and magicians and musicians entertained the crowd, and pop-up saloons offered drink and meals. Wooden towers dotted the landscape and Brandon assumed sharp-eyed watchers scanned the skies for any sign of a blood-rain attack.

Jamerson and Markie ran ahead of the crew to join up with the train, which sat idle several hundred yards from the pavilion on a spur emanating from one of the main tracks into the site. Though exhausted, Brandon put all his remaining strength into pushing his cart, his shirt sweated through and clinging to his broad back. Dirt ran in rivulets down his thick arms and into his wrists and hands. His teammates handling the wheelbarrows hung back, stopping every now and then to catch a breath. Jamerson hadn't let anyone sleep more than necessary. They'd pushed on until it was too dark to do so without the danger of an accident. At first light, after a meager breakfast, they pushed; yet, it was late in the day when they caught up to the train.

Elsewhere, ragged groups of men and women carried their wares on their backs, and even prosperous visitors, whose grease-smelling trucks belched noxious fumes, milled along all four open sides of the pavilion. Camps stretched for nearly a mile in all directions.

As Brandon approached, Jamerson led the judge towards him. Eager to show off the find, Brandon guessed,. The judge waddled on from Brandon's pushcart, onto the wheelbarrows lined up for her inspection.

"Where's Markie?" Brandon asked.

"Out of sight," Jamerson said. "I keep her hidden at these things. I ain't losing my good luck charm."

The train master wandered over and fingered the odd assortment of cloud refuse, some of which was sticky with blood-like gel. A few silvery worms still crawled in the bed of Brandon's cart, which made the train master suddenly jerk away in disgust.

"This is dangerous," the train master muttered. "Kill the worms before we take anything in for sale."

"We'll need the girl," the judge said, "to certify the two prisoners safe."

"No," Jamerson said.

"You got no choice," the train master put in, and the judge nodded her agreement.

"Did they say that?" Jamerson asked, and Brandon wondered who "they" were. The scientists? The prisoners' captors?

"I'm saying it," the judge answered. "I want a good price so our percentage is worth the trouble they gave us."

At that, Jamerson backed off, nodding, head bowed in acquiescence. The judge pressed her meaty hands together, pursed her lips and started to walk away. For a moment, her soft eyes found Brandon's and he hoped she'd speak to him, acknowledge his part in this venture. But she didn't. She moved on.

"If Markie has to go," Jamerson said, "you're going with her, Big Guy." With pursed lips, he walked away, but looked back and nodded. Brandon took the gesture as a silent signal to follow.

They walked deeper into the crooked lanes formed by the tents and piles of trade codes brought to the rendezvous. Guards kept watch on the valuable booty.

Markie sat in the makeshift kitchen in the center of the camp, a stack of dead rats at hand and a slop bucket between her skinny legs. The animals were the skinny type found in the fields, not the chubby creatures Brandon often came across in the sub-surface warrens, where he often hunted to earn day-work chits so he could labor above ground, sometimes at the top of the dome in the sunshine, where mansions housed the community's leaders, and where gardens adorned the artificial landscape.

"We're going with the prisoners tomorrow," Jamerson said. Markie raised her eyes from her work.

"I don't want to," she said.

"We want a good price," Jamerson said. "So we get a good-sized commission – "

"You don't need me," Markie countered.

Brandon saw tears well in her eyes. "I'll be with you," he said.

She snorted. "I don't need you to protect me."

"He's going," Jamerson said. "I'll go as well. You'll be safe."

"What happened to keeping me under wraps in the kitchen? Huh? Aren't you afraid they might know what I am?" She paused and took a breath. "Who I am," she added.

Jamerson folded his arms across his chest. Markie gutted a rat and let the innards fall in the bucket between her legs. She tossed the carcass over her shoulder and a small boy retrieved it and gave it to one of the older women at a table, where mallets and grinders prepared the evening meal.

"I don't care what they know or what they think," Jamerson said.

"That's right," she said, "we've got Big Guy here if there's trouble."

Brandon imitated Jamerson, folding his thick arms across his wide chest, legs spread. He pictured himself a worthy guard and he swelled with pride, confident that he would do everything expected of him.

#

Two women in long white robes with frayed cuffs and ragged hems inspected the two prisoners, who'd been released from their cages but bound with their hands behind their backs and their ankles roped together. They huddled in the middle of the large room, which looked to Brandon like a lab of some sort, very much like what he'd seen in books.

The pop-up building covered a large space under the pavilion, deep inside a maze of narrow stalls and closet-sized stores, all prefabs designed to be carted from place to place, unpacked, assembled, and put together to make rooms and corridors. This lab was one of many rooms. Brandon guessed there were dorms for sleeping and a kitchen, perhaps a clinic, and doctor offices.

Three guards from the settlement that had been holding the prisoners stayed close at hand, lined up along a wall of empty shelves. Brandon, though he tried to stay alert in case he was needed, found his attention drawn to the vats of worms in a corner of the room and the miniature cloud floating in fluid inside a goblet-like glass vessel.

The white-robed women traded whispered comments. Soon, several men in stiff, short white jackets entered. Brandon guessed they were all scientists of some sort. Why else would they be interested in the prisoners?

Jamerson hovered over everyone. Markie squeezed herself into a narrow space behind Brandon and a faux-porcelain white counter.

Outside the lab, under guard by another of Jamerson's team, a wheelbarrow full of the best refuse hacked from the dead cloud waited for inspection.

"Who brought this junk out here?" someone asked from an open doorway. He stood with his hands in the pockets of his waist-long white tunic, which he wore over red overalls that didn't quite come up to his neck. Tufts of pale body hair spilled out from the top of his one-piece suit.

"Not junk," Jamerson said. "It's all for sale. It's not junk. You the buyer?"

"Yeah. Let's look it over."

Jamerson stepped outside with the buyer.

"Those worms all alive?" Brandon asked, directing the question at no one in particular, but with the hope that someone would answer. "You get them out of people?"

One of the women grinned and said, "Don't worry. They won't jump out and get you."

"How'd you get them?"

The woman flipped her blonde tresses back from her long face. Brandon wanted to pose another question, get as many in as he could before Jamerson returned and made him be quiet. His curiosity run amok inside his head. But then one of the guards outside poked her head in and said, "Big Guy! You're wanted outside."

Brandon hurried out of the room. Markie stayed close to him, at his heels, behind him, hiding.

The buyer or scientist or whatever he represented, the one in the red one-piece outfit, examined the contents of the wheelbarrow. The two women joined him outside. Interested passersby stopped to peer over the low fence surrounding the prefab building. Guards kept people moving, grunting and gesturing.

"How big was the cloud?" the blonde-haired woman asked.

Jamerson provided the answer. Just an estimate, he insisted. They hadn't taken measurements.

The older woman sighed. "It's an original, Dr. Franz," she said to the other woman.

Dr. Franz picked up one of the narrow tubes from the bottom of the wheelbarrow. She produced a magnifying glass from a pocket of her robe and turned the tube over several times, studying it closely, her lips moving as she read the writing embossed across it.

"You don't get stuff like that all the time," Jamerson said, launching into salesman-mode.

"Who's that behind you?" the older woman asked. "Let me see you, girl."

"You find her, too?" Dr. Franz asked Jamerson.

"She's with me," Brandon said.

Red overalls took a step towards Brandon. "I know that girl."

Dr. Franz' face brightened. "Of course! Come on, Markie, stop trying to hide."

"Hey," Jamerson interjected. "I'm here to sell this stuff, not barter away my girl."

"Do you still feel the worms?" Franz asked Markie.

"We're selling stuff, not her," Brandon said.

The two women resumed their examinations, rummaging through the wheelbarrow, selecting one item to inspect, then another. "This looks like a pumping mechanism," one of them mused. "An original. Copies never get that good."

"Copies?" Brandon asked, and ignored the angry look he got from Jamerson.

Another scientist joined in. He dug into the debris, pulled out gears and wide plastic bands, examined them and then dropped them back into the wheelbarrow. This newcomer was elderly, with thick lips that dripped saliva, his cheeks glistening.

"You're right," he announced. "All original cleaner-bot material." He clapped his hands and smiled. "Perfect find. Good job. Well done."

"How much we getting?" Jamerson asked.

The elderly man stooped on bent knees, grinning. "Is that little Markie hiding there?"

"Hello, Professor Vale." Markie stepped out from behind Brandon.

"I'm happy to see you're still alive."

"I'm alive," she whispered. "And not crazy."

"You know," Vale began as his eyes roamed from one person to another, "the worms don't take kindly to the human body."

"Then why do they get inside people?" Brandon asked.

"Who knows?" Vale answered, and chuckled. "These machines were built for cleaning the atmosphere. To reproduce, sort of, by copying themselves. Prime examples of artificial life. Until they got out of control."

"And the blood?" Brandon pressed.

"It's not really blood. It's a cleaning agent. The worms spew it into the air. All very well designed a hundred years ago."

"I'm not here for a history lesson," Jamerson said. "Big Guy, keep quiet or go inside."

"We're not buying back the girl," Franz said.

"Like I said, she's not got for sale."

Brandon felt a hand tugging at the back of his shirt.

"Get me out of here," Markie said.

Jamerson nodded. "She's validated the two guys in there. You need anything else from her?"

"Just answers," Vale said in a quiet and sad voice.

"I got none," Markie snapped at him, and walked away. Brandon chased after her, into the surrounding alleys and crisscrossing thoroughfares.

"Stop," Brandon said as Markie stepped into a narrow pathway between two twisted rows of merchants. "Let's wait for Jamerson in case he needs something."

"You his lackey now?" Markie dropped to a squat.

"Did you work for those guys?" Brandon asked, nodding back at where Jamerson sparred with the scientists and the buyer in red.

Markie didn't answer right away. She looked up at Brandon with tears brimming in her eyes. "They raised me after my mother died," she said. "I was Professor Vale's prized specimen." She grunted. "Even though he always said I was more of a daughter than anything. Don't believe him. I don't. Never did."

"Because you're infected?"

"Are you really that dense?" she shot back. "Yeah. I've got worms in me and I've had them all my life. That's why they don't hurt me. That's why Jamerson keeps me around. I got some sort of second-sight with them in my head. Okay? Now you know."

"But they don't hurt you."

"Not yet," Markie said.

Brandon made an effort to speak with a kind voice. "Don't worry, I won't let them take you back."

Markie said. "I ain't worried about that."

Brandon waited for her to explain. When she didn't, he prompted with, "What then?"

She answered in a soft voice. "I'm afraid I'll want to. Want to go back."

#

Brandon didn't like the smell of the goats in the pen near the kitchen, so he shied away from guarding them, though that was his day's assignment. Why didn't Jamerson send him to accompany the judge and her assistants when they visited the market? With his size and strength, he'd be useful. Maybe he'd become one of the judge's favorites… if given the chance.

At least here, next to the kitchen, he was close to Markie, though she studiously ignored him while she worked, sometimes stirring the pot hanging over a charcoal fire and other times standing at a table preparing grease to be used for the trek home.

When Professor Vale appeared, she plunged her hands into a bucket of rotting meat. Brandon grinned, guessing she wanted to make herself unpleasant to be around.

"Is that what you want to do the rest of your life?" Vale asked. "You could contribute so much more." He withdrew as quietly as he'd entered, ducking under the kitchen's low hanging canvas roof.

"What's that about?" Brandon asked, stepping away from the goat pen and stopping at the edge of the kitchen.

Markie bowed her head. "Don't tell Jamerson."

Brandon nodded, but he knew he should. Jamerson understood more about this than he'd ever know on his own.

"I'm not going back there," Markie said, her eyes brimming with tears. Brandon waited for her to tell him more, but she didn't, and he returned to his guard post, his nose wrinkling at the renewed assault on his sense of smell.

Late in the afternoon, with Markie busy helping with kitchen duties, Brandon decided to offer a version of the truth to Jamerson, that wouldn't betray the confidence he'd built with Markie.

"I didn't hear what they talked about or what the Professor wanted."

Jamerson snorted. "He's no professor. Don't buy into it, Big Guy. Vale's just another lab tech making himself sound important."

Brandon weighed how much more he should say. "Markie didn't act interested."

"She just sat there making a vat of wheel grease?" Jamerson asked, sounding skeptical.

Brandon nodded. "What do they want with her?" he asked after a few moments.

"Whatcha think, Big Guy?"

Brandon shrugged. "Examine her? Maybe they want to know more about the worms in her body?"

"She's an anomaly," Jamerson said. "But you don't understand, do you? Everybody goes crazy when the worms make it to the brain, but not Markie. She's got them in her and I think – she thinks – they communicate with her somehow. I don't know. Nobody knows. That's why Vale wants her."

Brandon nodded as though he understood, though he'd need to run Jamerson's explanation through his mind a few times. He'd need to ruminate on the matter. Think about it.

"She ran away from them before," Jamerson said. "If she goes back she'll run away again."

"I wouldn't want that to happen," Brandon said, and hurried to clarify himself. "Go back to them, I mean."

"Yeah. Well, keep an eye on her, Big Guy. She's too valuable to lose. That's why I call her my good luck charm." Jamerson grinned. "Notice that we didn't get rained on once on the way here? That's her doing. She's got a way of warding them off."

Brandon wanted to know more, but he didn't want to ask too many questions. He didn't want to sound stupid.

"We're packing up half the train tomorrow," Jamerson said. "Sending back what we've bought. Don't let anyone grab you as a pusher. You keep close to Markie so she don't do something dumb."

"Got it."

#

"I've no choice," Jamerson said. He paced in front of his tent, while two of his crew packed his personal gear in crates. Elsewhere, teams of pushers, many of them as powerfully built as Brandon, muscled freight cars along the spur towards the railroad track.

"And Markie?" Brandon asked.

"She's coming with me."

Brandon nodded, mumbling, "of course," over and over. Tears welled in his eyes. He didn't want to be left behind, but Jamerson, who'd always seemed so important and in charge, had been ordered home by the judge. He'd be with the escort of the first train back. Pirate gangs often preyed on caravans and trains returning from a swap, and the judge wanted her best fighters and battle tacticians at hand for the slow trek home.

Jamerson turned away to supervise the packers handling his newly purchased souvenirs boys and personal gear. Brandon slipped away. At the kitchen, where he found Markie, he stumbled around looking for a way to seem busy. There were no heaps of merchandise to protect and no goats in the pen. Most everything, including the long tables where meals were served, had already been loaded onto the train's freight cars.

Markie stood at one of the remaining tables, her hands digging into a bowl of ground meat that she expertfly shaped into fist-sized balls that

49

she dropped onto a wood tray. A stew pot bubbled above a nearby open fire and a child stirred in handfuls of edible grass and roots along with a few cut tubers that looked like skinny versions of the potatoes Brandon enjoyed at home.

"Jamerson's leaving with the first train," he said to Markie.

Markie shrugged. She blushed only slightly. Her lips moved, but she didn't speak.

"You're going with him," Brandon added.

"I know. He told me."

With no specific duty for the morning, Brandon found a soft chair outside the kitchen's open-sided tent. Sitting back, his arms across his wide chest, he soon succumbed to sleep. It came easily, but he woke with Jamerson shaking him.

"Where is she?"

Brandon opened his mouth, but didn't speak.

"Come on, Big Guy. Where's Markie?" Jamerson fumed. He turned to the kitchen workers preparing the large midday meal. "The girl," he shouted at them. :The greaser. Where'd she go?"

Horns sounded. The trainmaster blew his whistle. One of the judge's crew called to Jamerson, urging him to hurry.

"Maybe she's with the train," Brandon offered.

"Don't be stupid. If she – I wouldn't be looking for her if ..." Jamerson shook his head. "We're leaving. I'm leaving. Find her and try to catch up."

Brandon nodded.

"Got that, Big Guy?"

"Yes. I'll find her."

Jamerson stormed off, swallowed by the dense camp.

"Anybody see where she went?" Brandon asked.

"Jamerson's pet?" one of the kitchen helpers asked, and the others laughed. They traded snickers and sneers.

"Where'd she go?" Brandon demanded.

"Maybe she's at the women's dorm."

Of course. She'd fallen asleep. As he had. Didn't Jamerson look for her there?

Brandon turned his back on a chorus of giggles and whispers and ran to the far side of the camp, past the litter of discarded clothing and other leftovers. More than one train had gotten an early start for home.

The dorm, located in a long narrow tent at the edge of the camp site, was nearly empty. Only a few wooden racks remained. Feathers and old rags, the stuffing that made up the thin mattresses, were strewn across the bare ground.

"You know Markie? She's a wheel greaser. A kitchen worker," Brandon explained to the matronly guard outside the tent. "She's one of Jamerson's."

The answer he got was a terse, "What about her?"

"I'm looking for her.

"She left."

"How long ago? Where'd she go?"

The guard shrugged. "She ain't here now. She had a sack with her, not that she had much to put in it."

Brandon felt something drop inside him. His face went pale and he blinked back tears. He looked towards the market teeming with merchants and buyers. Long strides took him to the edge of the pavilion. He plunged in. When he thought he'd lost his way he stopped to ask for directions. The overhead wood-reinforced canvas roof blocked the sun, so the dim light barely made the market's interior accessible. Oil lamps helped, but until his eyes adjusted to the shadows Brandon had little idea of where he was or how he'd find his destination.

After wandering through the alleys and narrow paths, of squeezing between closely set stalls to take shortcuts, he stumbled across something familiar, and then he saw it: the pop-up building and several guards standing in the surrounding open space.

"You got something to sell?" one of the guards asked, He pointed his thumb back over his shoulder. "Back that way."

"Vale. I need to see Professor Vale."

"The galley. That way. Easy enough to find. Follow the smell."

Brandon broke into a fast walk, pushing past anyone who got in his way. He drew stares and mild curses from the people he jostled. When he saw Markie, he slowed his pace. She hovered over a steaming cup of tea, her back to him. Perched on high stool, she looked like a child waiting for a parent to return.

He approached slowly, fearing she'd run if he startled her. He took note of a small knapsack on the ground, wedged between the bottom of the counter and the stool.

"What are you doing here?" he asked as he came to her side.

Before she could answer, someone else said, "A more important question… "

Brandon pivoted in the direction of a new voice. The tone, though friendly, came with a look of steely eyes and a grim face. Professor Vale stepped between Markie and Brandon and asked:

"More importantly, what're you doing here?" Vale asked.

"Markie's supposed to be with the train going back," Brandon said.

"And he sent you to find me?" Markie asked.

Brandon nodded. "We can still catch up. The train doesn't move that fast." He grabbed Markie by her skinny arm.

"Don't," Vale said. "Don't touch her."

Markie wrenched herself free with a strength that Brandon didn't expect.

"You don't want to go back to them," Brandon said, taking in the sight of the small backpack, putting meaning to why Markie sat here, why Vale was with her now, and why she hadn't joined Jamerson at the train.

"You don't know anything," she said.

"After what you told me? Why would you go back?"

Markie slipped from her stool. "I don't want to be Jamerson's pet. I don't want to be that grease-girl they talk about behind my back. There's a lot I don't want."

Brandon started to speak, to say, "That's your place." Just as he had his place in the world, Markie had hers, one she arrived at through choices made in the past. Running away from Professor Vale had led her to Jamerson and a grease-girl's life.

Vale spoke in a soft, elderly man's voice. "She can make up her own mind about what she wants or where her place is in the world."

"You didn't do her any good," Brandon snapped. "She's just an experiment to you."

Vale nodded. He pressed his pale lips together, puckering them for a moment. "Very true. With her help, I'd hoped to learn more about the blood clouds. Perhaps find a way to stop them. Find a remedy for the worms that infest the body and drive people insane. Find out why our Markie, teeming with the creatures since birth, is immune to their adverse effects."

"He's flattering you," Brandon said, whispering close to her ear.

"Jamerson does the same," Markie said. "Difference is, he doesn't need me. Professor Vale does."

Brandon snorted. "Professor of what? Is that just a title you gave yourself?"

Vale grinned. "We have a university on the other side of the mountains. It's for research, mostly, but I teach several classes on – "

"Okay, okay," Brandon sputtered. "I don't' care!" He took hold of Markie's chin and made her turn to look at him. "I don't want you running off."

"Her place with us is an important one," Vale said.

Brandon appealed to Markie again. "You wouldn't dare do this if Jamerson was here."

"You're right. I wouldn't. But he isn't, so I'll do what I've been wanting to do ever since ... Why do you think I didn't want to go to the lab in the first place? I knew I couldn't resist. I can't resist going back. I told you that!"

"She'll be safe with us," Vale said.

Markie picked up her backpack and held it to her chest.

"Jamerson won't like this," Brandon murmured.

Markie looked up at Vale. She turned to look at Brandon and said, "You can come as well."

Vale added, "We always need strong young men like you."

"I don't belong at some university."

"We have things to build. You could learn a useful trade."

"You need a pusher? That's my trade."

Vale chuckled. "We have engines to power our trucks."

Brandon shook his head.

"Don't think you're betraying him," Markie said. There was no animosity in her voice. No snarl. She didn't speak as though she hated "him" – Jamerson.

Brandon shook his head.

"You don't owe him anything," Markie continued. "He doesn't even call you by your name. What's he call you? Big Guy. He probably already forgot your name. Forgot it the moment he heard it. He'll forget all about you in a week."

"But he'll never forgive me," Brandon said.

"If you pass up this opportunity for a better life," Vale said, "you may never forgive yourself."

Markie and Vale turned away. Side by side, they walked into a crowd. Vale's head popped up as they moved along a lane bordered on both sides by vendors hawking their wares. Within seconds, the market absorbed them completely, and they disappeared from view.

She's right, Brandon told himself. Jamerson didn't know his name. But he didn't care about that. He liked being part of Jamerson's crew. Jamerson called him "Big Guy" out of affection.

Which would be gone now that he lost Markie. He wouldn't be "Big Guy" any longer. Jamerson would find some other nickname for him.

And he'd never call him Brandon.

Though Vale and Markie had disappeared into the market, he knew where they went. He pictured Markie looking back at him just before the market swallowed her. Had she? Really? She looked back at him in his memory of her receding from view, a question in her soft blue eyes and a plea on her face.

She needed him, he told himself. Needed him more than Jamerson needed another pet worker to nickname and coddle. Where she went, he could go. He'd go where Markie was more than just a greaser on the train and he another pusher keeping that train moving.

David Castlewitz retired from a long and successful career as a software developer and technical architect, and turned to a first love: fiction of all sorts, especially SF and fantasy. Living north of Chicago, he has wonderful winters that keep him inside and splendid (though short) summers for walking, biking, and fishing. All give him time to contemplate new story ideas.

Crimes Against Time

by Katie Kent

J udge Babcock is a distant but imposing figure, clad in robes and wig, his voice echoing around the wood-panelled courtroom. I clutch onto the small table in front of me so tightly that my knuckles begin to turn white.

"Hazel Thompson, you are accused of breaking the following Time Travel Laws, passed in 2096:

Section A, Clause 1: 'Travellers must not intentionally change the timeline.'

Section A, Clause 4: 'Travellers must not travel within 100 years of that day's date, in either direction. Travellers must not travel within their own lifetimes.'

Section B, Clause 1: 'Time travel must be used for leisure purposes only, and not for personal gain.'

Section B, Clause 2: 'Travellers must travel with an approved Time Travel Passport.'

Section B, Clause 3: 'All travellers must arrive and be processed at an approved Time Travel Centre.'

I quote: 'Anyone found to have broken any of the Laws shall be sentenced and subjected to incarceration in a secure facility without access to time travel, for a period to be determined by the Judge.'"

He peers at me over a pair of the latest smart glasses, his face stern.

The glasses are no doubt feeding him the results from previous court cases relating to time travel. There have been enough of them that a jail has been set up purely for offenders against the time travel laws, but this isn't a common crime at all. For most, to be without a time machine in this day and age is like being denied access to oxygen. The anti-time travel movement has its followers, but they only number in the hundreds across the world. Most people obey the laws, too fearful of the consequences of going against them.

"How do you plead?" Judge Babcock continues, snapping me out of my thoughts.

I look straight at him, determination set on my face. "Guilty."

A gasp goes around the courtroom.

I clear my throat. "Your Honour, I am guilty of breaking the laws, but I believe there are mitigating circumstances that should be taken into account when sentencing." Much to my mum's consternation I had waived my right to a lawyer, choosing to represent myself.

Judge Babcock is clearly taken aback, but he recovers quickly. "And what are these circumstances?" he asks.

I lean forward, closer to the microphone. Ready to make the speech that I have spent the last few weeks rehearsing. "It all started around a month ago," I begin.

#

Mum paced around the room. "Hazel, I need to go out. Look after your brother, will you?"

I looked up from my book, curling my legs underneath me on the sofa. "Again?" Mum was leaving me in charge of Jake more and more lately. It wasn't that I minded looking after him. Jake and I had always been close. When he was born six years ago, it had been one of the best days of my life. I had always wanted a sibling. I was at my mum's side, holding her hand, as he took his first breath, as he came kicking and screaming into the world. Unlike her loser of a boyfriend, who had cleared off when he learnt that he was going to be a dad.

I doted on my baby half-brother. I fed him, played with him and even changed his nappy without complaint. I spent my pocket money on clothes and toys for him. I was happy to help my mum. But over the past couple of years, it was like *I* had become his mum. She was barely there, either physically or mentally.

We were losing her to addiction. I could see it, and I felt powerless to stop it. She displayed all the classic symptoms of time travel addiction. Headaches, shaking, confusion, a loss of interest in everyday activities. Time travel was a ground-breaking invention, but for some, it was akin to drug use.

She picked up her lipstick and looked in the mirror as she applied it in a thick line. The bright red tone didn't suit her pale face. "I won't be long."

We both knew it was a lie. Mum spent so little time in the present these days.

"Okay." What else *could* I say? It was clear that she was suffering from depression. Time travel gave her a hit. She used to be really happy just after a trip, and those were some of the best times the three of us had shared in the past few years. She'd put on a movie, order pizza and we'd all snuggle up together on the sofa.

"Honestly, Hazel, there's nothing like it." I remembered how she used to describe time travel to me in the early days, while she was still capable of being lucid. Her eyes would shine as she tried to sell the benefits to me. "It's the escapism. There's something so great about visiting other time periods. It gives you a buzz."

But it never lasted long nowadays. Hours later the withdrawal symptoms would start, and she'd be almost climbing the walls until she could go off again. She'd be snappy and irritable. And lately, the ups were getting fewer and far between. The downs hit her far earlier than they used to, and sometimes that's all there was.

"I've got my exam on Monday morning," I reminded her as she gathered her things together. "9am." It was only Saturday now, but Mum had been known to disappear for days at a time before.

She nodded. "Don't worry, I'll be back in plenty of time." She opened the door of the basement and headed down the stairs as I went into the kitchen, took the cereal out of the cupboard and poured it into a bowl.

"When did Mummy go to this time?" Jake asked as I handed him the bowl. He was sat on the sofa in his robot pyjamas; Mum hadn't even taken the time to get him dressed.

I sighed as I ruffled his blonde hair. "She'll be back soon."

"Can we play VR?" His eyes lit up.

"Not today. Sorry buddy. Your sister has got to study for her exams."

He pouted, his bottom lip protruding.

"I'll put Robot Patrol on for you." I spoke the words in my head and the TV turned on and started playing his favourite show.

I settled down at the table so I could keep an eye on him, and started my revision. I rubbed my eyes and yawned. Studying wasn't going well lately. What with having to look after Jake, dealing with Mum and working weekend evenings at the local café, it was a struggle to keep my eyes open. But it was important for me to pass my exams so I could get into law school. Law was all I wanted to do with my life. Perhaps I could do something to change the Time Travel Laws, make it harder for people to become addicted.

#

Mum didn't come back that day. I had to call in sick to work, and not for the first time recently. It was a wonder I still had a job, to be honest. But I couldn't leave Jake on his own, and we had no family nearby. We could have done with the money—Mum was living on benefits, after being fired from a succession of jobs because she kept missing shifts—but at least I had the extra time for studying. I had to ace these exams.

I gave Jake dinner, tucked him into bed, read him a bedtime story and kissed him on the head before lounging on the sofa in front of the TV. My stomach rumbled as I tore open the wrapper of a protein bar. I needed to get back to the studying, but I was so tired. *I'll just shut my eyes for a few minutes*, I thought, as I rested my head against a cushion.

The sound of crying woke me up with a start. I glanced at my smartwatch. 8am. *Shit*. I felt better for the sleep, but I had so many modules still to revise.

Jake was crying his eyes out when I went into his room. "Mummy was being chased by a monster," he managed to get out, between sobs. He took a big gulp of air and launched into a coughing fit.

Patting his back, I tried to calm him down. "Hey, it's okay. It was just a bad dream, that's all. Mummy is fine."

He stopped coughing and looked up at me, his eyes full of hope. "Mummy's back?" he asked.

My heart sank. "Not yet, Jakey. But she'll be home soon, I'm sure of it." I gave him a big smile that didn't match what I was feeling inside.

Jake's dream of Mum being chased by a monster was close to the truth. Her demons were overwhelming her. My dad had died just after I was born, and then Jake's idiot father knocked her around, knocked her up and then left her as a single parent with a teenager and a baby. I wasn't much of a time traveller myself—Mum's addiction really put me off—but I'd been a few times and I could see why it was so addictive for someone like her. She was obviously using it to fill the emptiness.

I kept an eye on the time, hoping that every hour would be the one that Mum returned. Jake's nightmare had obviously affected him, and he was more hyperactive than usual. TV didn't settle him like it did usually. In the end I switched on the VR game, and finally managed to tire him out. As he fell asleep on my shoulder I breathed a sigh of relief, but was slightly alarmed when I saw it was almost 3pm. I quietly pulled myself away from him and settled him down on the sofa.

"Where is she?" I muttered to myself as I finally sat down in front of my tablet to study. I had so much to cover, and in such a short space of time.

#

I set the alarm early the next morning. As the piercing chime woke me at 6am, nerves flooded through me. I got dressed quickly, and then poked my head around Mum's door. She was nowhere to be seen, and she wasn't in the lounge or the bathroom either. I took a deep breath, and clenched my fists. *There's still time*, I reassured myself.

I made myself a quick cup of coffee. I really could have done with some breakfast, but there was no cereal left, and the bread had gone mouldy. Jake woke up, and I got him settled in front of the TV. I checked my watch. It looked like Jake wasn't going to school today—his was too far away and there wasn't time for me to take him and get back for my exam. Time was ticking away, and I felt a deep pit of despair settle in my empty stomach. I hadn't made any contingency plans, and I couldn't leave my brother alone, but I really couldn't miss this exam. There wasn't any point texting Mum; no one had yet worked out how to make communications across time periods possible.

"Shit!" I exclaimed loudly, running my hand through my short hair.

Jake giggled. "You swore! I'm going to tell Mum."

I raised my head and sighed. "That's if we ever see her again." The words were out of my mouth before I could stop them.

His eyes went wide, and his bottom lip trembled.

I reached my hand out to him. "I'm sorry, I didn't mean that. Of course she'll be back." I tried to smile. "I just hope it's soon. Your big sis has got an important exam today."

I was just debating ringing my school to tell them I was really sick and beg them to let me take the exam another time, when loud steps came up the stairs from the basement. The door opened with a creak.

"Finally! I told you I had an exam."

She waved my panic off. "I'm here, aren't I?" She looked distracted, her eyes bloodshot from lack of sleep and her hands shaking.

"Yeah, but it's 8.40 and my exam starts at 9. You really couldn't have left it any later."

"Well, go then." She flopped down on the sofa.

I knew I wasn't going to get an apology from her. She was too preoccupied these days, and I didn't have time to argue.

"Look after Jake. He had a nightmare the other night."

She nodded, but I wasn't convinced that she had actually heard me. There didn't seem any point asking her to take him to school. Muttering under my breath, I gave Jake a quick kiss and left the house, slamming the door behind me.

\#

I got to school just in time, running all the way. I could have done with popping into the toilet to freshen myself up first, and stopping at the water fountain to fill my bottle, but there wasn't time.

Three hours later my mouth was dry and my clothes felt wet under the arms from sweat, but I was happy with my performance. The exam hadn't been as difficult as I had feared, and I was pretty sure I had passed. I didn't rush home, stopping at a café on the way to treat myself to a cake and a long drink, but I knew I wouldn't be able to put it off for too much longer. I ought to go home and see how Mum and Jake were doing.

"Mum?" It was strangely quiet in the house. I frowned as I went from room to room. There was no sign of Mum, or of Jake, although some of his toys lay cluttering the floor—I winced as I stood on a piece of Lego. Had she taken him out? She didn't do that very often, unless she was just dropping him off or picking him up from school, although even then it often fell to me. Perhaps this was a good sign.

I loved my half-brother, but after several days of taking care of him I had to admit that it was kind of nice to have the house to myself. I went into the bathroom and ran myself a bubble bath, then lay back and relaxed.

An hour later, as I dried myself, I started to get an uneasy feeling in my stomach. It was unlike Mum to go out with Jake for so long. I descended the stairs to the basement, afraid of what I might find.

My heart sank as I approached the time machine. The red 'occupied' light was on, the glass was hazy and the display told me that Mum was 100 years in the future, visiting the year 2205, and that she had been there for nearly 3 hours.

I shook my head. "You couldn't even last a few hours in the present, could you?" I muttered to myself.

I wasn't sure why I was so surprised. The addiction had clearly been getting worse over the past few months. She didn't usually take Jake with her when she travelled, though. Time travel was possible for kids over the age of 5 traveling with a parent, but it wasn't recommended. Time travel took a toll on the body, and children were less able to withstand it than adults were. Jake certainly shouldn't have been out of his own time period for so long.

I hesitated, wondering what to do, but the longer I left Jake in there, the more dangerous it would be for him. I *had* to get him and Mum out.

I paused again as I reached out for the emergency stop handle. Every time machine was equipped with one, but the instruction booklet made it very clear how dangerous it was to pull someone back from a trip. I didn't see that I had much of a choice, though. Mum was deep in the grips of an addiction, and who knew when she'd be back if I didn't intervene. I had to look out for Jake.

My hand shook as I pulled the handle. A red light started flashing, along with an alarming siren. I covered my ears as it got louder and louder, until suddenly it stopped, the machine vibrated, whooshed and finally emitted a loud pop. As the fog cleared, I opened the door.

Mum was crouched down on the floor, her hands over her ears, trembling. I swallowed when I saw that Jake wasn't there with her.

"Mum?"

She looked up, seeming taken aback to see me. "Hazel?" She screwed up her eyes as if shielding them from a bright light. As she came to her senses, panic overtook her and she started repeating, over and over, "No! I need to go back!" She moved her hands towards the display panel. Her passport, edges dogeared, stuck out of the back pocket of her jeans.

I pulled her towards me. "Mum," I said, urgency in my voice. "Where's Jake?"

"Jake?"

I forced myself not to shout. "Yes, Mum—Jake. You know, little boy, 6 years old, blonde hair, about this high. Your son." I couldn't help but raise my voice at the end. Was she so far gone that she had forgotten who he was?

She looked at me helplessly, without saying a word. Her breathing was erratic.

I ran my fingers through my hair. "Did you take him with you?" I asked. "To the future?"

She shook her head decisively. "No, no. He's too young."

"Okay, so where is he?" Anxiety flooded through me.

She bit her lip. "I only left him for a moment." Her voice was quiet.

"You left him here, alone?! He's only 6 years old, Mum. Jesus Christ."

"I wasn't going to be long." She swallowed.

"It was nearly 3 hours!" I said. "And goodness knows how much longer you would have been."

Tears sprung to her eyes. "I had to go back." She sighed. "You wouldn't understand it, Hazel."

I shook my head. "Oh, I get it, alright. You're addicted. You need to get help."

She folded her arms. "I don't need help. It's just a bit of fun."

"I wouldn't understand it, but it's just a bit of fun?"

She just shrugged.

"Mum…." I tried to focus. "We can talk about this later. For now, we just need to find Jake."

Without waiting for her to reply, I ran up the steps back into the lounge and then out through the front door.

#

"No, I'm sorry dear. I haven't seen him." My elderly neighbour gave me a sympathetic smile.

I made myself smile back, although my stomach was churning. "It's okay. If you do, can you please let me know as soon as possible?"

"Of course." She reached out and touched my arm briefly. "I'm sure he will turn up soon. Kids are always running off; I remember that well enough myself from when my daughter was little."

"Thanks. I'm sure you're right." As I turned and walked away from the house, I felt my cheeks get wet and wiped the tears away angrily. I couldn't fall apart, not now. Jake needed me, and Mum was no use to anyone. But I wasn't sure where else to go. I'd now tried all the neighbours, and no one had seen him today. There was only one more option.

"I'm here to report the disappearance of my half-brother," I told the policeman behind the desk.

He asked me some questions, and I answered as best I could. As I spoke, my words scrolled across the screen of his tablet. When we got to the end, he clicked a button and the report was saved. He promised to look into it as a priority, and said he'd be in touch. As I left the station, I tripped over the doorstep and fell to my knees. Tears began to stream down my cheeks again, and this time I didn't wipe them away.

When I opened the front door, I didn't expect to see Mum. In the basement, the time machine glowed red again. She was in 1794 now. I turned and went up the stairs, slamming the door behind me.

#

The loud, insistent knock at my front door woke me up just after 8am the next day. I'd stayed awake the night before as long as I could, waiting for news, but eventually I couldn't keep my eyes open any longer. It had been a long day, and I was exhausted.

The house was so quiet. I opened the door, wiping sleep out of my eye and feeling slightly self-conscious in my striped pyjamas.

"Hazel Thompson?"

A policewoman stood on my doorstep.

"Yes." I swallowed, wiping my sweaty palms on my pyjama trousers.

"Can I please come in?"

"Sure." I led her into the house, and indicated for her to take a seat, but she declined and stayed standing. I sat down myself; I was so nervous that I wasn't sure my legs would support me.

She looked at me solemnly. "Did you report a missing brother yesterday?"

"Half-brother. Yes, I did." I held my breath. Time seemed to stand still.

She looked around the room. "Are Jake's parents here?"

I shook my head. "It's just me and my mum. And Mum is... well, she isn't here right now."

The policewoman frowned. "Do you know when she might be back?"

"Goodness knows." I sighed. "Look, just tell me, please. Is it good news or bad?"

"I'm really sorry." She removed her hat. "We think we found Jake's body in the river this morning. There were signs of a struggle."

"No." I clutched onto the nearby shelf on the wall. "No. There must be a mistake."

Her eyes were full of sorrow. "I'm so sorry, Hazel, I really am. We'll need someone to identify the body formally, but from the description and the photo you gave us, we think it's him. He was wearing the exact same clothes you said he was wearing last time you saw him and was the right height."

#

As I identified the body, I felt numb. Jake looked so peaceful, his tiny form laid out on the table. It looked like he was just asleep. I half expected him to suddenly open his eyes and start chuckling. He could be hard work sometimes, but I'd have given anything just to see his cheeky smile one more time. "Sleep well, little brother." I kissed him on the forehead, and tears spilled from my eyes again.

It was like the bottom had fallen out of my world. My mum was an addict, and my half-brother was dead. There was nothing left for me.

Back at home, Mum was still absent, and the time machine still in use. I didn't see the point in pulling her back again, just to tell her that her son was dead. She was barely holding it together as it was. Instead, I dug out my own time passport, left the house and walked to the nearest Time Travel Centre. The building loomed in front of me, the roof covered in solar panels. I opened the door and walked up to the front desk, approaching the android receptionist.

"Can I help you?" AI had come on a long way, but there was still something artificial about an android's voice. There was no warmth to the smile plastered upon its face.

"I'll take half an hour, please."

"I recommend you buy at least an hour. Most of our clients travel for several hours."

I shook my head. "Half an hour is all I need." I had no desire to spend any longer in another time period. I held out my payment card towards the scanner. It beeped once, and a green light showed.

"You're all set." The android handed me a smart bracelet. "Number 55."

I looked above me at the direction holograms hovering in the air, and turned towards the 50s room. These centres held rooms and rooms full of time machines. Most homes nowadays had a time machine, but if your household machine was occupied, no one else could use it, so going out to use them was still fairly common. Very few families could afford more than one machine in their house.

My bracelet got me through both the main door and then into the time machine itself. Only one other machine in my room was unoccupied when I entered. I shook my head; these were such soulless places.

Stepping into the machine, I located the panel and programmed in 2206. I didn't want to go too far ahead, but I knew Mum had recently been in 2205, and I didn't want to risk running into an earlier version of her. Although given Mum's addiction, there were probably versions of her in many time periods anyway. I'd just have to take that chance.

I pressed the button and braced myself for the trip, my feet planted solidly on the floor of the machine. The actual travelling part of time travel was a weird experience; I found it unpleasant, but I knew from what Mum had said that even that could become addictive. I imagined it was a bit like what astronauts experienced going into space, the G-forces pulling at their bodies. However, at least this was over a lot more quickly than space travel. Nausea hit me immediately, and I put a hand to my stomach, but a few seconds later I had arrived, and I was soon feeling normal again.

The panel on the machine flashed green and told me that I had reached my intended time period. Taking a deep breath, I pushed the door open and joined the queue of arriving passengers. A couple of androids milled around in case of problems, but the process was otherwise entirely automated. Luckily the queue moved quickly, and soon I was at the front. I placed my passport over the scanner and looked at the screen for my retinal scan. A few seconds later the gates opened and let me through into the main area of the building. I didn't hang around; there were all kinds of distractions here, from future duty-free shops where you could buy things that hadn't even been invented yet, to cinemas showing films featuring actors who hadn't even been born yet, but I had limited time, and I was only here for one thing.

Outside, cars zoomed around above my head, and shops beamed personalised adverts to shoppers, but I kept my head down and made my way to the Archives building. Once inside I hooked myself up to a screen and thought the words, 'Hazel Michelle Thompson, born April 22nd, 2087.' Seconds later my records flashed up on the screen.

What I saw in front of me made the nausea return. I turned and vomited into the waste bin. A few people looked across at the noise, and gave me disapproving looks, but most of them ignored me.

I straightened up and looked again at the screen. There was no mistaking what lay in my future. Mum would take her own life months after Jake's death, and I would spend several years in jail for theft and violence before living out my life alone. I looked for signs of a family, but there was none. No husband, no children. Just me.

I had seen enough. I had to fix this. My bracelet flashed, telling me that half my allotted time was up. If I overstayed, I'd be automatically charged double for every extra minute. I rushed back to the processing centre and travelled back to the present.

#

"Look, can you help me or not?"

I'd spent another night alone in the house. Mum was still AWOL, and it was so quiet there without Jake. He could be annoying at times, but I really missed his cheeky chuckles and his nonsense words. I'd spent most of the time since I got back from the future digging into the dark web. Eventually I managed to get a list of contact details for people who might be willing to help me, but I was on the fourth name so far and the others had all been unsuccessful. People were reluctant to break the Time Travel Laws because of the consequences.

"I might be able to."

I sat forward on the sofa, hands gripping my knees. "Are you serious?"

The voice in my earpiece was quiet but firm. "For the right price, I can help you."

I sighed, pressing the fingers of my right hand to my forehead. "How much?"

"Twenty thousand. Cash."

I gasped. "Any chance we could come to a compromise?"

"Sorry. It's this or nothing. I'm taking a big risk even by talking to you."

I shook my head and squeezed my eyes together. What alternative did I have? "Okay, you've got a deal. Where do I find you?"

#

A few days later I arrived at the address I had been given and pressed the doorbell. A thin man with greying hair opened the door, looked around me quickly and then ushered me in.

"Have you got what I asked for?" the man known to me only as 'The Traveller' said.

I nodded and took my rucksack off my back, unzipping it and showing him the notes inside. "It's all there." It had taken me many trips over several days to get it all. People rarely used cash these days and I didn't want to take it all out at once, or all in the same place, in case suspicion was raised.

I waited while he counted the money. I hoped he wasn't scamming me. I had just given him all the money I'd saved for law school, as well as the proceeds of selling a ring, a family heirloom that my grandmother had given me. This *had* to work.

Eventually he gave me a brief nod back. "Follow me."

He led me into a room full of books. Even though most reading was done online now, there were still a number of collectors who specialised in buying physical books. Reaching between a couple of them, he pressed a hidden button. The sides of the room separated like swing doors, exposing a flight of stairs leading to the basement. At the bottom of the stairs was a door with a numerical lock. Making me stand with my back to the door, he selected the combination. The door opened with a click and we entered the room.

On the back wall was a time machine. It was funny to think that this could be the answer to my prayers. It looked no different to any other time machine.

"Go ahead," he urged me.

I turned to him. "What happens when I travel? I presume I don't end up in a processing centre."

His face was emotionless. "No, indeed. You'll arrive in a building, but there won't be any staff or gates. Just get out of there as quickly as possible. To get back, make sure you take note of where the building is, otherwise you could easily miss it and get stuck. It's disguised as a block of flats."

"Thank you." I stepped into the machine, and the door shut behind me. My hands shaking, I selected my date of travel. 7th July 2099. The date of Jake's birth. The panel didn't blink and reset to the present date like it did in most time machines when a date within 100 years either side of that day's date was selected. I pressed the button.

#

There was a woosh, and I arrived. Stepping out of the machine was even stranger than usual. Time travel centres were usually bustling, noisy places. Here, you could have heard a pin drop. I didn't see any other people. My shoes squeaked on the wooden floor as I made my way to the exit as quickly as possible.

Outside, I took a moment to catch my breath, before heading to my house. I knew no one would be home; Mum was at the hospital giving birth, and my younger self was with her. I let the lock scan my retinas, and the door opened with a click.

My eyes went wide as I looked around the lounge. I had forgotten how tidy Mum used to be. I was so used to seeing Jake's toys all over the floor and dust on the shelves. I helped out as much as I could around the house, of course, but what with my study and babysitting and my part-time job, there was little spare time, and Mum was too busy travelling. Unlike most families these days, we'd never been able to afford an automated cleaning robot. It seemed like so long since Mum had been a normally-functioning human being.

I opened the door to the basement and went down the steps. As I stood in front of the time machine, I reflected upon the kind of place the world had become. There were few houses, even 6 years ago, without a time machine. It would be like having a house without a TV.

Even the machine looked cleaner than the one I was used to seeing. Mum didn't become a regular traveller until after Jake was born, when she realised how difficult and lonely it was to bring up a baby son and an adolescent daughter without any support. She'd started to make trips as a break from reality and I'd encouraged her, scared she was descending into postnatal depression. There's no way I would have done that if I'd have known how things would turn out.

I shrugged my rucksack off my bag, unzipped it and pulled a baseball bat out. As I swung the bat again and again against the machine and the glass shattered, tears streamed down my face. When all the sides were broken, I turned to the time panel. "THIS IS FOR MY FAMILY!" I shouted, smashing the panel continuously until the display blinked off and pieces fell to the ground.

I looked at the destruction around me, feeling hopeful for the first time in days. Back in the lounge, I reached into my bag again and took out an envelope with 'Mum' written on the outside. I went into Mum's bedroom and propped it up on her bedside table, against the lamp. Anxiety gnawed at my insides. I'd laid everything out in the letter, told her the whole truth. That I was writing to her from the future. That she became addicted to time travel. That Jake was murdered. That she killed herself. That our family was torn apart. I urged her to get help and stay away from time travel. But what if she didn't read it, or thought it was just a joke or that I'd gone crazy? I shook my head. I just had to hope this would work. There was no alternative.

#

"Done?" the Traveller asked as I stepped out of the time machine. He had obviously been stood there waiting for me; it was a good job I hadn't been long.

I rubbed my eyes, thrown by his disinterested tone. But then he was a criminal, what could I expect? He didn't care what happened to me. "Yeah."

He led me back up the stairs and sent me on my way with barely another look.

Outside, nothing looked any different. Had I actually changed anything? There was only one way to find out. It was time to go back home. I'd hardly been gone any time at all, but it felt like a lifetime.

A driverless car was parked outside our house. I walked around it slowly, peering in the windows. Was this our car? We hadn't been able to afford one for the past few years—Mum had sold our last car to fund her addiction. I hoped that this meant that she had a job, and that she wasn't in debt. Which would hopefully mean that she wasn't addicted to time travel.

I looked into the retina panel on the front door and it opened. As I walked slowly inside, my heart was beating so fast I felt lightheaded.

"Hi, Hazel."

My eyes widened, then filled with tears. "Mum?"

She was sat on the sofa, looking healthier than I had seen her in years. Her skin looked radiant, her hair was styled, and the black rings under her eyes had gone. For a brief moment, I wondered if I had screwed something up and come back to a time when she was younger.

When she smiled at me, I realised I hadn't seen that smile for ages. She patted the seat next to her. "What is it? You look upset."

"Not upset." I went and sat down, then threw my arms around her. "Just really happy to see you."

She looked confused. "But you only saw me a couple of hours ago…." She trailed off, and put her hand to her mouth. "Hazel, was this the day? The day that you went back and fixed everything?"

"Yes." I took a deep breath. "Did it work?"

She pointed towards the door leading to the basement. "Why don't you go and have a look?"

I descended the stairs slowly, Mum following. I emerged into a library full of books.

I turned around. "Where's the time machine?"

She raised her eyebrows. "When I came back from the hospital that day and read your letter, I vowed to have the machine completely removed as soon as possible. If I was prone to addiction, it was better to have the temptation removed. I decided I would rather live in the present."

I couldn't keep the grin from my face. "What about Jake?" I asked.

"He's having a nap. Why don't you go and wake him up? I'm sure he'd love to see his big sister."

I almost tripped up the stairs in my haste to see him. Opening the door of his room, I walked towards his bed and had to hold onto the bed post when I saw him lying there. Images of the last time I had seen him, lying there so still, his chest not moving, came into my mind.

"Are you okay?" Mum asked.

I swallowed. "Yeah. Seeing him so still just brings back bad memories."

She put her arm around me. "That's all they are now, Hazel. Bad memories. Your family is here; complete, happy, and healthy." She paused. "I'm so sorry for what I put you through."

I waved it off. "You were sick. I'm just so relieved to see you looking so happy and healthy." My voice wavered.

I sat down on the edge of Jake's bed. "I'm going to go to the Police Station tomorrow and admit to my crimes."

Mum gawped at me. "No, you can't! I can't lose you. Even though I didn't know that life, I know that I lost you both once before. I won't do it again."

I sighed, running my fingers through my hair. "Mum, I need to do this. I can't live a lie. I can't live every day wondering whether I will be caught. Everything will be fine, I promise. Maybe they'll go easy on me."

Jake stirred, and opened his eyes slowly. "Hazel?"

"Hello, Jakey." I felt my cheeks become wet again. I stroked the top of his head. "I love you so much, you know that?"

#

"Yes, I broke the law. But would I do it again? Yes, in a heartbeat. As far as I'm concerned, there was no other choice." I pause and look at the jury. Most of them are tearful, some are dabbing their eyes and others are openly sobbing. I turn around and look at Mum, whose own eyes are red. "Time travel destroyed my family, but time travel also restored my family. There's no doubt that I am guilty of breaking the Time Travel Laws, and I deserve the punishment that's coming to me. I just implore you to consider my circumstances and go easy on me."

I sit down. Judge Babcock is clearly affected too, and his voice wavers slightly as he speaks. "Thank you, Hazel." He turns and looks at the Judge for the Prosecution. "Mr Wilson?"

Mr Wilson stands up and clears his throat. "No questions, your Honor. The defendant has admitted to her crimes." He sits down again, with a sympathetic smile in my direction. I nod at him.

Judge Babcock rises to his feet and addresses me. "Well, Miss Thompson. You've given us the story of how and why you broke the laws. Now it's up to the jury to consider whether they find you guilty."

#

"On all counts, we find the defendant…." The woman pauses, biting her lip. With a sad smile across at me, she continues, "guilty. But…"

"No!" Mum's voice rings out across the courtroom, loudly. "Weren't you listening to anything she said? She did this for me. For us."

"Mrs Thompson, please. Let her continue." Judge Babcock gives Mum a stern look. She cowers back into her seat, but her face is pale.

"We, men and women of the jury, believe there is no reasonable doubt that Miss Thompson broke the Time Travel Laws. She's even admitted it herself. However, we were all moved by her story. We would favour a shorter sentence, because in our opinion, Hazel has suffered enough already."

I take a deep breath as Judge Babcock speaks again.

"Hazel Thompson, you have been found guilty of all charges. These were serious charges, and I have to sanction some kind of punishment. We can't have people breaking Time Travel Laws without fear of the consequences. There will be mayhem. Your refusal to give us details of the man who helped you also stands against you."

I bow my head.

"But I was moved, as the jurors were, by your story, and after all you've been through, I wouldn't want to keep you from your family for too long. Therefore, I am sentencing you to spend two years, in a secure jail, without access to time travel. The sentence will start immediately."

I turn around and smile at Mum. "It's okay," I say. I know it could have been much longer. I got off lightly, really. And it was worth it to get my family back.

As I'm led away to start my sentence, I think back to Mum's promise that she will start a petition against time travel and try and get more addiction centres opened. My case has generated a lot of publicity, and I know there are others out there who see that time travel can do more harm than good. I still hope to be a lawyer one day, and I know I will specialise in time travel cases and do all I can to overhaul the laws governing time travel. It's my hope that no other family will have to go through what we did.

Katie Kent is a writer of both fiction and non-fiction and lives in Oxfordshire in the UK with her wife, cat and dog. Her fiction has been published in *Youth Imagination, 101 Fiction, Flash Fiction Magazine, The Drabble, The Trouble with Time Travel (Smoking Pen Press'* time travel anthology), *Of Mistletoe and Snow (Jazz House Publications* anthology), *Tipping the Scales* and *Limeoncello.*

Hunter Tiger, Tiger Hunter

by Nickolas Urpí

Act I:

"Ilio!" a voice called out between the massive redwoods clutching onto the earth, remnants of dragon-times trapped in ink between the musty histories of monks.

"Ilio! Damn you! Where are you?" Koro cried out again into the shroud.

Mist choked the air, her words bouncing back into her ears.

"I thought the stripes would be a dead giveaway."

Ilio reappeared a stone's throw from Koro, a cunning smile painted into the corner of his mouth. Long white stripes disrupted the olive tones of his skin and cut their way all over his body. A long, grey leather poncho hung over his whole body and a flat hat formed a grey ring around his shaven head.

"Don't get too far ahead," Koro replied, bitterly remounting her horse.

"What's wrong? Can't trust a Thrakian?"

Koro did not reply. Water dripped down from the celestial branches of the redwoods high above the fog. A droplet clung to the short hair on the top of her head, the sides of her head shaved bare to reveal the blue geometric patterns and runes that cascaded down her neck onto her back.

"When did you plant your farro fields?" Koro asked, as they snaked around the redwoods, following Ilio's dog-like mystical perception.

"Changing the subject?"

"Yes," Koro replied. "When?"

"Spring."

"When in Spring?"

"Just as the magnolias bloomed."

"How often have you turned the farro fields?"

"Every so often," Ilio replied. "Is a senior knight of the Council of Manors really so interested in the workings of a farm while hunting down a murderer?"

"Perhaps."

"I suggest you find a different farmer, in that case. I am not one for conversation."

"I haven't found a farmer yet," Koro replied, her tone indicating a new leaflet of knowledge.

"Excuse me?" Ilio said, not bothering to turn around once to view his accuser. Instead, he focused on the minute vibration that tantalized the stretch of skin between his eyes.

"You heard me. You're not a farmer. You don't turn farro fields! You lied just to grab a handful of pity from the council into giving you this assignment."

A deep chortle rang out from Ilio's throat. Koro's skin shivered at the sound of his laughter.

"It worked, didn't it? I have the assignment now."

"I have half a mind to take you back to the council myself."

"Listen to the other half," Ilio replied. "My talents as a tracker are indisputable—"

"Through your—magic?"

"Aye, my magic," Ilio replied. "I've hunted down criminals, vagrants, libertines, any vile or base creature that can walk this earth. It's hardly a magic, more like sensations, or rather extra-sensory perceptions. I can see, feel, things that occurred, are occurring, usually malicious since that creates pain. Pain and terror are powerful feelings and therefore are the most potent, hence why it is not too difficult to track down murderers. The pain they cause sticks to them, something a magician can smell." He paused momentarily as the magic guided him in another direction. They changed course before he continued: "Magic is such a terrible word for describing the phenomenon. The word is no more than an excuse to paint a red triangle on the forehead and shout 'dark arts' until the magician is thrown into exile by his own, forced to take a cold world by the hand and let it drag him around."

"Do you catch liars too, or only murderers?"

"Very droll, Lady Koro—I did not lie about needing the work. A tribeless Thrakian is hardly a human at all. Let's be honest, just between us. Would the assignment have been granted had it not been for the fact that I claimed to be a farmer with a family who needed the money? That I just happened to be a wizard?"

"Probably not," Koro replied, unimpressed.

"And would you be here, dogging me, the only knight who opposed my taking this position, had it not been for the one fact that I was a Thrakian?"

"For one who dislikes conversation, your tongue never seems still. And yet, for a magician, you never seem to be working any magic."

"Oh, the magic works of its own volition," Ilio said, his eyes sealed as dew gathered on his forehead. "It is neither science nor art. It is not a philosophy, nor religion. It is feeling and technique—a perfect incantation has more effect than boyish foolhardiness."

Koro absorbed his words and let them play against the philosophy of her own, the order she had accepted long ago that fused spirituality with militarism in the hopes that one day the sword would only strike at evil on behalf of the powerless.

The flowers clammed up, stealing themselves away against the bitter cold of night's descent. Night had fallen down on them, pressing away the remaining light. Only their lonely campfire remained.

Ilio leaned against his saddle, the fire illuminating the figure of Koro performing a ritualized dance with her sword. The distribution of strength between her legs and arms illustrated perfect balance. She ended her ritual on a perfectly crafted swan-like pose without even a single stray step.

When she finished, she bowed to the fire in all its sacred mystery and fell to the ground. Streaks of sweat glimmered down her temples and nose.

"How exhausting," Ilio said with an emphasized sarcasm that Koro chose to ignore.

The following morning, she took what little pleasure she could in kicking Ilio's boot to awaken him. He groaned in protestation before muttering:

"It's hardly morning."

"It's morning enough," she said. "C'mon—find me a murderer."

The forest led to a clearing alongside the beach, where the wind howled ferociously against them. Their arms were lifted to protect their eyes against the hands. Stones of various sizes and indifference inhabited the shore, amongst which the horses were constantly losing their balance.

"Are you sure it's this way?" Koro screamed at the Thrakian whose eyes were closed, but whose face was uncovered so as to ensure his sense of direction was as strong as possible, even with the wind beating down heavily.

"No!" Ilio yelled back.

"Arjan lives close to here! We should take refuge at his cabin!"

Ilio's instinct to respond was cut short by the neighing of a horse consumed with fear. He whirled his horse around to witness Koro losing control of her beast. It reared up on its hind legs, a sand snake hissing beneath its hooves! Koro tried to restrain her steed, but she lost her grip with the wind throwing sand into her eyes, and she slipped from her horse, her head crashing against a rock.

"You promised," she said, riding alongside him, his red silk colors brightly contrasting with the grey fields of farro they rode through on the way to the castle.

"Did I? Things changed."

"Not that much, nothing has changed, you lied to me! You said the command would be mine…" she insisted.

"Not anymore. You have a talent for training men that is unusual, and vastly more essential than commanding an army in the field. You mold men into soldiers, and that is a talent I am hard pressed to find anywhere on this earth."

"You can't!"

"I have spoken. There is no more to be said. You will stay here," Lord Pithius snapped, letting his horse's hooves carry him away from Lady Koro, whose fingers tightened around her reins.

His knees broke his fall in the sand as he landed beside her. Koro's blood painted the stone behind her head. Even her tattoo was obscured in the obsidian-red liquid made mud in the sandy wind.

Ilio whispered songs of incantation, a trembling in his voice cracking his spell. He failed to produce enough ice to stop the bleeding at first. He tried again, focusing more on the words, and less on the villainous wind.

A breath of ice finally sealed the wound and stopped the bleeding. Ilio reached into his satchel and ripped out an assortment of rags. Crumbs still clung to them from the cakes they had wrapped, but he had no time to clean them. He bandaged Koro's head as best he could under the adverse conditions. One of his rags even slipped through his fingers and sailed off into the wind. Nothing more could be done as long as the sand was kicking into his back.

Koro's heels dug into the sand as Ilio dragged her, drawing a transient line from where she had fallen to where Ilio's horse stood, waiting in the wailing wind for its master.

The magician lifted the body onto the horse and mounted. The comforting hope of a nearby cabin reverberated in his ears and he spoke under his breath the spell of luck, in the hopes the cabin was not too far from the beach.

"Come, boy, take me thither," he whispered to his horse, an unnamed beast of honor, whose task it was to find a drop of water in the ocean.

And that is exactly what he found. The sweet saffron aroma of dying embers burned Ilio's nostrils. His horse had a certain magic of its own and had discovered the cabin of which Koro had spoken.

He looked up to see the wood-constructed abode, fields of farro radiating out from it, gently waiting out the fierce windstorm. Ilio paused as the horse approached the cabin, the farro leaves still just peeking their sallow heads up from the dirt.

The trembling in his forehead surged throughout his body, electrifying him with the knowledge that this cabin was pulling him. The riptide of energy that comes from the murder of another human being had drawn him towards this rustic farm.

Act II:

"Val! Val! Come here!"

Yila jumped over the farro fields to pull away the curious canine from a patch of dirt in the fields whose blackish hues battled against the soft grey of the dirt around it. Val obeyed the young girl whose dark curls bobbed metronomically against her back. A single piece of cotton with arm holes cut into it adorned her, held tight against her skin by a sash around her waist. Hanging from her sash was a charm made of bronze in the image of a wing: a traditional Leonid emblem meant to protect children from malicious eyes.

Yila noticed a pair of hazel-colored Thrakian eyes watching her from the kitchen window of the cabin. She pulled the canine away near to the woods to play, looking over her shoulder now and then: Ilio was still watching.

Ilio's eyes had been locked on her ever since she had stepped outside into the clear morning light. Blue clouds still lingered low, but bursts of sunlight burned away the mist on the far hills and converted green leaves to gold.

Ilio rummaged around the kitchen, opening the patterned clay jars looking for something he could munch on for his breakfast. They were all empty, except the penultimate one, which was one quarter full of small purple beads of farro, waiting to be boiled. He reached for the last jar on the counter when a voice stopped him:

"You'll find your own food. We don't have enough as it is for ourselves—much less for a Thrik."

The magician let his hands slip away from the jar and listened as the old man's hands reached out for the edges of the wall to guide his hands to the kitchen area where Ilio was snooping. Long white locks trailed down the back of his head in braids and his beard was unkempt. His rags appeared as old as he was, if not passed down as generational tokens of poverty. The skin around his eyes was blackish and drawn, with dead veins electrifying his cataract-covered eyes.

"I was surprised you discovered my race so quickly, being blind. I would be impressed if it were not for your hostility," Ilio replied, pulling out a chair from the kitchen table and seating himself as though he were a guest.

"It isn't too hard to smell a Thrik," Arjan said, emphasizing the derogatory name for Thrakians, as though the thought of one in his house left a bitter taste on his tongue.

"That would be solid reasoning if it were not for the fact that I have not been a tribal member for some years—I haven't eaten Thrakian food in even longer! No, it was my accent. A blind Leonid's ears are second only to those of a jackal, I've heard."

"Ha!" Arjan exclaimed, fiddling with the jar of farro and placing a handful in a saucepan with some water to boil. "No doubt Lady Koro told you I was not always blind. This was a recent attack. An old disease passed down from generations. Now it seems so long ago that I could see. Yes, I could see—"

"Enough to hate Thrakians," Ilio replied, taking notice of a board game arranged in starting position at the center of the table.

"I don't need to see to hate."

"No, you do well enough, I'm sure, without any reason at all," Ilio replied, reaching for the piece at the center of the board. He brought it to him to examine. An intricately carved, beautiful rendition of a tiger, wild and untamed, roared against the world that closed in on him. Such was the nature of the game, and consequently the game of nature.

"Oh, I have reason enough," Arjan insisted. "Thrakian raids—during the war—my wife wasn't a soldier, but they took her anyway. They—"

"She died?" Ilio inquired, his voice bare of any and all sympathy. He returned the piece to the center of the board, the hunter figures, painted red, surrounding it on all sides.

"Yes, she died."

"Pity," Ilio remarked. "Reminds me of my family. My parents were both killed in the Thrakian wars as well, orphaning a young son to the whole tribe to care for. And, quite naturally, no one did."

"Forgive me if I forget to pity you," Arjan replied, the same lack of empathy coloring his voice. The farro was just beginning to boil and spread its stale, steamed lack of appeal through the air.

"I haven't enough strength for forgiveness," Ilio replied.

"You haven't inquired even about Lady Koro—what kind of man are you? Don't you care about your companion?" Arjan asked, removing the hot pot from the stove and stirring the ingredients together, letting plumes of steam rise up like apparitions into the air.

"She isn't my concern. I assume she will live?" Ilio inquired.

"She will."

"What about that unfortunate girl in the bed beside hers? Your daughter, I presume?"

"That is none of your concern," Arjan snapped. He made his way to the door, less carefully than he should have, and smashed his knee into the table. Ilio let a smile cross his face freely, his perverse amusement unnoticed by the blind man. "Yila! Yila! Breakfast, my dear! Come in!"

He returned to the table and sat down opposite Ilio.

"She's very pale, even for a Leonid," Ilio said.

"She's starving," Arjan replied. "As if war hadn't taken enough from me."

"Oh, she's been to war then?" Ilio asked, sarcastically.

"A funny Thrakian, how novel," Arjan replied. "I meant Lord Pithius' wars."

Yila bounced into the room, stopping short as soon as she recalled the presence of Ilio. She stared at the Thrakian magician whose cunning smile, meant to endear, perturbed her. She walked around him from the far side, her eyes darting over to catch a glimpse of him, though keeping her head unmoved.

"Ah yes! The ambitious dead man," Ilio said.

Yila drained the pan of farro into four bowls, ensuring that not a single grain of the soppy mush remained. She then watered down the four bowls until the farro attained a soupy texture.

"I cannot say that the news was not pleasing to my ears—the end of wars, until the next ambitious warlord sings sweet lies of glory and victory in the council's ears."

"You had incentive then, to end the wars?"

"Me?" Arjan said, his fingers, worn and crooked, heavy at the knuckles with arthritis. "I already lost what I could from the wars. He came and took so much farro, we hardly had enough to survive on! When Meya became ill—and—and I promised him, too."

"Your promised Lord Pithius?"

"No! My son—Siltag—died fighting in the west. I promised him I'd care for his family. They never—they never even found his body."

Ilio nodded. "And you are telling me all this because?"

"Because you are the one here about Lord Pithius' murder. I can tell—why else would a Thrik be so damn inquisitive? And why else would he be traveling with a well-respected knight? I am an honest man. No one here killed him. No one here could."

Ilio watched Yila disappear quietly behind the door to the bedroom to feed her mother and the unconscious Koro.

"I'd watch yourself, Thrik," Arjan continued. "Lady Koro is a good friend to the people here—Now get out and find your own food. Don't let me catch you dipping your filthy hands in my jars ever again."

Arjan shakily stood up, planting his feet on the ground and his fists into the table to indicate that the conversation had ended. Ilio paused only long enough to take another breath before standing up as well. His feet rolled quietly when he walked, and it was difficult to hear him leave. But the door shut, the invisible breaths drawn by other humans were gone, and the irritating sense of Ilio's presence had subsided. He was outside.

Arjan crawled along the back wall with his hands, looking for the door to the other room. The security of Yila and himself was compromised as long as Koro dreamt in pink clouds in her recovery.

He listened to Yila speak to her mother, telling her the silly stories of Val's incoherent animal decisions: how he liked to dig in the garden, run around the trees, scratch his chin, and snap at fat bees that hovered too close to his nose.

Arjan's hand rushed to his mouth to muffle his crying. Only his tears betrayed him. His eyes did not work but the dam of tears he kept welled up every day was in perfect order. A rush of memories, all blurred and mangled, populated his mind all at once—and all at once, happy days when Siltag and Meya and Yila laughed and danced around the kitchen table he had fashioned from his own hands, returned. Even further into memory's well did he draw until he could see Siltag and Jeanetta sitting in a chair, the child held tight and asleep at his mother's breast, and the other, a young woman, who was beautiful to him, tired and worn from a day of work. Arjan bit his tongue and did not notice

Yila had stopped speaking until he felt her slip her miniature fingers into his. He could hardly feel them in his calloused hands, but their warmth permeated all the age-worn years of sadness that had hardened them, and he tenderly squeezed them back.

"All done?" he asked her, swallowing his tears to hide his them from the child.

"All done, grandpa," she replied.

Ilio, on the other hand, was not done. He had noted very quickly that Yila, the only conscious person with functioning eyes, was in the bedroom—the windowless bedroom. The wizard made his way over to the patch of dirt where Val had been digging and reached down into the dirt, using whatever magic he could to feel for (or see) an object. Another sensation, burning with a powerful malevolence called him into the mud. He pulled out a knife and used the broad side to dig down into the dirt. At first, he thought it was simply the anger of the old man that had buried itself there. Perhaps, it was the child's fearful hate and bitterness against a world that stole her parents away from her that was interred.

He had neared the point of exhaustion and despair when the harsh clang of metal on metal froze him mid shovelful. Did his ears deceive him? It was certainly a possibility—but he trusted his senses too much to delay any further. There was no drama to be had in the real pursuit of a criminal. A great lump sum awaited him. Enough, perhaps, to spirit him away to a better place, where Thrakians were not known—a place where he would be able to become a merchant or a baker without the oppressive arrows of hate flung at him from the Leonids and Thrakians—one for his stripes and one for his magic.

He pulled away the dirt faster, furiously scratching at the black mud, flinging worm and pebble alike into the air as he approached the object hidden beneath.

"Gah!"

Ilio drew his hand back from the mud. His index finger had been cut on a sharp object resisting being found.

He reached down into the pit he had carved more carefully now:

A knife.

He wiped the moist soil away from the weapon's blade, careful only to wipe away the external layer. What was once a shining, glimmering military weapon, issued to every soldier under Lord Pithius' command, now rested in his hands, a dingy dirty weapon of murder.

Despite the dullness of the weapon, which had no reflection to lend, Ilio felt the beaming light of revelation shine upon him as his imagination played the theatric murder of Lord Pithius. It was a reality sans magic. The blade, now dulled over with mud and blood, whispered to him the secret story.

A garden near the steep slopes of Highwater castle, upon whose stones the ocean had crashed for a thousand years.

"Why? How?"

"How what?" Lord Pithius replied, sitting on a stone under a magnolia tree, dripping its mellifluous white pedals onto his chestnut hair.

"How could you let us all die while you remained here in the arms of comfort? In the arms of your loved ones while we covered ourselves with the hot blood of men whose only desire it was to live in peace?"

"Is that why you came back? You left your fellow soldiers to come back?"

"There are none of us left! No more soldiers. I am no soldier. I am a ghost."

"You hold a knife in your hand, ghost. Can ghosts kill men of living flesh?" Lord Pithius inquired, holding an accusing finger up to his murderer.

"You will know soon enough," Siltag replied.

"Siltag," Ilio laughed. "Now, where are you? Where are you, tiger?"

He looked off into the petrified woods, the only witness to his words and thoughts.

Act III:

Arjan's hands wrapped around Yila's face, completely consuming it, before he leaned in to kiss her goodnight.

"Couldn't I sleep with Mommy?" Yila asked. Her heavy lids had already fallen over his eyes, and clasped shut, but her remaining thoughts still managed to slip between her lips.

"I don't want you to become ill. You are already near her too often."

"I want to be with her, Grandpa. Please."

"Maybe tomorrow, my dear, my pepperflower. Maybe tomorrow…"

Yila floated off to where conscious thought has no place, and Arjan left her in peace, closing the door ever so gently.

He felt a presence upon reentering the kitchen living area that shriveled the hairs on his back. The plague had returned to his house.

"I hope you don't mind if I cook some mushrooms, of my own gathering, over your fire? Would that be too much to ask?" Ilio said, pleasantly enough, but without leaving room for an answer. He simply dropped the fungi into a cast iron pan, smoking with heat. The cozy sizzling was only enhanced further by the earthy flavors that tantalized Arjan's nose.

"I don't think you are going to stay the night in this house again."

"I think that many things are going to change before the night is over," Ilio said. "Shall I go on?"

"No," Arjan replied, pulling out a chair and letting himself sit, yet again, opposite the wizard. "If you intend to bring me to the council, I would only be too happy to hear you explain how a blind man found his way to Highwater, murdered Lord Pithius, and returned. That is, if it weren't for the fact that Yila and Meya both require my aid."

"The child seems capable enough until your return," Ilio responded. "Nevertheless, you are mistaken. I have no intention of bringing you in. But perhaps you would care for a game of tiger?"

One finger played drumsticks on Arjan's arm before he responded: "Which am I? The hunters or the tiger?"

"That's the beauty of the game," Ilio laughed. "You can choose in the game—but you can't choose in real life. I'll let you decide, how about that?"

"I prefer the hunters, in that case," Arjan replied.

"Perfect," Ilio said. "A striped man plays the striped beast."

"Appropriate," Arjan said. "Tigers move first."

Ilio looked over the board and made his move on the square east of the center. The game was designed such that the tiger was surrounded by a number of hunters, each of whom could only move one square, whilst the tiger could move up to two. Neither piece could move diagonally. The goal of the game was different for each player. The tiger's object was to reach the corner of the board and "escape" whilst the opposing player only needed to surround the tiger on three sides, including the edge of the board if applicable. Arjan responded on the board and waited for Ilio's next move.

"They never found the knife, you know."

"What knife?" Arjan asked, innocently enough, as Ilio moved again.

"The murder weapon. You know what knife."

"Interesting."

"Then you'll find it interesting, no doubt, that I found it in your backyard."

"You're a Thrakian, you could have put it there."

"I think the council will find it difficult to believe I'd frame you with a military issued knife with blood on it. I have no motive."

"Don't you?" Arjan asked, moving his piece in from another side.

"None at all. It's part of the reason I was selected," Ilio replied. "Your son, however, would have an excellent reason—"

"What did you say?"

Arjan's interruption was sudden and filled with smoke. His knuckles trembled and his volcanic cheeks were pulled in as he held his breath, waiting for eruption.

"Your son—had an excellent motive."

"My son is dead."

"Is he?"

"Yes."

"Then how did a knife of military issue end up in your backyard? They never found your son's body, according to your own admission. He came back for his revenge, got it, and you are hiding him somewhere."

"This game is over," Arjan declared.

"I beg to dif—"

Arjan's fists slammed into the table, knocking the pieces over onto their side.

"This. Game. Has. Ended."

"For you, perhaps," Ilio responded. "I'm not interested in arguing the merits of my evidence. I simply want to know where he is."

"Even if what you say is true, and it isn't, I would never tell you. Now get out of my house."

"Tell me. Your Yila is a lovely girl. It would be a shame for something to—happen to her—"

"You beast—you wouldn't."

"Go ahead!" Ilio replied. "Test me! Test me! I have incantations so powerful she'll age to a hundred in day, a whole lifetime of age without a lifetime of living. She'll be gone before you. I have enough power to transform her intestines into an eel that will eat her from the inside!"

"Enough! If you had that power, you'd find him yourself!"

"And spend the next year in cold mountains dogging your son who could easily double back here or be waiting for me? Hardly likely. You will tell me where he is. You will tell me now. I have no patience for old Leonid men."

Arjan's trembling rattled the wooden table on the wooden floor. The fire cackled and hissed. Water dripped down the universe's water clock and Ilio waited for the hunter to make his move.

"He comes across the farro field every night when the moon is high for food," Arjan said, hurriedly, as though the words would not come if not all at once. How he summoned enough strength to remain standing as a mystery to Ilio who rushed to the kitchen window.

"Can you see him from the window, or does he return from another direction?"

He peered out into the blackness but heard nothing.

"I said—"

He heard the crash before he felt the pain.

Ilio collapsed onto the floor, shaken and unable to grasp immediately what had happened. Arjan was on top of him, his hands wrapped around Ilio's throat and clutching tightly. For an old man, Arjan's sum of strength was grand and the muscles on his biceps swelled with the memory of his youthful vigor. Ilio kicked and felt his face and eyes burning with lack of oxygen. His tongue was swelling, and he could not utter a simple incantation to save himself.

He surrendered to Arjan's hands, whose hold was unbreakable, and reached into his side-satchel.

He dug for the knife—the murder weapon that would now save his life.

At last! He pulled it out of his satchel to wield against his foe. His fingers were wet with sweat and his hands slipped off the handle!

The curved blade clanged against the wood floor, drawing Arjan's attention to it. The blind man realized what was happening and reached for the weapon simultaneously with Ilio. In doing so, he released his tight hold on Ilio by a single hand—but it was enough.

"*Gele-me-nolo-omo!*" Ilio yelled.

Arjan's head almost burst in two with pain as a thundering noise mingled in his brain with a shrill whistling. He covered his ears and screamed. Ilio kicked the old man onto his back and reached for the knife. He jumped for Arjan, ready to plunge his knife into the latter's chest.

His fall was broken by another thunderclap and he fell against the wooden floor unconscious.

Holding the leg of a chair in her hand was Koro, breathing heavily and sick with the wound of her own. Arjan recovered, reaching up for the warrioress whose exhaustion led her to slide down against the wall onto the floor, dropping the leg beside her.

"Do you—do you have rope?" she asked the blind man, who nodded. They both trembled for a while, letting their bodies shake away the dust of adrenaline into the air. Yila emerged from her bedroom, sobbing and panting with fear as though she had been wrestling as well.

"Yila—the rope," Arjan said, pointing to a far corner. Yila nodded her head and obeyed.

Ilio awoke to find himself bound to the chair. The knot sat just under his neck.

"The more you move, the more you squirm, the more you choke yourself."

"Clever device," Ilio coughed, noting how difficult it was to swallow with his Adam's apple pressing against the edge of the knot.

"It's you."

"It's the old man's son. It's his knife."

"Siltag is dead. It's you."

"It's not my knife."

"It could easily be purchased secondhand," Koro replied. Ilio's eyes took a quick lap around the room, noting that Arjan was not present during this interrogation. "Don't worry about him—he's asleep. It's just us now."

"His ear is pressed against the door," Ilio said, ever suspicious.

Koro stood up from her chair, opened the door as quietly as she could to reveal Arjan in Yila's bed with the young girl stashed away like treasure in his arms.

"Satisfied?"

"Never," Ilio smiled.

"You returned," Koro continued, returning to her chair, which was flipped around so she could lean on the back of it.

"What?"

"You came back to accept the assignment. It was a perfect plan. Commit the crime, kill the warlord, then become appointed to find his killer. A well-known tracker and magician like you would be perfect for the job, no?"

"I still am perfect for the job—"

"Then all you had to do was find the killer, which could be anyone you wanted to pin the murder on. Plant the evidence. And voila!"

"It could be you, as well!" Ilio shouted.

"What do you mean?" Koro said, almost laughing at he suggestion were it not for the racing tidal wave of thought she could see in the magician's eyes.

"Find the warlord, kill him, for prestige, power, money, position—any number of reasons. Follow the assigned detective around to concoct this very story! Pin it on him. Pin it despite the evidence! Any evidence he finds is evidence he could have planted."

"If you suspect it's me, why didn't your 'sensations' lead you to me?"

"I know it's not you!" Ilio shouted. "It's not me either. Don't you see how easy it is to pin a murder on someone by your reason alone? The evidence points here. I'm not the murderer and you know it."

"Maybe. Or maybe not," Koro replied. "But I just saw you try to stab a blind man to death after accusing his dead son of murder. I'm taking you back to the council. You can explain it to them."

She stood up from her chair and removed a ragged cloth from her satchel.

"Koro... stop! Koro! Go ahead! Pin it on the Thrik! You Leonids are all the same!"

She bound his mouth down and gagged him. He was mumbling wildly with the gag on, the knot tightening around his neck as he did so. Beads of sweat ran down his temples and he started to pant, moistening the cloth before she had even finished tying it around the back of his head.

Between the muffled noises of his protests, Koro leaned down in front of Ilio and put her finger to her lips.

"Shhhh..."

Act IV:

The wooden beams that held the cabin together groaned as the wind whistled through the cracks. Just the blue sound alone chilled the spine to listen. Ilio awoke to the burning of rope around his hands and legs. The knot around his neck had been loosened but not cut. His limbs were already numb and cold, having been motionless for hours. He concentrated on his fingers and whispered to them, hoping he could feel them stretch out. Enough, at least, to merit some hot blood to travel and reopen the empty channels of circulation. They were moving at last, though his wrists were constrained by the rope's tight hold.

"Molo-imi," he whispered, his words stealing away beneath his breath. The ropes loosened from his incantation.

"Molo-imi," he repeated to the same effect. His words were not crisp and clear, and hence neither was the effect of the spell. It had loosened the ropes enough, however, to allow Ilio to silently slip his hands out of the brash loops of hemp and experience the cold chill of the air on his wrists. Limb by limb he freed himself until he was entirely clean of rope. He took a refreshing, full breath, letting his lungs fully soak the oxygen air garnished with the stale ash of the still-warm fireplace from the night before.

The magician tip-toed his way to the door, using the Thrakian gift of silence as is necessary for hunters in pursuit of prey. Ilio opened the door only as much as was necessary for him to leave, and let his body cut through the empty frame until he was outside.

He hastened in silence to his horse, tied to the post just beyond the edge of the field. The distant beachhead with its everlasting crashing was just beyond his line of sight. He untied his steed's rope from the lonely post and prepared the horse for his escape.

Fwoop!

The pointed arrow bit and plunged right through the back of his neck. Ilio could see it through the bottom of his eyes, red and dripping with his blood, a proud testament to the eye of the marksman. Ilio fell to his knees, dropping his satchel and the reigns of his horse. The beast neighed wildly at the sight, and painted in pointillist drops with the blood of its master, it galloped away in fright.

Arjan's bow was still humming with the music of a successful release. Ilio, choking on his words and unable to utter an enchantment, witnessed, with horror, an old man, no longer blind, but with rich almond eyes staring back at him with the intensity of a vengeful wintered man.

Arjan approached rapidly, drawing a knife from his belt to finish the job on the Thrakian magician.

Ilio acted quickly, pulling the arrow through the back of his throat out into his hands. Arjan bent over to dispatch the fallen Thrakian. Ilio withheld his attack at first, his left arm weak with pain and blood spewing from his throat with every breath.

The moment when he felt his dreams die in his heart was the moment Ilio realized that his life was forfeit. He released Arjan's hand, letting the knife dig into his lower chest, penetrating a lung and letting the steel burn him from the inside out.

With another quick motion faster than Arjan could anticipate, Ilio returned the arrow to its master, and plunged the arrow into the old man's chest.

"Ilio! No!" Koro cried from the doorway, struggling to walk towards the two gladiators, wrestling and mingling in each other's bloods. She fell, dizzy with her headwound and unable to assist either of the fighters.

Arjan was a corpse, whose touch flared in Ilio a last vision of truth. Unable to utter what he had seen, and too near death to be concerned with survival any longer, Ilio summoned Koro to him. She was uncertain at first, but noting his weak state, assumed he meant no harm and even if he did, could do no harm.

She came to his side, lifting his head as mercifully as she could. "What is it, Ilio?"

He reached up and touched her forehead with his thumb. An image surged through her mind like a bolt of energy and imprinted itself on her memory.

His last remaining energy now spent, he perished. His hand fell limp into the dirt. Small sparks, like flame crackling over powder, the sacred magic of Ilio's powers, diffused from his body and dispersed into the air.

"Grandpa!" Yila cried, running towards her grandfather.

Koro reached out and grabbed the child, pulling her away from the corpse and tightly wrapping her arms around the struggling and inconsolable child.

"Grandpa…" she cried again in her tears as Koro shushed her.

Val emerged from the door, tired and unsurprised at the events that had transpired. He made a last visit to his master, and licked clean the blood from his face.

Act V:

"Come on, Mama, try to eat," Yila said, holding up her mother's head and letting the farro's liquid run down the chin of the sickly Meya. Koro watched, unsure if there any words that could let the child understand that her mother was gone as well. She clutched Arjan's knife tightly in her hands and thought of the last moment she had spent with Ilio. The image played again in her head, as clearly as he had seen it.

A garden near the steep slopes of Highwater castle, upon whose stones the ocean had battled for a thousand years…

"Why? How?"

"How what?" Lord Pithius replied, gently resting beneath the antique arms of the magnolia tree, white pedals languidly falling atop his chestnut hair.

"How could you ask any more of me?"

"Is that why you came here? To question me?"

"You are not a great warlord, you are a cruel oppressor. First, my son."

"Your son?"

Arjan let the knife of Siltag glimmer in the warlord's eye.

"It was all they found of him—it has Meya's name engraved on the handle. Now, you ask for her too. You ask for more farro than I can ever spare. My daughter-in-law is dying. My granddaughter needs her mother. Please. Wait until the next season to ask of my farro."

"Your farro? You have nothing. You are a worker on my lands. Everything belongs to me."

"I have worked it. I have owned it."

"You are under my protection. All yours belongs to me. I do not ask any more of you than of anyone else."

"I beg you."

"A ghost begs a lord! Bah!—Your words fall on deaf ears, ghost!"

The knife whispered its way into Lord Pithius' stomach, and the latter's insatiable bloodhunger was satisfied at last in his death.

Arjan rode furiously back to his cabin. A mixture of mud, lime, and a simple Thrakian spell he learned from the men he hated—this he applied to his eyes. Immediately, they were blackened and gave the appearance to all who looked upon him that he was blind.

He kept the mixture in a jar by the kitchen window, the last jar—the jar close to the farro.

A tear woke her from her musings. In their last moments, mingled in blood and pain, the memories of Ilio and Arjan merged, Ilio's magic allowing him to retain the image just long enough to transfer to Koro's. Arjan could never let Ilio return with the knife, or at all. His sensations had been true, but his inferences had been wrong—and thus led to his own demise.

"Come, Yila," she said, drawing the child away from the corpse. Yila had no more tears of her own to cry. Her sadness wrenched at her heart, each hammer blow more painful than the last. There was a point at which so much death no longer felt real, and all reality felt like a nightmare she simply had to let expire.

Koro buried the three bodies near the farro fields while Yila packed some farro grains for their journey home. Koro did not want her to see the bodies anymore. They were not the family she loved.

Koro looked at the knife, crusted with blood and dust, scraping away until the word "Meya" inscribed on the handle saw the light once again. It was a lonely memory.

She wrapped the knife in a cloth and put it away in her satchel.

"Come, Yila."

Yila obeyed, carrying the bag of farro over her shoulder. She did not turn around to impress upon her memory any last sight of the cabin. Whatever the cabin was to her, was defined by the past; the present had no charm over her, no enchantment. In a single day all her remaining family had been lost.

Val watched Koro carry off the child in his care. He was an old hound. Arthritis clicked in his knees and he was hard of hearing; but he was also stubborn and loyal. He followed from a distance, unknowing of and unmoved by the workings of men.

Nickolas Urpí is the author of the literary war fantasy novel *The Legend of Borach* and has been published in *Tell-Tale Press, Page and Spine, The Copperfield Review, HCE Review* literary journal, *Ripples in Space* magazine, amongst others. A Hispanic author, his writings fuse his studies of ancient history, literature, and philosophy with his crafted prose to immerse the reader in the world of his fiction through vivid settings and characters. An alumnus of the University of Virginia, he resides in Charlottesville, Virginia.

What Should Have Been

by Alex Minns

The wall opposite was bare rock. Ben had been staring at it for longer than he could remember. As he sat on the stone floor, with just a wicker mat keeping the cold away, he swayed gently back and forth as he tried to get his panic under control. He needed to figure out what had happened. The machine had been working normally, he was sure of it. Nothing had seemed out of the ordinary until he'd initiated the run protocol, then a blinding flash had consumed him. There had to have been a malfunction, an energy feedback, except...

He ran through the events again in his mind. He'd never actually touched the keyboard. His hand had been hovering above it when the flash happened. It was impossible. Something else had intervened.

Whatever had enveloped him, seemed to have transported him to some other place. He had been so disorientated when he had landed that he hadn't managed to take in any details or clues. Before he had had time to gain his senses, hands had grabbed him and dragged him down rock passages and he'd ended up locked in some dingy cell. Translocation had never seemed possible to him in all his research so he had nothing to base any theories on. And yet, he definitely wasn't in his workshop anymore.

Perhaps he had gotten it all wrong. The flash had actually been a stun grenade, that made sense. Some organisation had gotten wind of his work and they wanted his knowledge to use for their own purposes. They knocked him out and dragged him off to some hideout of a foreign government, or perhaps even his own. Surely someone would look for him, Ellie would call someone when he didn't come home wouldn't she? Work would want to know where he was when he didn't show up

Monday. They'd start hunting for him; they wouldn't want him talking about their research.

As long as no-one found his workshop. Panic rose up as he tasted bile at the back of his throat. His hands rubbed over his face as anxiety surged up like a wave threatening to overwhelm him again. Apply scientific process, he told himself. He needed to gather data and then figure out where he could be. There wasn't any room for panic. He made himself get to his feet to examine his prison a little closer. There were no windows. The walls were grey rock, but not built, the floor joined seamlessly with the floor. It was like it had been carved into the rock. Veins of red traced spiderwebs across the surface of the walls. As he pressed his face closer, it seemed like the threads of crimson were pulsing with life. His finger traced along one path; it was completely solid but a tingle seemed to tickle his skin. Could it be conducting some kind of electricity? It was like no ore he had ever seen before.

He moved to the entrance. The door was metal, almost definitely iron. It was an irregular shape but fit the opening exactly, custom-made. An experimental push told Ben that there was no give, not even a little wiggle. The lock wasn't even visible from this side. There wasn't even a peep hole. He was completely sealed in. His breathing started to get shallower as claustrophobia started to take hold. He sat back down, hitting the wicker mat with a bump. His head fell back against the rock wall as his eyes travelled upwards to the only source of light in the room. It was impossible to look directly at it, the white glow was too intense. There was no way Ben could look closely enough to even figure out what was causing it.

Eventually, as the sobs of panic made his throat convulse, he let his eyes close until reality drifted away.

#

Hands were grabbing at him again, roughly shaking him awake as he was hauled to his feet. Automatically, Ben resisted, his body jerking to try and free himself even before he remembered his situation. As the memories came back to him, his eyes flashed open. His head whipped round to try and glimpse his attackers but he couldn't see their faces. There were two of them and they lifted him up and dragged him backwards to the doorway as if he were no more than a rag doll.

"Who are you?" Ben's voice came out no as a hoarse whisper. The figures ignored him completely. They didn't even react to the sound of his voice. Underneath him, his legs tried to get purchase so he could walk for himself but they didn't give him the chance. In the end, he gave up and let them half carry him round the labyrinth of rock tunnels.

Eventually, his captors stopped and let him drop to the floor. They both took a step backwards. Ben glanced up at them. His body recoiled out of instinct. They had no faces. Ben's hand clamped over his mouth partly to stop himself screaming and partly to stop himself hyperventilating. He stared harder, hoping it was all his mind playing tricks on him but all he could see was blurring. Even the edges of their heads seemed undefined. Was it some kind of disguise technology? The rest of their bodies looked normal. He was about to creep forward to see if there was some kind of edge to the blur when they both sharply bowed their heads and retreated back down the tunnel they had come from.

Silence descended in the space as the echoes of the men's footsteps died to nothing. Ben stared down the now-empty opening for as long as he dared. Eventually, he turned his attention to his new surroundings. He was in a large room, another cavern carved out of rock. Curved benches of stone ran either side of him around a large polished circular space. The circle was not the focus of the room, however. Three large seats opposite him were raised up on a platform. It reminded Ben of some kind of throne room, looking down on the court. Each seat was completely different. The one on the far left had a base of marble with black wicker woven into a back piece. The middle seat was wooden, intricately carved so that each strut spun round and twisted round others. Figures danced around the base of the seat; their features clear even from Ben's position ten metres away. At the top of the back, a head of a tiger seemed to leap from the distance, ready to watch over whoever sat upon the chair. The last seat, however, was the one that looked most out of place. In a room carved from rock, the metallic construction should not have existed. Polished chrome reflected light, piercing all areas of the room, no shadow hid untouched. A fan of strips created a strange peacock effect at the back. Pipes thrust out of the base at strange angles and disappeared around the back, strange hissing seemed to be coming from them, almost laughing at him.

Ben hauled himself to his feet and moved forward tentatively. As he crossed into the central circle, the whole world seemed to shift beneath his feet. He tottered, reaching out for the stone bench to his left but then everything settled and back as it was, apart from the three women now occupying the seats ahead of him.

All three faces glowered at him in stony silence and he realised his mistake. This wasn't a throne room; it was a court room.

Ben looked away from the women, the intensity of their collective gaze too much to bear. He spared a quick peek over his shoulder, toying with the idea of running.

"Unlikely," one of the women spoke. Ben turned, ignoring them as he scoured the back wall. He'd just come from there. The tunnel should have been right there. He spun on the spot; the whole room had not just been sealed, but there was no evidence there had ever been any entrances.

"Poor feeble mind can't take it." A different voice spoke this time, the mockery and scorn echoing round the chamber.

"This is the one who interferes with the fabrics of reality?" Ben turned back to the platform to see the woman on the metallic chair was the one speaking. Her face distorted with disgust. "I expected someone taller."

"Who are you?" Ben wished his voice sounded stronger than it did.

"You are not here to ask the questions boy. Not that you would understand the answer." The old woman sat on the stone chair dismissed the idea with a flick of her withered hand. She looked ancient. Her black robes hung to what was left of her wiry frame. She reminded Ben of the dolls one of his neighbours would put out on Halloween with the skeletal hand poking out of the black cloak. Grey hair hung limply around her angular face but her eyes still held the vibrance of life and a clear intelligence.

As Ben glanced nervously at the other two women, he saw she was clearly the oldest. The woman on the central chair seemed more of his age, perhaps slightly older but the one on the end was barely more than a girl. As he looked at her, her eyes narrowed in anger and she brought the end of a metal staff crashing down onto the rock floor. Thunder seemed to engulf the whole cavern bringing Ben to his knees, his hands covering his ears.

"He has no respect." Her voice rolled over the thunder, hitting Ben with another shockwave. The young woman was standing, her blonde hair seeming to glow white. The woman on the central seat put her hand in the air. She sat serenely, obviously not affected by the noise in the slightest.

"Perhaps," her voice managed to reach his ears through the din, a soothing sound that served to ease some of the pain in his head, "you should not call Aisa, girl." Ben's eyes widened in horror: he hadn't said anything out loud. The woman merely nodded at him.

"I'm sorry," Ben's mouth moved but he wasn't sure if any words came out through the crashes that reverberated round the cavern. Then, as soon as they began, the stopped. The blonde woman, Aisa the other had called her, tilted her head, gave an indignant sniff and sat back down.

"He learns quick though." The older woman laughed. Ben let himself drop down to the floor and sat staring up at his audience in disbelief. The woman who had been wearing rags only seconds before now had close cropped grey hair and was wearing a women's business suit, complete with pinstripes.

"Am I having a breakdown?" Ben hugged his legs up to his chest.

"No," Aisa sighed. "Nor are you dead, been drugged, abducted by aliens or on some reality tv show."

"A hundred years ago everyone would know who we were." The old woman muttered.

"Klo," the woman in the centre, the one Ben had already pinned all his hopes on, shook her head. "Try closer to two thousand. I told you, you were out of touch." She took a deep breath, straightened her purple dress and locked eyes with Ben. "You may call me Lak. Do you have any idea as to why you are here Ben Hibard? And do not lie, we can see all in your mind."

"Any idea? I don't even know where here is. Where did the…" He pointed back towards where the doorway had been. His brain was spinning so fast with questions he couldn't manage to string any more words together.

"The world is not bound by your elementary science rules like you like to think it is. Not that you stick to them mind you." Aisa managed to make every word drip with scorn.

"Who are you?" His brain was rebelling, refusing to acknowledge what was happening. There was no logical explanation. It could not be real.

"We told you our names." Klo tapped her fingers against the rock base of her throne, a rhythm of four repeated over and over again. "But you would not understand who we really are. Beings such as ourselves do not fit in your world of physics. You have no space for the old ways, for beings of power and influence. Each generation of mortals tears down more layers of the past and tries to assert domination over the universe."

"Mortals?"

"You see the impossible before you and yet still you cannot accept that there is more in the world. What more can we show you?" Aisa descended the few steps and moved closer to him. He spotted Lak stiffen but she stayed in position despite his imploring expression. He resisted the urge to shuffle away from the fierce woman; he had to stand fast. Her blonde hair was no longer free by her face but plaited in a thick braid hanging over her shoulder. At some point she had gained a helmet of chromed metal. Jagged strips followed her cheekbones until they ended in sharp points above her chin. A fin swept across the top of the helmet, curving round from the back of her head to her above her left eye. Patterns were etched into the surface of the metal. The precision was incredible. For a moment, his fear was forgotten as he marvelled at the intricate designs that were minute. It had to have been done with a nano-laser he posited. She closed the gap between them further. Her hands moved to the hilt of a sword Ben had noticed before. A distant part of his brain noted it was the same metal as her helmet and he found himself wondering if it had the same etching but his thoughts were disturbed as her fingers dug into his chin and dragged his attention back to her face. Her eyes blazed blue, not simply bright but unnatural. It looked like electricity passed across her irises. "You are but one. And we see you all. Every mortal. Every single one. Those that have been, those that are, those that will be. All of them. We see their lives, their loves, their hate, their wars. We see the potential, both bad and good and we give it space." She pulled his face closer. Her nails dug deeper as he gave a yelp of pain. Ben watched as flashes of blue and white danced across her eyes. "Shall I show you?"

"Aisa!" Lak's tone was commanding but the warrior before Ben ignored her. The electricity in her gaze crackled faster and flashed, blinding Ben.

For a few seconds, all he could see was white. The heat was what hit him first.

"The Fall of Troy. So many lives." The sound of Aisa's voice managed to penetrate through the shock. He realised his eyes were screwed up tightly against the white. A slow breath steadied him and he managed to ease his eyelids up but only a fraction. The sun was high in the sky, beating down on the sand around him. Ben spun round searching for the room he was just in but he was in the middle of an open patch of sand, up on a hill. He ran his fingers through the sand. The grains scratched at his fingers as they fell over each other to cascade back downwards. It felt real enough. Her words finally made an impact on his brain.

"Troy?" He struggled to his feet and shuffled a few steps further forward to stand near the warrior woman. Her chrome armour only shone brighter in the sunlight, although he could swear there were now hues of blue visible at certain angles. His attention was pulled away from admiring her seemingly impossible metal armour when he saw the walls reaching up from the sandy ground before him. A whole city surrounded by an impressive wall stood proud. Men were stationed at points along the structure looking down on the men who stood outside, swords at the ready. "This isn't possible."

"I would have thought you more believing than most," Aisa sniffed. "I know each and every man, woman and child down there. I have seen the choices they make and where it leads them."

"You have studied their history."

"There is no history for a being such as I. Everything is immediate. They are as contemporary to me as you are. I would show you people ahead of you, but I would not let *you* see their advances." She turned to face him as a roar went up through the crowds of men below. "Their lives and yours were mapped out at the moment you were born. It is a simple system. One you toy with daily." She grabbed his shoulder. He prepared himself this time and was ready when the world around him went white. The temperature plummeted suddenly, making his whole body convulse as he adjusted somewhat violently. "Points are fixed. Everyone at Troy was fixed, events happened as they should. It is how the world works."

Something was starting to click in the back of his overwhelmed mind. As his muscles finally started to relax, his brain began to catch up with him. "You mean fate. Everything is pre-determined? That is nonsense."

"You call us nonsense boy?" Klo's voice was menacing enough to make him regret his tone instantly.

"I have free-will," Ben countered, more subdued than before.

"You have free-will." Lak spoke this time, although as they all stood and approached him, he found it hard to focus. The women hovered over him as he sat on the floor, one leg wedged unceremoniously underneath him. "You made all the choices, we simply see them before you make them. We plan and document those choices. And most of all we protect those choices." The woman's voice dropped lower, striking a chord in Ben's brain.

"Methinks the penny has dropped," Klo cackled. Ben fought to keep his face neutral. There was no way they could know about his project; he had told no-one.

"And now he's starting to realise we are real, what he sees is real." Aisa leaned in close to him, a wicked grin on her face. Her helmet had disappeared. He scowled, could they not at least stop changing things in front of him? He massaged his temple, closing his eyes for a split second for respite.

"Poor Ben, is everything changing too fast for you? You don't seem to worry when you change things for everyone else." Aisa shook her head before retreating, turning her back to him as she walked away. She drew level with Lak. "I say we throw him to Tartarus and be done with it. We waste our time. He cares not about the damage he's caused."

Lak was watching him intently. Her red hair cascaded over her shoulders as she tilted her head to one side. The purple dress had morphed into a purple blouse and navy jeans. She looked like a regular woman he'd pass in the supermarket. "Time is something we never run short of though is it Aisa. You refuse to let time master you either do you Ben?"

His insides turned to ice. They did know about the project. This was insane. The project was a scientific breakthrough, all physics not magic. He hadn't broken laws of physics just read them in a different way, re-interpreted them. There was nothing magical about it so why were there three magical women staring at him in an impossible place having had him abducted by faceless men?

"This can't be real," he muttered as he put his head in his hands. "Magic is not real; science is real and you..."

"Perhaps," Lak crouched down to meet his eye level but his own gaze refused to meet hers. Simple stud earrings sat on her ears: silver Celtic knots that Ben's eyes traced round in loops. "Perhaps, we are following science too, you just don't know how to interpret it yet." She smiled kindly but it didn't make Ben feel any easier. She was in his head. He kept his palms fixed to the sides of his temples as if that would stop her from getting in. Lak gave him a tired look before standing up and moving back to her throne.

"Maybe Aisa is right," Klo piped up. The old woman was back on her throne, sat sideways with her legs swinging over the side. "Ship him down below."

"I haven't done anything wrong!" Ben shouted, a sudden indignation giving him the courage to speak. All three women stared at him; Klo looked amused, Aisa furious but Lak was impossible to read. When she spoke, her tone was guarded.

"You really see no issue with your, project?"

"My project?" It sounded pathetic even to himself. Lak suddenly threw her hands in the air; her face consumed by anger. A ring of flame spontaneously erupted from the floor in a ring around Ben. He yelled and dragged himself more into the centre. Sweat beaded all over his body at the sudden intense heat.

"Okay fine!" Ben yelled. And then, the flames just as quickly died away to nothing. Ben hugged his knees and stayed very still just in case. He thought of his workshop, how careful he had been to keep everything a secret, not even his wife knew of its existence. He had planned on showing it to his colleagues, publish papers on it. It would have made him the most famous man on the planet but he just wasn't ready to share yet. "You mean the Temporal Inverter."

"Yes Ben," Lak sighed. "I mean your time machine."

Ben's gaze dropped to the floor. "I never used it to hurt anyone."

"It's easy to say that when you don't look closely Ben. But you made your decisions. You don't get to take them back and try again."

He refused to look up. He felt like a child again being told off by his mother. So he gave himself another chance to make things a little better for himself. It's not like he stole the lottery numbers and became a millionaire. It was only ever small things: take a second shot at a meeting, make sure he wasn't late for things – inconsequential.

"You're not an idiot," Lak started.

"You sure?" Klo interjected. Ben was certain he heard Aisa snigger.

"You've heard of the Butterfly effect. Did you really think the things you changed would have no other knock-on effects?" Lak carried on, ignoring the other women.

"Knock-on effects?" He repeated incredulously. "So, one day I was late for a bus and went back and got a taxi instead so I didn't miss a meeting. What knock-on effects could I have caused? Other than me not being yelled at by my boss?"

"I'll show you." Lak clicked her fingers and the room disappeared. Air rushed around him as he felt like he was falling. As the world coalesced around him again, he was more prepared than he had been before.

He was stood at the edge of a park; it was one only ten minutes from his house. There was a slight breeze bringing a bit of a cool wind but Ben found it refreshing compared to where he had been. He let out a deep breath and looked around at the greenery. There were quite a few people around, mostly adults out for a stroll but there were a few groups further away kicking a ball around.

"Do you see her?" Lak asked. He screwed his face up; there were lots of people. "The woman in the wheelchair." Ben sighed and looked around again. There, off to the left, there was a woman in a wheelchair being pushed by a younger male.

"I see her."

"Seen her before?"

"What? How..." Ben flinched as an image flashed into his head. Lak must have been in his head again. He saw himself; it was the morning he'd been talking about. He was heading for the taxi sat idling in the layby. A woman was heading in the same direction but she had a massive bag in one hand and her handbag hung over the other shoulder. Ben watched as his previous self put on a burst of speed and got to the taxi ahead of her and leapt in. The car pulled away, taking himself off to his meeting. The images kept playing out in his head as the woman who had been racing him for the taxi got a little closer.

"It's her," Ben mumbled in surprise. The woman was muttering to herself, probably calling Ben some choices words.

"That was her taxi. Before you decided to play God with time, she got in that taxi and got to the office. Now she has to make a new choice. The taxi has gone and there aren't any around. Does she wait or does she struggle round the corner to the bus-stop? This is choice she was never supposed to have to make."

A crawling sensation starts to creep up Ben's spine. The woman in front of him was walking towards the edge of the path, no wheelchair in sight.

"She decides to get the bus. And as she gets round that corner," Lak pointed ahead of them, "her bags make her overbalance and fall. The driver never sees her." Ben watched in growing horror as the woman tottered off in that direction. Mercifully, the images stopped and he was back in the park, listening to the birds chirping overhead. "The man pushing her is her son. He was supposed to go to university but he couldn't leave her so decided to stay instead. The life he was supposed to have is all changed as well. Same for the girl who he was going to marry. All because you didn't want to get yelled at by your boss." The trees faded around him as he kept his eyes focused on the woman until the last possible moment.

The light dimmed as he returned to the cavern. He could feel the three knowing gazes upon him without having to look up. No noise could penetrate the sealed cavern and the three women stayed silent. The only sound Ben could focus on was his own breathing. He wanted to tell himself it was all some trick but he could remember reading about the woman in the paper; it had never occurred to him that he had been so close by. "How was I to know?"

"You couldn't possibly know," Lak admitted. "Which is exactly why you should not be toying with things beyond your comprehension. By improving your own luck, you destroy the fortunes of those around you. They are the ones that feel the catastrophic consequences of your actions."

"But it was such a small thing…" he looked up to protest but cut himself short as he saw the stares on the three judges before him.

"But not all of your changes have been so small have they Ben?" Klo straightened herself on her throne. She leaned forward tracing underneath her own chin with her pointed fingernail absently. "Do you remember your interview for your research position? The original interview?" She didn't wait for Ben to reply. She leaned forward and steepled her fingers together as if ready to tell a bedtime story. Glee danced in her eyes as she began. "You completely messed it up didn't you Benji? Fluffed your entire presentation and couldn't answer that difficult question about particle acceleration whatnot. Didn't have a chance. So poor little Benjamin is stuck in the job he's had for fifteen years ever since university. Can't have that, now can we? So, what's a boy to do? Well, depends on whether that boy has a convenient little time machine that will let him jump back a few hours and have another go. After he's asked his colleague the answer to that tricky question mind you." Klo threw her hands up and clapped, leaning back against her throne as if it were a sun lounger. "What's the past to you eh? No more is the past a fixed thing, it's fluid whatever you want to get the present that you want."

"I deserved that job." Ben regretted speaking instantly, despite how true it may have been.

"Do you know who else deserved that job? Mr Caine, the one who was offered it before you went back and had a second go. Mr Caine who had wanted to move to be near his family." Lak had sat forward now, taking over the narrative. Her hands lay on the armrests but her fingers were clawed around the ends resembling the tiger carving above her head, ready to pounce. Each word she spoke was more clipped than before, just as his mother's voice always turned when she was mad at him. "So now you have the current life you want and you're more than happy."

"He got the next job that came along." Ben stood up, fed up with being talked down to. He had accomplished something wonderful and they just couldn't understand.

"Yes," Aisa nodded. "He did. But what about the person who was supposed to have that job?"

"The only other applicant was some student." He flicked his hand in the air.

"Some student. Like you were once. The one-time student who accomplished something wonderful?" Aisa smiled cruelly. They could all get in his head. How was he supposed to argue with them?

"Why are you doing this to me?" His voice echoed around the chamber as he yelled.

"Still you ask all the wrong questions." Aisa shook her head. "You only think about your life, here and now. What about the future? All the future events and possibilities you cut off at the head. That student was going to design a green battery that would change energy production across the world. No more fossil fuels. But he didn't get that job. So he couldn't afford to stay in this town and went back home and got a job in a shop until he found the right place. In the end he gave up. You stole that from the world Ben. You. You stole the world's future so you could enjoy the present."

His fingers ran through his hair, damp with sweat. Could it be true? They saw all decisions, so of course they saw the future. "I didn't mean for any of that." His head shook, wobbling side to side subconsciously. "I only tried to change a couple of things. Things I thought I deserved."

"Like your wife?"

He froze. "I just tried to make her happy."

"By surprising her with romantic gestures, gifts and trips away each time she was going to tell you she was leaving?" Klo had lost any trace of humour.

"I didn't want her to go."

"And she didn't want to stay." Klo's clothes has changed again. The business suit replaced by royal looking robes. A thin golden band circled her head, contrasting starkly with her silver hair.

"I was always busy at work, I wasn't the best husband but I tried, I should have done those things all the time but I just…" The three women looked unmoved. "She changed her mind. She could have still gone; I just had some warning to give her another choice a couple of times."

"Nine," Lak snapped. The word made the whole cavern shake. Ben's balance was thrown and he lurched over to one of the stone benches beside him. "You made her stay nine times. Do you even know how many times you have changed the past?"

His mouth opened but he had to think. It wasn't that many, he just needed a hand every now and then. He'd finally managed to get the machine working eleven years ago. And in that time? He grasped for an estimate but before he could speak the air shimmered in front of him.

A strange silvery surface began to hover in mid-air, his haunted reflection hanging in the middle.

"What do you see Ben?" He wasn't sure who was speaking now.

"Me." He shrugged and watched the reflection mimic his gesture.

"How old are you?"

"Forty-one."

"No, you're not."

His face twisted in a sneer. He knew his own age. The gesture highlighted the wrinkles forming on his forehead. When had he gotten so grey? His hand reached up at his right temple.

"You've used your machine so many times Ben, sometimes you went back multiple times to get it right. Like the time you needed to get your calculations done for the group meeting. And the time you needed to 'borrow' some ideas from your colleagues talk. You know the one, the one who got accused of plagiarism after someone noticed the similarities? Each time it got a little easier to go back didn't it? Each time it seemed like less of a big deal. You've gained another seven years. You're actually forty-eight Ben." His eyes widened in shock as he looked closer. He was older. How had he not noticed? How had he not realised that would happen? He should have been keeping track. Seven years?

The mirror disappeared in a cloud of smoke, leaving him facing the three women again. They all had face paint on now, black patterns traced across their skin. Past, present and future, he thought. He let out a mirthless laugh as he realised that wasn't all they represented. His eyes moved from one to the other: judge, jury and executioner. His eyes landed on Aisa's sword.

"Why did you let me do this for so long?"

Lak smiled, "Time, it is a fickle thing and it's not linear for us. Where we got you from, we could not control."

"Are you going to kill me?" He could not help but notice Aisa's blade glinting blue in the dim light. He could swear the young woman's arm flexed instinctively towards it.

"And how many decisions will be changed if you are not in your time. No Ben," Lak shook her head. "We're not going to kill you. We're going to hit reboot." She smirked at her own joke. "We've undone all of your decisions."

"Took a long time to unpick all of those disasters I tell you," Klo's hands were full of pieces of string, all knotted and frayed. She let them fall to the ground and kicked them under her throne. "We will put you back where you should be, how you should be. But don't worry, we'll leave your memories intact, so you'll remember everything."

The room started to shake. Rock scraping across rock made his teeth set on edge. He turned to see the tunnel reopening. Two faceless figures stood in the widening gap.

"What's to stop me using it again?"

"Oh, you don't want us to bring you back here." Aisa stroked the hilt of her sword. He felt hands grab his shoulders and he was enveloped in a flash of light again. He pulled against the hands, trying to jerk free.

The light disappeared and a jolt of pain went through his shoulder as he landed on the floor. Coarse nylon scratched his face. He blinked. Nylon? He was laying on carpet. His body jerked upright and his head snapped round side to side. He knew this room. Red carpet, tired concrete walls painted white, an old swivel chair next his third-hand grey desk. This wasn't right; he'd left this place years ago. Ben dropped his head into his hands as he realised they had really done it. They had undone everything he had changed. Everything in his life had played out exactly as it would have done without his machine. There was no way he could stay like this; he couldn't go back to working in this dingy old lab with these idiots, he was meant for better. A righteous fire lit in his gut and he stood up with a sudden energy. The machine would be right where it always was. He'd show those old hags.

The door opened making Ben leap backwards and knock into the filing cabinet. The half-dead potted plant wobbled perilously.

"There you are Benji-man!"

Ben nearly began to twitch. He'd escaped this fool and his ridiculous nicknames years ago.

"Dude you look like you've seen a ghost."

Ben bit his tongue before he said something mean about seeing a forty-year-old man-child still dressing like a teen out of a sitcom and actually, a ghost would have been more pleasant. The urge to get to his machine increased tenfold. Christoph, as he insisted he was called, filled the doorway. He still wore the garish shirts Ben remembered him wearing, yellow and red swirls that were more suited to a Florida beach than a research lab. The only difference was the man now wore a handlebar moustache. Ben instantly hated it.

"I'm fine."

"Look me and Troy are going for some lunch, he's new, thought I'd show him the canteen. You coming?" Christoph stepped to one side to give Ben a glimpse of the new scientist.

Ben's heart nearly exploded in shock. He pressed himself harder against the filing cabinet, the metal handle digging into his back. The man Christoph called Troy was standing dressed in beige 'nothing' colours. His head was cocked to one side in some weird mockery of curiosity as he could not show it one his face. Where his features should have been, there was only a blur.

"Are you alright?" Ben heard the words but there was no mouth visible on the man. A metallic tang filled his mouth as he clamped down on his tongue. Christoph was looking expectedly at him, somehow oblivious to what was standing next to him.

"Fine." Ben's voice had all but vanished.

"You coming then? Or you got somewhere else to be?" Christoph grinned inanely at him but the other man seemed to lean in slightly. It was as if he knew what Ben had been thinking of doing.

"No," Ben shook his head and the faceless man pulled back. A fog of hopelessness descended on Ben as he realised the awful truth. "I'm right where I'm supposed to be."

Alex Minns is based in England and has worked in forensics, teaching, PR and been paid to wield custard flamethrowers. She writes sci-fi, fantasy and steampunk and can be currently found forcing her mother to listen as she tries to untangle the timelines of her time-travel steampunk novel. You can find her obsessively creating blog stories and micro-fiction on https://lexikon.home.blog/ and on Twitter under @Lexikonical

A Quest for Lemons

by Daragh Kennedy

Vinny awoke in his cabin with a coughing fit. He sprayed black mucus and gunk across Rolo the parrot who was sleeping on his masters chest.

"Oi, watchit," said Rolo.

Vinny lurched over the side of the bed, coughing and spluttering and rubbing at his gums.

"Sorry old chum," said Vinny.

Rolo flapped across the room and perched on top of a jar containing a dried up octopus.

"You're getting worse, Vin," said Rolo.

Vinny wiped away the bile from his face and rubbed it on his trouser leg.

"Aye, I know it," he said.

Rolo preened himself, trying to clean off the blood before addressing Vinny further.

"If you don't find some fruit soon you'll die."

Vinny didn't answer. He knew the bird was right. He stood to his feet, stretching his aching joints. He pulled his frock coat about him and grabbed his feather cap, stumbling towards the door. He shouldered and kicked at it, ignoring the busted handle, till it opened. He tasted salt and the glare of the sun as his eyes adjusted. When he acclimatized to the light he surveyed the ship and the state of the crew.

He scanned his eyes across the small vessel. The sails flapped indiscriminately with no particular design. The cannons lay limp and impotent at the sides of the boat, their ammunition spent. Members of the crew shambled about coughing and spewing up bile and blood, their legs filled with pus sores and swollen joints.

They'd been lost at sea ever since the navigator had fallen overboard during a party some months go. Vinny had ordered the rest of the rum thrown overboard after the mishap, to teach the crew a lesson. But he had given the order while the airs of intoxication still permeated all faculties of senses. The men, in their drunkenness, had thrown overboard the crate containing the vital lemons instead of the rum. Vinny had shot the man responsible, and proclaimed to the crew, "He's killed us all."

Rolo flew to his masters shoulder, flapping his wings and looking across the ship, following Vinny's eyes.

"What you gonna do today ?" he asked.

"Same as every day. Look for lemons."

"You gonna give the motivational speech again?"

"Perhaps," said Vinny.

Vinny took from his pocket his spyglass, and flicked it out, extending it and putting it to his eye. His thought his naked eye had caught a stray glimpse of a tiny speck on the horizon. Through the spyglass he could just about make out the shape of sails in the distance, several miles starboard.

"The gods have heard us," he said.

He put the spyglass back in his pocket and for the first time in months, felt energy and excitement and the lure of the sea. He stood up on a rotten wooden box and cleared his throat, wiping away the accompanying blood.

"Men!" he said.

The men did not react swiftly to their captains address. Some of them glanced in Vinny's direction and rolled their eyes, awaiting another pointless morale-boosting speech.

"I say Men!"

The men turned with slightly more haste to observe their bedraggled captain.

"There is to be no speech on this day men. To the starboard, a ship on the horizon! If you value what little life you all have left, do all in your power to make it there before we lose our legs and our teeth to this dreadful sickness!"

The men stood and ambled across to the starboard side of the ship, straining their eyes to get a look. And sure enough, the men could see something in the distance; a dot of indiscriminate shape and form. And with that realization a murmur of desperate hope caught in their hearts, and they moved to action to ready the ship for a chase. The crew unfurled sails, pulled at rigging, and Vinny being satisfied with their haste made his way up the ladder to the helm where he might have better vantage to direct the quest for lemons. Larry the helmsman lay slumped across the wheel, so drunk that he had lost the ability to breathe. Vinny booted him in the leg with his plush velvet slippers, one gangrenous toe protruding.

"Starboard Larry!" he shouted. "Don't make me shoot you!"

Rolo landed atop the wheel.

"He's dead," said the bird.

Vinny moved closer to inspect, took out his saber and stabbed at Larry's guts, which emitted a blackish yellow ooze.

"So he is," said Vinny. "I shall steer this thing myself." Vinny grabbed Larry off of the wheel, hoisting him up onto his back and moving to the side of the boat before dumping him overboard with a grunt and a groan. Such was the regularity with which bodies had been thrown into the sea of late, not one of the men stirred from their post at the splash of another corpse spilling into the water. They were focused on their tasks, and watching the dot on the horizon. Vinny watched it likewise as he gripped the wheel. He allowed himself a moment of reflection, praying to the Gods of the Seas and asking that they may grant him a sweet bite of lemon before the day was done. He turned the wheel starboard in the name of citrus.

The ship pushed through the calm waters at steady pace. Vinny would have liked to have been going a bit faster but with the crew stricken with scurvy, they were making acceptable progress. Rolo flew about from one side of the helm to the other, helping Vinny to negotiate the waves. Both the navigator and the helmsman may have died, and while Vinny felt their loss he knew in his heart that it was the bird that made his life on board the ship tolerable. He wouldn't trade all the navigators and helmsmen in the world for that talking parrot.

"Doing well, Vin, doing well," he said. "Port five paces. Starboard one."

The bird's chattering in his ear soothed Vinny into a trance where all that existed was just him, the sea and the wheel. It had been so long since he'd actually steered a ship himself, but he hadn't lost his masterful touch. He instinctively guided the vessel through the waves, moving closer to the dot which had now become something more similar to what one thinks of as a blob.

"Three hours Rolo, three hours," he said.

"Two Vin, we have the wind now," said Rolo.

The Crusty Sword, Vinny's ship, which had been named rather euphemistically after a famous Pirate who had contracted gonorrhoea, cut through the waves and the salty air. Vinny's thoughts turned to what manner of vessel they might encounter. Regardless of whether it was to be friend or foe, they would have to take it. The men were far too weak to win in a straight fight. There would have to be some measure of cunning and craft employed if they were to acquire the goods on board. He only prayed that it would not be a fellow scurvy ship that they would encounter. He tried to push such thoughts from his mind. He resolved that they would take the ship no matter who manned it, and no matter what cargo lay on board they would acquire it. Either they would find lemons on board, or die trying.

"Any ideas how we take this ship, Rolo?" he asked.

The blob had now become a blur of a ship on the horizon.

"Guns and sword."

"We have guns and sword, but not the strength to wield them."

"Pity about the cannons," said Rolo.

The Cannonballs had perished during the party along with the lemons. The men had been holding a competition to see who could throw them farthest. That was how the navigator had fallen in.

"Let's both have a think," said Vinny.

With that Rolo left Vinny to his thoughts, flying to his favourite perch atop the highest mast in the middle of the ship. Below the bird, the crew struggled and strained against the scurvy and the sea itself to power the ship to its target. They were getting closer with every passing minute. Vinny clutched the wheel and swung it left and right, cruising over the waves coming against him. He thanked the gods that while the men may have been dying, the ship was still strong. Vinny racked his brains trying to think of some way that they could wrangle the ship from whoever occupied it without the need for a fight. He knew that dread and terror were a pirate's greatest weapon. He recalled an old sailor's tale of a cursed ship occupied by a race of squid men. It was said that the squids had risen from the sea to combat the fishermen who scooped up the fish they lived on. They had taken to eating human flesh. It was regarded as a myth, but he knew that sailors lived and died by their superstitions. A plan began to form in his mind. And though he knew it was insane, he could think of nothing better. He whistled loudly, and pointed to Barry the oarsman, who was clutching at the rigging of the sails.

"Take the wheel!"

"Aye, Captain!"

Barry moved as fast as the scurvy would allow, and when he reached the helm after several minutes, Vinny gave him the wheel.

"Keep the bow pointed at the ship, Barry." he said.

"Aye Captain."

Vinny left Barry at the helm, and climbed back down the ladder. He walked into his cabin, with Rolo flying in after him.

He looked about the room, surveying the loot and ill gotten trinkets and curiosities he had assembled over the years. There was a lock of a witches hair, which he had won in a card game in Pirate's bay, there was an array of swords and guns and knives, and a turtle shell that he had fashioned into a brandy decanter. But his eyes lay on the jar with the octopus soaking in brine.

"You alright?" asked Rolo.

"Oh I don't think I've ever been alright," he said.

Vinny walked across the creaky cabin and plucked the jar from the desk. He had pilfered the octopus from a gang leader who had been cultivating and growing poisonous octopi from the devils swamp. The thing was black with red rings and Vinny had found it aesthetically pleasing and thought it would go nicely in his cabin should he ever have to entertain guests or impress some fair maiden. The Octopus always caught the eye.

"What's your game?" asked Rolo.

Vinny took the jar and hurled it to the floor, smashing the glass and soaking his feet in slimy brine. The octopus wriggled free, emitting a foul stench of decay and rot.

"This thing smells worse than us," said Vinny.

"What's the plan?"

"Today, I shall be a squid God."

"This is an octopus."

"Nobody will know the difference. Come on. We must be close."

Back on deck, the crew had made great progress in closing in on the ship. Vinny moved to the bow, and with his spyglass looked into the distance. He could see no signs of life on-board the target ship. Indeed he could see now that they were close enough, that the ship wasn't even moving. It was drifting. His heart fell slightly at that, as he theorized that it could be another ship that had been devastated by scurvy and that it would be lemonless. But he did not allow it to dampen his spirits. It could just as easily be a trap. It was a technique he had often used himself. Hide the crew below deck, pretend to be drifting and wait to be boarded, only to burst out and exact bloody murder unto whoever dare climb aboard. He turned with spyglass and octopus in hand, and addressed the crew.

"Men!"

They turned to their captain, with hungry eyes and diseased bodies.

"Men, we are weak, we are weary. But we have found something. A ship! This is our chance to survive. The Sea Gods have answered our prayers. But there is danger. We must use cunning to succeed. The boat appears to be deserted, but we must not take any chances. It may be a trap. Thus I will go aboard first, wearing this."

Vinny held the octopus aloft, as if it were the head of a rival freshly taken.

"I will wear this head and prey upon their fear of the squid people!"

The crew looked to each other nervously. Vinny had expected triumphant cheers, but they were not forthcoming. Jerry the quartermaster spoke up.

"Captain, it doesn't do to impersonate an evil being such as the squid king. It's bad luck."

The crew murmured in agreement.

"It also doesn't do to throw all of our lemons overboard while piss drunk , but alas men, this is the situation we are in. We are in dire need. And this is what will grant us victory, I assure you."

The crew continued to murmur and glance at each other nervously. Some put their hands together in prayer.

"Pirates," said Rolo, sighing behind the Captain.

Vinny gave one last order.

"Now sail! Get us closer."

Then he stood down and took his knife to the back of the octopus, and set about carving himself a space where he could place it atop his head.

They were almost upon the drifting ship. There was no sound that came from it that hinted at any life. They pulled up alongside, and the crew threw the ropes and boarding hooks, securing themselves to the ship, making a tether. Vinny took several deep breaths, before putting the stinking rotting octopus over his head. The tentacles seemed to wrap about his neck, and the stench made him want to wretch. But with all of the crew watching, and terror and dread left to instill in his enemies, there was no time for hesitation. He could barely see through the eye holes he had poked out with his knife, but with Rolo guiding him, and through his peripheries he could just about take hold of the rope ladder extending from the Crusty Sword to the drifting ship.

"Left, Right, left, right," said Rolo. "Now jump!"

With that Vinny landed, wincing, on the deck of the other ship, his scurvy legs weak. The crew crouched low, waiting for Vinny's signal to call them to board.

Vinny looked about the ship, and all was silent. Now was the time for theatrics. His intention, was to put almighty fear into anyone who may be lurking below deck. Vinny held his arms aloft and started delivering the speech of the squid god.

"Murglepurgleflangem shnaw," said Vinny, lifting his betentacled head to the heavens.

Silence.

"Magglepagglegurkamok."

Nothing.

"Scraw!"

"Vinny!" said Rolo.

A door creaked open behind him. He let out a roar, a kind of gurgling guttural bellow that he thought a squid or octopus king might make and fired his guns in the direction of the creaking door. And with that , the crew roared and they too slowly climbed aboard and fired their guns at the door of the cabin.

Amidst the smoke and chaos and roaring and screaming, Vinny's Octopus head slipped off and fell to the ground. His men stood about him with smoke lingering in the air, their ammunition spent. Vinny, along with his men, looked down the narrow door of the cabin, as the smoke cleared, to see who they had just emptied all their shots at. Blood seeped through the doorway. Vinny strode forward, his men behind, Rolo hovering above. A stray hand, covered in blood, robed in white garments, lay across the doorway.

"Pull that body out," said Vinny.

Two of the crew went and dragged the corpse out. The man was clearly no soldier, pirate, or merchant. Rather, he seemed to be dressed like a monk, with a robe and prayer chains draped about him.

"What you make of him?"said Rolo

"I'm not sure," said Vinny.

Vinny reached a hand inside the monk's robe, looking for something of value. He found nothing, but as he was looking he noticed a small tattoo, a triangular symbol with two interlocking spirals.

"The goddess of plenty," said the bird.

"Yes," said Vinny. "What are they doing so far out to sea?"

"Fresh air?" asked Rolo.

"I think not," said Vinny.

Vinny knew that the advocates of the goddess of plenty had pledged themselves to cultivating food, wine, and all the other amenities that fed the world. Vinny turned about, and addressed the men.

"This is a plenty ship men, there's bound to be food. Check the hold."

The men hastened to follow Vinny's orders. But even if an an order had not been forthcoming their hunger would have led them to search every corner of the ship. The crew disappeared inside the cabin and went below deck, and after some brief moments a chorus of cheers went up.

"Lemons Captain! A whole crate!" said Jerry the quartermaster.

Vinny stood away from the corpse and the octopus head on the ground. He walked to the port-side railing and leaned against it, giving himself a moment to thank the goddess of plenty and all the other gods of the sea to which he had prayed to for delivering bountiful lemons unto him and his crew. He shook the railing and tapped his feet in a private joyous celebratory dance.

"We will not die yet, my friend," said Vinny as Rolo landed on his shoulder.

He stroked the bird a tad and Rolo enjoyed the quiet touch of his master on his feathered back. The crew returned from below deck with the box of lemons, and placed it at the captains feet. The box had been half opened, such that the crew could gaze within. They were practically salivating at the thought of putting the juicy lemons to their lips. But Vinny would not give them the satisfaction yet, until they had searched the rest of the ship. He wanted to go below himself to have a nosey about for this whole business of these seafaring monks intrigued him. And he would be lying if he did not say that he felt some trepidation at the mystery of what the ship was doing here, transporting foods and wines across the waters without an escort and why it had been simply drifting with the wind.

"Get the crates aboard the Sword," said Vinny. "I'm going to look below, when I return we shall leave, and then we shall eat. No man is to touch a lemon until I return."

The men fought the need within them to grab the lemons at that instant and gorge themselves. Vinny could see the desire in them to disobey him. "Go, that's an order." he said.

"Aye captain," said the quartermaster.

Vinny went to make his way below deck.

"And bring that octopus as well," he said, before descending into the hold of the ship.

Below deck it was cramped and stuffy, and filled with boxes, which his men were cracking open and checking to see what they contained. Some had dried meats, others bottles of wine and rum. Several more monks lay dead, covered in blood, victims of the gunfire. Vinny ignored the crates and the bodies, spotting instead a door towards the rear of the ship. The door was unopened. The men, in their hunger and desperation had neglected to search it. Vinny drew his saber and walked past the row of crates till he stood in front of it.

"Careful Vin," said Rolo.

"I know," said Vinny.

With his ever failing strength Vinny mustered a kick and busted the door open.

The room was small and dank, and filled with tomes and vials and incense burners unlit. But the smell of incense seemed to have seeped into the wood itself in the room. Vinny covered his nose, such was the aroma. He was not averse to the smell of incense, but here it was put to religious purpose and he disliked the connotations. A large book lay on a lectern, bolted into the wood, so as not to be dislodged during rough seas. Vinny wondered how these monks could even know how to navigate the ship. But the book drew his thoughts from their stray wanderings. He limped over, his legs aching with the exertion of the last few hours in pursuit of the ship he stood in the belly of. He rubbed the weathered leather cover, and turned it open. Strange writings and diagrams were inscribed throughout. There seemed to be no sense or rhyme to it. But then he came to a last picture, which consisted of two lemons, one small, one large, and some kind of arrow pointing from the small lemon to the large one.

"What's it mean?" asked Rolo.

"I know not compadre, but I don't like it."

Vinny looked about the room at all of the vials. Filled with reds and greens and purples and all other sorts of multicolored liquids. He didn't know what they contained. But they looked to be brimming with magic. The liquids almost crackled inside the bottles, as if they were electric. He could picture himself flogging them at the bazaar when they got back to Pirate Bay. He didn't need to know what they did, he knew with charm and some concocted story he could sell them to some hobbyists of the occult.

"Best leave them alone," said Rolo. "We got the lemons, let's get out while we're in luck."

"Just one," said VInny. His eyes settled on a blue green vial, which was small enough that he could easily carry it on his person. He took it, and put it into his frock coat.

"Bad idea Vin,"

"I know what I'm doing."

"Do you?"

"I do. Don't chastise me. I got us the lemons didn't I?"

"Pure chance. I really don't think you should tempt fate."

"Too late," said Vinny. "It's done."

With that the conversation was over, and Vinny made his way back on deck. The last of the boxes were being carried up and onto the Crusty Sword. Vinny made his way across the rope ladder, where the crew were waiting, their stealing of the cargo of the plenty ship almost complete. The lemons hadn't even made it to the hold. They still lay half opened now on the deck of the Sword. But something made Vinny's blood boil. Maybe he was being pedantic. He could have just let the men have the lemons as soon as they got them. But he knew that to do so would ensure that they wouldn't last long. No, he knew they had to be rationed if they were to be worthwhile. And while he too held a desire to quaff as many as possible as quickly as he could, he knew that restraint would give them a better chance in the long term. They were still without a navigator and were very much lost at sea. All they had done was ensure they could stave off the scurvy. And for that, they needed the lemons to last. Also, he had given an order that the lemons were not to be touched until he said so. A direct order. And he knew, as any pirate captain knows, that if you let one thing slip, even one little order, no matter the circumstances, it was a fast track to mutiny, and next thing you know you would be taking a swim with the sharks. He was alarmed and enraged when he saw a lemon rind on the deck of his ship. He drew his saber and pierced the lemon rind with the point of the blade, lifting it up and pointing the evidence of disobedience at the crew. The skin of the lemon flapped in the wind, and Vinny's eyes opened wide and he snarled and foamed as he spoke.

"Who ate the lemon?" he said.

There was silence amongst the crew. Most of them looked at the ground or off into the sea. Others stared at the box of lemons. Only a few looked at the captain.

"Who ate the lemon?" Vinny asked again.

Again, he was met with silence, as the last of the crew climbed aboard behind him.

"Is no man brave enough to admit he disobeyed me and took a lemon?"

The crew did not speak. There was no backing down now. He would have to do something. This was a precarious situation. They may have got the lemons alright, but this disobeyal of a direct order was a stepping stone to mutiny.

"If no one owns up, I'll throw the whole blasted lot of them into the sea," said VInny.

Rolo appeared on his shoulder and whispered.

"Let it go Vin."

But VInny knew it was too late. He had taken this fight and he couldn't back down. To do so would be to relinquish all of his authority.

"Can you blame us?," said Jerry the quartermaster. "Look at the state of us!" he said.

Vinny cast his eyes across his disease ridden crew. He didn't want to blame them. But he could not and would not let it slip. He held the lemon rind up in front of him, and wondered how all of the decisions in his life had led to him in a standoff at sea over a lemon. He held it up and shouted to the crew.

"I know it's been tough men. And we were so close to salvation. To saving our weakened ruined bodies. But disobedience will not be tolerated. You already once threw lemons overboard due to your own stupidity and ignorance. I think it's only right that this time I'll throw them overboard!"

Vinny didn't know, as he picked up the box of lemons, whether he was actually going to throw them overboard. But he didn't need to wonder long, because as soon as he went for the box the crew swarmed him. They pulled and grabbed at him, and the box fell to the floor, lemons rolling everywhere over the deck. Vinny fired his pistol, shooting the quartermaster in the commotion. But as he struggled amongst his crew in a mass of bloody spewy pus-filled pirates, the vial he had taken from the ship of the monks of the goddess of plenty slipped from his coat pocket and fell to the floor of the Crusty Sword, rupturing and spilling the viscous liquid onto the lemon covered deck. And as the liquid covered the lemons, an alarming thing occurred. The lemons began to grow. They expanded, like sponges full with water. They grew and they grew and they grew, till there was barely enough room for any man to stand on the deck of the ship. The lemons caused the masts to splinter, the sails to tear, and the ship to bend and buckle under the enormous weight of the rapidly growing fruit.

"Abandon ship!" screamed the crew, as some were knocked overboard by the lemons. Others jumped over the side by themselves. Some of the lemons split in half as they grew, others exploded, showering the ship with bitter pulpy mass, and some lemons spat their seeds so hard and fast that they killed some of the crew members stone dead. In among the chaos, Vinny had sprung free from the mutinous hands. And he was now in no doubt as to what the vial was intended for. The goddess of plenty. Providing the living with food. Clearly these monks had perfected some kind of growth serum to feed the masses with gigantic fruit. However, Vinny surmised, clearly the correct dosage of liquid administered was of essential importance.

"Jump Vin!"

Rolo dragged Vinny from his thoughts. The lemons continued to grow, some exploding, others falling over the side, into the water. Vinny ran to the side of the ship and dived overboard without looking. He landed splat in the middle of one half of a lemon. This particular one had exploded in such a way that it made a kind of makeshift raft to sit in. Fortune had favoured him once again. In all the chaos, some other members of the crew were floundering in the water, trying to grab onto the lemons to stay afloat. Some were lucky, and were close enough to some of the half exploded ones. Others, scrabbled and scratched at the gigantic yellow skin of the full lemons, unable to make any kind of dent. The turbulence of the lemons falling had created such powerful currents in the sea that Vinny found himself driftly rapidly away from the scene of the lemon mishap. Part of the magical liquid had clearly fallen on the Octopus head as it too had grown to an enormous size and was drifting away from the scene of the accident. Years later, this Octopus would be the foundation of myths of a giant kraken that would terrorize Pirate Bay.

Rolo hovered about above Vinny, looking at the chaos as they floated further and further away. Vinny too, could see the ship disappearing from view, and to his left and right, some other half exploded lemons, with pairs of hands and heads of crew members who had been lucky enough to land inside them. They were now at the mercy of the sea once more. Rolo landed on Vinny's shoulder.

"I told you that vial was no good," said the bird.

"You're wrong. It was too good."

"You think they were trying to help with world hunger or something?"

"Probably. It would have never worked."

"Why not?"

"Bureacracy and capitalism Rolo. Money has to be made."

Vinny reached down and took up a big mouthful of juicy bitter lemon, which was like heavenly nectar to his scurvy riddled gums. He took the juice and rubbed it all over his sores. Rolo too flew down and landed on the inside of the lemon and took his fill. After gorging themselves for a time, they lay on the lemon, man and bird, floating aimlessly along with the tide. Vinny broke the silence.

"It's not so bad actually. We got away from the crew, they were really starting to piss me off you know? We can get a new crew. A better one. Back in Pirate's Bay. All we have to do is drift with the tide till someone picks us up. No ship is going to ignore a whole bunch of gigantic lemons floating around with people inside. They're gonna wanna know what happened. And until then, all we gotta do is sit here, and eat us some lemon."

"That sounds like a good plan" said Rolo. "But I have one question."

"Shoot," said Vinny through mouthfuls of lemon.

"What happens when the lemon's all gone?"

Daragh Kennedy is a writer from Dublin, Ireland. He is an English Literature and Philosophy graduate and is currently working on his debut Science Fiction novel, inspired by his time spent travelling in Brazil. He also writes songs and short stories and his work will be published in the upcoming Horror/Crime anthology From the Shadows.

The Break-Up

by Max Turner

The shuttle from Io City ran as efficiently as ever, giving Nico only twenty minutes to consider what he was going to say to Laurent. This couldn't go on any longer.

He'd agreed to meet Laurent at the Natural History Museum. Agreed against his better judgement, with the fact that this had been where they'd gone on one of their first dates not at all lost on him.

They had met initially at a state celebration and immediately enjoyed each other's company. Being friends with an Ionian had been eye opening for Nico, but more than that, there had been an attraction. Laurent enjoyed sharing his work as a geologist, and the history of the terraformed moon on which the Ionians had evolved. Everything about Laurent simply fascinated Nico. But that wasn't enough.

Nico found Laurent sitting on one of the benches in the viewing dome overlooking the small volcanic area that eluded to the moon's original state. It was otherwise empty, and Nico noticed the slight turn of Laurent's head signalling that he had heard Nico's approach.

Nico sat, resisting the urge to reach out and touch the man he had become so close to in the months he had been on this moon. Their gazes met for just a moment before Nico had to look away.

"You're as beautiful today as ever, Nico," Laurent's words were sentimental and to be expected from an Ionian, but genuine nonetheless.

Nico took a breath, wishing things could be different. This was never going to work between them, they were from two different worlds, literally. Two peoples that never mixed in this way for both cultural and practical reasons. When his boss had become aware of the romance, he had told Nico he must end it. Nico knew in his heart that was the right thing to do.

Looking at Laurent now, it was easy to see how different they really were. The style of their clothes and jewellery spoke of their differing pasts.

Nico was shorter, a little thicker built having grown up on the Lunar Terra where the gravity was stronger. His skin was a light brown and his eyes dark. Laurent was almost unnaturally tall and slender, his skin was so pale as to seem almost an eggshell blue. Nico looked like farming stock, a worker, a doer. Laurent was like all Ionians, intelligent and passive. Almost regal compared to other species in the solar system. They were a peaceful people, where Nico's kind were built to fight and conquer.

Even if they might overlook all of this, there was no ignoring the Ionian bonds.

Laurent, as all Ionians, released a natural chemical when he encountered a potential bond-mate. Something that had evolved in their once small population as a way to signal that they were ready to be paired or grouped. Ready to form a family unit. In the beginning it had been a way to ensure the Ionians only took lovers who were unrelated to them, but as the population had grown, it had become steeped in a rich tradition.

Nico grit his teeth knowing that he had to deny what was clearly between them even as he felt that metallic tang in the air of the chemical Laurent was producing. He would never sense it in the same way an Ionian would, never be able to form a chemical bond.

"I'm glad you agreed to meet with me," Laurent spoke softly, "it feels like I haven't seen you in years. Being apart makes time drag."

Nico ached at the words and shook his head.

"I wanted to see you one last time. I couldn't be a coward, I had to do this in person. I needed to be clear that this is over and we should have never let it get this far. You want me to be something I can't be."

"I never wanted you to change," Laurent replied.

Nico noticed how Laurent's hand twitched as he clearly stopped himself reaching out.

"This is beyond just us—" Nico started, wanting to reiterate the upheaval this could cause in both their lives, but Laurent interjected.

"It is beyond us, beyond you and I. I can't explain it all right now, but there are studies we're going to publish and—"

"Laurent, please don't make this harder."

This was worse than he'd hoped it would be. They should have ended this sooner, or never started it. Nico wasn't about to step on generations of cultural tradition that practically mandated that the Ionians not form attachments to any other species. To do so could destroy both their lives and careers, and he couldn't do that to Laurent.

In hindsight, Nico should have never come to Io. Diplomatic relations be damned, there were plenty of others that could do his job. He was a small cog in a large machine that kept the solar system in some semblance of peace. A peace he knew he would never feel again without Laurent by his side and in his bed, but there was nothing to be done about that.

"I'm returning to Lunar Terra," Nico choked out the words. "This is over, Laurent. I—"

"Do I get no chance to speak?" Laurent's tone was caught between anger and sorrow. "We're all—"

Laurent was cut off as noise filled the air.

A rumble, growing louder and louder like an earthquake coming closer.

There was an explosion that felt both distant and intensely close, filling the air with a static charge. And then more noise, like the moon they stood on was screaming.

It all stopped abruptly, or Nico couldn't hear it, he wasn't sure which was true.

Nico's eyes went wide as the ground began to shake uncontrollably. He reached for Laurent instinctively, taking the Ionian's arm as the whole building started to break apart, with cracks slithering through the glass skin of the dome.

"Laurent," Nico called his lover's name just as the building started to crash down around them.

#

"Nico, wake up!"

Nico felt Laurent shake him gently and he slowly opened his eyes.

They were still in the half buried basement that they had been sheltering in for the last few days whilst searching the area to replenish their supplies. He blinked.

"Another bad dream." Laurent's words were soothing but not a question, Nico nodded all the same.

The world had ended weeks ago and here they were, trying to survive amongst a people gone feral. The usually passive and timid Ionians that had survived were quickly turning on each other.

Nico had held out hope for the first two weeks that help would come. He hoped that the EM blast that had disabled the entire moon's technology and caused countless overloads and explosions had been nothing more than a horrific accident. But as time moved on and no one came, he had enough insider knowledge to understand what had happened. That, as they had always dreaded, peace in the solar system had ended.

The chances were that every inhabited planet and moon in the system had suffered the same fate as Io. Those that survived the damage wrought by the initial blast, would find no working technology, no civilised comforts. Any still partially terraformed body would quickly become unlivable entirely.

Io wouldn't suffer that fate at least, but this was all there was now.

Ruins and bad dreams.

And each other.

They had dug themselves out of the Museum, their conversation moot for a moment as they clung together. And yet, they were not together, they were not lovers.

Logically, Nico knew there were no cultural conventions to stop them now, and yet it felt like allowing this one sided bond would rob Laurent of something that Nico could never replace. He could never bond as an Ionian could, and that was what Laurent deserved.

As society deteriorated, being able to bond with a stronger, well positioned Ionian, could mean the difference in Laurent's continued survival. Nico could not take that from him.

"It'll be daylight soon," Laurent noted, sitting up in the mess of blankets. "Do you still wish to try for the docks?"

Nico nodded.

Laurent hadn't understood at first when Nico had mentioned it, thinking of the spaceport rather than the pleasure docks where you could sail out onto Io's Great Ocean. It had once been a volcanic crater, long before the Ionians had evolved but now was a vast ocean full of life.

The ocean had been artificially created and seeded less than a century ago, resulting in no real maritime history for the Ionians. But Nico had learned to sail as a child. His grandfather had learned decades before as a young man on Terra, before the planet became uninhabitable, and had passed on his skills. Nico could fish, could repair and maintain most vessels, all hobbies he had continued after his grandfather's death, right up to his move to Io.

He had only been to the pleasure docks once, but he knew there would have been many vessels there before the blast. What remained was yet to be seen.

If they could find a serviceable boat they could live off the sea, forage along the coast line and see what fate might await them.

"Wait," Laurent put a hand on Nico's arm as he made to get up from their bed.

Nico stilled and yes, there were the faint footsteps of someone passing above in the alleyway. They both froze, listening as yet another Ionian tried to locate the source of the Laurent's chemical. So many of them seemed driven to try and claim and rebuild the civilised lives lost to them.

Finally the footsteps resumed, the Ionian having given up, and the pair relaxed a little.

Nico began to pack up their few items into a bag as Laurent moved from the blankets and bundled them to tie up.

"You can stop this from happening, Nico." Laurent said softly, yet Nico could feel the Ionian's anger radiating. He couldn't blame him, because he was completely right. Laurent was only releasing the chemical because his anticipated bond-mate was nearby, and it would stop if Nico allowed Laurent to bond with him.

"I can't Laurent. It's not right. We should never have been together, and the end of the world doesn't change that."

"It does!" Laurent said, firmly. "And I wanted it before all this. But you have decided the choice is yours alone."

"Don't I have the right to that choice?" Nico snapped back.

"Not when your choice is on my behalf. You won't allow me to bond with you because you feel that you are robbing me of something, or robbing my culture. And I'll tell you again, I only want you. I've only ever wanted you. A whole moon full of Ionians and I only ever chose you."

There was a harsh edge to the pleading tone and Nico couldn't blame Laurent for the resentment there. Laurent had made it clear in many ways. In both words and actions he had confessed his love for Nico and his desire to bond. But it wasn't that simple.

Now more than ever Nico had to think about the effect this might have on Laurent's life. To be bonded to a Lunar Terran, the species that had likely caused the blast in the first place. To not have his availability to bond as a potential bargaining chip should he need it.

Whatever rose from the ashes of this planet, Nico would do everything he could to ensure Laurent was safe.

"I can't." Nico said quietly, silencing the topic for another day.

#

It was a cold night.

127

It was always cold at night since the world ended.

Nico knew that it would be easier if they could maintain a distance from each other, but every night the cold drove them together, huddling under blankets, body's wrapped around each other for warmth.

In the mornings Nico would wake early, usually unable to sleep for more than a couple of hours, and would free himself from Laurent's grasp, leaving him to wake alone.

When Nico did sleep, the dreams came.

Dreams of Laurent lying dead in the Museum, or of himself setting off the blast and being responsible for all of this. The worst were the ones where he was still on Lunar Terra and discovered what had happened to Io, feeling a sense of loss that tore his body and mind apart without knowing why.

This morning Nico woke to the echoing sound of bricks being torn down.

They were at least another day walk from the pleasure docks, and had been lucky so far in avoiding people and finding shelter. But that luck seemed to have run out.

The small room they were in was little more than three walls and no roof, and the sounds came from behind them, the other side of the wall they'd slept against. With the bricks falling Nico had thought the building was coming down, he moved to wake Laurent, but then stopped. The noises ceased for a moment, then the sound of footfalls and voices became clear.

Nico clenched his jaw.

"Laurent," he urged softly as he shook the Ionian's shoulder.

Laurent's eyes sprang immediately open, taking only a moment to focus in on Nico's face.

Nico held up a finger to his lips to silence him and then nodded his head towards the direction of the sound. They both listened and then there were jeering voices. Not loud enough that they could make out all the words, but the few that were spoken with a little more conviction came through. Words like _bond_ and _family_.

Nico felt Laurent bristle. But there was no fear in his eyes. There was only a rage filled determination. The way in which the Ionians were losing their famed civilities seemed to be affecting Laurent too.

Nico took in a sharp breath.

He had assumed that they had merely reacted to the situations they found themselves in, but what if this was what lay at the heart of all Ionians? A society that abhorred sports with physical contact and seemed to have strict moral codes. Perhaps that was all a veneer to stop them being just as aggressive as the rest of the species in the system?

He couldn't dwell on it for now, there were more pressing concerns. And whilst Laurent could perhaps repel unwanted attentions, even if it became physical, they had gone weeks now with sparse amounts of food. They were both exhausted and run down. Neither of them were in any shape to fight, they had to run.

"We need to move," Nico spoke quietly, grabbing their few items and stuffing it into the backpack he'd acquired. But Laurent sat there watching the direction of the noise.

His eyes seemed almost completely dilated and there was a low rumbling sound from his throat that spoke of Laurent's desire to attack.

Nico grabbed Laurent's arm roughly, and spoke quickly and quietly, "we have to go. We don't know how many. How strong. Don't be a fool."

It was those last words that snapped Laurent's attention back to him. He blinked and then nodded, getting to his feet and following Nico out through the half fallen wall.

"Hello." A deep voice crooned, menacingly.

Nico whipped around to see a man who might be considered heavy-set for an Ionian, now stood where a short while ago they had been sleeping. Before they could respond, he was barreling towards Nico and Laurent as they scrambled over the broken down wall.

Nico barely made it, falling onto the broken bricks with a thud. He grit his teeth against the pain of it, stunned for just a moment before trying to get to his feet.

The bricks gave way and slid beneath him, making it difficult to stand as he tried to regain his bearings.

All the voices were closer, now in the room he and Laurent had just left, and making their way to the fallen wall.

In the early morning light he could make out Laurent grappling with the stranger that had been on their heels. When the Ionian lunged for Laurent, he dodged and then shoved a foot sharply at the bricks. They started to cascade and the Ionian lost his footing, falling with a thud next to Nico.

Nico grabbed hold of the bag again just as the other Ionians appeared at the gap in the wall.

"Stay back!" Nico snarled, but the two Ionians looked unimpressed and chuckled at him.

Their fallen friend chuckled too and started to try and sit and grab for Nico as he stumbled away from the man's grasp.

Laurent launched himself at the fallen Ionian, pushing him back down onto the bricks and pinning him.

Laurent called out over his shoulder at the amused Ionians.

"Decide his fate. Don't come closer."

One huffed dismissively and the other laughed again and then they started to clamber through the gap in the wall.

Quicker than Nico could even track, Laurent pulled the man up and then slammed him back down against the bricks, causing the man to cry out in pain.

Stunned at the sudden violence, it took a moment for Nico to register what had happened. And by then Laurent had a hold of him and was dragging him away from the crumbling bricks as the other Ionians saw to their friend.

They ran and didn't stop until they were streets away. If they could even be called streets anymore.

Then Nico stopped, leaning against a wall to catch his breath. He watched as Laurent stalked back and forth, agitated in a way Nico had never seen before.

"What were you thinking?" Nico growled through grit teeth. "You could have gotten us killed. We should have just run."

Laurent raised a brow at him, "We probably wouldn't have out run them."

Nico had no reply to that. It didn't matter if Laurent was right or wrong, all that he could think of was how terrified he'd been at the thought of losing Laurent.

He wanted to let Laurent bond with him there and then. More than he'd ever wanted to before. And not just because of the fear of losing him. But because it was Laurent.

Laurent who was beautiful and elegant, and wanted to visit museums with him. Laurent who had fire in his eyes and had just attacked someone to ensure their safety.

Instead, again Nico forced himself to reject the thoughts and feelings, just as he knew he should reject Laurent.

With a growl Nico pushed away from the wall and stalked to the Ionian, clasping his hands to his side to stop himself from grabbing him.

"We shouldn't be together." Nico snapped, wanting to pull Laurent to him. Wanting to push Laurent away. "Being together puts us both in danger."

"If you'd let me—"

"No!" Nico shook his head. "No, Laurent. We've already had this discussion."

He could practically feel the anger burning in Laurent, but then the Ionian composed himself, taking a few breaths until he was as he had always been.

"You're quite right, Nico. Perhaps it is time we go our separate ways." Laurent's expression and tone were completely blank. Not even sadness in his acceptance of what Nico had been trying to say for what felt like a lifetime now.

Laurent turned and began to walk away.

Nico resisted reaching out to him, knowing that this was the best way to keep Laurent safe. To stop his chemical production, to give him a chance to use his bond for an allegiance if he needed to. This was the only way.

#

It took most of the day to get near anywhere near the docks and in the end Nico sought shelter as the sun went down. He hunkered down in the shell of a burnt out travel pod, not quite dozing as every sound made him startle and wonder where Laurent was and if he was safe.

His Laurent. He would ache for him forever, but had to be satisfied with knowing he was safe.

The next morning, exhausted and hungry, Nico scavenged for food but found little more than some unripe tomatoes on a vine growing in what had once been a garden. They made the acid in his stomach reflux but they filled it a little all the same.

He thought about Laurent as he ate them. Of his laughter the first time Nico had tried Ionian grown tomatoes on their fourth or fifth date. He had not been prepared for the strange, sweet and sour taste of them, making the soup he had ordered quite unpalatable for the Lunar Terran.

Such a different time that had been.

Nico shuddered. His stomach growled and he moved on.

His only hope now would be to find a seaworthy boat at the pleasure dock, and hope that Laurent found equal safety.

The closer he drew to the docks the worse the world seemed.

There was barely anything left this close to the city. What was left had been picked over by groups of marauding Ionians that he barely avoided.

There was a metallic scent heavy in the air that Nico had to guess was the combined chemical release of a huge number of unbonded Ionians. Their bodies reacting to this situation in the time honoured tradition of their people. Bond, build families, build civilisation.

Every noise made him jump, every footfall he knew could mean danger. Even if those he might encounter held no animosity towards him for being Lunar Terran, he still wasn't one of them. There was a loneliness to it that he hadn't even begun to address within himself.

Everything he'd grown up with, his family and friends back on Lunar Terra, he would never see again. It hadn't felt quite so bad with Laurent at his side. Not just the company, but the love between them.

As Nico approached the docks, it looked deserted.

Boats were adrift, some sunken in dock or further out.

All of the floater pods were completely fried, the blast having shorted them out whilst on water, with explosive results.

The boats that were still floating had been ransacked and one was still somehow afloat after having been half burned out. Whatever had been in these boats was long gone. Provisions, food, medicine. Anything and everything that could be scavenged would have been taken and, most likely, the rest destroyed. Nico and Laurent had seen it time and again in the days and weeks following the blast.

Nico was cautious as he made his way towards the moorings.

The boards groaned under him and he wondered what structural damage the docks might have taken and how safe this was. He tread carefully, staying alert for anyone that might still be lingering. The boats groaned, cabin doors knocked open and closed with the motion of the water. There was nothing to salvage of any of them so Nico continued, hoping that by the time he got to the end of the dock there might be something.

He was nearing the end of the dock when he saw her.

One of the pleasure boats designed to be rented for vacation trips. With both sails and a motorised engine, it was designed to look like a Terran antique whilst offering all modern comforts.

She was adrift, almost out of the harbour. From where he stood, Nico couldn't see that she had any damage. There were a few others out there floating further out, maybe unmoored by the initial explosions, or perhaps by people trying to escape?

He was prepared for that. Prepared that there was every chance he'd climb aboard and find people with no knowledge of boats, just drifting there. Hungry, scared, possibly violent.

Nico hoped they'd be violent. It would be easier then to fend them off and get them overboard. If they were just sitting there in a pitiful state what would he do?

What choices might he have to make?

He was done with choices. With choosing whether to be with Laurent or not, and the shifting reasons one way or the other.

And yet if Laurent were with him Nico knew he wouldn't hesitate to do anything he had to to protect him.

He ached.

Nico let out a growl and removed what remained of his tattered jacket and let it fall to the ground. It was cold, the water was going to be warm, heated by the moon's remaining volcanic activity, the coat would only weigh him down once it became sodden and then chill him through once out of the water.

Nico made his way to the end of the dock, or at least what was now the end of the dock, the rest having been completely destroyed. And from there he took in a deep breath in preparation and then jumped.

It took long minutes to fight through the slightly thick Ionian water and he was exhausted and aching when he reached the boat and took hold of the ladder on her side. He rested for a minute, catching his breath, trying to restore his energy as much as he could after weeks of near starvation.

When he pulled himself up out of the water, the cold of the air on his wet clothes hit him and he shivered. It would have been easier to endure if he was well fed and in good health.

Nico grit his teeth, trying not to be concerned about what might await him, what he might have to do, and he began to climb.

It was the scent that hit him as he pulled himself on deck.

He'd been prepared for the scent of blood, and perhaps of decomposition. He'd been prepared for the scent of a number of endings this boat might have seen. But that wasn't what hit him.

The scent was metallic. It made his stomach tie itself in knots and his jaw tighten.

It was the chemical scent of an Ionian seeking a bond mate. It was the scent he hadn't realised he was able to smell quite as strongly as he had until Laurent had left.

He hesitated as he continued on deck, everything a mess, but it wasn't clear if it had been ransacked by a person or simply tossed around by the events that had unfolded. It seemed from the thick state of the thick ropes, the boat had pulled loose in the initial explosions. Had someone been on board the whole time, their chemical release signalling for others to find them? Or had they only just arrived too?

Nico placed his hand on the half open cabin door and gave it a tug.

The scent was stronger. A tang that he could taste at the back of his throat.

It took a moment for his non-Ionian senses to register that the scent was a familiar one.

"L-Laurent?" Nico pushed his way into the mess of the cabin, seeking the Ionian. The scent was all the stronger. Sharp and clear and so obviously Laurent now that he had realised it.

"Nico." A whimpered lament, and movement from the bunk.

It was hard to distinguish from the mess, where all the cupboards had emptied into the cabin, some now hanging off their hinges. But yes, there in the bed, amongst clothes and blankets, was Laurent.

Nico clambered over the mess and practically fell onto the bunk, cupping Laurent's face in his hands and looking him over. As much as he'd wanted Laurent to be safe, he didn't know if he could let the Ionian go again.

"You're shivering. Did you swim? Are you cold?"

"I-I swam, last night. I saw the boat and I hoped. But you weren't here. I hoped some time apart—" Laurent shivered as he said the words but Nico pulled him close to share their heat.

"I'm here now," Nico replied, softly.

So many other words running through his head, but he still couldn't bring himself to say them. And that was what made him the worst bond partner for Laurent.

He grit his teeth and turned away.

"Please, Nico. I had to come find you. I don't want to be without you." Laurent practically begged.

Nico closed his eyes and pinched the bridge of his nose, "I want to, but—"

"Nico, you have to stop." Laurent struggled to get the words out, placing a hand on Nico's face and turning him to look into each other's eyes. "I know you think you're doing what's best for me. But what's best for me is you. It was always you."

Nico tried to pull away but Laurent kept hold of him.

"I tried to tell you about our studies that day in the museum. You know there is a reason my scent means something to you and why myself, and all Ionians seem to have lost some self-control. There is a truth here that has been ignored so long that it seems to have torn this system apart. Don't let it do the same to us."

Nico's throat ached and he sobbed at Laurent's words.

"When I first met you, I was intrigued because you're Lunar Terran. I thought knowing you could be beneficial to my studies," Laurent admitted. Nico frowned, he had said things along these lines before but it sounded different now, more manipulated. "But then I fell in love with you and it only confirmed more what my colleagues and I already suspected. What, deep down, you know too.

"History started so abruptly here, where we count it in centuries as on some other planets and moons, but in millennia on Terra. Time and again we return to the same truth, or the same lie. Ionians did not spring from the primordial swamp of this planet that the terraforming created. And the same for Mars and Europa, and Ganymede and more. We're all terrans. All from the same original planet."

"We're all terrans." Nico repeated the words and wondered if voicing it would break reality even more. But it didn't, everything stayed as it was. He was a Lunar Terran on Io, descended from some of the last native Terrans, realising that so much history must have been lost on the various exodus's from their home planet that the truth was lost too.

"I wanted to explain so many times since the EM blast. I wanted to finish what I'd tried to tell you at the museum. The theories we had and the papers we were publishing. But... I needed you to understand it first. Not to think that I was just making up a fantasy and saying anything just to keep you." Laurent let out a heavy sigh, "because I would say or do anything to keep you."

Nico sucked in a breath and tasted Laurent on the air. The chemical almost overwhelming in this small space.

"The bond would still be one-sided?" Nico asked, despite knowing the answer and wishing it was different.

Laurent nodded.

"Yes, it evolved in the Ionians due to the social and environmental conditions here, just as those on planets and moons closer to the sun evolved darker pigmentation and skin more resistant to the sun. Just as Venusians have developed a nictitating membrane. All different evolutionary paths of the same species."

They were quiet for a few moments, still holding each other to ward off the cold.

"Let me bond with you," Laurent asked softly.

"Laurent," Nico breathed out his name as he released a shuddering breath.

When Laurent moved, the air around him seemed distorted, almost a yellow hue to it.

"Say yes," Laurent urged.

"Yes," Nico nodded and pulled Laurent into a kiss.

It was soft but passionate, full of the longing they had both felt all these weeks.

As they kissed, Nico could feel Laurent moving, tugging until both of their sleeves were pulled back and he was able to rub their wrists together.

Nico broke the kiss to look down, the air almost citric now as he felt the bumps, the glands under the pale blue flesh of Laurent's wrists and the sting of pain in his own.

He pressed back, knowing enough to understand that were he Ionian his own glands would be releasing his own chemical, blending the scent so all would know a bond had been formed.

The scent didn't change, but it lingered on Nico.

Laurent drew back with darkened cheeks and a shy smile, his wrists looking inflamed.

"You're mine now," Laurent smiled.

Nico looked down at his own wrists and saw a slight inflammation there too. A sort of chemical burn that stung and would likely leave marks. And he wanted them to, he wanted it to be clear that he and Laurent belonged together.

\#

Three Months Earlier

_Your Excellency,

Thank you for your recent letter addressing your misgivings regarding my ongoing romantic involvement with your employee, Nico Musa. Whilst I appreciate that you have concerns regarding the appropriateness of a relationship between our two peoples, please rest assured that I believe this to be moot.

You will find attached an advance copy of a paper co-authored by myself along with colleagues in other lunar and planetary sciences corroborating something we believe to be known to the Lunar Terran leadership. That all life in this system originated on Terra.

Please read the paper thoroughly, and be aware that we intend to make this information known. And whilst it may cause initial destabilisation, we feel this can be weathered and will not result in the break-up of the mutually beneficial agreements across the solar system.

To that end, I urge you to be selective in who you share this information with at this stage. I have provided it to you in advance in the hopes that you will retract the sentiments you have voiced to Nico regarding our relationship, given that the reasons behind those sentiments will soon be meaningless.

As is now likely evident, I will do anything to keep myself and Nico together.

Sincerely,

Dr. Laurent Adnet_

Max Turner is a gay transgender man based in the United Kingdom. He is also a parent, nerd, intersectional feminist and coffee addict. Max writes speculative and science fiction, fantasy, urban fantasy, gothic horror and LGBTQ+ romance, and more often than not, combinations thereof.

The Weight of Rebellion

by Barend Nieuwstraten III

Willus Daulmont stood on the high balcony, cold and alone, well ahead of the evening's gathering. His back to the city below him as he leaned on the stone balustrade, watching his family's servants bring firewood for the braziers, and wine for his brothers and parents.

Though he never showed it, it embarrassed him when they bowed. He always gave at least a nod back and an awkward smile. As the middle son of Norcaster's lord, he didn't consider himself worthy of the bowing. They were paid to be there, and they lived under the same roof.

He felt guilty. Just by being there, he was unintentionally compelling them to bow and act as they do before members of the city's ruling house, instead of however they'd normally act while setting up an area for his family and guests. He imagined they'd normally be making jokes, sharing gossip, or talking of whatever pursuits and entertainment brought them happiness in their spare time. Instead they were shifting iron fireplaces and furniture into position in subservient silence, avoiding eye contact with their social better.

Showing up early to the traditional winter gathering seemed the only way to steal a little solitude and let his mind wander through the past. He had fond memories of this small annual event. It was, after all, where his father had first allowed him to taste wine. His older sister had always been the best part of them though. When they were children, it had been here, this time of year, when they would plot all the great structures, they intended to build out of the snow soon to fall. Her wicked sense of humour made every gathering worthwhile. Something they had all lost when she was married off, several years ago.

The fires were soon lit, and wine poured. Willus was handed the first goblet for the night as he heard his brothers approaching from within the keep. Each were handed wine as they emerged.

"Evening, brother," Daemen said, raising his goblet. "You're already here. Trying to get ahead on the drinking?"

Willus looked to his cup and shrugged.

"We'll catch you up either way," his oldest brother said, lightly elbowing their youngest. "Right, Geord."

"I didn't realise there was a competition at hand," the slender young man said. His dark but humble garments inching ever closer towards the devout clerical calling he seemed to be destined for.

The pair spread out, flanking their middle brother on the railing as he turned to face the city of Norcaster with them. The people on the streets below made their way home quickly to escape the cold while others made for their nearest inn. Houseguard walked the keep wall while cityguard walked the city walls, and men of the townswatch patrolled the streets in between.

As much as he loved his brothers, Willus hoped the silent observation of their city would last. He'd been avoiding them of late, knowing they wanted his opinion on matters that had been plaguing their family of late.

"Why are you always so cynical?" Lady Selysa asked her lord husband, as they stepped out into the night air to join their three sons on the balcony.

Willus looked back to see his approaching parents. Their layers of finery buried under fur cloaks as they arrived, dragging their discussion with them like mud on boots. Sir Dunold accompanied them, giving the young man a cheerful nod, despite the concern that his lord and lady's conversation was clearly bringing him. It brought Willus some comfort to know he wasn't the only one being distressed by the matter.

"It's not cynicism, it's caution," Lord Aethred replied as a cup bearer handed him wine. "Much is being asked of me, my love. There is a great deal to carefully consider."

It was the same discussion that had been plaguing Norcaster Keep for days. Willus dreaded the topic filling another evening. Just one night, speaking of anything else, would have been a most welcome change.

"A shooting star, my lord, look," Sir Dunold said, raising his silver chalice of wine up towards an orange light moving across a rare patch of clear night sky. A crawling vale of cloud had concealed most of the stars from the city that night, with only a pair of dull glowing orbs where the moons should be.

Willus smiled at the distraction, enjoying a deep breath of air cooled by night and winter.

"How delightful," Lady Selysa said, stopping to embrace her tall muscular husband for warmth as she slid her arm inside his furs and around his broad back. "You should make a wish, Aethred. Just the thing to prove me wrong."

"Should I?" Lord Daulmont huffed, amused at his wife's suggestion as they hovered towards their sons. They stood on the other side of a brazier, burning to facilitate their winter use of the balcony. "Very well. I wish for the gods to send me a sign or send me aid. If I'm to join the Knights of Paliodor in open rebellion against my king, then I would have the gods send me something to ensure victory."

Willus let his short-lived smile sink and wandered away from the barrier, physically distancing himself from the topic.

"Your king?" Daemen scoffed, stepping around a servant feeding wood to the brazier between them. Daemen, the eldest of three brothers, was a younger version of their father, barely in his thirties, tall and strong, with the same thick dark brown hair that still blessed their father in his early sixties. "Your king was Tholmis Armont the Third, before this King Garaug Aeligis turned up with Froskheim marauders from the frozen south and murdered him eleven years ago. He is a conqueror, not a proper king."

"Every king is a conqueror, or the son of a conqueror, or the grandson of a conqueror, some long passed down progeny, nephew, or adopted ward of a conqueror," Lord Daulmont told his first born. "Royal birthright is nothing more than the legacy of conquerors, murderers, and usurpers." He took a sip of his wine.

"Very well then, Father," Daemen said. "If that is the way of things, why not support the Knights of Paliodor in supplanting one conqueror for another? At least House Rosendor supports the faith of this land. They follow the first gods as we do. Just as the Knights of Palidor do, being soldiers of the Citadel of Light, chosen by the vilician himself."

"And what year is it, my son?" the lord asked. "Remind me."

The future lord looked at his father with a tilted head and a suspicious squint. He knew some lesson was coming, but first he had to answer the question put to him, to find out what it was. "Two-hundred-and-seven," he answered reluctantly.

"Which marks...?"

"Two-hundred-and-seven years since the fall of the Kestrian Empire," he sighed, at the tediousness of the masquerade in which his father made him engage. Though, Willus always suspected his older brother secretly enjoyed it to some degree.

"Precisely," their father said victoriously. "An empire supported by the Citadel of Light. An empire that was, more or less, the servant of the Citadel. But now all that remains of that empire is the name of the continent it once ruled and the order who built that empire, supported it, and watched it collapse." Lord Daulmont turned to face his eldest son, turning his side-embracing wife with him. "Why does the vilician decide who should be king of Southmarch? Who does he pick? House Rosendor. A house of keep-lords at Arcanhold. Caretakers of Arcani temple. They mean to make district lords bow to a lesser lord and name him king because he presides over a fort built around an ancient holy ruin? Do they intend to replace the kings of all the kingdoms of the Umberlands with temple lords who are nothing more than glorified deacons?"

"So why not support one of the other district lords?" Willus asked, thinking aloud.

"And make enemies of both the church *and* the king?" the Lord asked his middle son, incredulously. "Why not just declare myself king, and Norcaster the new capital of Southmarch? That way I can have my own rebellion, learning which other houses favour or detest that idea while I'm out on the battlefield already fighting between two enemies of superior numbers and resources."

Willus twisted his face and turned to the nearest fire. He began vigorously rubbing his hands at it, regretting joining the conversation, as he always did.

"And what of my youngest?" Lord Daulmont asked, turning again to face Geord. The thin nineteen-year-old had seemingly listened to the whole conversation in silence, despite having clear loyalties to the Faith. "Do you have any questions for your father, struggling with this dilemma?" Lord Aethred asked, with an inviting raised brow.

"Yes..." Geord said, pointing to the sky. "Is it just me or is that shooting star getting bigger."

Everyone looked to see what Geord had been watching the whole time. A hurtling ball of bright yellow light flew through the sky tearing through cloud as it fell to the earth. They all watched as a tail of smoke followed it, rumbling as it fell out of view somewhere south of the city.

There was an almighty thunderous crack, they all felt as much as heard. It sounded as if the sky itself had been torn asunder. There came a brilliant flash of light from behind the hills, like a blink of daylight. They all looked to each other in panic, as loud cracks continued across the land as sharp rolling thunder. It slowly faded like a guard dog's barking, receding to a lazy growl before finding something else to occupy itself.

"I think you wished that star down, Father," Geord said.

Slipping out of his wife's hold, Lord Daulmont looked beyond the city, leaning over the balustrade as a light snow began to fall. "Gather some men and a cart or two. Have my horse readied," he commanded Sir Dunold.

"My lord, it is winter, it is night, and snow falls," the knighted commander of his houseguard cautioned. "I think you should wait till morning."

"Aethred, please," Lady Selysa begged him. "Listen to him. There are too many beasts that stalk the lands at night. And the cold weather makes them bolder."

"I can have some of the men go after it instead, my lord," Sir Dunold suggested. "They can find it and guard it until we meet them in the morning."

"Very well," the lord reluctantly agreed. "But we leave at dawn."

"Can I come?" Geord asked.

"All three of you," their father instructed his sons, as he left. "But I want to rise early, so ensure you're well rested." A command disguised as a suggestion, to send his adult sons to bed early.

#

As the three brothers eventually had their fill of the fire, wine, and view that made the balcony so inviting, they retired for the evening as their father had instructed.

"What think you of all this?" Daemen asked his brothers, stopping them in the cool stone corridor before they could get to their heated rooms. "This rebellion, the Order of Light would have us join."

"I think it would have been nice to spend the night drinking wine and speaking of less concerning matters," Willus admitted, further fortifying his reputation for flippancy.

"Do you not think it time you took this matter seriously?" his older brother scolded, firmly gripping his shoulder. "Or anything, for that matter?"

"Geord is the religious one, you're the heir, and I'm the spare," Willus explained. "Your jobs are to make and influence decisions from halls and altars. Mine is to follow the orders that eventuate, leading more experienced men than myself to their deaths in the name of our father and the Twelve."

Daemen's firm brow softened. "You think yourself unimportant, is that it?" he asked, concerned.

"We are all important in the eyes of the Twelve, Willus," the youngest of the three said. "They have a place for us all, and you sit far higher than most in the kingdom."

"I don't care about my importance," Willus assured them both.

"Then what do you care about?" Daemen asked.

"Stability," Willus said. "I was eight when we first heard of raids upon the south coast. Remember? Within a year, those raiders took control of the kingdom's entire southern coastline. In two more, their leader was our king."

"After much blood was spilt," Daemen added. "Blood of people we knew. People who served us and people whom we served. Including our King."

Willus nodded. "Make no mistake, I loved King Tholmis. He attended three of my birthdays and told me he was going to make me captain of the royalguard one day. I had as much reason to hate the conqueror as any, but he became our king, and Father told us that was the way of things. Then that conqueror went on to spend years fortifying towns and restoring old Kestrian Keeps, turning them into strong cities. He improved-"

"Yes, Father has educated us all on the works of our current king," Geord stopped him. "Of course, there has been merit to his rule. Elsewise, rebellion would have happened far sooner. But the Avanomicon warns us of those who would win our hearts with works while they secretly work against our souls."

"I'm not arguing for or against the claims of the faith," Willus said. "Whatever rumour and accusations are whispered of heresy, we still worship the Twelve, and none have made to prevent us. Until someone does, leaving well enough alone seems far more lawful a course of action than rebellion. But, as I say, it serves no purpose to influence me, one way or another. For I shall do as bid. Decisions are not my domain."

"But if they were, what would you do?" his older brother asked. "For that is all I wished to know."

"The only evidence we have of our king's proposed dabbling in necromancy, comes from the hearsay of some new chapter of holy knights who've been training to combat it," Willus said, patting his pious younger brother on the back. "While that might be enough for dear Geord, here, I would ask for something more directly damning.

Sharpening the blade, with which you intend to stab your wife's lover, is not evidence of the infidelity itself."

Daemen pulled his head back with an impressed smile and rested his hands on his brother's shoulder. "So, there *is* a mind hiding in there."

"One that can be probed on the morrow in transit, where I won't have a warmer place to be," Willus said, slipping out of his brother's embrace to return to his hearth-warmed room.

#

By morning much of the land was covered by a thin white blanket of snow, crunching under hoof as Lord Aethred Daulmont rode with his three sons, Sir Dunold, and a squad of houseguard. They rode to camp, following markers left by their soldiers the night before.

When they found the men, who had waited the night, they were packing their tents and boiling some broth over their campfire. Others stood around a crater in which a large broken boulder lay in fragments. The debris had cooled in the night and snow had fallen into much of the pit, along with the rest of the surrounding land. Though several pieces of the broken fallen rock were haloed by an absence of snow, as if it refused to fall closer than a foot to them. Most notably within the crater itself, where the main bulk of fallen sky-rock had seemingly evaded snowfall as well as the grey metallic substance that had leaked out of it, onto the ground like poured lead, cooled and hardened.

"It's metal, my lord," one of the camped men said, handing him a steaming wooden cup of broth. "It was still glowing, smelt hot, when we got here. But by sunrise, it was hard as iron."

Two of the men were loading a small cart with the hardened pooled metal and rocks from which they could not separate it.

"A metal from the heavens?" Lord Daulmont contemplatively said, circling the crater on foot. He slowly sipped at his warm broth as he eyed the curious find with intrigue.

"Untouched by cover of snow," Sir Dunold said, in wonder. "It is as if to call attention to itself, demanding to be seen and found, my lord."

"What was it you wished upon this falling star again, Father?" Geord asked, snapping his father out of his haze.

"I said I wished for the gods to send me a sign that I should join with the Knights of Paliodor," he recalled, "That I would have the gods send me something to ensure victory."

"And then this metal fell from the heavens in answer to your request," Geord surmised.

His father turned and smiled at him. "A silly wish, upon a light in the sky, nothing more," he said, offering cynicism to challenge and supress his own excitement at the prospect.

"A pious man's wish said aloud is a prayer," Geord said.

The lord huffed, impressed. "The book of Aulm," he said, recognising the quote from the second book of the holy Avanomicon. He nodded gently and looked to his youngest son with enthusiastic assessment. "Your brother Daemen will one day rule Norcaster, your sister Jaenella has been married off, and Willus," he shrugged, "will find his place, I'm sure. He is gifted with a sword, after all. But you, young Geord, I'm more than certain, will end up a priest, then a divinion, then arch divinion, and perhaps one day even the vilician himself."

Willus, ignoring the vagueness with which his father seemed to regard him, grimaced, confused at the pride the lord of Norcaster had for his youngest son's piousness and devotion. Especially after their father voiced so much mistrust for the order's motivations the night before, the night before that, and just about every night since the holy Knights of Paliodor had last visited.

Willus felt his older brother's eyes upon him from his left. Either sympathy for the lack of confidence his father had publicly expressed or possibly optimistic encouragement as he focused purely on the back-handed compliment about swordplay. Willus turned away, disinterested in discovering which and patted his black horse instead.

#

Weeks later, it was the keep-smith's apprentice who brought the sword, made from the fallen metal, when it was complete. Presented to Lord Aethred Daulmont in the main hall of Norcaster Keep. He brought with him the tanner who made the scabbard and the fletcher, with a bow in hand and quiver by his side. The lord sat in his throne watching their presentation with curiosity and excitement.

"My lord, Theos sends both his regrets and me in his stead," the apprentice announced.

"Is the smith too busy to boast of his own work?" the lord asked.

"I fear he's been taken ill, my lord," the apprentice said, apologetically as two assistants carried in a wooden practice dummy stuffed with hay and armoured in a full faced helm and breastplate of iron. "He sends his apologies, as the healer has strictly recommended bed rest."

146

"I'm sorry to hear that," Lord Dalmont offered. "Should he require anything, he need only ask, of course. But let us see this handy work of his, while we're all gathered here."

"Very good, my lord," the apprentice complied, handing the large sword to Daemen to take to his lord father.

"A two-hander?" Lord Daulmont said, surprised.

"Yes, my lord," the smiths apprentice said, with a hint of boastfulness in his voice. "Theos said you had always favoured claymores and greatswords in your youth, before inheriting you lord father, Maelon's, longsword. He had intended to make it a flamberge, but he was working with a new metal and thought a more traditional blade would be a safer course."

Lord Aethred nodded approvingly as he gripped the sword. His eldest son pulled the scabbard away. "The blade is quite narrow," he observed, intrigued.

"Yes, my lord, but the metal is quite heavy."

"As I can feel," Lord Aethred said, bouncing it in his hands to get a feel for it. "So, the narrow blade is to mitigate the weight?"

"Indeed, my lord. It is almost twice as heavy as iron and incredibly strong. It will still not be an easy sword to swing, but the edge is quite sharp, and my lord a notoriously strong man. Only one swing should be needed."

"I am strong. I'll adopt no modesty there," Lord Aethred said, with a proud smile. "But one-swing strong? I'm not so sure."

"If someone would care to spar with you, while you restrict your blows to his weapon, you will see what I mean," the smith's apprentice assured him.

"Very good," the lord said, tickled by curiosity.

Willus made to step forward to assist his father in the testing of the new blade.

"Ulex," his father said, instead calling to one of his houseguard. "You're a strong lad. Give me a challenge."

"An honour, my lord," the burly houseguard said, falling out of his squad as Willus retracted his unnoticed advance.

Ulex drew his bastard sword before the throne, waiting as his lord descended the stairs that elevated it.

They tapped the flat of their blades together and began circling each other. The watching houseguards were excited. It seemed a fight they had been keen to see play out, though they shouted no support to either party. The pair pulled back and swung their swords to meet and, with a great shriek, the great sword cut through the bastard sword like it was a candle. Ulex pulled his head and shoulders back, faster than his leg had time to react, avoiding the long blade he should have otherwise been able to deflect. As Ulex fell to the floor, the top half of his own blade cartwheeled through the air, clanging onto the floor where gathered men quickly parted.

There was a stunned silence as the lord held out his hand for his faithful guard and pulled him back to his feet. "Are you alright?"

"Yes, my lord," Ulex said, looking at his own sword sliced into a short sword with a near perfectly square tip. "But my sword has seen far better days."

"I'll get you a new one," Lord Daulmont assured him with a laugh as he patted the houseguard on the shoulder.

"With what was left," the smith's apprentice said, "Theos thought arrowheads would be the best thing to make. Though there was enough to make quite a few."

"Then why not make another sword?" Lord Aethred asked. "Or a matching dagger?"

"I will show you, my lord," the smith's apprentice said, taking the quiver and holding it for the fletcher.

The bowmaker pulled an arrow into his bow, facing the armoured practice dummy at the far end of the hall. He aimed carefully at the target, many yards away, before slightly raising the bow to point the arrow higher.

"That's going to go over our wooden friend's head," Willus smugly predicted. "Do you mean to offer him a warning shot first?"

The surrounding guards chuckled with him, but the fletcher smiled slyly at the lord's second youngest son a moment, before letting loose the arrow with a twang of the bowstring. The shaft flew in an arc weighed down by its arrowhead of sky metal, and with a deep pair of short tearing clangs, the arrow pierced the armour through the heart, out the back, and chipped the polished stone floor where it crashed.

The entirety of the hall's gathered men quickly shifted to the other end, to examine the armour. A few hands wrapped their knuckles on the breastplate and fingered the hole to make sure it wasn't a trick.

"It's hot," one of the guards said, blowing on his finger.

"What sorcery is this?" Sir Dunold asked.

"No sorcery, sir," the smiths apprentice said. "I mean aside from the fact that this metal fell from the sky when called upon by Lord Aethred. The metal is merely very dense, which drives its point much harder. Any archer using it would need much practice using them over a greater distance, for as you saw, it requires a high aim because the metal wishes to return the ground sooner than iron would." He then pointed to the sword. "Just as the weight of the metal in the sword drives its edge, making every point the weak-point on any armour your enemy wears."

"It would seem that the course ahead has been made abundantly clear, Father," Geord suggested.

Lord Daulmont nodded in agreement as he marvelled at his new weapon. "Then I name this sword, Heavens Blade and the arrows, Angel's Teeth," he declared, to the approval of the room. "And the Knights of Paliodor will have their answer when they return in two weeks."

Willus looked to his brothers but said nothing to dissuade their enthusiasm. With all that had taken place, and the momentum driven by this sign, all saw as divine intervention, he felt his opinion was of less consequence than it ever had been before.

#

The Rebellion, planned through winter, began in the spring. "A new year, a new spring, a new king," was the catchcry of the holy alliance as the northern houses of Southmarch rallied under the orange banner of House Rosendor, once House Daulmont declared for them. Though, no lord would name Orland Rosendor King before he sat upon the throne.

They attacked the loyalist forts and outposts manned by Aeligis soldiers. Lord Daulmont always fought in the vanguard, slicing through his enemies with Heavens Blade as his best archers, armed with Angel's Teeth, pierced the most heavily armed men on the battlefield. Men slowed by iron upon their chests and heads when they may as well have been wearing cloth. Word grew of Lord Daulmont's unstoppable nature on the field, cutting through swords and armour. The opposed king's soldiers faltered in their formation whenever the black and blue banners and tabards of House Daulmont appeared on the field of battle.

#

The fight continued through the year seeing the king retreat to the capital of Whiteborough in late autumn. While Lord Aethred Daulmont and his firstborn, Daemen, led their men against the forces of the southern loyalist houses, it fell to Willus to pursue and besiege the king's city with the host of men under him.

Not wishing to spend the approaching winter camped outside the city, in a war he'd never welcomed, Willus lead an aggressive assault. He and his men soon breached the city walls and defeated the men defending the city.

As his home defences fell, King Garaug Aeligis surrendered to save lives, though he had had the foresight to evacuate his own family before the fight had even reached his doors.

Though perhaps regaler than most, King Garaug looked like any normal man, save for the unusual feature of two small horns upon his forehead. They protruded forwards and bent upward. A strange, and rare, attribute that had been documented in journals of several prominent figures throughout history, without adequate explanation. They led to a unique design in his tall golden crown; a thick and elaborate headdress that would be far too heavy for most to comfortably wear.

As it was Willus Daulmot, whose commanded force breached the keep of Whiteborough, it was he to whom the king directly surrendered. King Garaug unfastened his belt and lay his sword across the arms of his throne, smiling as he presented his upturned wrists, ready to be clamped in irons.

"Young Willus, isn't it?" King Garaug made to confirm, only earning a nod in response as the iron cuffs were handed to the lord of Norcaster's second son. "Seems a shame to surrender so peacefully. From what I've heard, of what little makes it past tales of your father, you're quite the swordsman. I should have at least opted for a duel."

"Perhaps next time, your grace," Willus suggested, as he locked the restraints.

The king gave him a perplexed smirk. "So, it's still 'your grace', is it?" he asked, seemingly focused on the formality within the joke. "I thought the point of this rebellion was to appoint and anoint another."

"That was my understanding," Willus admitted.

"Your tone and attitude lack conviction, my boy," the king said, surprised. "I was expecting more passion, more objection to my title. Isn't that the point of rebellion? Does it not fulfil you to personally place me in irons?"

"Did your son, Prince Garykk, choose to vacate the city with the rest of your family or did you send him away, by order?"

"I sent him, of course. Against his will."

"Then, if the path of a firstborn prince is chosen for him, by what conviction do you imagine a lord's middle-son to be driven?" Willus asked, as he led him away.

The incarcerated king offered a conceding tilt of his head at the observation.

#

The Knights of Paliodor accused King Garaug of associating with a necromancer, in accordance with rumours that further incriminated him as one himself. He looked to the assembled lords of his kingdom and shook his head. "And which of you will now be king?" he asked them, as the holy knights and their wardens shackled his feet to further restrain him. "Take my crown, if any has a worthy neck to support it. Rule, knowing that a bent knee from any of the rest of you is worth no more than a dozen years loyalty."

"You killed our king," Lord Daulmont said, in their defence, adopting his eldest son's protest of many years. "And you worship lesser gods," he added, adopting the words of his youngest.

"And who made the lesser gods to begin with?" the surrendered king asked. "Was it not the Twelve? Why make them if they did not intend to delegate their godly duties? Do you even truly know the Twelve? They left this world long ago, and believe me, I have far closer ties to them than anyone here could ever hope to claim or understand."

"An absurdity," Lord Daulmont said, stepping closer to his former king who looked back at him with curious pity.

"Why, Lord Aethred, I barely recognised you," King Garaug said. "I had hoped to remind you that you had no protest in your heart when I helped rebuild your city's defences from years of neglect by your previous king. But to look at you now, I can't help but wonder if all this war and treachery robbed you of your appetite. Also, the colour in your skin, the meat on your bones, the flesh in your face, and the hair on you head. What has become of you?" King Garaug sounded genuine in his concern as his appraisal had been accurate. For Lord Daulmont had become gaunt, his face shaped like a skull, the skin around his eyes grown red and sickly, and his long brown hair now grew quite thin. "I had heard tales of you these last months. 'The Twelve's Chosen' some call you, reaping through men like a scythe through tall grass. But the figure I see before me, cannot be the object of such terror and doubt to undermine such stalwart hearts."

"I have seen healthier days," Lord Daulmont said. "With all that I have heard of you of late I wonder if this is not some spell of yours to curse me for rebelling?"

"If you believe that of me, then your mind has gone too," the king said, as he was surrounded by soldiers of the Order of Light.

"There will be a trial of the faith," one of the Knights of Paliodor announced, stepping forward in his white enamelled armour. "During which, you will answer for all your crimes."

"*Answer* for my crimes?" the king scoffed. "Did I already miss the trial? I thought the purpose of a trial was to *determine* guilt, not declare it. I assume then that you have a punishment already arranged?" the deposed king asked.

"The trial will be fair and just."

"Oh, so if you find me innocent, you'll let me go back to my throne, and we'll all pretend the last year didn't happen?" the King jested, with spiteful confidence. "The only crime here is treason, and your trial is nothing more than a mockery of justice designed to justify regicide, usurper," he yelled, as they began to drag him away. "I take it those orange banners mean you're all bending the knee to the citadel's puppet?" He stopped in his tracks a moment as if purely to demonstrate that his manhandling escorts were successful in moving him strictly through his cooperation. "At least for twelve years," he added, with a smug smile, winking at Lord Daulmont before allowing his captors to escort him further.

#

And so, stand trial he did, in exchange for an end to the war and the agreement that his loyal subjects and family in Aeligsand not be pursued or punished for loyalty to their king. The trial was held within the Rosendor stronghold of Arcanhold. During that trial that lasted more than a week, King Garaug was subjected to little more than hearsay and rumour by those of the faith, before being found guilty and sentenced to death upon a standing pyre. The trial was conducted and concluded so precisely as he had predicted, that Garaug seemed far too vindicated to take in the horror of his impending execution by fire. Willus almost admired the man's defiant attitude in that moment, as his father and older brother were merely confused and disgusted, taking his flippancy as some madness or mania.

The condemned king was walked without incident to the place of his execution in the city square. He held his head high, proud and unafraid, almost smug. He turned only to look at Lord Daulmont with pity as Daemen supported his father's failing frame.

"Perhaps next time, your grace," he said to Willus, recounting the young nobleman's subtle joke, uttered during his apprehension, with a chuckle before he was taken up a ladder and fastened to the post.

The assembled lords watched well into the night as the former king was swallowed silently by flames on a high pyre in Arcanhold square. As if driven by pure spite, he suppressed his screams, leaving his accusers with only the crackling of the burning wood and wind-rippling of the flames to satisfy their ears. The fire burned through the night but Lord Aethred Daulmont's declining health had him leave early to return home with his sons and men.

It wasn't until he did return to the north that the accusations laid against the former king were finally justified.

Ikhvisial, a frost elf necromancer under whom King Garaug had been accused of studying, took vengeance on the cities, towns, and settlements of the north with an army of the dead. Growing his forces with every fallen soul of Southmarch who fell against them, he raised them to add to his own number as they marched raggedly and rotting across the land without rest or fear.

And so, while the lords and captains of the northern cities and towns celebrated with the Citadel's priests, wardens, and knights of Paliodor, the death of a wicked king, his unholy forces had been shredding their lands in their absence. An attack that undid much of the restoration of which that king had boasted.

Lord Daulmont and his men fought their way back to Norcaster against foes they had already defeated once before and men they had lost in the war. Men they had called brothers, now rotting and lumbering from beyond their shallow battlefield graves. Dead men, again on their feet, who now feared nothing and suffered no pain from injury to their flesh turned carrion. An indefatigable force who had to be broken and dismembered to be at all halted and defeated, not merely run through or bled like living soldiers.

With sufficient force, the returning party carved their way through the throng of walking human horrors, to Norcaster Keep. A fight that cost many lives and took a toll on the nerves of men, made to face their fallen brothers and returned foes. When the homeward battle was done, Willus could see in the men's eyes and trembling hands the same malady of unease that had plagued him since talk of rebellion had first begun. Though he had mastered the art of concealing it. The façade of an iron will that gave the men under his command the strength to fight their way home.

They made to send word of warning to the lords gathered at Arcanhold. But when they finally arrived home, it was word from their intended recipients, that instead already awaited Lord Daulmont.

"By the morning that followed the execution, the men guarding the pyre were killed," Daemen read, from the message to his gathered family and Sir Dunold. "Camps of the assembled forces were put to the torch before dawn, killing a third of their number."

"Does it speak of the recently risen dead?" an exhausted Lord Daulmont asked, to his son's shaking head. "Then we must warn them."

"Not all were recent," Willus observed. "I saw the rotted tabards of house Armont on soldiers that were barely more than bones."

"Also colours of some of the houses that used to rule upon the coast," Daemen recalled, old enough to remember their heraldry.

"Some of this army has been in production then for what, fifteen years?" Willus said. "So perhaps every soul that ever fell to Garaug Aeligis's conquest. This army must be enormous by now."

"And to think, before this begun, you spoke of stability," Geord reminded Willus. "Look what has happened to our kingdom."

"Yes stability," Willus said, with a bitter smile as all eyes were upon him. "I cannot think of a better word to describe that moment before one decides to shake a hornet's nest. Aren't you all glad we did?"

#

The Knights of Paliodor and lords of the north took their remaining forces to aid the northern half of the kingdom. They rallied at Norcaster, where Lord Aethred Daulmont's health declined beyond his ability to fight or even leave his bed. His once mighty frame became so light, he could now be lifted and carried by any single guard to his throne when needed. He conceded to his wasting illness and fast fading strength, naming his eldest son, Daemen Daulmont, the new lord of Norcaster.

They received further word from the south that the Aeligis loyalists had retaken Whiteborough and Ikhvisial the necromancer had taken the keep of Arcanhold as his tower. They had robbed the faith's chosen house of their stronghold before there was even time for a coronation, or to relocate them to the now reclaimed capital. Furthermore, there was now no rule nor influence of the old faith in the kingdom of Southmarch. The Citadel's army were forced to return to the west, where the neighbouring kingdom of Cliffguard had now fallen under attack by Ikhvisial's army of the dead, in retribution for their part in instigating rebellion.

#

Lord Aethred crept slowly to his death fading with the word, that despite what he saw when he watched the man burn, King Garaug Aeligis had retaken his throne.

"Perhaps the gods sent me the sword for some other purpose, and I misunderstood. For I have withered away losing hair and teeth and flesh, while the king I betrayed has risen from fire like a red dragon and retaken his throne. Perhaps the undead are a plague sent by the gods to punish us for laying such accusations at our king's feet. Perhaps I was meant to use the sword to protect the kingdom from the ambition of the Citadel of Light." Those were his last words, leaving the world in doubt and regret, slipping away before he could ask the gods for forgiveness or before his devout youngest son could reassure him of the righteousness of his allegiance.

#

In the years that followed, the lords of Southmarch fought in new conflicts as their kingdom warred with their neighbour to the west. The kingdom from which the Knights of the Order has issued. For the Lords of Southmarch were all made to once more kneel and swear fealty again to the king they had betrayed. One, who had survived execution by burning and now commanded the dead in open defiance of the religion that instigated rebellion and inspired their treason. A kingdom united again, but now in fear and dread as dark rumour became reality.

Lord Daemen Daulmont had replaced his father, as the man to be feared by the enemy, carving through iron and flesh with Heavens Blade. After six years of conflict, he was summoned to the capital of Whiteborough. There he witnessed a treaty made between King Essebert Bellethon the Second, of Cliffguard, and King Garaug Aeligis, of Southmarch, to end the conflict that saw the western kingdom bereft of sufficient forces to continue warring with Southmarch. Even after their holy forces had turned the tide on the undead that plagued their lands there was not enough of them left to face the living, as the men of Southmarch fought for their king in penance. The treaty was made on the provision that the Citadel of Light and the Kingdom of Cliffguard never again interfere with the rule of their neighbouring kingdom.

#

Being a devout servant of the Twelve and proud disciple of the Citadel, the lord of Norcaster's youngest brother, Geord, believed there was no longer a place for him in a kingdom in which the Order of Light was no longer welcomed. So, he left for the Citadel of Light, in the distant northern kingdom of Orbreath.

"I do not know what the gods want of this kingdom, or what they want of you, Brother," Geord said, before leaving, "But I know this is no longer a place for me and I'm not so sure it is a place for you. For you have begun to look more like father in his last years than in his youth, as I remember him when I was small. He died believing the gods cursed him for turning on his king, but now you have inherited his affliction as you fight for that very same king."

It was true. Lord Daemen had become thin of body and gaunt of face. His eyelids reddened, his skin seemed dry, and sores appeared about his person as his hair thinned from its once proud lion's mane of thick brown hair.

"I will seek answers from the books of the citadel's library to see what course may reverse whatever has befallen this house and these lands," Geord told his older brothers. "And I shall take the northroad by the mountains, instead of the more direct path, to be away from this cursed and godless place all the sooner. May the light of the Twelve forever find its way to you under this shadow of death."

Lord Daemen and Willus watched their brother leave the city where together they had grown. A long silence sat between them as their youngest sibling's carriage slowly shrank out of view.

"And what now remains of us, brother?" Lord Daemen asked. "Our house continues to diminish and suffer regardless of our loyalties."

"Do you doubt Geord's return?" Willus asked.

"All of the light he saw in this kingdom is gone," Lord Daemen sighed. "Father is gone. Mother, lost to her sorrow, skulks in the shadows like a ghost, dining alone in her room, rarely seen in our halls or corridors. Jaenella is bound to another house, and another kingdom, at least far from this mess. Now Geord is on the journey he was always going to make, one way or the other. With the faith driven out of Southmarch, and the works of darkness fortifying our king, there is nothing left here for our brother."

"Each of us won every battle, in each direction, but it feels as if we lost both wars, somehow," Willus said.

Daemen put a hand on his brother's shoulder, growing tired. "Damned either way, I suppose," he said. "You're too kind to say it, but perhaps if we'd stayed out of the whole affair as it seemed you desired, we could have avoided the storm."

"We were the faith's justice, then the king's," Willus said. "If we had been neither, what would that have made us, now? Cowards? Traitors to both through inaction? No, brother. As much as I wanted it, abstinence was never a luxury we or father could have chosen. A side had to be picked and terrible consequences were inevitable."

"Always loath to make such decisions, but you believe we chose wrong, don't you?"

"Perhaps if we'd declared for our king, there'd have been no rebellion at all and everything would have stayed as it was," Willus said, with a shrug. "And while their accusations proved true in the end, almost coincidentally so, given their lack of evidence or solid testimony, there was nothing but sheer ambition behind their desire to usurp. Father saw it. That's why he struggled so. Perhaps father's mockery of me on the balcony, the night the star fell, might have been the best choice after all. To claim the rebellion in our own name and make house Daulmont the new kings. We did fight both factions in the end. Yet here we are. Still standing. Perhaps the faith might have even backed us, if we'd let them listen to Geord talk for half a moment."

Daemen issued a now rare smile upon his gaunt face. Amused, he breathed heavily through his nose. "Yes, if we'd let him speak for us, it might have made house Rosendor look downright heathen by comparison."

Willus laughed then shook his head before pointing to their brother's carriage in the distance. "Let's go back inside before one of us tries to make a break for it as well."

Daemen gave his brother another smile before being helped back into their keep.

#

In the absence of conflict over the following years Lord Daemen wore Heavens Blade by his side sparingly. He took it to official ceremonies and public gatherings, but the greatsword grew too heavy for him as the withering disease that had claimed his father was now too taking its toll on him. He had one young daughter, producing no male heirs after her. He eventually found himself bedridden, loosing teeth and hair, and so named his second youngest brother, Willus, lord of Norcaster in the year Two-Hundred-and-Fourteen of the New Kestrian calendar.

"Well brother, the time has come for your opinions to count," Daemen said, through shallow breaths. "Time to lead, time to use that mind, you like to hide behind that dry humour of yours."

"The heir has made the spare the lord of Norcaster," Willus said, by his brother's bed. "The Twelve help us all."

"You'll do well, I know you will. You once said something about leaving well enough alone when the rebellion came knocking at our doors. Perhaps if anyone had listened, at the time, things might have turned out better."

"Stable."

"As you say."

"As I said, years ago," Willus recalled. "But as stable as it might have been, it would have been in blissful ignorance of the dark undertakings of our king."

"A dark king who thinks favourably upon the new lord of Norcaster," Daemen said, offering a weak smile.

"Whatever do you mean?" Willus asked, confused.

"When I oversaw the treaty with Bellethon in Whiteborough, I told King Garaug, that you were the one voice against rebellion. So, whatever happens under his rule, at least know that you'll be the one lord he trusts."

#

In the following months, Lord Willus Daulmont had summoned apothecaries and scholars of medicine from far and wide to cure his brother. One of them suggested that perhaps the sword, made from an unknown metal, might be to blame in some way beyond the measure of his knowledge. He was therefore instructed to consult Kai Ghoruus, the wizard of the Umberlands. After all, similar symptoms had begun to plague the archers who handled the Angels Teeth arrows.

Willus, favouring a longsword anyway, travelled instead with his grandfather's sword by his side. He brought only a single shaft of the Angel's Teeth arrows, wrapped in many cloths and stored in a wooden chest. He rode for the far north of the west kingdom of Cliffguard, with Sir Dunold and several men. They made their way to the white tower of Pereon, a four-hundred-foot tall structure with four flanged fins that that supported four high balconies facing north, south, east, and west on each of the four highest levels, like the top of a giant spiral staircase.

The tower was made most unusual by the extension of a single long arm that protruded west with an open room like a round covered fifth balcony making the tower seem as if it should topple from the imbalance.

The tall wizard greeted him at the door and took him up many stairs to his alchemic laboratory. "So, you made weapons of a metal that fell from the sky," he said, taking the arrow and placing it in a clamp. He swivelled a series of large glass lenses on hinged black iron arms. "You should have brought it here before you started forging weapons. How many weapons did you make?"

"A greatsword and quite a few of these arrowheads," Lord Willus Daulmont told him.

"A greatsword? the wizard asked. "Would this be Heavens Blade?"

"You know of it?"

"A sword that cuts effortlessly through other forged metals would of course have a reputation. Its name now makes more sense to me. As I suspect your father and brother's illness will shortly," the wizard said, trying different combinations of lenses, some clear, some frosted, and some tinted. "What a terrible mistake your father made," he said, pulling his head back alarmed.

"What is it?"

"This metal was not meant for living hands to wield," the wizard warned, as he unscrewed the clamps and returned the arrow. "Did you carry this all the way here from Norcaster yourself?"

"Wrapped in layers of cloth, secured in a wooden chest, yes," Lord Willus said, certain he'd taken every precaution.

"Cloth?" the wizard scoffed, "Cloth will not protect you. Nor wood. Give it to one of your men to carry on the journey home. Then perhaps another. Limited exposure should not seriously harm any of you. But when you return home, put it with the others and your Heavens Blade. Place them in a great box made of thick lead, that seals tight and locks. And put it in the deepest hole you can dig, surrounded by stone, that leads to no water."

"Why, what is it?"

"Beyond your understanding, is what it is. This metal's weight and density comes at a great cost to things around it. Especially living things. If you must keep this sword, put it as far from where you sleep as you can, where no one will find it unless they are meant to. Use it to defend your keep only in the direst of need but do not carry this thing with you. Do not wear it at your side. Do not show it off to visiting lords. Do not touch your own face or eat after you have touched this metal until you have scrubbed your hands near raw. Can you remember all that?"

"Yes, Kai Ghoruus," Lord Willus agreed.

"Good, then write it down on some parchment and leave these instructions in the box in which you place the sword and these arrows," the wizard insisted, "That sword will see the end of your house if you do not do as I say."

"My father believed the gods sent him that sword."

"I can assure you they did not, and even if they had, it would have meant the gods did not look upon him kindly. Gods are not so elusive and vague when they want something from you mortals."

"Then who did send it?"

"No one sent it," the wizard abruptly said, shaking his head. "It just fell. Sometimes burning rocks just do. The next time you catch a falling star, tell me first before fashioning it into an heirloom."

And so, Lord Willus Daulmont returned to Norcaster and had the smith craft him a thick-walled crate of lead that left no gap when shut. He then had a deep dry well made within the lowest crypt of the keep where a long chain attached the box to a lead lined wooden door that sealed the deep stonewalled shaft. There Heavens Blade was laid to rest until its power would need to be called upon. Lord Willus hoped that that time would never come, and that the legend of this sword that claimed his father and brother would be forgotten by his heirs. "Heavens Blade, a sword so destructive it even kills the ones who wield it," he said, as he closed the doors to the crypt.

He stood over it and stared, lost in thought. Everything that had gone wrong, had begun with the arrival of that celestial metal. It convinced his father to join a doomed rebellion, drained him of life, and, after a counter rebellion, claimed his firstborn heir.

Now it felt as if the chaos of the last few years had been buried with that grave sword. It cost him dearly, but it seemed Willus finally had the stability, dark as it was, that he had always craved. There was sorrow. But the ever-present panic that plagued him had finally departed, as if lanced from his soul.

Leadership was thrust upon him and, for the first time, he did not fear it. He left the deep place of Norcaster Keep, sealing the entire level, to take his place as it's lord.

Barend Nieuwstraten III was born in Sydney, Australia, to Dutch and Indian immigrants. He's worked in film, television, music, and online comics. Primarily expanding his high-fantasy world through stories spanning from shorts to novels, he's also exploring science fiction and steampunk worlds. Usually dipping his toes in horror.

The Solar King

by Kara Race-Moore

A flower.

The building was shaped like a flower. There was no other way to describe the structure looming ahead as anything but flower shaped. If the king, Louis XIV, had ordered his royal architect to build him a palace in the shape of a lily, it might have looked something like this, if the architect was also a magician, to make the impossibly large panels of glass and mirrors that made up the fantastic petals.

The merchant glanced back. Beyond the avenue of flowering trees the humming wall of light that had let him through was now closed. Beyond that the snowstorm still howled, but muffled by that impossible wall of bluish, shimmering light. Against all modern reasoning he thought magic probably had something to do with this. Or perhaps, his sluggish brain tried to argue rationally, this was a fever dream of a summer garden before he died of cold and exposure in this unexpected spring blizzard.

The horse trotted forward and the merchant, his left wrist still tangled in the reins from when he tumbled off the horse in exhaustion, was dragged along. The horse had pragmatically divided the world into 'cold' and 'not cold', and wanted to be in the 'not cold' section, however uncanny.

The man lurched along a few steps, grey spots dancing before his eyes, before his knees buckled and he collapsed, lacking the ability to even laugh at the irony that he would still die from the storm, even after finding this magical shelter. As he slid into unconsciousness he was aware that some*thing* was loping towards him, and then he knew no more.

He awoke from a strange dream of losing his entire fortune and having to leave the city. Then the memories of the past year came sweeping back, and he realized he had momentarily thought it all dream because he had been sleeping in something as soft as the great bed back in his lavish mansion, long since confiscated by his creditors.

163

He stretched and sat up, amazed at how refreshed he felt. Throwing off the strange silver blankets and swinging his legs over the side of the bed, he stood up. He could see by the sunshine pouring in through fantastically large windows that he had slept later than his new country habit. As he felt the warm air on his skin he realized he was naked, and he grabbed up the silver blanket before he shocked some chambermaid.

He saw was alone, but there was a suit of clothes draped over a chair and a table bearing a tray of covered dishes. He pulled on the new clothes, marveling at the softness and fit, then turned his attention to the covered dishes. Upon examination he found a meal set out by an eager, if uncertain, host, with what appeared to be a little of everything. There was a bowl of fruits, a dish of figs, a pot of honey, a dish of soft cheese, a carafe of fresh milk, a basket of rolls, a crisp salad, and a clutch of boiled eggs.

The sight and smells made him ravenous, and he resolved to sit down and eat. If some ogre wanted to fatten him up, surely he would not have been given new clothes? It wasn't a refined feast like the banquets he had once hosted, back when he had been the wealthiest merchant in the city, but it tasted better and was more satisfying than any meal he could presently recall.

Once satiated, he stood and surveyed his surroundings. The room was pleasant, if strange. It was large and airy, like the room of a palace. He had the sense of a hurried reassembling; things seemed to have been moved recently. He was reminded of the time he had hosted a minor prince at his mansion, at the height of his glory, and giving up his own master suite, overseeing the servants in hastily removing personal items.

There was a sigh behind him and he turned to discover a portion of the wall had opened to reveal a doorway. He waited, but no fairy queen or demon lord appeared, and so, nerves singing with tension, he peered out.

He saw no one, merely a dim hallway with walls of a dull metal color. A light appeared above from a vine stung along the top of the walls, like an odd Christmas decoration left hanging long after the season was done. The vine grew fat purple flowers, some of which were glowing, the glow intensifying as he stared, and moving along the vine towards another doorway down the hall as one flower after the other on the vine began to glow.

He hesitated. The trail of glows became an annoyed flicker, shining brightest above the other doorway, a strong hint of where he was supposed to go. He stepped out and followed the glowing flowers through the twisting, turning passageways of a magic castle that looked like no castle he had ever set foot in. The lights lead him to the castle's foyer where an entrance stood open. There was no sign of any door here either, and he wondered if it was a portcullis design, the door rolled up to allow unimpeded movement to and fro.

The vine above the entrance blinked rapidly at him, encouraging his exit. The way was open, he had been well rested, fed, provided with fresh clothing, and just outside he could see his horse tethered, looking similarly fed and freshened, loaded with a saddlebag that bulged fuller than it had the night before, suggesting he had even been given provisions for the rest of his journey. *Leave*, was the clear message.

But he hesitated, his gaze lingering on another nearby doorway that spilled out bright green light and hothouse fragrances. The smell brought back memories of faraway travels in his younger days, a beautiful bride standing beside him on the ship that had sailed through clear blue water past islands of bright, bright green.

He told himself he would just be a moment as he moved towards the tantalizing doorway. He stood on the threshold and breathed deeply, relishing the scent of the seemingly thousands of flowers that crowded in front of his eyes, in trays on the tables and on shelves along the walls. Some he recognized, both local and foreign, but others baffled him in their strangeness.

Strangest of all was a rosebush sitting by itself in a small tub of dirt on a little table with odd bits of metallic strings attached to the branches, the blossoms emitting pale halos of golden light, and the leaves shining with strange markings. Peering closer, he saw a scrawl of living gold ink was shaping foreign letters across the leaves.

Beauty has to see this, he thought, and snapped off one particular perfect rose.

Lights from nowhere began to flash all around and high pitched whistles rang out, a calumniation worse than a town bell clanging an alarm of fire or invasion. He froze, the rose clutched in his hand as the alarms shrieked and flashed, the entire palace alerting that a theft had occurred. There were faint vibrations through the floor and a sound of pounding feet as something came running towards the hothouse. The man was rooted to the floor with fear, silently berating himself for his stupidity to think he could steal from such a powerful place.

A creature galloped in. It stood like a man, and dressed, somewhat, like one, in pants and shirt that resembled peasant's clothes but made of some odd shiny material. The creature was incredibly hairy with a lion-like mane and ears, but with horns like a mountain goat, and a mouth and jaw uncomfortably like a man with disturbingly intelligent eyes. The creature shouted something in a roar of unintelligible, harsh words. The merchant gaped at him, mouth opening and closing helplessly.

The creature took a deep breath in and out, closed his eyes, and pinched the tips of his horns, looking like a parent exasperated by a misbehaving child. The creature opened his golden eyes and asked, slowly and carefully, "What. Have. You. Done?"

The man looked down at the stolen rose. "I, uh, I am sorry for taking one of your flowers, ah, my lord, please forgive me."

The creature frowned. "I am not a lord. I am a Beast."

"My apologies again, Beast," he said hastily. "I meant no offense. I can see you are powerful, and your home is wondrous. This flower…" he looked down at the stolen rose. "I would have loved to have studied it, and shown my daughter so we could compare it to other horticulture oddities…"

"You are curious," said the Beast flatly.

"This is a most curious place," he gulped.

"Are you," the Beast paused and murmured a few words to himself, searching for the right one, "a man of science?" he asked finally.

"I am only a merchant," he gabbled. "My fortunes have taken a bad turn, but-"

"Merchant? Buy and sell? But you study flowers?"

"The goods I have imported have often included plants from the New World and the Far East. My youngest daughter and I enjoyed studying them." He chuckled with a father's pride. "She actually came up with some intriguing new ways to keep them alive longer in transit. She has quite a clever mind along with her mother's beauty, not that her sister's aren't beauties themselves, just more concerned with more feminine matters-" he stopped, remembering he was not talking business with another merchant. He went back to examining the floor with great interest. "You have a lovely home and I am the most flattered and humbled of guests to have seen it and apologize again for taking the rose."

The Beast made an exasperated huff. "If I had gone completely native," the Beast grumbled, "I would just kill you now and be done with it. But, knowing my luck, your people would come looking for you and find me and my problems would expand exponentially. Also, I am resisting the pull to act like my barbarian neighbors. So. You see my dilemma."

"Please don't kill me," the man blurted. "I vow by the Virgin Mother that I shall never return or tell anyone what I have seen. I am truly sorry I took the rose. I just thought my daughter would want to see-"

"This would be the one you studied plant shipping with?"

"Um, yes, we just have the vegetable garden now and she misses the park flowers, but would dreadfully miss her father more if he did not come home and-"

"Bring her as a hostage for your good behavior."

"What? But, my own daughter, my youngest, she cannot-"

"How old is she?"

"She is only 17 and-"

"Old enough to be separated from the family unit, by your culture's standards."

"I-"

"Either bring her to live here or come back alone and die here," said the Beast flatly. "That is the extent of my generosity these days." He bared his sharp teeth in a horrible grin. "Life has rather ground out the mercy in me."

The merchant stumbled back in an instinctive reaction to the teeth. "I-" he began, not even sure what he was going to say, only that he must make some protest.

"I will send a guide to lead you back." The Beast said something foreign, and after a moment a strange bird flew in.

'Bird' was the first word that came to mind to describe the small thing that sailed through the air to land on the Beast's shoulder like a trained parrot, but it was like no bird the man had ever seen. He realized with a start the thing was made of metal, a construct of some sort.

"This will accompany you home and guide you back. And you can be sure what it sees, I see. Be back in three days."

"Ah, yes, my lo— ah, Beast," capitulated the man.

The Beast nodded at the rose still clutched in his hand. "Give that to your daughter," he commanded, "since you have already broke it off. If she is as interested in plants as you say, she'll want to see it. Now go."

Numbly, the man stumbled outside towards his horse, where it was placidly eating grass as if nothing had happened. Ahead, an opening appeared in the humming wall of light. Mounting hastily, he urged the horse forward, away from the crystal palace to head home to what would surely be a most unhappy homecoming.

Homecoming was as miserable as he anticipated. As he stood in the cottage, dully reciting the incredible tale of how his journey had ended, there were round eyed looks of disbelief. However, his daughters were unable to dismiss his tale as a fever dream as the odd device settled on the mantelpiece, malevolently watching the family.

"Of course I will go," said Beauty when he had finished, looking at the rose.

The man felt all arguments die on his lips as he saw the look on her face. He knew his daughter. Presented with such a curiosity, he would have to shackle her to a dungeon wall in order to stop her from exploring further.

Three days later they left, Beauty's baggage, such as it was, strapped to her horse. Before they departed she had taken the rose from the little jug she had kept it in to slip it in her pocket. Now, as they followed the metal bird through the forest, she touched the flower now and then, wondering what to expect from a place that grew such roses.

Deep in the forest they arrived at the humming wall of blue light, just as her father had described it. An opening appeared, and they entered the hidden domain.

As they entered Beauty looked around to see what was being so carefully guarded. There were an abundance of fruit trees, a lush vegetable garden, a lovely expanse of green grass, and an unexpected sense of movement. There was a slim windmill spinning merrily, ordinary square sheets of cloth flapping on a clothes line, and flowers everywhere, little heads bobbing in the breeze. But most eye caching of all was the building at the center, indeed looking like a giant silver flower, the mirrored petals stretching out in worship of the sun.

"Only a king could afford so many mirrors," Beauty breathed out, thinking of the single large gilt framed mirror that had hung in the main salon of their old mansion, one of her father's most expensive purchases.

They dismounted as the mechanical bird flew into the flower-shaped palace. A figure appeared in the entrance, concealed by a hooded cloak.

"We are here!" she called out. "My father has explained all." She found herself with her hands on her hips, irritated that the exchange was to be dragged out by theatrics.

Their host loped over, soon mere steps from them. A pause, and then he swept off the hood and looked down at her, awaiting her reaction.

She had an impression of a lot of hair and a powerful jaw, like a lion she had once seen in a menagerie, but she found herself staring at the enormous emerald twisted in glass and wire that hung from his cat-like ear. She looked closer and realized, no, it wasn't an emerald; it was a plant. A little green plant sat comfortably in a tiny glass vial and looked like it was still growing in its little case. Of course girls often weaved a crown of flowers to adorn their hair, but *live plants* as a decoration? A Beast that lived in a flower shaped palace and wore living plants for decoration – what sort of demon lord was this? Was he Persephone rather than Hades? She almost giggled.

Her father interrupted her reverie with a stilted speech about her insistence on coming and his hopes for her safety. The Beast waved his words away. "She will be safe. I will respect her as *you*," he glared at her father, "will respect my privacy."

Her father bowed his head and Beauty frowned, anger overcoming her own fear and wonder to see her captor making her father afraid.

"Also," said the Beast, "I am aware of your marital customs and will be sending you home with compensation for her loss on your marriage market."

"What am I worth?" she inquired. Once she had been worth a fortune that would have been the envy of princesses. Of late she was worth the clothes she stood in. But now, how was she valued by this Beast?

"I have gifts that I believe will be of use to your family without causing any harm." He indicated two bulky saddlebags waiting near the entranceway. "Be careful, they contain mirrors."

"Mirrors?" father and daughter exclaimed.

"Just small ones," he said, indicating with a stretch of his hands an expanse big enough to reflect a full head and shoulders. "Useful but harmless," he shrugged, as if such a gift was nothing.

Beauty wondered if her sisters would allow her father to sell such valuable items; she guessed not. She removed her meager luggage and the Beast strapped on his bags, making soothing noises to help calm the horse as it whickered unhappily at being so close to the unknown scent.

Beauty embraced her father awkwardly. He had been vocal in his love for his children, but never physically demonstrative. "Take care, father," she told him, trying to smile.

Her father looked miserable, similar to when he had announced to his daughters that his money was gone and their lives would be forever altered. "Be well, Beauty."

She nodded, understanding. It was all he could say in this bizarre situation.

As he rode his horse away, leading hers, keeping both animals at a slow walk as they approached the blue wall, she saw the Beast press something small in his hands and the entranceway appeared again. Her father glanced back. She raised one hand, he did the same, and then he left.

It was silent once they were alone. "Well," she said quickly as the silence threatened to become awkward, "what now, my lord?"

He frowned. "I told your father, I am not a lord. Call me Beast, for that is what I am."

"Very well, Beast, but my question stands."

"Allow me to show you your rooms." He turned and she followed him into the mirrored palace. In the entryway he removed his cloak and tossed it over an odd manikin made of a bubbly suit, with a head like a glass bell. Underneath the cloak, the Beast wore pale green billowing pants like a sultan and a vest with vine-like embroidery that matched his earring.

They walked through the twisting metal hallways her father had described, decorated with the glowing purple flowers, until they came to a section of wall of no particular distinction that Beauty could make out. The Beast placed his hand on the wall, causing it to draw back smoother than a curtain.

She walked into a bright and airy set of rooms decorated with more of the glowing vines around the ceiling as well as several other strange plants growing in nooks and niches, with one wall completely covered in a waterfall of greenery. The bed was large and looked comfortable. There were several large chairs, well-padded and solid enough to hold the Beast as well as several little tables, some holding more plants. She glanced around, noting what was missing amongst the luxurious setting.

"Where is the fireplace?"

"There isn't one. The heating comes from the walls."

"There is fire in the walls?"

"No! No fire! Fire is horrible in- in a place like this. I can explain, but first, let me show you the basics. In here," he touched a part of her bedroom wall and another doorway appeared, "is where you can clean and take care of body functions."

She looked at him blankly. She ventured near the doorway and peaked in as he went on, "I'm sorry, I'm not sure which words to use. To relieve yourself? Is that right?"

There was a very complicated looking and clean chamber pot and Beauty realized what he meant. "Oh, yes, of course, thank you Beast." She felt herself blushing to have a man, even such a strange one as the Beast, showing her where the chamber pot was kept, but she also appreciated the luxury of privacy again after sharing with her sisters in the cottage.

He made a careful demonstration of how to use the instruments that provided water to wash her face and hands, the glass stall that would provide water from above to wash her whole body while standing, and how the chamber pot would dispose of waste for her, with the use of the right dials and buttons.

After using the dials herself to make water, hot and cold, appear and disappear from various sources, she stared at the Beast, astonished. She was reminded of histories of the ancient Roman Empire and their feats of engineering. "This is not magic," she said slowly. "This is mechanical."

"Yes," he said, sounding relieved.

"Show me more," she demanded.

He took on a tour of the whole palace. The spiraling hallways lead to many strange rooms, which the Beast did his best to explain and she did her best to understand, but one room made her shrink back, certain she was in a dungeon torture chamber, despite the bright lighting.

"What do you with these... things?" She gestured at what looked like a small gallows.

He grabbed a dangling rope and pulled, lifting a metal counterweight it was attached to. "I practice movements," he said, after a moment's thought.

"But... why?"

He considered, then said, "If you were on a ship, sailing from one end of your oceans to the other, would you sit the whole time or would you need to walk around the deck sometimes?"

"Yes, I would need to probably stretch my legs now and then. But we aren't on a ship now."

"Actually, we are."

She blinked at him. "But we're nowhere near the sea. Why build a ship so far from water?"

"I flew the ship here."

She opened her mouth to object, but decided against it. If she were to protest every strange thing that she saw or he said, every conversation would be twice as long as needed. Instead, she asked, "Why make landfall here?"

He shrugged, "Low seismic activity, lack of major meteorological events, a temperate climate, more than adequate rainfalls and groundwater but low flooding, flat terrain, excellent chemical balance to the soil, abundant local fruit, vegetation, grains and wildlife. It hits most of the check points for setting up camp. From an environmental view point, southern France is a lovely place to live. The natives are hostile, but that's what force field fencing is for."

She decided to ignore the 'hostile native' comment to get to more important matters. "Where are you from?"

"Far away."

"And?" she prompted.

"And I do not want to melt your brain with too many new ideas within the first hour of knowing me. More about me later, I promise."

"That's fair," she conceded. "Please continue the tour. I would like to see your indoor garden."

He smiled and led her to the hothouse where the trouble had started. She walked around the room, impressed by the quality of the plants she recognized and intrigued by the ones she did not. She made her way to the notorious rosebush and made a careful study of the augmentation. "What have you done to it?" she asked, without looking up. "I don't think it's harming the plant, but I can't see how it helps."

"It's an experiment, to see if I could use the local flora for my needs."

"What do you need it to do?" She gingerly poked at the lights dancing above the leaves, causing distorted imagery to dance across her fingers.

"To act as backup display boards."

She turned to look at him, unsure what he meant.

He gave her a bitter smile, rightly understanding her blank incomprehension. "I introduced chemicals that make up a highly conductive polymer to the roots and the polymer itself was assembled inside the xylem channels as conducting wires, while still allowing the xylem to function normally, which meant the rose created an electrochemical transistor in the steam, converting ionic signals to electronic output. I infused a second variant of the polymer into the plant's leaves using vacuum infiltration, which formed pixels of electrochemical cells around the veins. When the plant generates energy through photosynthesis, the infused polymer sends an electrochemical signal through the veins which causes the original polymer to interact with the ions in the leaf, and subsequently changes the color in those leaves like a display. The plant in effect becomes a self-sufficient display device."

She frowned. "You are making fun of me."

"I am making a point that my answers won't make sense if you don't have a foundation to understand them."

"And you are making fun of me."

He ducked his head, abashed. "I apologize. Just because you are not a Beast is no reason to be rude."

"I want the foundation. I want to understand about this ship and garden and- and- and all of it. Please," she heard the begging in her voice and tried to remain composed, "I want to learn." Her heart beat faster at the thought of learning more about what he was doing with his plants.

"There would be a lot to cover," he said hesitatingly.

"I currently have no plans," she said dryly. "And you?"

"I do believe I have the time," he agreed. "In fact," he smiled as he thought of something, "this could work out well. The sleep-state auditory program allowed me to learn the local spoken language, but I am still struggling with reading the books I have acquired to try and learn more about local history and customs."

"You want me to teach you to read?"

"I can read," he said defensively. "But yes, I would like to learn more."

And so they taught each other language, and many other things besides.

He had, as he had said, already studied quite a lot of hers, but she was able to explain nuances as well as allusions and idiosyncrasies that he had did not have a reference for.

She was somewhat chagrined that he gave her baby stories to start while he was already reading much more advanced texts, but the tales she read were so amusing she couldn't feel too upset as she deciphered the text, laughing when she comprehended jokes and smiling at the gentle lessons the stories taught to be kind.

The routine became a start of a light breakfast in the mechanical kitchen, eggs or fresh fruit accompanied by a drink similar to coffee. It was lighter on the tongue but left her eye-poppingly awake after just a few sips, ready to begin the day's chores.

The little kingdom the Beast had built inside his blue walls was amazingly self-sufficient. The rain, the wind and the sun were all harvested like any other crop, and used to keep everything working. He had some spoiled chickens ranging free, a pampered nanny goat, and an old warhorse that he said he had offered "noble retirement" to when he saw it being mistreated by its former owners.

Instead of servants, there was an amazing array of machines – a machine that created clothes like a printing press, another machine to wash the clothes, machines in the kitchen to make meals, and machines that did the cleaning. Beauty was so delighted to not have to sweep floors that for the first few days she followed the diminutive floor-cleaning machine around her new home, just to be sure it was true. The Beast was also assisted by plants for lights and many other things besides food. They tended the gardens, inside and out, making sure all the plants were healthy, cared for the animals, and he showed her the proper maintenance to insure all his clever little machines kept working.

They would have a light lunch, often outside if it wasn't raining, and then, after a break to change out of clothes made grubby by gardening and machinery repair, and a glorious wash in the marvelous bathing room, they would meet back up in his study to muddle through lessons as they both tried to teach each other a lifetime of knowledge. Whenever they reached the point the Beast called 'critical mass,' meaning his was afraid of one or both of them having apoplexy from too much studying, they would give the mind a rest and work the body instead with his 'exercise' machines.

"The most important skill to learn," he puffed as he leaped though a complicated series of steps in one exercise routine, "is to fall correctly."

"Fall? As in trip and fall and land on your face, fall? That's a skill?"

"Ah, but if you practice, you don't land on your face. You land," he twirled in the air, "on your feet!" he exclaimed, flourishing his hands.

Intrigued, Beauty allowed him to show her how to use the different machines and tried the different exercises. She found herself the most at ease with one of the more simple ones, a platform that moved as she ran in place. In the light clothes he had provided her, unrestricted by skirts or corsets, she was delighted to learn how fast she could go, feeling as though she was almost flying as she ran faster and lengthened her stride.

The evening meals were more formal as they sat at a table near the kitchen, large windows letting the starlight pour in, the purple flowers providing a gentle light over the table. The dishes were a mixture of her foods and his and a fusion they experimented with, with sometimes delicious and sometimes disastrous results. After dinner they would often sit outside with a glass of cider or wine and watch the stars.

One night as they stargazed she took a leap based on what she had read and asked him, "Which one is yours? Which star is your sun?"

"That one," he said without hesitation, pointing out a small prick of light along the left wing of the Cygnus constellation.

She looked at the tiny sparkle. "That… is a far distance to sail."

"Well, the ship goes very fast."

"How fast?

"Faster than light," he stated.

"Faster than the light?" That hadn't come up in lessons so far. "How?"

"Well," he clicked on the lantern they used to find their back in without stumbling, "this light lets you see your hand in the dark, yes?"

Smiling, she held up her hand, twisting it about to play with the light and shadows flitting across the skin. "Yes, the light lets me see me hand," she repeated. "But what does that have to do with speed?"

"Light is a thing, a tangible object, and it takes time to journey from the lantern to your hand. Not much time, just a tiny fraction of a moment, but that is still a unit of time. My ship goes faster than the time it takes for the light to journey to your hand."

She looked from the lantern to her hand. "Quite fast," she said, aware of the understatement. "What does it feel like, to go at such speed?"

"Faster than the fastest horse you have ever ridden," he told her, holding her gaze with his own, a challenge in his eyes.

"I think King Louis would ban such a thing if he knew of it," she said airily, choosing to ignore that challenge, whatever it was, for now.

Soon after they had settled into their routine, she was reading a slightly more advanced text, a book of myths from his culture, and had just reached a point when two sisters overcame incredible odds to reunite with their parents, when she had to look away to squeeze her eyes shut and sniff.

"Are you all right?" asked the Beast, looking up from his own reading.

"My sisters are silly and vain and my father is obsessed with his old ledgers, but... but I miss them," she admitted.

He muttered something in his language; she knew enough now to understand it was a mild oath of self-recrimination. "I forget," he told her, shifting back to her language. "You can see your family here."

"What?"

"In here." She followed him to a small room that held several large square black mirrors. She reflected only dimly in them, which seemed to defeat the point. From her studies she understood this room was the equivalent to the ship's helm.

The Beast sat down and began hitting his fingers on the desk, not randomly or with frustration, but with an odd purpose. She was distracted from his odd hand movements by the black mirrors flaring into bright, colorful life. Images flashed across them, hard shapes, strange symbols, and all sorts of pictures.

"I apologize for the lack of ethics, but the mirrors I sent were not just a gift. They have cameras built in to allow for remote viewing."

"To spy?" she asked, vaguely aware she should be outraged, but too distracted by the wondrous mirrors to spend too much effort on it.

"I wanted to be sure your father didn't start babbling about the monster that stole his daughter and round up some mob to kill me." He shrugged. "I decided to prioritize my safety over informed consent issues. Technically this isn't even illegal."

"Oh?"

"This planet is outside the Empire, so it's not in the jurisdiction of my people's laws. And your people don't have laws to cover something they haven't invented yet. And, ah, yes, here we are, live feed of your father's house."

A few more determined taps, and one of the mirrors showed her the inside of the main room of the cottage, as if she was looking through a window. Her father was slumped in his chair, reviewing a ledger book. Her sisters were on either side of him, mouthing words.

"Sorry, I left it on mute last time I was using this," said the Beast. He adjusted a small dial, and suddenly words poured out of her sisters' mouths:

"Are your investments no better?" asked Pomona.

"How much longer will we be buried in the country?" asked Marguerite.

Their father waved them away with the familiar refrain that his latest investments needed time to come to fruition, especially since his last venture had come to nothing. It was the typical daily conversation. Suddenly weary, Beauty waved a hand, "Enough, please. Thank you for showing me my family."

"You may use these to see them anytime you wish."

"Thank you," she said again.

She did, on occasion, use the mirrors to see her family, but the mirrors only showed whatever was right in front of them, and even when someone was in the room, there was usually not much to see as they went about their routines. She found herself checking on them less and less as she learned more about the Beast's background.

One night as they stargazed she asked, "If where you're from is so wonderful, why are you here?"

"Politics," he said, and explained about being of a faction that had challenged the ruling power and, losing, being forced into exile. He had been assured by friends that they would work for his return, but so far, he had received no word. He sounded resigned.

His talk of exile prompted her the next day to check on her own family. She turned on the mirror and tapped in the commands to see her home. To her surprise, there was a great deal of chaotic movement, and a doctor was bending over her father as he sat huddled in a blanket in a chair close to the fireplace. He was gray and the doctor was shaking his head with regret.

Beauty gave a cry of horror that brought the Beast rushing into the room.

"What is it?"

"My father is ill."

He looked at the image. "You must go to him," he said, without hesitation.

She nodded. "I... just for a short while. I'll come back."

He shook his head. "Your return is unnecessary."

Beauty felt as though she had been struck in the stomach. "What? I do promise, I'll be gone just for a short while to see him recover and-"

"There is no reason to keep you here. None but my own selfishness. I acted rashly to demand you as a hostage. Go back to your family and forget all this."

"Yes, I'll just forget the most amazing experience of my life," Beauty said scornfully.

"I'm serious, you must go. It is wrong to keep you here. I want you to go home and not feel guilty about feeling safe with your family."

She glanced between the mirror and the Beast. "I will visit my father and then come back."

He sighed. "Promise you will at least give it some thought. Staying here means missing opportunities to live a normal life with your own kind." He held up a hand as she opened her mouth to object. "Please consider what that means before you casually dismiss normalcy as boring."

She scrunched up her face. "Sometimes it is annoying when you guess my thoughts like that."

He smiled. "You are an open book. One I love reading."

She smiled, then glanced back at the screen, her unease returning. "I'll pack now and leave immediately." She put her hand in his and squeezed it. "I promise while I am there I will give serious thought to... priorities."

"Thank you," he said.

She rushed to her room and dug up the bag she had brought with her a lifetime ago, still containing most of what she'd brought. She hadn't needed them here, with everything provided, and so much better.

177

Outside, the Beast was putting a package in the warhorse's saddlebag. "I've packed some medicines that should help. Promise me to keep your doctors away and he might recover."

She nodded. "I promise." She clambered onto the warhorse and settled in the saddle. "I will remember all of my promises," she told him, and kneed the horse into a fast walk, not even stopping at the blue wall, knowing the Beast would open the gateway for her.

The horse brought her home quickly and she ignored most of the exclamations and questions from her sisters to rush to her father's side and administer the Beast's medicines. Within a day he was much improved and all attention turned to Beauty and demands to know what had happened.

She struggled to explain the Beast. "He's lonely," she finally said. "He may look strange but he's smart and friendly and misses having people around. We mostly just talk and do chores," she finished helplessly. She hesitated to tell them too much about his home and devices. He had described the dangers of his devices in the wrong hands, and she was afraid of what might happen if her family realized how valuable his things were.

Marguerite was appalled by the clothes she had arrived in, insisting it was a waste of whatever fabulous silk the material was. "Trousers! Peasant trousers!" she exclaimed. Meanwhile, Pomona bereted Beauty for going about without a bonnet or parasol. "You don't look fashionably sun-kissed," she told her sharply, "you look sun-*ravished!*"

Beauty made it worse by laughing.

The next morning, already thinking how soon she could leave without looking churlish, she took out the little two way mirror he had given her and went through the carefully learned steps to show her the helm room. She smiled in anticipation of seeing her Beast.

Instead, she gasped at what she saw. In the room were several other Beasts, looking military in their dress, and they appeared to be arresting him. Hardly daring to breath, she activated the sound. They were speaking in quick, clipped tones that confirmed to her that whoever they were, they were military. They spoke the Beast's language, and she couldn't understand more than half the words, but it was clear he was in trouble.

With horror, she realized if any of them were to glance at his mirror they would see her in the corner frame. She hastily turned off the mirror, as much as she wanted to keep watching. If they saw her, her Beast might be get into even more trouble.

She flew down the stairs, nearly running over her father.

"Beauty?" he queried, confused by her haste.

She was halfway to the stable, but made herself run back, give her father a quick peck on the check and declared, "My Beast is in trouble. I love him and I must go to him," and took off running again.

She already had the saddle on the horse by the time her baffled father made his way to the stable. "You love him?"

She swung herself up, but paused to try and explain. "He is smart and kind and different but beautiful and I love him with all my heart," she said, nudging the horse into a walk.

"But why such hasty—"

"He needs me," she said fiercely. She encouraged the horse into a trot and called over her shoulder, "No matter what, I love you!" Not the most eloquent of farewells, but it would have to do.

She urged the horse to a gallop most of the way and once in the center of the woods she was both relieved and dismayed that the blue wall was gone. She slipped off the horse and moved closer, cautiously peering about to see the Beast's magnificent little kingdom rapidly being dismantled.

He had mentioned it was designed to roll up quickly and leave no trace of his presence besides a pleasant clearing that would gradually grow back into wild forest. Now she saw other Beasts doing precisely that as her Beast stood next to a high ranking looking one. He had a slump to his shoulders and looked defeated.

Next to his ship was an even larger structure. If his ship was a flower, then this was a thorn, all lines and sharp edges. There was a suggestion of fire and smoke near the bottom, and several Beasts were hurrying up a gangplank, carrying large crates, like sailors readying a ship for a long voyage.

She watched, horrified, as the flower she had lived in began to close up its petals, all traces of the Beast's life packed up. The Beast was lead, dejected, onto the larger ship and everyone else began to go inside.

Beauty flung up her cloak's hood and, bold as brass, grabbed an overlooked potted bush and marched in behind one of the stragglers. The ramp closed behind her and, putting down the plant, she crouched behind a large crate. She glanced around the hold, desperately trying to think of what to do next. Too late, what she guessed was some sort of pistol was pushed into her back with a growled inquiry in Beast's language about who she was, ruder than the formal version she had learned, and she was prodded forward.

She concentrated to understand what they were saying. "*I found something, sir,*" the one who was prodding her said to the high ranking Beast standing next to her Beast.

"Beauty!" her Beast exclaimed, shocked.

She gave him a sickly grin as she was prodded to stand next to him. The high ranking one glared at her Beast.

"*Should I throw her off?*" the one who had found her inquired. She saw his hand hover over a bright red button. She guessed that would open the cargo hold gangway.

"*We've already taken off,*" snapped the high ranking one. "*We'll be out of the atmosphere in a few minutes.*"

She glanced around the hold and with relief saw the emergency packs along one wall. She had studied them when she had studied his ship design in general. She knew how they worked. Theoretically.

"*A simple arrest,*" the high ranking one was sneering. "*Except the pickup of one prince turns complicated when we find him holed up in a solar system littered with asteroids and set up with a shelter barely confirming to non-interference laws!*"

"Prince?" she muttered.

"Not now," he begged.

"Well, your highness, you're going to have to fall correctly," she whispered, trying not to move her lips. From the corner of her eye saw him give a barely perceptible nod.

"*And on top of that,*" the leader continued to berate, "*you've taken a local barbarian as a lover!*"

Enraged by his insult, she screamed in his own language, "*I'll show you barbarian!*"

She whirled, pounded her fist against the bright red button, and the floor dropped down. The Beast tumbled away before she could grab him. She grabbed two emergency packs and jumped. She was immediately flipped around in a dizzying spiral, ship, sky, land, ship, sky, and then managed to steady her fall, packs clutched tight, one in each hand, and she saw the vast horizon spread out below her.

And there he was, already far below her, but she could see he was splayed out, facing upwards, arms and legs out wide, using his own bulk to slow the fall.

She straitened her legs, stretched out her arms, let the pack straps rattle around her armpits, and dove after him; she was an arrow, shooting straight and true to her lover's heart. "Virgin Mary, please let this work," she begged.

She spread out her fingers as she came closer. The ground was rushing towards them. She stretched her hands out to him as he stretched his hands to her. She grabbed his hands and flung herself forward to grasp onto him, clinging to his large frame. She managed to get a pack on as the Beast shrugged into his. The ground was terrifyingly close.

"Now!" he yelled, pointing at the bright yellow cord on her left shoulder strap. She pulled and with a loud flap there was suddenly a great deal of white sheet above her and she had turned from a plummeting stone to a floating leaf.

The Beast joined her floating along the breeze and showed how the other cords worked to steer their direction and gently fall the rest of the short distance to the ground and land back where they had begun on the bright green lawn.

The flower home, now sealed tight as a bud, was all that was left. "We have to hurry," he said, as he shrugged out of the fall-slowing contraption and gathered it in his arms like dirty bedding and headed towards the ship, with Beauty doing the same. "My ship was set to an auto-sequence to follow once the prisoner transport was out of orbit." He stopped and turned to her. "You have to make a choice. I have to leave this planet and never come back. I'll travel for a while and let the political situation sort itself out. It means never seeing your family again-"

She kissed him. "You are my family," she told him. "I love you, Beast, and I am coming with you!"

He grinned. "I love you too. Now let's go before the ship takes off without us!"

Onboard, they strapped into the helm's chairs. Beauty adjusted the large straps to fit her smaller frame as Beast set a new course.

"Are you ready to travel faster than the light?" he asked her.

"Yes."

Kara Race-Moore studied history at Simmons College to read about scandalous British royals. Ms. Race-Moore first came to fantasy and science fiction through the works of Anne McCaffrey and still loves stories of riding dragons and adventures on faraway planets.

The Kill Switch

by S. C. Burns

C hief Scientist Dr. Jamal Jackson tensed his jaw as he entered the secure area of the three circumscribed rooms that had become all too familiar. The outlying viewing room was reserved for the upper echelon of Clean Energy Technologies (CET), or their customers who toured the facility. The control room housed the computer equipment and safety measures that kept scientists safe during testing procedures. The inner room contained CETHER, Clean Energy Technologies' Hybridized Electromagnetic Reactor.

Reliable nuclear fusion, both an enigma of modern energy and the ultimate dream of obsessed scientists, could change life on Earth insurmountably. The advancements of the Korea Superconducting Tokamak Advanced Research (KSTAR) reactor in Daejeon had rippled through worldwide clean energy markets. Universities everywhere accepted record numbers of budding fusion scientists as government-run energy departments poured trillions of dollars into fusion technology research and development. Companies materialized from nothing and snatched up the resources to form the foundations for endless possibilities.

Jamal had entered the fray a decade ago after earning his doctorate in hybridized electromagnetic reactors (an upgrade over magneto-inertial reactors) and had worked for CET for the past five years.

His choice to pursue reliable and stable fusion energy had begun at his father's bedside in his small town's hospital. A series of events had led him there: a mother who had given her life to birth his brother, who had given his life for the country's senseless military goals. The pain of loss had eaten away his father's organs over years, throwing his health into turmoil.

"What will you do with your life when I'm gone?" his father had asked. "Over the years, I've learned we can't have everything..."

Jamal, the oldest, still had yet to decide on a career while his brother had already enlisted to serve the country, proving himself useful. While he struggled to answer his father's question, unrest over skyrocketing oil and energy prices had peaked. Ecoterrorism had taken a dark turn, and coordinated acts of sabotage brought power stations offline around the world. The hospital generators could barely run the lights, let alone keep his father alive long enough for Jamal to figure out what exactly he wanted. The disruptions in critical care had proven too damaging. Jamal's only course was to pull the plug. His father would never get the answer to the only question in life that had mattered to him anymore: the value of his son's contributions.

Jamal gripped the main control room console. A network of twenty computer systems arced across the space in two rows. The x86-64 workstations operated on a Linux distribution the team had customized to fulfill the specific requirements of their experiments. They considered it a barebones setup that would reliably perform the standard operations of their work, but the unspoken complaint was about their lack of funding for a much more powerful supercomputer setup. Too much had been allocated to CETHER's structural design. The computers beeped like life support attached to a dying beast as the nightly safety checks completed their routines and subroutines. Jamal had ensured there were more redundancies and fail-safes than were necessary. A power outage was now nearly impossible. Nothing would stop his hope from living.

The network was rigged up with switches, breakers, and relays, both physical and virtual, but the main system kill switch lay encased in glass next to Jamal's right hand. Several fail-safes could be triggered before he'd ever need to smash the box and press the button to divert all reactor input power to separate grounds. It had never come to that, but if it did, could he really kill CETHER by his own hand? Perhaps if other lives were on the line.

Jamal looked past his ghostly image reflected on the shatterproof glass at the front of the room and focused on the key to his life's goal. A behemoth built for greatness, CETHER stretched thirty-two cubic feet across the forty-foot inner room, six and a half times larger than KSTAR and just a fraction larger than the International Thermonuclear Experimental Reactor (ITER) in France. Jamal cared more about the science than the size, but CET's management wanted the device to break records early on so the organization could secure more funding. Jamal's college rival, Dr. Andre Basset, took CETHER's size personally and worked tirelessly to further ITER's functionality faster than Jamal had thought possible. The two reactor projects were the vanguard of large-scale fusion science.

Acoustic cushions covered every nook and cranny within the inner room, though the deep growl of safe mode reverberated through the control room's floor. The doors were sealed, flanked by the dormant emergency lights. The sophisticated ventilation and filtration systems hummed, ready to pull the stinging metallic scent caused by slivers of plasma touching the reactor walls.

CETHER's titanium body resembled a sphere of water spinning in space, able to withstand adverse pressures of full vacuum, isolated from any hint of vibration. A metallic toroidal ring encircled the chamber. The coils were wound tightly as a means to impart a magnetic field strong enough to prevent superheated plasma from vaporizing the metal walls. An array of tubes guided countless collated laser beams into the reactor. The tubes traveled from the isolated glass chamber to several rooms away where the lasers were guided and cooled. The three layers seemed simple in theory, but blasting pebble-sized deuterium-tritium capsules to split atoms at nearly 100 million degrees Celsius was no simple feat. The system survived when each leg worked as designed. Once mastered, enough energy to power a small city could fit in the palm of one's hand.

Again, Jamal eyed the red kill switch. He contemplated the worst-case scenario. If the coiled tubes failed to prevent the tritium plasma from hitting the walls...well, it would be bad news for everyone. The gaseous fuel would seep out. The system's safety measures would put the inner room on lockdown to prevent the gas from escaping. Dr. Wilkinson had designed the room to withstand an explosion, but the sonic wave would injure everyone within the control room. Upper management, however, would remain more or less safe in the viewing area behind Jamal's station.

The twenty-member research and experimentation team trickled in, starting with the dedicated workhorses: laboratory technicians and master's students in material science, software engineering, and nuclear physics. Then the more senior members representing specialized and emerging areas entered, including Dr. Lucius Raymond, an expert in pinpoint laser targeting at atomic scales. Jamal shook hands and greeted each member of his team. They returned his professional comradery with grins and nods before they took their seats.

The past few weeks leading up to this test had pushed the team to the edge, but their eagerness to show their progress glowed upon their faces. Jamal hoped they would overcome the discouragement of their many failures, but failure hovered unremittingly over all fusion scientists. None of the thousands had ever succeeded, but Jamal had his family etched behind his eyes. He'd prove himself worthy of his father's gift of choice, of CETHER, poised and ready, behind the inner room glass.

Dr. Riley Wilkinson entered. For a brief moment, Jamal's worries vanished at the sight of his first study partner. She had risen alongside Jamal during college and obtained a distinguished graduate designation for her dissertation on metallic deconstruction from plasma impingement. While Jamal managed the project's testing procedures and overall research quality, only Riley could lead the team of manufacturers capable of building a device as technologically advanced as CETHER. Their duality kept both teams level-headed.

In college, they'd spent some nights locked within the physics library. Other nights, she'd drag him to a swing dance at a local jazz bar. His heart and mind warmed at her presence during their college years, but his father's gaze would bore at the back of his head and his brother's casket would trip his feet. This never failed to spur him to return his focus to energy, to fusion, and he would shove his face back into his textbooks.

Riley's positivity, her ear-to-ear smile and unrelenting optimism, calmed everyone under Jamal's command. The mere thermophysical improbability of her existence—of all existence—instilled hope in him. Today would bring them the breakthrough they needed. She had said she wanted nothing more than to break the barriers of fusion alongside him. They had the same goals as partners in science, but sometimes she'd look him dead in the eye only to turn away as though leaving something unsaid.

Jamal turned to the glass window at the back of the control room. CET's senior management often took turns viewing these tests, but the stakes had changed. Funding was on the line, and the room was now packed beyond fire safety regulations. The nation's wealthiest venture capitalists and the illustrious board of directors were seated comfortably as they swirled mixed drinks. They appeared to be talking shop and were likely hoping the next few minutes wouldn't be a waste of their precious time and money.

CET had trusted Jamal and his team with the seemingly improbable feat of developing and implementing marketable fusion energy. They already dominated the market in other energy sectors, including wind and hydro, and even provided the world with the most tritium by way of lunar robotic excavation. They had aired commercials year round, hyping the concept while propagating their company creed:

Imagine...
a world sustained
by limitless energy...
a world where no
one lives in darkness...
Light for all.
Warmth for all. Life
for all.

But they were playing with the power of suns now. To date, the hottest fusion confinement of 100 million degrees had lasted for a record-breaking twenty seconds only, and CET's chief economist wanted twenty-year costs to meet $70 billion dollars. Current projections had climbed past $100 billion, which made the board restless. To them, the CETHER project meant throwing good money after bad, and they couldn't have that. Not after nearly four hundred failed tests over five years and none of them outperforming Dr. Basset at ITER.

Among CET's upper echelon, Jamal interacted only with his manager, Frank Conrad. Mr. Conrad had a suit for every day of the week and never hesitated to draw people's attention to the fact. His overdone coiffure and designer glasses made him look wealthier than the investors he gabbed on with between sips of gin and tonic. The man always played an angle and was probably sliding his business cards into coat pockets in case Jamal's team failed him for the last time. At CET, with a test of such pivotal importance, if a scientist failed, the manager failed, and the company would toss both to the curb. Everyone had seen it happen a couple of years ago when the electrochemical division's rapid-charging car battery exploded during a customer's road trip. Conrad had never been fired, had never lost, and he seemed to have a keen sense of self-preservation, but Jamal noticed when his boss loosened his tie as though to release steam that had been building up unseen. They locked eyes. Conrad's lip quivered a moment, his winner's mask fading momentarily as he downed the rest of his drink.

For fusion scientists, failure was an occupational hazard, but no company would hire Jamal to lead anything again if today's test were to fail. Managers, on the other hand, risked losing face irreparably, risked being blacklisted and barred from the best managerial positions. Conrad's anxiousness made sense, but Jamal's own thoughts turned more to his father's memory than to his career trajectory. The failure of this test would mark the end of Jamal's dreams and would harm the livelihoods of the talented scientists around him who trusted his leadership. His failure would trickle through the energy industry and would make skeptical anti-science investors pull funding from other attempts at humankind's ascension toward harnessing the power of stars.

The investors themselves looked anxious now, having finished their drinks, and they now paced the back room, waiting for the demonstration. Then Conrad finally turned to face Jamal squarely, standing inches from the glass, arms crossed in self-conscious anticipation.

Failure was not an option, and his ruminating had Jamal sweating underneath his white lab coat. He turned away from the impatient corporate and financial types who'd rather treat scientific discovery as a sprint instead of a marathon.

Riley shrugged as if to tell him, "Who cares about them? You've got this!"

Jamal grinned, anchored by his longtime partner. "Arm doors." Even if he didn't fully succeed, he need only appease them with the scent of money. "Begin test three ninety-four."

"Doors armed." Riley pressed a button, and a light above the door turned red as a siren wailed briefly before shutting off.

Given the makeup of Conrad's cadre, this test was far more important than any other. He knew his team understood this, as he could feel the tension in the room among the vibrating hums of the system's startup procedures. He could sense the tightness in their faces and noticed their reserved movements. It was he and Conrad who had the most to lose in the event of a catastrophic failure. Such failure would be his burden, not theirs.

Anxiety would accompany each test for a feat none in the world had yet achieved. The tests opened gateways to the unknown, for an unfortunate price, but Jamal cared about his team. After a failure, he'd occasionally invite a member over for dinner to make sure they hadn't lost their drive. He had last dined with Dr. Lucius Raymond, the resident laser specialist. Lu's wife, Amy, had kept locking a stink-eye on Jamal throughout the meal and grumbled about the long hours. It was then that Lu revealed they wanted children but couldn't bear to move forward with it given the unpredictable work-life balance. The Raymonds' predicament had resonated with Jamal as he contended with his own thoughts of children, but over time it had become clear to him that each member of his team had postponed one life goal or another in their dedication to science. Some had sacrificed friendships or relationships, while others had lost or gained weight from the stresses of pursuing stable fusion. Despite it all, Jamal knew, none of them had lost hope in him.

"Set the final vacuum level," he said. "No pressure, team."

Laughter livened the control room. The simple joke had broken the cloud of negativity hovering over them. Their minds were locked on the present moment, and nothing else mattered.

"You've no doubt seen the crowd behind us…" Jamal's terse pronouncement turned heads. His team faced him. "We've spent five years building CETHER, the largest fusion reactor in the world. We've worked hard to break the smallest atoms by raising them to unimaginable temperatures. No matter what happens, you've done outstanding work, and I couldn't have asked for a better team, better partners, or better people." He nodded toward their moneyed observers. "Present company aside."

The glass rattled behind him. Conrad gestured to cut the crap. The manager was framed by crossed arms and deep scowls. They were done with waiting. Jamal refocused, somewhat shaken until he noticed the team's expressions had changed from impassive to resolute and determined. He knew they all had his back, that they believed in CET's creed more than the board members who'd signed off on it.

"So, let's show them a breakthrough!" Jamal had gained a burst of energy. "Let's show the world we work for more than CET. We work for everyone who wishes for power, for the plants and animals who wish for us to stop destroying their lives for the sake of clean water and selfish freedom. When this works—and it will—you'll be heroes. We have a power that rivals thermonuclear energy: the application of our joined minds."

The last ounce of anxiety fluttered away as heads bobbed in agreement amid courageous chuckles, but Jamal sought approval from the distinguished graduate above anyone else.

"You're awesome," Riley mouthed before facing her monitor screens. "Near vacuum, reached."

"Power the coils," Jamal ordered.

One of the techs slowly raised the slider at her terminal to maximum. The spooling power to the magnetic field coils hummed low. The room rumbled as the hum raised in pitch and volume then quieted into an almost inaudible whine.

"Is the B-field barrier secure?" Jamal asked.

"No plasma will breakthrough this field," Riley stammered.

"Charge lasers."

Dr. Raymond powered up an array of lasers one by one to avoid oversaturating the terminals. A low hum emitted throughout the protected control room.

"How're we looking, Riley?" Jamal asked.

"Balanced across all systems."

"Then it's time." He swallowed. "Insert fuel pellets and fire lasers on my mark."

Everyone went silent. As he observed the test, he listened to the beeping of terminals, the humming of machinery, and the clacking of keyboards. Jamal wondered if CET's management and potential investors had their faces glued to the glass, but he kept his eyes forward and prayed for favorable probability.

It seemed like every member of the team collectively held their breath like the audience in the still moment before the start of an orchestral performance.

"Mark."

A handful of pebble-sized fuel pellets filled with deuterium and tritium atoms were suctioned from the fuel ports into the vacuum. As the lasers clicked on, the pellets passed through the line of fire. At 100 million degrees, the outer atomic shell stripped away in a flash of ionic power that raised readings across every sensor to godlike levels. Free from the imprisonment of their electrons and filled with the heat of suns, the atoms evolved. At the edge of the torus, the soup of energized molecules swirled. They jetted faster around the reactor, as the show had just begun. A pair of energized ions slammed against each other, sending out a flash of awesome power visible by no human eye. And yet the atoms did not die. They evolved, fused together in a new helium form.

In less than a second, countless reactions of the same had occurred in a flickering display of flashing light, of innumerable fusions, of immense calculated power from very little fuel. The power of suns. The smell of money. The hope of freedom.

The team of scientists cheered as the power steadied. The observers clapped, high-fived, and shook hands. Mr. Conrad released his crossed arms and relaxed his face. The union of science and money had sustained fusion for more than thirty-one seconds. It was a new record for the fusion industry, but was it enough to keep the CETHER project going?

Jamal gripped the edge of the control console, tighter than before. While the others cheered, he stared through his reflection. The reactor showed no signs of malfunction, but his guard remained tightly wound in the absence of Riley's positivity and congratulations.

Riley's face contorted as she bounced between the two monitor screens displaying the sidewall temperatures. Over the past few years and over hundreds of tests, the same structure had withstood the small handful of fuel. The team had routinely performed X-ray examinations to check for microscopic structural imperfections, but over the past few years, slivers of the hottest soup had slammed against the metal barrier. Degradation was inevitable.

Jamal squinted through the protective glass as a pinprick of red flashed against the side of the reactor. The cheers of those in the room had been premature, as the flash grew against the sidewall and began to speckle. Plasma threatened to burst through the thick metal wall, threatened to break through the protective glass in a prismatic expulsion of destructive beauty. They had tried to contain the power of nature, but CETHER revolted.

Jamal locked onto Riley's wide and fearful eyes as bright streaks of plasma zigged across his sight. How could he see plasma streaking at the speed of light? But it was everywhere, piercing through the reactor room glass, swirling around Riley's cowering body, passing through the computer consoles.

Time slowed. Though he thought to slam his fist against the glass and lay into the red kill switch to disrupt everything, his body froze. The plasma, bright and hot, grew even brighter beside an ear-piercing whine.

#

Jamal blinked at the light from the living room ceiling fan and shook his head as the piercing whine died down.

Must have been dreaming, he thought.

The sound of rambunctious children pattered across his eardrums. Though he recognized the voices and knew in his core that he was their father, an odd feeling had detached him from reality. Through a fraction of his thoughts, he felt little more than a passenger within his body, burning against a sullen drive to fulfill his lost dream.

His son of seven years had dressed in Jamal's lab coat, a trail of dangling cloth behind him. "I am Reactor Man!" The child raised his small hands skyward, fingers curled like grasping claws.

His daughter of six and son of four giggled and swayed as they watched Reactor Man strutting about the living room. His oldest child, his daughter of fourteen, rolled her eyes as she tapped away on her phone.

His younger daughter sprang forward, her mother's rubber biosafe gloves reaching past her elbows. "I'm Wonder Weactor Woman!"

"That's not real!" her oldest brother teased.

The giggle bug had overtaken the younger son as he kicked away, sideways on the floor, rolling as his face reddened.

"Yeah, it is!" The younger daughter scowled and focused behind Jamal. "Right, Mummy?"

"Anything can happen." Riley leaned against the doorway, smiling wide. "You can be Wonder Weactor Woman if you want."

"See!"

"She's more powerful than Reactor Man." Riley smirked at Jamal.

Tendrils of plasma streams flickered across Jamal's sight, sent him dreaming of the past. He had long forgotten about CETHER and how he had failed to stabilize it. He had aborted the test in front of the investors, perhaps saving the lives of everyone in the lab. These big-time investors had come to observe the worst test—the one where the reactor casing had nearly been compromised. His decision to put safety first, to accept his failure, had cost him both his job and his dream. If his father could see his family now, however, would he have been proud of his choice? Another unanswered question...

If Jamal hadn't aborted the test, would it have succeeded? If the reactor had somehow stabilized, no one would have died. Their tests would have continued, and the world might now praise him for the gift of power: the end of oil, gas, drilling. But no. The wars still raged on overseas. Activists had upped their game and continued to siphon power from wealthier cities, sometimes provoking firefights with law enforcement. The completion of his lifelong dream would have changed the world insurmountably, but those dreams were gone now, replaced by the family he never had growing up, while others died for theirs.

"Where are you?" Riley laid her hand against Jamal's face.

"What?" He blinked and then focused on his family. Each of their faces was scrunched with concern and consternation. "Oh! Sorry."

The six-year-old laughed. "Daddy, sometimes... So weird."

"He spacing out a lot." The seven-year-old rubbed his eyes.

The giggle bug had thrown the four-year-old to the floor again, and he continued rolling and kicking. The commotion had grown too intense for the oldest child. She grumbled from the distractions and marched herself upstairs. Against her wishes, her younger sister attached herself to her big sister's hip as their footsteps bumped through the first-floor ceiling. So many balls of energy were hard to keep track of and couldn't be controlled, like atoms streaming through a reactor.

Jamal grinned anyway.

"Daddy's tired. Off to bed, boys." Riley flicked her hand, pulling the boys toward her as though she had mastered gravity.

"Aw, but it's only eight thirty."

"Yeah, Mum. Aw... Eight thirty?"

Riley rolled her eyes. "You can wake up early and watch your shows."

"*Battle Dragons!*" The two boys jumped and yelled, scampered upstairs ahead of Riley toward their bedroom.

She snickered at Jamal and chased after the kids.

Jamal got up from the couch. Although it seemed new to him at that moment, he followed a familiar bedtime routine. He locked the door and armed the security system, enveloping his home in a field that protected everyone within. He killed the main lights, and the red nightlights throughout the house blinked on. The kids would sometimes scramble downstairs late at night for snacks or juice boxes they weren't supposed to have. It was better to light their way than have them tumble. He finished his routine by brushing his teeth and donning his pajamas, and he happily slid under the covers of the spacious bed.

He could hear the commotion of his adventurous and hilarious children, fighting against the call to sleep. They too fought nature and sought comfort in choice, but nature had its own way. Living beings must sleep eventually. Jamal had learned many things the hard way, and his children would learn no differently. Each child, smart and heroic, would take on the world and perhaps carry Jamal and Riley's dream to new heights as scholars of the next generation. They could even develop the next CETHER for the good of humankind.

Riley entered the bedroom, glowing as she had always glowed.

"You're so great with them," Jamal said.

"We got lucky." She entered the bathroom. "I know we didn't plan on having children, given our career choices, but of all my regrets? They certainly aren't one."

She exited the bathroom, dressed in the shiniest nightgown. Even though they had four kids and had been happily married for fifteen years, Riley's figure still mesmerized Jamal. The nightgown flowed across her curves like water. After fifteen years, he looked upon her as though for the first time in his life he had truly seen not Riley the plasma impingement specialist but Riley the woman. Both were his trusted partners, but had she always been this beautiful or had motherhood contributed to her glow?

Riley slid under the covers and blushed once she caught Jamal's spellbound expression. "Why are you looking at me like that?"

He couldn't help but hold her face, kiss her lips, leaving her with a bright smile.

"Wow…" She touched her lips, flashing the scar on her hand from when she had touched the sun they attempted to control. "You haven't kissed me like that since… What was that for?"

"You're beautiful." He took her hand into his, knowing his negligence had caused her injury fifteen years back.

"Staring out into space. Staring deeply at me." She turned the lights off and slid farther under the covers, melting into him. "Seems your mind is untethered lately."

"Maybe." Jamal ran his fingers through her hair. "Seeing the kids in our clothes had me thinking about CETHER."

She looked up at him. "Are you okay?"

"No, I'm fine. No worries."

Maybe he did worry.

Something streamed and flashed through the dark room like photons married against ionic charges. Jamal traced it, determined it was probably a trick of the light.

"Are you here?" Riley prodded. "Sometimes I wish we hadn't stopped the reactor. I wish we would've seen what might have happened, what might've been. Sometimes I feel I ruined your dreams. I ignored protocol and entered the inner room. Standing so close to the escaping plasma made you smash CETHER's kill switch."

"What? No!" Jamal shook his head. His voice shuddered. "I'm so happy here."

The flicker waved from the corner of his eye as he faced the window. The moon had often shined through and brightened the bordered seal, but this light transformed into thin fractures glowing in plasmatic orange.

"What's that?" Riley sat up, gripping her hand. "No… I've seen this before."

Jamal's body had moved on its own, attracted to the window by CETHER's pull. He reached forward.

"Don't touch it." Riley reached for his wrist.

"I'm not." But Jamal's hand moved against his words in stride with his wishes.

"If that's what you want." Riley's scarred hand fell to the comforter. "I won't stop you."

Jamal loved his wife, loved his kids, but he needed answers to the sullen call in his heart.

The window shattered, sending speckles of orange plasma through each piece of glass, each a reflection of an alternative perspective. The plasma swirled throughout the room, growing in density, and reclaimed Jamal's perfect family life.

#

Camera shutters cracked against Jamal's ears. Like gongs, the sounds lingered deep within his bones. He shook his head to free himself from the dizzying sensation of the cocaine he had just taken, but he had grown accustomed to the feeling after fifteen years of self-medication.

He blinked, forming a fraction of clarity. Mr. Conrad spoke to the crowd, riled them up before Jamal took the stage. The shaking in Jamal's legs reminded him of Dr. Raymond at the start of a test sequence, even though Lu's lasers never failed. Riley, Lu, and eight others had died because Jamal cared more about his goals than the lives of his team members. The dinners he'd had with them were manipulative, stunts to keep them loyal, keep them working.

He patted his suit coat but knew they had taken away his flask before he entered the facility. His regular buzz dipped slowly toward socially acceptable as he heard his name ahead of a torrent of applause.

His boss scowled at him knowingly but shook his hand as they traded places.

Jamal swayed from the disorienting lights beaming down from the vaulted, white ceiling, reflecting from the polished floor patterned with indiscernible shapes and filled with gala-style round tables. It was a room meant for royalty, not an addict, a failed son, a failed friend.

Bright figures dimmed into a small crowd of well-dressed doctors, Nobel laureates, diplomats, aristocrats, military officers, governments officials, representatives from science organizations, and likely numerous news reporters and bloggers. All of them smiled up at him, but none of them knew what he had truly done to arrive at this time and place.

Nausea welled up as his buzz faded faster than he'd otherwise expected. He wondered how he had left his home, his wife and children, and arrived before this enthralled crowd. His life had changed as he held the small capsule of heavy water in his pocket, a component to fusion reactor fuel. The capsule helped him remember what it took to stand in front of the American Physics Society's annual conference and reception. The image of Riley's smiling face in his mind rekindled his courage. He released the capsule and gripped the edges of the podium, sending his nerves straight through to the grounded floor.

"People of Earth!" His voice seemed to strike at the hearts of the audience. He had no memory of writing or practicing a speech, but he knew it by heart as though he had rehearsed it while somewhat inebriated more often than he liked to admit over the past fifteen years. "At long last, we at CET have conquered the realms of imagination, surmounted the obstacles of our physical world, and tapped into the power of the sun."

So many words spewed in succession had built gas up in his stomach, so he paused and turned from the microphone to let it out slowly. He had the sense that he didn't know anyone in the audience very well, but he was sure they had heard the rumors. No doubt his current swagger tilted the scales toward the negative side of any of their perceptions of him.

"Twenty years," he said. "I began this journey with CET twenty years ago. We had quite a few setbacks at the beginning. Quite a few...casualties."

Casualties, he thought. *How appropriate to describe my research as a war on energy, fought by hardened soldiers and scientists alike. But soldiers signed on for death. None of my team enlisted to die. I had the power to press the kill switch, kill the dream.*

"But *I* am here. *We* are here to carry the torch for those who could not be, for those who paved the way for this new future."

Jamal's thoughts then turned to his team and what they had sacrificed even before their lives were taken by CETHER's miraculous catastrophe. He thought of their unfulfilled desires, their neglected friendships, their missed romantic connections. He thought of how no one could replace his partner in science, his other self, the woman he had not known he loved until it was too late.

"One test uncovered the key to stabilizing fusion," he told the crowd. "Not even a year later, CET developed a stabilized mini-CETHER, a twenty megawatt reactor!"

Jamal let the subdued energy of respectable people ride over him, but he couldn't prevent the wrench twisting in his gut over what had happened. The price of developing reliable fusion energy had been so terrible that he still hadn't recovered from it fifteen years later—still chopping lines by day, suckling bottles by night.

The crowd calmed.

"A new age of power beckons us toward a new age of life!" He faked a convincing smile. "CET is finally ready to distribute a family of fusion reactors throughout the world, varying in power outputs and size from the micro-CETHER to the five hundred megawatt CETHER Max!"

All powered by innocent souls, seethed in radioactive soup.

"And with help of governments everywhere, we aim to provide all people, all places with the means to bring light to darkness, warmth to the freezing, and freshness to the sweltering, to live in comfort where living has long been a struggle. We've found a way, but not just for me or you." He shook his head, raised his hands. "Fusion is for all!"

The applause roared louder than before in a wave that cleared Jamal's mind regarding who was in attendance: physics professors from his alma mater, counterparts who had traveled across the ocean from KSTAR, and Dr. Andre Basset, the chief scientist at ITER. Jamal couldn't blame Basset for resenting him, as CETHER had solidified fusion jobs across the world. Jamal should have been proud, but he didn't have Riley at his side. He had lost his confidant, the one person in his life with whom he wished he could share this moment.

Jamal shook the event coordinator's hand as he walked down the center aisle, waving to those he passed. CET had asked him to provide a brief speech so the world could see the face of their success.

Thoughts of escape pounded against his skull. He barreled into the men's room, locking the door. He exhaled. His mind had dammed his body's needs. The building stress of coming down and the rising heat of an arrhythmic heart punctured through his lips like plasma escaping a weakened cage, like a failed CETHER gearing to explode. The sadness, the pressure in his chest, increased because the walls around him now blocked out all expectations. A cold chill slithered down his back. His face dripped as his reflection spun across his eyes. Scrambling on the floor, he rolled down his sock to retrieve his only comfort. The bag of white gold was empty except for trace amounts. He licked his finger, dragged it through the inner surface of the bag, and collected as many atoms as he could before rubbing the coveted remnants across his gums.

If Riley were here, what would she say?

He stuffed the bag back into his sock. His body and mind were fooled into normalcy. He splashed water on his face, washed his hands, dried them. His eyes had reddened to a hue of emergency lights, but the reception continued, and Conrad had ordered him to be in attendance.

By the time Jamal returned, the gala tables had been removed, and several cocktail tables had been set up in the center of the room. A small jazz band wailed good vibes across it all. Riley had danced throughout college. Part of him wished to visualize her body spinning on the dance floor, but another part of him knew his soul couldn't bear it. Then he eyed his saving grace: an open bar in the far corner.

Gin and tonic in hand, Jamal turned. He froze as Conrad approached him with two flashes from his past: his rival, Dr. Basset, and Dr. Raymond's widow, Amy. He had hoped to avoid anyone he knew, hoped to slip through the rest of the reception with little conversation and a lot of alcohol. The three of them reached Jamal all smiles. After what he had done, why would they have any reason to smile at him? Did their smiles hide their pain? Had they somehow found happiness through their loss?

"Look who I found." Conrad presented Dr. Basset and Ms. Raymond, his Saturday suit making him look more relaxed than usual.

Amy laughed. "It was we who found you, Mr. Conrad."

"I guess you did." Conrad chuckled. "I need a drink." He escaped behind Jamal to the bar.

"And to think," Basset said, "that I turned down the position at CET. They had no plan and no vision—only cash. You certainly weren't top of the class, but you always knew how to develop a process to reach an answer."

Jamal ignored the backhanded compliment and sipped at his drink.

"I wanted it to be me, but it's fine," Basset continued. "Had *I* taken the job, we might not be here. CET succeeded because of you. Great job on CETHER, man. It's amazing what you've accomplished."

"Oh…" Jamal shook his hand. "Thanks, but if it weren't for you pushing the boundaries at ITER, Mr. Conrad wouldn't have pushed me so hard."

"Yes, well, push too hard and we risk losing something." He patted Jamal's shoulder and turned to line up for his own drink. "Hang in there."

Jamal clenched his teeth and downed half his drink, hoping it would make the next conversation more bearable.

"Hello, Dr. Jackson." Amy Raymond smiled joyfully but clutched her purse. "I don't know if you remember me. I'm—"

"Yes, of course I remember. Lu was such an amazing physicist."

"He did have a way with lasers." Her smile flickered. "Listen, Dr.—"

"Jamal is fine…"

"Jamal." She cleared her throat. "We—the widows and widowers—formed a support group shortly after it happened. At first, we hated you, hated CET, and we pinned their deaths on your negligence."

Jamal's heart raced as he recalled the court hearing: The People v. CET. The People had lost. They didn't stand a chance. He blamed and hated himself so much that he ended up anonymously paying off their court fees in full. If he'd had a support group of his own, maybe he wouldn't be spiraling out of control. He swallowed his drink as water pooled in his eyes.

"Yes, it's my fault. I know." The words slurred through his mouth so fast that he surprised her. "I can't say sorry enough. I can't—"

"It's okay," she whispered, smiling.

Why would she smile? If I pressed the kill switch, if I pulled the plug, they'd still be alive.

"Dealing with hatred is one of the first steps on the road to healing one's grief," she said. "If you still hate yourself, you're still grieving. We've moved past it. Look at all of this." She spread her hands. "You didn't lose our loved ones. You materialized their hopes and dreams! We all consider science a profession without hazard. You're not going to some Middle Eastern warzone, you know. But they fought to change the lives of everyone in this world. We didn't see it at first, but when you locked yourself away in CET's labs for years and when word of the prototype was leaked, we saw how the world reacted. The actions of you and your amazing team have changed the face of humankind. I hope you receive a Nobel Prize for your efforts."

Jamal's heart sank as he held onto a nearby cocktail table. Him? How could he, a reckless massacrer, receive such recognition? How could he be recognized as Earth's savior? He hated himself and fought between justification and self-deprecation every hour of every day over the past fifteen years. Perhaps the world was better now, but he still let ten amazing souls die a horrific death.

A soft hand grasped his shoulder. He looked up at Dr. Raymond's widow. She had the audacity to hug him tighter than he'd been hugged since Riley was alive. Then she let him be.

Sadness shook him with guilt. He had to go, had to escape farther than the restroom. His mind forced him upright, sent him lurking through the shadows of the event building until he busted through a set of side doors into the dark city streets. Cars waited along the venue's edge. He lumbered toward one and hopped in.

"First and Mary." His voice felt scratchy, so he cleared it.

When they drove off, the driver squinted at him in the reflection of the rear-view mirror. Jamal looked away through the dark window next to him.

"Hey," the driver said, "aren't you that energy guy…?"

Jamal continued looking at nothing in particular through the glass. "I'm sorry?"

"The energy guy! You're that famous fusion guy!"

"No, I'm not," Jamal said. *I'm a killer.*

The driver paused for a moment, watching Jamal through the mirror. He squinted again as he eased the car forward.

Jamal had used up his energy to rile the crowd, to satisfy CET, and he had nothing left to give. His body sat untethered to the seat, swaying as the car rolled across uneven asphalt and then a cobblestone bridge. The motion rocked him like calm waves on a sea, but even with his eyes fixed on the back of their lids the stream of plasma had returned.

"First and Mary, sir," the driver said.

Jamal stepped out of the car and slammed the door. "You can go."

"But we're in the middle of nowhere."

"Go!" He tossed the man all the cash in his wallet, far more than the ride's worth. Guilt money, a gift to someone more deserving of it than a man who'd kill for the sake of dead man's question, no matter what some widow or rival might say. They hadn't been there. They didn't have to stare ten deaths in the face as Jamal had.

Jamal swayed through the rows of stones as the car vanished into the growing mist of lightly falling rain. He had crossed this threshold so many times that his body now moved automatically. He kneeled before Dr. Riley Wilkinson's headstone. He kissed and then hugged Riley's stone before wrenching himself away toward the cemetery's exit.

Looking over the edge of the cobblestone bridge, his vision pulled in as his mind grasped the distance between him and the liquid metal river. His heart pounded as he gripped the heavy water pellet in one hand, the bag of empty promises in the other. His hands opened.

The pieces holding him together swirled around his hapless reflection, begging to alter his perspective once again. A hint of orange spiraled through the water, excited by the pellet and the bag of magic dust. The plasma had returned to claim him as it had claimed his friends and family.

"I am energy's martyr." Jamal smiled. "Just like Lu. Just like Riley. Like my father."

He hovered for a moment, defying gravity like a master of the physical world. His stomach churned as he descended, aimed steadily on the glowing doorway swirling around his reflection. The plasma streamed through the water, building in its disastrous torrent, engulfing him.

#

As the flashes died, Jamal locked onto Riley's wide eyes. He remembered it all: his fulfilled family life, his dream that changed the world. The same recognition was written all over Riley's face as she ran toward the inner room, retreading Jamal's fear. Would she shut CETHER down? Would he smash the kill switch, sacrificing years of work and a chance at world peace?

Riley smiled at him, eyes wet, then she disarmed the door against the most stringent of protocols. She ran into the room of flashing plasma and scrambled for the pile of metal plates and extra wires.

"Riley, what are you doing?" he yelled. "Get the hell out!"

She continued working, tears pouring down her face, connecting high-gauge wires from one plate to the next.

Dr. Raymond led eight others from the front row. All faced Jamal as his soldiers, prepared to vanquish the enemy at the cost of their lives. They joined the frontline, assisting Riley with the wires and plates. Had they all seen their futures as Jamal and Riley had? Did they *know* fusion and peace hung in the balance?

Jamal's heart pounded as he eyed the kill switch within the glass. He raised his hand, building energy for the crash. The rest of the team stood there and watched the others within the inner room. They each held a metal plate connected to wires.

Mr. Conrad entered, arms sprawled, face frozen into an expression of shock. His eyes cycled between CETHER, the metal plates, and the team. The man who Jamal had thought had no heart and only a love of winning and money, ran for the inner room. What did he think he could do? Save them by himself? It was a valiant effort, but the team wasn't on board with it. The master's students and the technicians grabbed hold of the clambering Conrad to stop his meddling.

Jamal swallowed the knot in his throat, eyeing the team members focused on him. He trembled with horror from the choice each of them had made. Any one of them could start the process, could dismantle CETHER, but they stood firm – feet planted and waiting. Their stilted expressions said, "We leave it in your hands. We trust you and your choice." Upon Riley's face was, "I want this for you."

The ten dedicated scientists in the inner room turned their backs to Jamal, plates facing CETHER's revolt. They marched forward like a phalanx, resolved to protect their commander.

Jamal broke down at the waste from the flashes of Riley in bed beside him and his children wearing oversized science gear. The pain of losing four beautiful children was so great that he broke open the kill box. The key to their lives was now free for him to press despite the glass shards lodged in his hand.

But what futures had they seen? Had they seen love from lost dreams and pain from dreams fulfilled? There were no words, only action as they slammed the metal pieces against CETHER's side.

CETHER's damaged wall interacted with Riley's pristine metal plates, merging enough to block microscopic imperfections. The wires between each plate amplified the electromagnetic field, a final push to keep the plasma from impinging against the metal shell. Riley specialized in metal interactions with plasma, but this test had reached levels beyond what anyone had analyzed. If she hadn't acted, if she had chosen not to fight, the machine would have failed along with Jamal's dreams.

As it happened, Jamal had finally pieced together Riley's goal was the same as his only because she loved him. Who was he to pull the plug on someone's love? He moved his hand from the kill switch and fell to his knees, bracing for the end.

A shockwave traveled through the ten scientists at lightning speed. Their bodies fell limp in an instant, glued to CETHER, which hummed as though contented.

S. C. Burns works as an astronautical engineer by day and delves into infinite universes by night. His studies in astronomy and engineering armed him with the power to conceptualize treacherous planets and advanced technologies. He writes to expose the awesomeness of space exploration and scientific discovery through worlds teeming with difficult choices.

Collusion

by David Richie

Part One: Catastrophe

"Anyone else having issues with their command codes?" Lieutenant Commander Davies slapped the side of the mobile command device.

"Percussive maintenance hasn't worked on Earth-Tech devices for at least 15 years, Bob." Lieutenant Franks, his watch commander, replied dryly. "Head down to see the IS team on Deck 27, probably just needs an update."

"100 Light Years from Earth, wormhole engines, and yet still bloody updates…" Davies muttered as he headed out of the door.

Zeek didn't look up from his work. He was frantically hunting for a fault in what looked like a navigation sensor. He guided nanobots to their target with interface gloves, hunting desperately for the issue on his VR unit. Alfred came out from the back room.

"Wassamadda?" Bob was never sure if Alfred's accent was the product of his alien biology, an affectation or genuinely how he had learned English. If it was the latter he must have learned the language from watching James Cagney and Humphrey Bogart films. Bob held up his MCD.

"Command Codes aren't being accepted. Franks thought it might need an update."

"Franks did, did he, eh? Ain't no update due, so it ain't dat."

"Leave the device." Zeek didn't stop working. Something in his tone seemed colder than usual to Bob.

"I need it for my work."

"Tell Franks I told you to leave it, he'll give you another task." Zeek did look up this time and pushed his VR unit out the way. "Just leave it."

Bob popped it down on the desk and left with a nod. Not the best exchange he'd had with the tech team, normally they were a lot more helpful to him.

The corridors were quiet on his way back to his station, usually he'd expect to see the command staff around, he hadn't come across any of them today, odd.

"Where's your MCD?" Franks asked as soon as he arrived back.

"Zeek told me to leave it, and said I had to ask you for other duties."

"Did he, okay," he got out his own MCD and scrolled through the task list. As he looked for something he could get Davies doing, Commander Forsyth arrived. She nodded at Franks and turned to Davies.

"Lieutenant Commander, with me please."

"Ma'am, the duty shift?" Franks asked.

"Rearrange it Lieutenant Commander, Captain's orders." Forsyth was normally one of the warmest officers on the crew, as Second Officer she was in charge of a wide range of matters including staff morale. She left immediately, knowing Davies would follow and not looking back or slowing to explain.

"Ma'am?" Davies asked, jogging slightly to catch up.

"With me." Her tone made it clear that there was nothing more forthcoming. Bob's heart started to race. What could he have done?

Then it hit him.

But it couldn't be that. If it was that then, he stopped the thought, keep it out of mind, if you don't think about it then it never happened. They had yet to encounter a species that could read minds but that didn't stop the old suspicion that those around you could hear your thoughts if they were too loud.

The Briefing Room was in secure mode. The doors opened and inside sat the most senior crew and an officer, an Admiral, he didn't recognise. The order of seating was odd, the Admiral sat at the top of the table and instead of being flanked by the Captain and the First Officer it was Commander Hicks, the Head of Security who took up the seat on the other side. Forsyth indicated to the chair opposite the Admiral and Davies sat.

Fight, flight or freeze. They looked at him and could see he was stuck in the loop, adrenaline pumping, the fear of the unknown. Skin clammy, heart pounding, digestion shut down, shaking with a surge of hormones. Fight, flight or freeze. Higher brain functions shut down and pain dialled to the lowest setting. Training kicked in and Davies breathed through it, dissipated. Zeek entered, handed the MCD to the Admiral and whispered in her ear. Zeek left as quickly as he arrived. Davies realised he had stopped breathing and fought to start it again.

The walls, the walls were wrong. He had been in this room hundreds of times but he just realised it, the walls were wrong. The room was cuboid, but it was at the edge of the shipe, a spherical ship. Why had he never noticed that, it must be offset in. The cuboid walls, like a long tunnel converging to a vanishing pinpoint as they close in and close in. Breathing walls.

Freeze it is then.

Breathe.

The senior officers patiently waited. Every single one of them had been through 8 years of training and had at least 20 years of experience as officers on Tunnel Ships. They knew how to handle a crew, they knew when there was no point engaging. Eventually the Admiral slid an armoured tactical MCD to Hicks.

Hicks was huge. Despite having grown up on a high gravity planet he still managed to reach nearly 180cm tall but he looked nearly as wide again. Although most of the work of Head of Security was tactical it was very clear that Hicks was equally as capable physically.

Hicks was as close to a friend that Bob had on the ship.

'Was', it seemed, was the right word. This wasn't his friend walking towards him, he was being stalked by the Head of Security. Hicks' eyes never left him and he slammed the device down in front of Bob and walked away in silence.

"Review the device please," the Admiral's voice was silky smooth, professional, neutral. Everyone else either glared or avoided Davies' pleading looks, the Admiral just smiled. It was far from a warm smile but it was a welcome island.

He picked it up and scrolled.

The smile wasn't an island, it wasn't the security of even a life raft. The smile was that of a shark. No need to be rude, no need to be aggressive, the prey was caught so why make things any more unpleasant than they needed to be.

"I have only one question planned. If you answer one way this meeting immediately ends. If you answer another we may have a lot to follow up on."

Davies nodded, then mumbled.

"I sent them."

"Thank you for admitting to that, it saves us a lot of work."

"But I want to…" The admiral raised her hand and the smile dropped.

"Excuses or reasons will be dealt with elsewhere." The Admiral placed her hands on the desk and looked straight at Davies. "Lieutenant Commander Robert Davies you are found guilty of gross misconduct and as such are immediately dismissed from service. You are stripped of all rank, all privileges and all benefits. We are responsible for transporting you and your personal effects to the most appropriate Earth Colony," she checked another MCD in front of her, "ahh, that would be Earth itself for you, correct?"

"Yes."

"My ship is heading there. I will have quarters assigned to you. You will not be confined to the quarters but there will be nothing else on board you can access. You will have civilian access to the ship's systems but will not be permitted to use even the civilian communication software. You can therefore have entertainment and food. Hicks will take you there immediately."

"But my things, my friends." Davies looked desperately at the Admiral but found no sympathy, no island any more. The look that came back was clear, he should be happy with what he had.

"Your things have already been packed. It is best that you do not communicate with anyone onboard, we will need to investigate if anyone else is involved."

"There is nothing to be involved with, nobody else did anything. I wasn't betraying," Davies was drowned out as the Admiral raised her voice.

"You'll excuse me if I don't take your word for it, and as for your intent, well, as I say, others will discuss that with you. It doesn't matter to me, the outcome is still betrayal. Dismissed. Please change into civilian clothes when you arrive on my ship and leave the uniform outside the room for destruction."

Part Two: Aftermath

Alone.

The journey was not long, relatively speaking. The Admiral's ship was capable of creating a wormhole to Earth that would make the journey in a matter of hours but the Admiral was a busy woman and had a number of stops to make along the way. Nobody came to see him. He had been assured that the whole incident had been dealt with privately but the only time he left his cabin he felt everyone looking.

Real or paranoia, he didn't know or care. Every stare made him flashback to his actions. He felt naked beneath their gazes and he swore the security devices in the ceiling tracked him.

Alone but not alone. Silence was an enemy. Silence led to thought, thought led to the spiral of recrimination and regret. All the people he would never speak to again or could never face. The family he had let down so badly. What would he tell them? What could he tell them? Would they let him explain? Was there any acceptable explanation? Would it be made public, would everyone know?

Why? Why did he do it? Why did he send them?

One simple thought came over and over. I would not do it again. If time travel could have been willed into existence then his regret would have created it.

Books required more concentration than he had. Films were hard to follow but they would sometimes tire him enough for fitful sleep. Cartoons though. He couldn't laugh but they produced a barrier in his mind, cartoons helped him reach a zen state of non-thought. Two hundred year old images that had been painstakingly painted by hand of a rabbit, a mouse hunting a cat, a duck, and so many more helped him to just exist. Living was too hard, existence let time pass without him needing to be part of it.

He kept the light at the lowest level and lived on the sofa. If it hadn't been for the cartoons he may have completely gone over the edge. For now he rocked, asked himself why over and over, and scratched his arm. Everything itched, his whole body just wanted to explode. He shook, felt trapped, couldn't breath but couldn't react. If the cartoons hadn't pinned him to the spot he was sure that he would be raving, howling at the stars, scratching at the walls and hurting himself properly. Instead he scratches, just a little, and a little more. It doesn't feel like it should, it doesn't despite the blood, really feel of anything, he scratches on.

He had no idea how long he had sat alone in the dark. Sometimes he ate, not often. Discarded plates and cups littered the cabin but there should have been so much more. It had actually been 16 days that had passed when the door chimed. The visitor didn't wait for an invitation and came in.

"Jesus." It was a tall man that Davies didn't know, a Lieutenant, possibly, it was too dark to see properly. "Civilian Davies. You are hereby informed that an investigative panel will convene tomorrow at oh-nine-hundred hours in a private room. You will be escorted there at oh-eight-fifty tomorrow. In the meantime tidy this shit up and have a shower."

The officer left.

"This hearing is voluntary. If you refuse to comply you will be transported to Earth and our investigations will continue, we may have to involve Earth-Fleet security or other law enforcement as necessary. If you comply we may still involve them but if we are satisfied then this may all end today. We are in orbit of Earth."

His cabin didn't have any windows, not surprising in a sphere, only the senior staff, honored visitors and various formal or recreational spaces did have a view out. This room was not one of them. It was some form of secondary briefing room that looked neglected. The corridor it was on, in fact the whole deck, as far as he could tell, was in mothballs. This wasn't odd in itself, Earth-Tech built its ships with massive redundancy and multiplatform capacity, at any one time only around 30% of the usable space was in active service. What was unusual was to utilise a room like this within a deadspace.

The desk this time was circular, the space was cold and almost as dark as he had kept his cabin. Three men, not wearing uniforms, sat opposite him. Outside the door a guard waited to be called. The middle man spoke again.

"Earth-Fleet has concluded that you were acting alone. They believe that they have uncovered the full extent of your treachery too, that is their business. They are concerned with the what. our's is the why."

"This hearing is to find out if you are what we think you are," the man to the left sneered, "traitor or idiot?"

"Shall we begin?" The man on the right asked quietly.

He had no idea how long it went on. With the long-sleeved shirt he had chosen for the occasion he couldn't access his arms so the sensitive skin on the backs of his hands took the brunt of it. The questions didn't ever seem to stop, each answer was dissected and rejected until it had been taken to pieces over and over. Every single line he had written was studied in exquisite detail.

Tears came, he had no excuses, no reasons, no escape. He simply had done it. It seemed that the questions would never end, and then they did.

"Idiot it is then." The man on the left said cruelly. "Your biggest lie was to the Admiral, 'what about my friends?' It is clear you have none, you isolated yourself, unable to cope with deep space exploration since your divorce you sought a friend. Your pathetic story about a gradual deepening of a relationship, your need to impress, it all fits."

"You were selected, targetted, and then played." the person on the right said, "you were led out onto a ledge and left there, your friendship became more important than anything else."

"But still," the voice in the middle, "still, you betrayed the locations of wormhole entrances, movements of the fleet and you endangered the lives of tens of thousands. You are guilty of an act that can only be described as collusion with the enemy."

"All because you thought it would get you laid," said the voice on the left.

"And because you were in the middle of a sustained breakdown," added the voice on the right

"Our biggest sticking point wasn't so much that you shared the information, that was bad but you had been manipulated. The real issue is that you continued your act of collusion even after you suspected that all was not as it seemed. Your mental illness at that time made you double down and share information that had not been asked for." The voice in the middle, clearly the leader was scornful but had a hint of empathy. "No further charges will be brought. We do not want there to be public knowledge of such a breach. We have moved our ships, we are creating new wormholes and it is imperative that we continue to have the confidence of the people. You will not see law enforcement and your record is clear but you will fail any enhanced security checks, should you need one, you can never contact anyone from the fleet again, and you will get no reference. We very strongly urge you to get some mental health support."

"How do I explain a gap of 15 years in my work experience?"

"That is your problem," growled the person on the left, "you get your apartment for life. You get the living wage. If you want to get a challenge, improve yourself, whatever, it is up to you."

"You will be taken directly to a transport, your belongings have been packed for you."

Bob's first few weeks on Earth were some of the worst he had ever endured. The apartment they had arranged for him was in a nice neighbourhood, it was well appointed and thanks to the government having made the global transport tube network free whilst he was away, he could go anywhere on the planet in less than an hour. He couldn't afford big luxuries but could save for them. His standard of living would have made anyone before the twenty second century green with envy.

But he had seen the stars. He had walked on alien worlds. He had clung to the outside of an Earth-Tech Tunnel Ship as it barrelled uncontrollably, cutting a new wormhole through unexplored space. One hand clamped to the machine, desperately trying to oppose the forces at play, the other repairing the reality shield that prevented them from becoming pure energy and part of the wormhole itself. He had killed with his bare hands and with ranged weapons. He had assisted others to save lives by the millions.

All of that was gone. 8 years of training, 15 years of service. When he looked out of his window at night the Milky Way seemed to taunt him, so close he could almost touch it, yet shut off from him forever. Round and round thoughts came and troubled him. Every action, every way he had been manipulated. He was convinced that noises in the corridor were either his former employers coming to give him his job back, or to tell him they'd changed their mind and were pressing charges; he didn't know which idea scared him more.

The rocking returned. Isolation, recrimination, the full weight of what he knew were crimes. He was the worst person in the world. He didn't deserve the humanity he had been shown. All these luxuries, he should be dead or imprisoned.

Part Three: Reflection

He didn't hear the knock. He wasn't aware of the door opening. He sat staring at a blank screen, the same way he had for days, just rocking. The gasp of his ex-wife behind him should have been a shock but instead it was just one more thing to worry about, he pulled the covers over himself and curled up to be as small as possible.

"Stacey, go outside please." Brian was here too, her husband, of course he was.

"Brian, look at him."

"Stacey, go, just for a minute or two."

She left, Brian sat next to Bob (causing him to retreat into the corner even more) and sighed.

"She has never stopped loving you. I am okay with that as I know she never wants you back. The thing is, that she does love you, so that means she cares, which means I have to. Now I've never disliked you, in fact until you started to lock yourself away from everyone after the wedding, I thought we might end up as friends." He pulled the blanket down and ignored the whimpering it caused. "This is what is going to happen. You will go and shower now, with the door unlocked. I will find clean clothes for you. Stacey will make coffee and a snack for us all if you have anything in, or just use the processor if you don't. We will then talk. We will listen. You will tell us it all."

"Can't."

"I wasn't asking, Bob. I am telling you what will happen. It can be pleasant or I can drag you in there and wash you myself. We will sit outside, none of the other balconies on this side could overhear us. It'll be nicer to talk in the open air."

The shower, he had to admit, was wonderful. He always enjoyed washing but could never be bothered to get round to it that often any more. Shamefully he dressed and slumped out to the balcony. The coffee was nice, the food made a good ornament for his plate.

"You are out of the Earth-Fleet, we know that. I'm guessing you're no longer even employed by Earth-Tech. In your own time, all of it. We are your friends. Stacey loves you and I love her, we are here for you regardless. We may not like you for a while, we may need some space but we will still always be here. Right now we are assuming you got someone killed or something like that. Take it from the top in your own time."

Bob stared out over the city. He hadn't realised that he could see the railway museum from the balcony. Swindon, the unlikely home of international space flight. He was thankful that the Earth-Tech building was behind his, he never needed to look at it.

Slowly he started his sad tale. How lonely he had been, how unworthy he had felt to have any relationship. Stacey looked to Brian who smiled supportively at her 'not your fault' he mouthed back silently. Bob laid out his spiralling symptoms and how he contained them by being extra friendly and cooperative at work, the closest to a friend being Hicks. He detailed how old issues, childhood issues became magnified and that abuse that he thought he had long-since overcome dominated his psyche.

He had seen the doctor and was on powerful antidepressant and mood suppressing drugs. Sat alone in this apartment the drugs had come to mind a lot. He searched not for excuses but for possible reasons. Both of these had high incidences of lowered inhibitions amongst their listed side effects. Both were known to potentially magnify feelings of weakness and isolation in some. He had been like that, he didn't see it until now, when he was clean, but it was clear. They made it easier to cope but it was all a lie, just like everything the woman he'd met on the Rema trading post had ever said to him, a lie.

Everything came out. His manipulation, his response, how pathetic he was. How he had betrayed the human race. How he was not worth their sympathy. It was clear that he was not making excuses, not blaming anyone or anything but himself, he was just looking for reasons why he would do something so awful. He then asked them to leave, he understood that they couldn't be associated with him, he knew they were sorry they asked, please could they leave without saying anything, he was saying enough in his own head for everyone.

"Saying too much, you mean." Brian said firmly. He saw Stacey roll her eyes and realised what he had said. "Sorry, no, wait, I don't mean that, I mean you are saying too much in your head. You did something wrong, very wrong but it is not the worst thing in the universe. I deal with people who leak information, much more valuable information, for profit. People who deliberately seek to cause harm to others, or are utterly indifferent to that. You," he looked to Stacey again and silently mouthed 'sorry' in advance, "are really not that big a deal. A blip, on the scumbag scale you barely get off the X axis compared to what I see."

Stacey placed her hand on Bob's arm. Somehow he managed not to recoil.

"What my husband is trying to say in his own fashion is that you are not scum, not evil. You did more than make a mistake, yes, but you did not actively seek to cause harm." Bob started to speak but she squeezed his arm. "Listen for a minute. You have hit the nail on the head. It isn't an excuse and you need to accept that. The only way forward for you is to fix yourself. Part of what drove us apart, and I'm sorry to say this, is your need for external approval, you needed to please me and tried to put others before yourself all the time. You set yourself impossible standards and fell to pieces when you didn't reach them. Hell, Greta said to me that you almost seemed to go along with the affair because you just didn't want to let her down after your flirting had gotten a reaction. I can believe that. You pour on the charm and get locked. You don't like to pass up opportunities because you fear you are unworthy and may never get another. You need to please others to validate yourself."

"When did you become a therapist?" Bob said with a weak smile.

"She married someone on course to be a Tunnel Ship Captain, then one of the top civilian security officers on Earth, she has always needed to be a therapist." Brian said, blowing her a kiss.

"If I'm wrong, tell me, either of you." Brian and Bob looked at each other with a degree of fear and just shrugged. "Bob, you need to sort your life out, learn to love yourself again, if you ever have. Opportunities will come, take them but don't be afraid to say no if they aren't right. Brian is going to visit you everyday."

"I am?"

"You wanted a workout partner." Brian looked at Bob, then at himself, then back to Stacey. "Don't make me say it again." Brian shrugged. "I will look for some jobs that don't need references or don't care if you don't have them. I might grease some wheels. It'll just be basic stuff, teaching, or tech repair. You get a few of them under your belt and they become your references. Did they tell you the story they were using?"

"Burn out."

"That is a little on the nose, does allow them to ask officers not to contact you though. I'll put feelers out but I won't do anything for a week or two."

"Don't suppose you need pilots or engineer's, Brian?"

"We do but it sounds like you'd fail the Security Checks. I will keep an ear out just in case anything suitable comes up."

"You are up now. One day at a time. Have you left the apartment at all?" Stacey was all business now, more of a mother than former lover.

"No, I tried to go to the shops but I found it too overwhelming so I've been ordering in or processing."

"You promised to take me to Sri Lanka."

"I did, I hear it is paradise."

"It is, Brian and I went. There are a few global network points on the island. Give me a second." She flicked through menus on her wrist and made a selection. "The dawn train from Badulla to Kandy will be leaving in about two hours. You can be in Badulla in 20 minutes from the hub at the end of the street. According to what I've read it is a 15 minute Tuk Tuk journey from there to the train. They've switched from the Diesel-Electric train back to a classic steam engine to enhance the experience further. It is an eight hour journey up to Ella and the hub for the global network is right by the train station."

"I spend all day sat down, it hasn't been fun."

"Shut up and listen. This is the most beautiful train journey in the world. I don't care what others think. Look out of the windows the whole way. They do a basic ramen noodle lunch but I've arranged for an upgrade so you will get string hoppers for breakfast and rice and curry for lunch instead, as well as all the tea you can drink. Your carriage has a little outside seating area at the front, feel free to use it, smell the air, enjoy the sights."

"I don't think I can." The idea of leaving the house was terrifying to him. Brian checked his wrist, typed madly and nodded to Stacey when he was done.

"We loved the journey. It is exactly what you enjoy. You've never seen or been part of the culture of Sri Lanka or that whole region at all. It will literally be like an exploration."

"I've lost that Stace, I don't think I can."

"We have booked the carriage behind you, Brian has re-arranged his day."

"Which did not take a lot of persuasion, it is an amazing trip."

Part Four: Recovery

It was amazing.

It turns out that Stacey was being literal, she had completely booked out two carriages which allowed Bob to relax about how crazy he felt. Every now and then he would go back in to speak to the two of them about the ever-changing views but, on the whole, he just marvelled at them. The track turned a corner and a valley of jungle was laid out below on one side with European-style woodland on the other. Tunnels seemed like wormholes taking the train to strange new locations and habitats. Tea plantations give way to vegetable gardens, which in turn become scrubland. The train endlessly slowly climbed whilst snaking around the hills and mountains that it ascended. If Stacey had intended to show him that there were still wonders to explore on Earth she had succeeded in dramatic fashion.

As they approached Kandy, Bob felt a sinking feeling in his gut, he didn't want it to be over. Brian arrived and sat next to him as if he'd just read his mind.

"Tomorrow I'll arrive at 6am to get you. We'll take the global network back to Sri Lanka and our exercise will blow your mind."

Sigiriya was mind blowing. An enormous, impossibly ancient rock with the ruins of a palace on top and formal water gardens laid out below. Feats of engineering so old it seemed unreal. The climb up the stairs, jogging in places, was tough, especially as the sun started to rise, but the view from the top made it all worthwhile. He hadn't magically recovered in two days thanks to Stacey and Brian, but it had been a hell of a kickstart for him.

Every day without fail Brian arrived and they went somewhere amazing to run or workout. They had the whole planet to play in. The world that had felt like a trap, a tiny pale blue dot of a prison, became huge to him. He felt like they could do this forever and never see it all. Why did people even need to leave the planet?

Then he looked to the stars and remembered.

"How has work been?" Brian asked as they jogged up Jebel Hafeet. The mountain's steep roads were only ever used by joggers or cyclists now, especially as there were global hubs at both the top and the bottom of it.

"The same."

"How long has this one been?"

"Six months. They've promoted me twice and keep trying to get me to go for the regional manager job."

"Why don't you?"

"It's tech work, everything I've done so far has been back office, next step up requires a security check."

"Ahh, but surely they aren't going to be requesting an actual security check, it will be just criminal records and the divergent behaviour register."

"I can't be sure, besides, it isn't what I want to do. I've had three jobs for a reasonable amount of time since coming back to Earth, nobody is asking to see my Earth-Fleet service record any more. I've shown me accepting anything initially and then the last few jobs look like me acquiring new skills or testing the water in different fields." He stopped talking for a moment as they jogged on. It had been a lot to say at once. The air was just thinning a little but enough for him to notice as he jogged up a very steep road whilst trying to talk.

"What is it you want to do?" Brian asked after a few more turns in the road.

"I'm still not clear. Since I arrived I've improved their efficiency, instigated new procedures and policies and increased their profitability. It was supposed to just be a two week placement from the agency helping with a backlog of repairs to decommissioned Earth-Tech devices but I can't help coming up with ideas."

They jogged in silence for a little while until finally reaching the summit. Both slowed down and walked the perimeter fence, taking in the views from all sides.

"Normally people with your training settle off planet after longer service, many join other companies to continue as senior officers for some of the haulage or security firms out there. Those who don't make it often wash out before getting your experience, many of those simply return to Earth to just exist."

"Maybe you and Stacey should visit all of them, a lot of skill going to waste."

"You joke but there is enough to make a living off of, if someone could figure out how."

"How do you mean?"

"I'm really not sure but as you've shown you can pretty much fill in and excel anywhere. What was the last place? Something in farming, right?"

"Close enough." They looked out over the desert and rocks.

"And you made it so efficient that your job there wasn't needed."

"Heh, yeah." He smiled, it was rare to see but gradually becoming more frequent. "The old me would grab this and run with it, create a team of problem solvers or find a private company willing to take a risk to start their own exploration division. I like leading, I'm good at it but I don't need to do it any more. I don't need to prove myself, currently I see it as just doing a good job. Half the stuff I do nobody notices."

They walked to the network hub.

"I'll keep looking all the same. Stacey wants to know if you're coming round for dinner on Saturday?"

"She hasn't got another friend to introduce me to has she?"

"Man, I'm staying outta that." They both laughed. "It does sound like you need something that challenges you."

"Are you telling me something about my blind date?" Brian thumped him gently as their queue moved forward.

"I'm serious, you need something with challenge and variety. Like you said you don't need to strive for the position or the wealth."

"Wealth would be nice."

"Man, I see you everyday. You've yet to spend a single cent you've earned above your basic living wage."

"I suppose, I suppose. I'll think about it some more."

"Saturday?"

"Why don't you tell her I promised to let you know tomorrow?"

"Are you trying to break us up?"

"Okay, okay, Saturday."

Part Five: Rebirth

"Well, what do you think?" Stacey had stopped even trying to be subtle in her matchmaking duties. She pounced on Bob as soon as he brought the empty plates into the kitchen. Bob, on the other hand, was less thrilled.

"She knows," he replied coldly. He had managed to stay polite and had avoided having a panic attack at the table but his heart was racing so hard he could hear it. It was all he could do not to throw the plates at his ex-wife. He put them down with exaggerated care. "Tell her I felt sick. Tell Brian not to bother with tomorrow." He turned to leave.

"Bob, we didn't say anything to her."

"Bullshit."

"Not initially, look, she works in the emergency relief sector. She gets a lot of trouble so she has taken to running a security check on people she meets. We didn't know. She was a little annoyed at us so I explained it to her, she accepted and still wanted to meet you."

"Dance monkey, dance. Watch the pitiful fool who let himself get so sick he betrayed his people."

"No. Watch the brave man overcoming his trauma to use the skills he has whilst healing himself." Becky's voice was smooth as silk. She lent against the door frame drink in hand undressing Bob with her eyes. "Would you recognise the symptoms of a breakdown again? Would you be able to talk to someone now about any other issues that come up? Are you confident enough in your decisions to not seek approval for them?"

"That is a lot of questions."

Stacey put down her towel and squeezed past Becky without a word.

"They are all asking the same thing."

"Have I learned from my mistakes? Absolutely. Have I tried to change how I live because of it? Definitely. Am I there yet? Not at all. Would I let it happen again? I'd like to say no, but I think it would depend on the support I have around me."

"Good enough for me." Becky didn't so much walk across the room as gently flow in an undulating motion. She linked arms with Bob and gently pulled him back to the other room. "I have to be careful. Agree to tell me how you are feeling, be honest with me at all times and I think I've got something for you." Bob stopped and pulled his arm away.

"You are stunning but I am confused here. It sounds like you are offering me a job, and are discussing a relationship. After all I've been through, all I've done do you really think this is in the best possible taste?"

"Honey, I don't care. I see so few people I can trust in either capacity. Let me tell you a bit more about what I do and what we plan to do and you might see why. As far as a relationship goes, it would be nice but isn't a dealbreaker. I've seen how you are with Stacey and Brian though, I'm convinced that we could still work together if it didn't work out."

"You are insanely forward."

"I have to be."

"I'm not sure that I need," he indicated up and down her body, "this in my life right now. Sexy boss lady I desperately need to please, it is the opposite of the medicine I should be taking."

"Bullshit. You recognise it. If it helps I'm talking about offering you a role as an equal partner and most of the time I'll be covered in grease and gore."

"I feel like if I take your arm again now I'm admitting to some weird kink about dirty ladies." She laughed and grabbed him.

"Let me get this straight, none of your staff gets paid?" Brian asked incredulously. Bob felt it was a mix of surprise and a touch of drama to remind Bob of their conversation a few days before.

"We cover expenses, have top of the line medical cover, our processors are Earth-Tech top spec models and if we have shore leave on an alien world we often negotiate reasonable sums of local currency to allow our crew to enjoy the culture. All that said, nobody gets paid. The central government agrees to maintain our apartments on Earth and to continue to pay our basic living wage as if we were on-planet, this can actually help a number of our crew to appear quite well off as they have so few opportunities to spend their money."

"Space travel is expensive. Governments gave it up centuries ago. How do you do it?"

"We live on the scraps. Decommissioned vessels, discarded tech, discarded crew." She took a sip and stared at Bob. "We do the jobs that Earth-Fleet won't touch and they pay us in technology, equipment and, occasionally, money. Central government supplies us with the medical kit we need along with a more regular supply of cash that is often eaten up by repairs or bribes. Then we have charity donations on top."

"Do you use the existing wormhole network?"

"We can't afford the sorts of vehicles that cut their own. Our ships are mostly just jumpers. We have, however, just acquired a new vessel from Earth-Fleet. We are going to make it our flagship and possibly use it as a hub to deploy some of our other vessels from."

"What is it?"

"Mark 7 Tunnel Ship."

"Believe me now?" It was the first time Bob had been in space for nearly two years, the jumper shuttle had taken longer to get them into the orbit of the Moon than the global network took to get him to Japan, longer than a wormhole journey to hundreds of the nearest star systems. In the bow window the ship loomed, it seemed impossibly big from this angle. The jumper shuttle was ovoid, with the tapering tail behind them. Earth-Fleet deployed vessels like this to explore planets or to drop off crew to side missions further along a wormhole corridor. Few were capable of opening a wormhole on their own but these had been adapted to. What lay before him was something very different.

His heart pounded at the sight of the ship. Fear, panic, terror. Becky looked over to him, worried.

"What is it? Be honest." Bob turned away and sat facing into the observation room, as if he could will the vessel away.

"Panic," he said quietly. "Fear of discovery, rat in a trap, don't feel worthy, shame, lots of things I'm struggling to process."

"What does your training and experience tell you to do?"

"Process, observe, analyse."

"Do it then." Bob slowly turned round, remaining seated. He tried to view the ship as an object of study rather than a symbol of failure.

"The vessel is spherical as with all true tunnel ships, being a Mark 7 it is the first to lack any ring around the sphere. The vessel is considerably smaller than the Mark 23 I served on, very little redundancy built in. The missile ports appear to have been replaced by additional docking rings and the weapons array has been updated to the same emitters as a Mark 23 but in a substantially reduced number. It seems as if you've added ablative armour and energy shield emitters from a range of species, and it is white rather than conventional Earth-Fleet grey."

"We've gotten agreement from all the space-faring races for a white ship with a red cross to be considered a noncombatant, there is an ID tag to go along with that. They've agreed on a maximum defensive array of energy weapons and they all contributed defensive technology." On the surface of the ship robots started to paint their own red cross. "A number of different races will be using the same guidance for their disaster relief ships."

"It's huge."

"I thought you said it was small?"

"Compared to what I was on, but that was too big to get your head around, like a moon or something. I've never stopped to look, my training didn't really permit it. They are enormous ships."

"With a lot that can go wrong."

"Do you need an engineer? Is that it?"

"I need an engineer, a training officer, a tactical consultant, an operations manager and a Captain. What I have is you."

Bob turned away and looked at the ground. Suddenly her words hit home.

"Say that again?"

"It is your ship. I run the rescue ops on the planets or to crippled vessels; with your advice, and you run the ship."

"Becky, I can't even look at it. God knows what I'll be like when we go inside. Captain? What crew do I have? It takes 8 years to train an officer to serve on one of these, I'm guessing I don't have that long."

"You have a month, the time that they've estimated the refit will take and you may lose some of the crew to rescue missions in that time. It takes 8 years to train someone to command one of these, to be able to operate every system on it as well as to lead a crew. It takes 8 years to indoctrinate people with a sense of purpose and a belief in the great Earth-Tech company and how this adventure they take will turn a profit for them. Your crew are all experienced on civilian or rescue vessels."

"They are also volunteers, Beck. How the hell do you order someone around who is only there because they want to help? How do you tell them off?"

"Do you never ask for volunteers for missions? For projects? Have you seriously not been trained for similar things?"

"I suppose, it is just everyone I've worked with before knew everything I did, we were a team, cogs in a machine."

"And being a cog broke you. You know more about this hunk of junk than anyone onboard it now. You know the right way everything is done but you won't have the tools, the back up, the additional crew or kit. You have to find new solutions."

"Even the smallest thing is going to be a challenge."

"Are you afraid of a challenge?"

"Every single day will be unpredictable and ever-changing."

"And?"

Part Six: Redemption

"It is going to take six days following the network, Madam Director. We can be packed with all we need to relieve the crisis within the hour but by the time we get there we might as well just pack tools to dig graves." Ga'Tag was an Ungan, a very humanoid alien who spoke English perfectly. His species were known for their ability to process complex issues quickly, the average Ungan being faster than all but the most highly trained and experienced humans. The delay in human processing, however, was both a problem and an advantage; it was their imagination.

"We will go directly, wormhole cutting will double the travel time for the distance but it will take no more than 12 hours." Bob looked at the star maps on the holographic display, then at Ga'Tag. "Prepare the equipment, get any additional vessels you need onboard."

"Captain, you can read a star chart as well as I. The direct route goes through highly disruptive space, we would be subject to the influence of at least 5 major gravitational disturbances, 3 of those are mega-black holes."

"Bob?" Becky looked at him. The past three years had been more than just a challenge. They had saved countless lives but every mission had been a struggle, every journey fraught with unknown problems. One thing that had become apparent though was that she had made the right choice in her Captain and partner.

"The reality shielding will need to be manually adjusted from outside the vehicle. We will need to constantly adapt it through certain sections."

"Oh come on." Ga'Tag laughed dismissively. "Nobody has ever done that, it is impossible."

"On the Commodity we once strayed too close to an uncharted black hole. We lost sections of the hull and were about to join the energy stream. I got sent out as part of a last-ditch attempt to save the ship. It worked, but it was tough. I'll write you up the specs of what I'll need to make it easier."

"Bob, you're the Captain, you can't do this."

"Nor can I expect anyone else to, plan your side of the mission and leave me to mine. Dismissed." His confidence had returned, an arrogance that was necessary to lead had developed but it was one born of experience and ability, more of a surety than the front many Earth-Fleet officers had. He projected leadership naturally, he didn't show off or otherwise feel the need to let everyone know about his abilities. Underneath it all he remained vulnerable, raw. Everyday was a chance to prove himself worthy of this second chance, but worthy to himself, not anyone else.

"We leave in an hour, how long will it take you to supervise what you need to make the trip?" Becky's voice was filled with concern. Bob, in contrast, just casually pressed a button on his MCD and smiled.

"Already done. I planned it out last night as I looked at the problem."

"With us docked on the orbital network you could be anywhere on Earth in minutes. Why don't you meet up with Brian for a run somewhere nice before we go?"

"A lovely idea but even with the adaptations it is going to take all my strength and attention to keep all of it going."

"What about an arctic spa?"

"Will you come along?"

"I'm going to be busy. You've been promising you'd go with Brian for a while."

"He just doesn't have the guts to jump into that ice water without me holding his hand."

"Well then."

The spa had been exactly what he needed. As he came back aboard and inspected the work his team had done on the hull he felt invigorated and refreshed. They headed off immediately taking a well-worn path to deep space, unlike most travellers they peeled off along the way and headed towards what many knew as the 'troubled space'.

"I'm going up top. Nigel, you have the conn."

It wasn't easy. The reality shield had that name for a very good reason, that close to it Bob wasn't always part of his own universe, occasionally part of him, his conscious mind, would skip between dimensions. Few people had experienced what he had when he saved the Commodity. In the old days it had been considered a side-effect of faster than light travel, earlier shields protected the ship but leached badly. The earliest explorers from Earth had to be rigorously selected for their mental stability. In the modern era only a handful of people saw what he had. As he jumped between alternative realities he came to see his own more clearly. This very mission, this act had been one of many factors that contributed to his breakdown. With his self-imposed isolation the visions he had experienced created a little crack that the drugs, his anxiety and a host of other issues could widen until he was ripe for manipulation. This time what he saw made him stronger. Sometime in the third hour he started to scream in pain, despite this he held on and continued to make adjustments until they arrived.

With the reality shield disengaged he stood literally alone atop his own vessel in alien space. With a smile he noted that he was surfing his ship to the rescue. As they approached the planet and its apparent size grew to be larger than that of the sphere he surfed in on, the problems became more than apparent. This was Hadrian's World, an independent

Human colony that was part of the breakaway faction. Hadrian's World had no connection to Earth, it, along with its allies had seceded over 70 years ago starting a cold war that occasionally spilled into violent exchanges with Earth-Fleet.

Hadrian's World was also dying. Pressure was building in the mantle and noxious gases were spreading. The Alliance's own ships were engaged in a fierce battle with Earth-Fleet on the other side of the galaxy and couldn't spare a ship, not even one, to save the hundreds of thousands of colonists. Bob watched the gas cloud expand and, as they reached orbit, felt, then saw, the Jumper Shuttles detach and head down. He stood for a while considering the unfolding disaster. The planet had an unfinished transport network. They had the equipment onboard to complete this which would allow the whole population to be moved to the opposite side of the world but this would only delay things by a few days. It was hoped that those few days would be enough to transport them all offworld in batches to nearby Alliance worlds.

"Ga'Tag, what is the pressure under that crack?" Bob asked through his communicator.

"I'm not going through this again, sir. There is too high a risk the whole thing will explode as it is, if we try to seal it that risk increases."

"What if we open it?"

"What?"

"If we open it in the right place the gases could be released at once, the risk of explosion would go and the planet might be saved for habitation."

"You didn't present this at any of the planning meetings, sir. I'll need to run it through the simulators and the population will need to agree to it."

"I didn't present it because I didn't have a view like this. I'm watching that mantle bulge right now, I'm wondering if we open it in the right way it might have a high enough velocity to release most of the toxins into space."

"Yeah, or we'll cut our rescue window down from days to hours, the earthquake would probably tear the transport network to pieces too."

"Plug it into the machine, I'm coming in, I'm going to grab a quick shower and change and I'll meet you in the logistics lab."

"Well?" Bob's hair was still wet as he came into the lab. Ga'Tag was frantically typing, his hands were actually prosthetics that allowed him to function in a human vessel.

"I've had it spit out 20 scenarios based on the data so far."

"Have you done an invasive scan?"

"Only a minute ago, it took the Director a while to get agreement from the ruling body below, I've just found why." A new image appeared on the screen of machinery within the fissure. "They were mining the mantle, probably to help with equipment for the war, and it went wrong."

"Never mind that, what does the new data do for the scenarios?"

"There is a distinct bubble of highly compressed gas, the pressure from below is causing it to leach through but, I don't know, give me a minute more."

The hologram showed many different possible outcomes with the mathematical models running along the edge of the screen too fast to read. Too fast for a human, Bob thought, Ga'Tag was taking this all in.

"It can be done but we can't do it."

"Explain."

"Our weapons wouldn't be able to deliver the energy needed quickly enough, we would most likely cause a tear that would rip itself open, the gasses would expel under pressure but along the surface and they'd kill everyone in a day or two."

"What is the nearest ship with the firepower to do it?"

"The Alliance has nothing in the area that could manage it, and Sir, the model thinks that we will not be able to complete the evacuation before that crack blows, probably taking half the planet with it. Our previous estimates were wrong."

"Who else is nearby? The Alliance would pay any pirate or privateer handsomely for saving their world."

"There is nothing, accept the Commodity."

"What?"

"I don't know why but it is two jumps away right now."

"Package the whole scenario up and get Becky up from the surface, we will need her to swing this."

Bob stayed out of sight as Becky communicated with the other ship. He sat by the screen and sent her messages via his MCD. The Earth-Fleet vessel was not happy to have been detected, they had been on a covert mission to cut their enemies supply lines. Becky had previously arranged that all vessels from all space faring races would be visible to her organisation in case of emergencies. The actual communication was only the first problem, the mission caused an explosion of venom.

Sat where he was everything Becky had said about his former employers was so clear. He had never considered himself a bigot or indoctrinated, perhaps he had never really been, which had made his catastrophe so much more inevitable. Becky laid out details of treaties, interstellar law and Bob supplied her with Earth-Tech regulations to back up her arguments.

The Commodity's mission had been to hasten the end to the current active conflict, whether by forcing peace or a return to the former cold war. Becky passionately argued that even if you put all of the regulations and laws that obliged the Commodity to act, even if you ignored that it was the morally correct thing to do with a humanitarian crisis, it also made tactical sense. They could save the planet, such an act of decency and charity could help with their explicit orders.

"Or you could just transport them yourself." She sighed finally. A message came from Bob. "Let's flip this on its head, what if they discover, and this isn't a threat, but through their own means discover that you were here and did nothing. What if a crewman speaks out of turn in a bar in a neutral territory, or a listening station has picked all this up, or whatever? What do you think your chances of there ever being peace will be then? Hundreds of thousands of innocent civilians, Captain."

The idea of the Alliance civilians being onboard was unthinkable to them, but in the end, after their modelling computer agreed the plan would work, they arrived in orbit. The Commodity remained for as short a time as was necessary, it fired two shots with perfect accuracy and the gasses were mostly vented into space. A couple of carefully aimed missile strikes, an option that the rescue vessel hadn't had, burnt off most of the remaining gases in the atmosphere. They scanned deeply with their more powerful sensors and declared the crisis over, then left without a word.

"You could have said hello at the end."

"What, and let them know it was my idea? Confirm in their mind that I'm a traitor, or try to make them feel silly for letting someone as smart as me go?"

"I suppose, I see your point."

"This was your mission, you are our face to the world. Where next?"

"I was going to say for us to head back home but there is a drought on an Earth colony, the equipment we had to build the transport network could be adapted to create an irrigation infrastructure to overcome the issue and avert a famine later in the year."

"Don't they have processors?"

"Religious objections."

"Okay, give Nigel the coordinates and get Ga'Tag working the problem. Time to go save another world."

David Richie is a British author who lives in a small cottage with a wife and a number of children. The children are his and he will get round to counting them one day. David has had short stories published in the past and has just finished his first novel, #NewNormal, the tale of a serial killer striking a Cornish city during lock down.

The Ministry of Sacrifice

by Elana Gomel

I *have been lucky my entire life. This is why I am going to die tomorrow.*
When the results of the Lottery came in, I carelessly tore open the red envelope stamped with the Dragon's official seal, ripping the single sheet of paper inside. My father had kept a sharp letter opener for official mail. Not me: too untidy, too rebellious. But lucky, always lucky.

I had had another fight with Elvin the evening before, and I was still thinking about it as I picked up the letter, scratching at the inflamed wound of my pride, angry that he would be so evasive about the date for our wedding. The Lottery was the furthest thing from my mind, even though I realized I would have to glue the letter together.

They required that you signed at the bottom and sent it back to the Ministry of Sacrifice. Otherwise, people would claim that the letter was lost, or stolen, or eaten by the dog. People who won the Lottery. The lucky people who suddenly discovered that *How sweet it is to die for our city* slogan was meant literally. The lucky people like me.

After I read the letter, I suddenly found myself on the floor, looking up at the ceiling. It was as if I could see Him through the brick and mortar of the tower's top, resting His heavy bulk on top of the city, cradling us all under His wings. Security always came with a price.

But why should it be paid by me?

There were no whys in the Lottery. Somebody had to win it every year. This year, this "somebody" was me.

I was the city's Ransom.

#

"This was how our city was saved," the teacher said.

Why were my classmates' faces rippling in slow green as if we were underwater?

He pointed to the large poster he had pinned to the blackboard. He was wearing a tatty belted robe that disclosed his chicken-thin legs: not very appropriate for a teacher.

The poster showed a sinister black figure in a crested helmet on a black steed menacing with his lance a huddle of drooping refugees. But standing between the oversized figure and the helpless women and children was the winged silhouette of our savior.

"The Dragon," the teacher said. "When our city was sacked, our people massacred, and the Adversary was about to take control and turn the survivors into slaves, the Dragon came like a thunder from the sky. His raven head dispensed wisdom; His eagle head inspired the people with courage; and His vulture head demolished the bodies of the slain. Thus, our city was saved and renamed the Dragon's City as a token of our eternal gratitude. And the Dragon has not abandoned us but is watching over us, defending us from enemies within and without."

My desk was pushing down on my knees as I was trying to get up, and the door to the classroom banged open, and Elvin strode in ...

Elvin?

I woke up.

How did I fall asleep? Of all the possible reactions to my imminent death, that was one I had never envisioned. I had always been active, even hyperactive, jumping into action, confronting misfortune heads-on. But it was before my parents' disappearance. Before I learned that the Adversary did not ride on a black steed but stole into your house in the middle of the night. Before I knew that misfortune was as irresistible as the snowfall that softly freezes you to death.

A noise came from the outside. I dragged myself to the window, squinted into the gathering dusk. The Dragon's City was formed of concentric rings of staggered towers that rose toward the highest of them all – the Dragon's Eyrie. My tower was located in the second ring, close to the curtain wall that surrounded the city, Maybe, because my head was still muddled with the residue of my dream, I stared at the wall as if seeing it for the first time. Why did we need it at all if the Dragon was watching over us?

Your social standing was proportionate to your closeness to the Dragon's Eyrie. The first ring was blackened and dilapidated, populated by riffraff. Mine was just a bit better, while Elvin's family occupied spacious quarters in the innermost ring. But at least from my socially dubious perch I had a great view of the top of the wall where uniformed sentinels moved with the precision of marionettes, and beyond it, the broad featureless plain infested by the Adversary's marauding gangs. In summer, it would be a patchwork of green and brown, threaded by the silvery stitchery of creeks. Now, covered by snow, it was as white as the sky above. For a moment, I forgot the Lottery, my mind curling up like a hedgehog, protecting itself. I woozily contemplated the scene before me.

Black dots were swirling against the white background. I squinted and saw that groups of people were coalescing into a column that moved toward the Gate. This was strange. The Adversary's attacks usually took place in spring or summer. Surely no horse could gallop on the frozen crust of snow without floundering and throwing off its armored rider!

And then I saw that there were no horses. The attackers were gliding on skis over the drifts like water-spiders on a lake. They were not wearing the heavy fireproof armor that we were used to seeing on the Adversary's warriors. These people were dressed in furs and armed with crossbows and javelins.

I pushed the casement window open. The cold air cut my face and finally woke me up. Opening a window was frowned upon—too easy to jump out—but I suddenly realized there was certain freedom in being marked by the Dragon as His own.

The sentinels of the Wall scurried around in disarray, looking ridiculous in their ceremonial padded cloaks and tripartite headgear. A couple of guards were hauling a barrel, containing pitch to be set aflame or maybe just slops to pour at the attackers, but before they could get their act together, an invader below lifted his crossbow and nonchalantly shot a guard who crumbled like a discarded ragdoll.

How sweet it is to die for our city.

Meanwhile the attackers dragged something big and heavy toward the Gate. I leaned halfway out the window. It must be a battering ram! I had seen pictures in my history textbooks but never one in real life.

The attackers were well organized. Until now, only ragtag bands of desperadoes had tried to sneak in during summer months, sometimes doing no more damage than plundering an outbuilding or setting fields on fire. The Adversary was running out of fools who had succumbed to his blandishments, as preachers in Dragon shrines were wont to say. So, who were these people?

The ram swung against the iron-bound Gate and I felt rather than heard a mighty blow. The Gate shuddered.

In adjacent towers, windows were opening like startled eyes, people leaning out, pointing, screaming.

Another push. The Gate was trembling. On the wall, the sentinels were scurrying around in disarray. The short winter day was curdling into twilight.

And then the Dragon came.

A sudden night fell as His shadow mantled the sky. The ragged silhouette churned and spread like an inkblot. The three heads blended and separated, a confused shadow theatre of bird-skulls and gaping beaks. His many wings were beating spasmodically, raising darkness into the air like the slit from the bottom of a muddy pond. The wings were shedding black feathers, each the size of a man, that plummeted down and found their victims, piercing their bodies with the unerring precision of a nail driven by a workman's hand. Scarlet splotches bloomed on the snow.

The raven's head emerged from the tangle of shadows, as big as the world, blocking the weak radiance of the new moon. The serpentine neck wove through the brittle air. The beak gaped, the black hole in the pale sky, as the Dragon cawed His victory.

The Gate clung shut. No way in, no way out.

#

Elvin refused to come with me to the Ministry of Sacrifice.

"They'll want you alone, Sophie," he said, avoiding my eyes. "They won't even let me in, I'm sure."

We stood so close that I could touch him for the last time, could put my hand on his cheek, feel the roughness of his stubble, trace the contours of his full lips. But I did not. I was seeing him as if through the wrong end of a telescope, immeasurably distant.

As I walked up the steep cobbled street that led up to the Dragon's Eyrie, the torn halves of the letter in my pocket, I felt hollow. It was bitterly cold; a sharp, short winter day.

The last day I had seen my parents had been warm and sunny, flowery smells wafting on the wind from the fields and orchards outside the wall. I had yelled something angry and stupid and stormed out, slamming the door.

Our fight had been about Elvin. They disapproved of our relationship. Elvin's father was a highly placed official in the Ministry of Procurement, and Elvin himself was perfectly placed to climb the bureaucratic ladder as soon as he finished sowing his wild oats. My parents insinuated that I was just a grain among those oats. Of course, I was convinced they were standing in the way of true love.

I spent that night with Elvin and his buddies, sitting on top of the wall, drinking tart wine and watching the slow-moving lines of lights on the plain below as guardsmen patrolled the fields, protecting them from the depredations of the Adversary. The fields were heavy with corn, and the Adversary would often send saboteurs to set them on fire or steal the harvest. Of course, the Dragon would not let His people starve but the less we appealed to Him in everyday emergencies, the better. Because every time He saved us, the Lottery ran a little more often.

At the time, the Lottery was something that happened to others. I did not think about it as Elvin's hand sought mine in the dark. He wanted me to go back with him to his family's quarters. I was not sure why I had said "no": perhaps my parents' warnings had more effect than I acknowledged. But I was proud of that "no"; proud of the fact that I had come back alone that summer morning to find the door torn off the hinges and my parents gone, snatched by the Adversary. Just as I was alone now, trudging toward my final destination on the frost-slippery cobblestones.

My overcoat was too thin for the weather, but it had capacious pockets. The Lottery letter lay in one. The only thing I had inherited from my father in the other.

The Dragon's Eyrie loomed into the colorless sky. Old snow lay in dirty drifts along the plaza. The heart of the city looked dingy, and I felt offended that my last day should be so ordinary. Couldn't it at least snow, so the city would wear the bridal white to honor my sacrifice? There was an apocryphal tale that once upon a time, only pure maidens and virginal youths had participated in the Lottery. The cynical consensus was that the rules had been changed due to the shortage of suitable candidates.

I lingered at the entrance, staring at the tall bronze door decorated with a bas-relief of the Dragon triumphing over the Adversary. The Adversary was depicted as a menacing faceless figure in a crested helmet, his broken sword lying at his feet. Above was the slogan that decorated every classroom, every shrine, every official building.

How sweet it is to die for our city.

I did not want to read the familiar words. Instead, I looked up, following the majestic sweep of the Tower's rough stonework. It was the tallest building in the Dragon City. But what made it stand out even more was its top. Alone of all the towers, the Dragon's Eyrie was mushroom-shaped, crowned with a wide flaring cap several stories high.

The cap was not stone but metal; smooth, windowless, and unmarked, shining like polished gold even in the dull winter light.

"Can I help you?"

The elderly guard was muffled up in a greatcoat, his nose red and dripping.

"I'm…" I stuttered. For some reason, I felt embarrassed to tell him why I was here. "I need…Ministry…"

"Which one?" he smiled with the evident pleasure of offering help. He looked about my father's age. "I can take you up. It's a proper maze inside, and no mistake."

"The Ministry of Sacrifice,"

The light in his face went out and he stepped back, as if I was contagious.

"It'll be fifth floor," he said briskly and avoiding my eyes, opened the bronze door.

#

He was right: it was a proper maze inside. Winding corridors lined by identical doors with obscure sigils instead of written signs. The scuffed carpeting the color of vomit. Ramps led from one floor to another so after making a couple of rounds, I did not know where I was. The dull, lifeless light of lumens fixed too high up on the walls, so shadows puddled on the floors like unclean water. Lumens were one of the Dragon's gifts to His city, and every room had at least one, but shouldn't His Tower be better illuminated than ordinary dwellings? Especially because the slit windows were covered by shutters that let in only scant drops of daylight.

All doors were closed. A low humming permeated the Tower, composed of the overlapping sounds of whatever bureaucratic activities were going on inside the offices. Occasionally a figure laden with files would emerge and scurry across the corridor but they disappeared through another door faster than I could catch up with them. I tried to call after them, but they did not seem to hear me. I was beginning to doubt my own existence. Was I a ghost already? Was this the shore of the Three Rivers, which the righteous souls had to cross to enter the Dragon's Lair? If so, it was nothing like the soothing images in the Book of the Dragon.

Finally, I had had enough. I pushed one of the doors at random. Its sigil was a stylized pen with a feathered end.

Inside was a cramped office with a large desk burdened by the untidy scatter of papers. There were some pictures, which I could not make out because the only lumen was so old and exhausted that its light was brown like stewed tea. At first, I did not see the office's inhabitant: a wizened man in a black suit, groping under his desk. He jumped up when I walked in and dislodged an avalanche of files that fluttered onto the floor.

"What do you want?" he asked in an aggrieved tone.

I marched toward the desk and leaned toward him so close that our noses almost touched.

"I won the Lottery." I growled. "And I expect a better reception for the Ransom of the city!"

His face underwent an instant metamorphosis, the peptic scowl relaxing, and something ambiguous stirring in his faded eyes. He came out from behind the desk and looked me up and down.

"May I see your winning letter, please?" he asked.

I handed it to him. His eyebrows shot up when he saw its torn state, but he did not comment. He carefully perused it.

"Very well," he said. "We are a different department, but I can take you to the Ministry of Sacrifice. Please follow me."

I was about to but the pictures above his desk drew my attention. Despite his impatient huffing, I stepped closer.

There were four of them. The biggest one was a standard poster of the Dragon in His majesty: His wings outstretched into a semblance of a thundercloud; His raven-head crowned with a circlet composed of stylized towers, while His eagle-head and vulture-head bore golden coronets. But below the poster were three smaller pictures that were unlike anything I had ever seen. At first, I thought they were private family portraits, though why would they be allowed in a workplace? But they were too well executed to be dabbles of street painters and had an unmistakable aura of officialdom. On the left was a grey-haired, straight-backed, black-suited official holding some sort of a seal. In the middle was a general of the Dragon's Guard in a dress uniform, with a sword and a harquebus. And on the right was a teacher, standing with an open book in front of his class. The strange thing was all three had the same face: smiling, vapid, and vaguely benevolent.

The man coughed impatiently, and I reluctantly tore myself away from the pictures and followed him.

"What is your department?" I asked.

"Education," he said.

#

The whole thing was a letdown. When we had studied civics in school, much was made of the whole idea of the city's Ransom and of how the Lottery allowed each citizen above the age of sixteen to compete for this highest of honors regardless of their sex, social standing, and economic status. Our teachers spoke with tears in their eyes about the sweetness of laying down one's life for the survival and prosperity of all. We were shown pictures of previous Ransoms – always the best-looking ones, starry-eyed girls in white gowns and square-jawed boys in fetching uniforms – and assured that their souls had no fear of crossing the Three Rivers as they would be ushered straight into the Dragon's Lair, while the rest of us, mere mortals, would be subjected to the terrors and punishments of the underworld. We sang happy songs and stood at memorial assemblies. And it was just life: as natural as breathing; as taken for granted as the wiles of the Adversary; as ubiquitous as the golden mushroom of the Eyrie seen from every Tower. Because of course, winning the Lottery always happened to others.

The Ministry of Sacrifice was no different from any other department in this bureaucratic anthill. The same faceless doors, exhausted lumens, and mountains of paperwork. Any hopes I had had of touching ceremonies and soul-stirring speeches was instantly quashed as I was processed, and stamped, and entered in ledgers, and asked the same questions over and over again by a legion of faceless clerks. At least, it was efficient. Once my guide from the Ministry of Education deposited me in the reception room and scurried away without a backward glance, I was quickly taken charge of and maneuvered from office to office with an impersonal speed of a conveyor belt.

Once it was finished, I was ushered into a room that reminded me of the school infirmary. The lumens here were brighter here, and there was a vase of generic flowers on the table. And prominent on one of the walls were the same three pictures I had seen before.

I was examining them when a woman came in: stocky and middle-aged with a kindly face. To my surprise, she gave me a hug.

"Goodness gracious!" she exclaimed. "You must be starving, Sophie!"

I nodded gratefully. I was indeed famished, having eaten nothing since breakfast.

A server brought in a cart laden with delicacies such as I had never seen before. The City prospered under the Dragon's wings; the famines of the pre-Dragon past were a horror tale. But our food was often plain as we relied mostly on ourselves in producing it. Neighboring cities were under the sway of the Adversary and refused to trade with us. The Dragon would occasionally bring exotic wines, spices, and fruits from His forays into faraway places, but we could not, of course, ask Him for steady supply. So, I had never before tasted anything like the melt-on-your-tongue slices of cured meat; round yellow honey melon; sugared apples and plums; cinnamon-scented warm bread. And I had never drunk anything like the red wine with the aromas of blackberries and cardamom that relaxed your limbs and filled your head with the softness of a summer afternoon. At the beginning, I felt vaguely ashamed of drinking too much because the woman, who had told me her name was Emma, looked like a school-nurse, and those disapproved of alcohol. But she topped my glass and toasted what she called "my good fortune".

The meal was over too soon, and Emma got up and grasping my elbow, led me through a curtained doorway into another room that was filled with wardrobes and cupboards of various sizes.

"We need to get you ready, honey!" she chuckled.

The wine glow instantly dissipated and I was cold-sober.

"What? Now? But I thought…"

I had thought – insofar as I allowed myself to think about it at all – that I would have some period of grace to get ready, a day at least, maybe as much as a week. Time seemed infinitely elastic now: a week's postponement would be an eternity.

"Why to delay? He is waiting."

She lifted her eyes to the ceiling and suddenly I realized with a piercing clarity that He was indeed waiting, sitting on top of this Tower like a brooding hen, covering with the shadow of His many wings the entire City. My whole life had been in that shadow: my parents, Elvin, everything, and everybody I had touched, loved, hated were marked by His presence.

"What? No…" I started backing off, toward the door. "No, I can't! I'm…I don't want to!"

Emma's hand clamped around my wrist like a steel trap and her kindly eyes shone with a glint of the same steel.

"Come on, honey!" she said. "You know we have to do it."

She pushed me onto a padded bench and hustled through the cupboards, pushing dress hangers around. I wanted to get up and I could not. My knees were suddenly weak.

_How sweet it is…

I am going to die. And it is not sweet at all. It is dreary, and sordid, and ugly.

How sweet it is to be a sweet morsel on the Dragon's plate!_

See," Emma was chirping, "they are going to name a school in your honor! Kids will sing songs about you. Everybody will be envious – you know what they say, how sweet it is to die for the Dragon…I mean, for our city. And after all, it's not like you have much going for you. This boyfriend of yours, I mean…there are easier ways to break up, don't you think?"

"What?" I went cold all over again. "What did you say? Elvin? What about him?"

Emma hauled out a long white gown with a beaded sparkling bodice and a gauzy train.

"This will do nicely," she said with satisfaction. "He likes white. And yes, honey, that Elvin…I mean, you know who his father is. You should have been more careful. Why would he take a girl from the Second Ring, I ask you? A little common sense goes a long way. Now, try it on. If it doesn't fit, I have another one for you. We'll make you pretty, honey, don't you worry!"

The gown fit. I folded my old clothes carefully, putting them away in the corner. Emma was urging me to hurry; I suddenly realized that she was impatient to get back home, to her husband and two grown daughters. She told me all about them, as I was putting on the gown, my back turned to her, as she chatted on. I filtered out as much of her happy-family stories as I could. I didn't think I had hated anybody in my entire life more than this bustling motherly woman. Except one person.

Elvin had rigged the Lottery to get rid of me.

It was so transparently obvious that I despised myself for not seeing it before. The Lottery was rigged. My parents were dead. My boyfriend had betrayed me.

And I was going to die, eaten by a monster.

#

The ramp leading up was carpeted with some heavy golden fabric and the lumens were new and fresh. The air swirled with sparkling motes. I went up, holding the train of my gown over my arm. I was alone. Why to waste guards when there was no possibility of escaping? The heavy door at the bottom of the ramp had slammed after me, and I heard the click of the lock. There were no windows, so I could not even throw myself out and deprive the Dragon of his meal. There was nowhere to go but up. And up I went.

The train was cumbersome, and a couple of times I tripped and almost fell. But its heavy folds provided the disguise for what I clutched in my sweaty palm.

There was another bronze door on top of the ramp, decorated with a familiar frieze of the Dragon Triumphant that brought a fresh wave of nausea to my throat. I hoped I would throw up, splatter the immaculate carpet with the half-digested remnants of my last meal, but the nausea subsided. I pushed the door.

I expected a bloody cave littered with bones. Instead, there was an ordinary room. Not quite ordinary, I realized, as I took in the exotically carved sideboards groaning under crystal goblets and beaten-bronze trays; overstuffed armchairs piled up with embroidered throws; knickknacks and gewgaws littering every available surface. Each object alone was rare and striking; together, they looked like the hoard of an indefatigable magpie.

I slowly walked around the room, picking up a figurine here or a painted tile here. My fear dissipated. There was nothing left but hollow disgust.

And then I saw something gleaming under a curvy-legged table. I bent down...and then the door I had not seen before opened and a man walked in.

I quickly straightened up and tried to make my expression blank but did not quite succeed. Because I knew the man.

He was the one depicted on the three portraits I had seen. I could not be mistaken. That bland face had the strange ability to insinuate itself into your brain, lingering in your memory like a bruise.

He was wearing the black suit of the bureaucracy and he smiled broadly when he saw me.

"Hello, Sophie," he said.

His voice was not quite as ordinary as his appearance. It was syncopated, underlain with stealthy whispers and sibilant noises as if he had more than one windpipe to produce it.

"How do you know my name?" I asked stupidly.

"I know the names of all my children."

"You are the Dragon." It was not a question.

"I am the First Head of the Dragon," he corrected.

And at that moment, I knew.

"There is no Adversary," I said. Again, it was not a question.

The First Head shrugged.

"There were many. At the beginning. Your city resisted. Stupid people: hungry, poor, beset by enemies. Still, they resisted. What for? I brought security, prosperity, civilization. I made the former Tower City great. The wall had not been breached in a generation, even though your superstitious neighbors are still trying 'to defeat the monster'. What fools! They live in stinking hovels while you live in bright towers. Their children swell with hunger and never learn to read, while your children are well fed, loved, and educated. And what do I ask in return? Just a bit of patriotic pride, loyalty, and selflessness. *How sweet it is to die for our city.* I came up with this slogan myself. Doesn't it have a nice ring?"

I moved a little, so my full skirt masked the table.

"What are we waiting for?" I asked, the quiver in my voice genuine, but producing the effect I wanted. The monster should believe I was entirely cowed. He smiled, the corners of his mouth curving up into his cheeks, stretching wider than humanly possible.

"For my Second and Third Heads. They will be here soon."

"And then you'll eat me."

"And then I'll eat you."

The hidden door swung open and the Second Head walked in. He was wearing the general's uniform covered in golden braids, clanking medals, flashy insignia. I realized that the sentinels on the Wall strove mightily to imitate him with their clumsy outfits that were unsuitable for combat. Why would they care? They had a monster to defend them against the would-be monster slayers.

The Second Head had the same face but puffier, coarser, flushed with dark blood. It looked even less human, quivering on the edge of an unspeakable transformation.

The two Heads turned toward each other.

"Where is he?" the First Head asked petulantly. The Second Head licked his slack lips. His pointed tongue lapped at his chin. Strange how seconds stretched and filled with my own time of frantic heartbeats. My mouth overflowed with metallic saliva. I had a moment to wonder at the fact that they needed to talk to each other as if they were not the same entity – and perhaps originally, they had not been. But that was not important. The important question could still be asked – and I did ask it.

"What happened to my parents?"

The two Heads burst into titters like mean schoolgirls, but another sibilant voice answered.

"They were eaten, of course."

The Third Head just walked in. He was dressed in the modest tunic of a teacher, the same as the teachers in my own school had worn. And his face was the most inhuman of the three: blank and unfinished, with barely sketched-in features, his eyes like buttons: dull and opaque, with no whites.

"But they did not win the Lottery!"

"They were traitors," the Third Head explained as patiently as my headmaster had done throughout my childhood. I remembered those hours in his office. My headmaster had been kind and dedicated. His voice had been soothing. He had taught us to be selfless and sharing. And he had shaped us into offerings to the monster, sweet morsels to be consumed by the creature that has stolen our humanity.

"Traitors have doubts. Their names are forgotten. The Lottery winners are patriots. Their names are remembered."

"But they are eaten anyway," I said. 'How sweet it is to be the fodder for the Dragon."

The three Heads nodded in unison and then they started changing.

The three bodies flowed together into a ragged black mass, a pile of moldy feathers, swelling and growing precipitously, shoving aside the junk that the room was littered with. A webbed claw pushed from under the mass, yellow and scaly. The stench of a chicken coop, of acrid bird shit, and rotten bones, filled the room. And three scrawny necks rose out of the pile. Each bore a swelling head that was changing, melting, and reshaping itself. The bureaucrat's bland features flowed into a vulture's bald head; the soldier's swollen visage transformed into an eagle's cruel beak; and the teacher's blank mask flushed with darkness and sprouted the oily feathers of a raven. They were cackling maniacally but I could see that the transformation was not easy for them. It was proceeding in fits and starts, with the huffing and puffing of an old man trying to climb steep stairs, because they *were* old. The Dragon, our god, was old, and molting, and pathetic.

I whipped out my father's letter opener.

It was small, its blade tarnished. But it would have to do because there was nothing else.

I rushed at the Dragon, catching him in the precise moment when his transition was tottering on the cusp between three entangled men and a three-headed monster. It was a matter of pure luck that I caught him in this moment of vulnerability. But I was lucky, wasn't I?

The blade went into one of the wildly swaying necks, slashing through the pimply skin. I was deluged by a fountain of tarry blood that smelled so foul that I coughed and retreated. The other two Heads screamed. The opener flew out of my hand and disappeared into a pile of junk in the corner. The scream bowled me over, so I fell and rolled on the carpet, entangled in my own skirt. I ended up facing the curvy-legged table I had noticed before. As the Dragon roared his rage, I reached under it and pulled out a sword.

It was not much of a sword; not like the two-handed blade in those pictures of the Adversary confronting the Dragon Victorious. Its edge was dull. It must have ended in the Dragon's collection because of the jewels encrusting its golden hilt, and these jewels, slippery with cobwebs, made it unwieldy and difficult to hold. But it was a weapon.

The raven head opened its beak wide and vomited a ribbon of flame that sputtered and died out before it reached me. It set a bolt of fabric aflame, filling the windowless room with acrid smoke. I dove through the smoke, the sword held aloft in a two-handed grip. I had never been taught to handle arms, but all those endless pictures and descriptions of the Dragon's Fight had been useful for *something*.

An iron arrow whistled past me, almost taking off my ear. The creature – half a monstrous three-headed bird, half a dark-suited swelling parody of a man – was gurgling as its severed artery pumped out blood. It was plucking out its own feathers with a taloned hand and launching them at me. They metamorphosed into arrows in midair, but its aim was poor. The smoke helped to disorient the creature, swirling before me like a screen.

I ran the sword through its feathered chest, and it got stuck. As I was tugging frantically to get it out, the Dragon swiped at me. Its talons tore through my shoulder. A moment of sickening, gushing warmth – and then I was blinded with pain.

But the pain only fed my fury. The hot blood felt like a soldier's cloak around my shoulders.

I was yelling something as I was hacking at the quivering pile of feathers, fabric, and flesh. And I only stopped when I realized that the thrusts produced no response.

I spat at the tripartite body that lay, quiescent, on the floor.

"How sweet it is to die for our city, you bastard," I said. "Glad you got to experience it."

I poked the corpse with the tip of the sword. It looked like a melted sculpture of a bird fused with the sagging corpse of an old man. The three heads had melded into a distorted bubble of a beaked skull.

I dropped to my knees and slashed through the head. The stench of blood no longer felt nauseating.

Under the bird-skin was a human face, the same one as in the portraits. Except now it was old and worn-out, its glamor gone. And yet, for the first time it looked real.

The Dragon must have been human once.

I felt lightheaded. My gown was no longer white. The blood gushing from my torn shoulder had painted it in swirls of red. I rummaged through the junk in the room until I found a couple of scarves that I pressed to the wound to staunch the flow.

I went down the ramp and pushed at the bronze door at the bottom. It swung open.

Emma was waiting outside. Her face grew white when she saw me. She retreated, pressing her hand to her quivering lips.

"Didn't expect me, did you?" I rasped. "What is it you were waiting for? The leftovers of the Dragon's meal?"

She said nothing but, in her eyes, I saw what I needed: fear.

And I vividly imagined the same fear dawning in Elvin's face.

"Take care of my wounds, woman!" I commanded. "Move! There has been a change on top. The Adversary is now in charge!"

Elana Gomel is an academic and a writer. She is the author of six academic books and numerous articles on subjects such as narrative theory, posthumanism, science fiction, Dickens, and serial killers. As a fiction writer, she has published more than eighty fantasy and science fiction stories and three novels. She can be found at https://www.citiesoflightanddarkness.com/

Thank you...

Thank you for taking the time to read our collection. We enjoyed all the stories contained within and hope you found at least a few to enjoy yourself. If you did, we'd be honored if you would leave a review on Amazon, Goodreads, and anywhere else reviews are posted.

You can also subscribe to our email list via our website, Https://www.cloakedpress.com

Follow us on Facebook http://www.facebook.com/Cloakedpress

Tweet to us @CloakedPress

We are also on Instagram http://www.instagram.com/Cloakedpress

If you'd like to check out our other publications, you can find them on our website above. Click the "Check Our Catalog" button on the homepage for more great collections and novels from the Cloaked Press Family.